Vito Durante

A Fairly Honourable Defeat

Also by Iris Murdoch

NOVELS

Under the Net

The Flight from the Enchanter

The Sandcastle

The Bell

A Severed Head

An Unofficial Rose

The Unicorn

The Italian Girl

The Red and the Green

The Time of the Angels

The Nice and the Good

Bruno's Dream

CRITICISM

Sartre, Romantic Rationalist

IRIS MURDOCH *A Fairly Honourable Defeat*

THE VIKING PRESS / *New York*

Published in 1970 by The Viking Press, Inc.
625 Madison Avenue, New York, N.Y. 10022

SBN 670-30533-2

Library of Congress catalog card number: 75-89509

Printed in U.S.A. by The Colonial Press Inc.

Second printing February 1970

To Janet and Reynolds Stone

PART *One*

❀ | ONE

"Julius King."

"You speak his name as if you were meditating upon it."

"I am meditating upon it."

"He's not a saint."

"He's not a saint. And yet—"

"What about him?"

"He's in England."

"I know."

"Who told you?"

"Axel."

"I didn't know Julius knew Axel."

"That is characteristic of both Julius and Axel."

Hilda and Rupert Foster, celebrating their twentieth wedding anniversary with a bottle of rather dry champagne, were sitting in the evening sun in the garden of their house in Priory Grove, London, S.W.10. Hilda, a plumper angel now, reclined limply, exhibiting shiny burnished knees below a short shift dress of orangey yellow. Her feet were bare. Her undulating dark hair showed some needle-thin lines of grey. Her burly boyish-faced husband, whom she had at last persuaded to stop wearing shorts, sat open-shirted, cooking in the sun. He was red, hoping later to be brown. His shock of abundant fair hair had faded with the years, becoming unglistening and dry while still undeniably blond. They were a handsome pair. They were altruistic, but treated themselves judiciously to luxuries. The latest one, to which they had not yet become accustomed, was a diminutive swimming pool which made a square of flashing shimmering blue in the middle of the courtyarded garden. The garden was enclosed by an old red-brick wall which was surmounted by a trellis bearing an enlacement of Albertine and Little White Pet, all now in outrageous flower. The air was dense with smells of roses and of the camomile which Hilda was attempting to grow between the paving stones.

"Who told *you?*" said Rupert.

"The *Evening Standard.*"

"Of course. I suppose Julius is rather famous now. And there was all that publicity when he gave up the biological warfare game."

"What was Julius working on exactly?"

"Nerve gas. And a kind of anthrax which resists antibiotics."

"You were all praising Julius for chucking it. I blame him for ever getting involved in it."

"You have to investigate the stuff in order to find the antidotes."

"I hate that old argument. All evil lives on it."

"These borderlines in science are often rather shadowy, Hilda. A biologist may be pursuing something useful or something just interesting and he may happen to make a discovery of military interest. And by then he can't switch off his curiosity. Anyway, I suppose it's better to paralyse people temporarily than to blow them to pieces."

"I'm not so sure. It seems such a betrayal for a biologist to meddle with warfare. And some of those diseases aren't all that temporary. I think I'd rather be cleanly blown up."

"You might be mutilated."

"Oh, don't *argue*, Rupert. It's too hot and I can't think. You seem very anxious to defend Julius."

"Julius doesn't need defending. He acted on principle."

"Men seem to imagine that that's a justification of anything. He hasn't made any sacrifice. He's a distinguished biochemist. He can get a job anywhere in the world. And he has money of his own. Where did Julius get his money, by the way? Did he inherit it?"

"Yes. I believe his people were bankers. You must remember,

Hilda, that he had a marvellous lab and every facility and limitless funds at that place in South Carolina. What's its name?"

"Dibbins. College. It's written on my heart."

"Because of Morgan."

"Yes. But his work was financed by the military, wasn't it?"

"True. But the lab didn't only deal with biological warfare and I know Julius was interested in a lot of other projects. He may never find such good working conditions in impoverished old Europe."

"Well, he doesn't have to stay in impoverished old Europe. He told the press he was giving up the work because he was bored. He didn't talk about principles. His high-minded friends over here have dreamed up the principles."

"Julius is an ironical sort of chap. He wouldn't bare his soul to the press."

"Well, I liked him for saying that. And actually I think Julius is someone who might do anything because he was bored."

"You mean the love affair with your dear young sister?"

"No. I wasn't thinking of Morgan. That may have been serious for all I know."

"It certainly was for her."

"Yes. But I could never manage to see how Julius felt. Morgan's letters were frantic but totally uninformative."

"What *did* happen between those two in South Carolina? And who left whom?"

"I don't know, Rupert. When my dear young sister arrives she will doubtless enlighten us."

"I wonder if Morgan realizes that her former lover is going to be in London too."

"Yes, it's odd that they should both turn up here about the same time."

"You don't think they've got a rendezvous in London?"

"No. Morgan was so positive about their having parted. That at least was clear. I suspect it was all over some time ago really. I've no idea if she knows Julius will be around. It may be a nasty shock."

"Just when one's trying to get over somebody."

"Well, we still don't know who's trying to get over whom."

"There's no reason why they should meet, Hilda. Morgan will be staying here, I presume. But if Julius rings up I'll entertain him at my club. By the way, does Tallis know that Julius is arriving?"

"I doubt it. He has no contacts with Julius's world. And he doesn't read the evening papers, they aren't serious enough. Does Tallis know that Morgan is arriving? That's the prize question."

"Morgan didn't say she'd told him?"

"During the last year his name has not been mentioned!"

"Well, I think Tallis ought to know. After all, he and Morgan are still married to each other. She's still Mrs. Tallis Browne."

"I think we'd much better wait until Morgan is here and see what she wants."

"She may be coming back to live with Tallis."

"If he'll have her after two years' unscheduled absence and a stormy love affair."

"Tallis would forgive her, Hilda, as you perfectly well know."

"Oh, forgiveness, forgiveness, what's the use of that? Morgan needs a strong hand."

"All her things are still over at Tallis's place, aren't they?"

"I know. Tallis wouldn't let me take them away."

"I suppose he reckoned that was still her home!"

"Pathetic. But I felt it was rather thoughtless of him really."

"Or thoughtful."

"Assuming he wants to see her, yes. All her work manuscripts are there, that book she was writing on glossy what was it?"

"Glossematics."

"What a word! How clever of Morgan even to know what it means!"

"Well, I think we must keep an open mind here, Hilda, and if Morgan shows any signs of wanting to go back to her husband we should give her every help and support. It is not for us to judge whether these wounds can be healed or no."

"I agree. But I can't quite see Morgan returning to hubby after all that excitement in South Carolina. Well, she might. But please, not a word to Tallis, Rupert. After all, we don't even know if Morgan is proposing to stay in London. She may be just passing through on her way to somewhere else."

"She may not find it all that easy to get a job. Biologists are universally welcome, but philosophically minded philologists are getting a bit expendable in the modern world."

"It was that philology conference at Dibbins that started it all, wasn't it. She met Julius on the second day. She went for a fortnight and stayed two years. And it was all your fault."

"Well, it seemed quite natural to suggest to my old college friend that he should look up my visiting sister-in-law and show her around!"

"I wonder if Tallis will try to see Julius. They've never met each other, have they?"

"No. I shouldn't think they knew of each other's existence before Morgan took up with Julius. But do you mean Tallis should see Julius to make an outraged husband scene? That hardly seems in character!"

"No, just out of curiosity. Just to inspect the man who's wrecked one's marriage."

"But you kept saying it wasn't Julius's fault, Hilda. Your theory was that Morgan and Tallis were breaking up in any case."

"And you always disagreed. You are too sentimental about the marriage bond, Rupert."

"What a thing to say to me today of all days, my darling!"

"Well, *sentimental*. You get so soppy about couples. One's got to be realistic. You're even soppy about Axel and Simon."

"I believe they're happy, if that's what you mean. I want them to go on being happy, if that's what you mean."

"But do you think Simon is really homosexual?"

"Yes."

"I suppose you should know your own brother."

"And after all, I've known Axel a long time too. As a student, then as a colleague in the department. I think those two are all right."

"How does Axel know Julius?"

"They were graduate students at Oxford together, we all three were."

"Funny, I'd forgotten Julius was at Oxford. He's such an exotic foreign object. How secretive of Axel not to say he knew him. I suppose queers are always a bit sly."

"My dear Hilda, being homosexual doesn't determine a man's whole character any more than being heterosexual does! Axel's just a rather silent man. And probably the matter simply didn't come up. Axel's silent, Simon is a chatterbox. Did Simon come for his swim today, by the way?"

"Yes, he was splashing round like mad just before lunch. We had a few words. It's nice that the pool brings Simon here more."

"He did know they were supposed to be coming round tonight?"

"Oh yes. You know they're always late."

"We must remember to ask his advice about redecorating the bathroom."

"For an eighteenth-century expert his taste in bathrooms is rather lurid. Dear Simon. What a pretty pair he and Morgan made at our wedding, do you remember? It's hard to believe that's twenty years ago, Rupert darling."

"They were children then. And you were already making plans to marry them to each other!"

"Yes. Your brother and my sister. A little incestuous, but it would have been rather neat."

"And they really did get fond of each other."

"They did. But I remember once, later on, asking Morgan what they'd been talking about so intimately, and she said Simon was recounting his homosexual adventures! I think they talked a lot about sex. Morgan wanted information. I suspect she would have liked to be an adventurous boy hunting for other boys in Piccadilly Circus station."

"Hilda!"

"Rescue that bumblebee from the pool, will you, Rupert. That's right. I do wish insects had more sense of self-preservation. I do hope our hedgehog won't fall in. Have hedgehogs got any common sense, I wonder. Is it awful of us to have started drinking champagne before our guests arrive?"

"No. Anything is permitted to us."

"Is it disgraceful to be so happy?"

"A grace, not a disgrace, Hilda."

"Too much at home in Zion?"

"Natural Zionites."

"Do you think it makes us the teeniest bit selfish?"

"Yes. But we ought to forgive ourselves, don't you think? Today of all days."

"I agree. Rupert, it's so super that after all these years you don't want anyone else. Most men of your age run after younger women. It's so super that you wear a wedding ring and still write me love letters."

"It's so super that you still keep them."

"And I'm older than you—"

"Forget it, Hilda. You aren't really."

"Did you remember to send this month's money to Oxfam?"

"Yes. I see the connection of thought!"

"I know. It's silly to feel so guilty about one's luck, isn't it?"

"More champagne, darling? Heavens, it *is* hot. I'm sweating like a pig. You don't think I drink too much, do you, Hilda?"

"Well, we both put away a good deal. It doesn't make us any slimmer. I hoped·the swimming might."

"Swimming refreshes the soul, but does not affect the waistline, I'm afraid. Anyway, drink is good for my insomnia. Thank heavens I'm happy. Insomnia must be hell if one isn't."

"It's so luxuriously sunny, Rupert. I'm quite glad we didn't go to Pembrokeshire after all."

"It would be nice at the cottage. But it's quite like the country in our garden today."

"Perhaps it was silly to invite Simon and Axel to drinks this evening."

"Why? It's a moment for family."

"Axel is so anti-family. He's the sort of queer who doesn't like to be reminded of normal relationships."

"I could hardly invite Simon without him. They are so very married."

"I sometimes feel Axel hates to see a successful heterosexual marriage. He would like all men to leave all women."

"Nonsense, Hilda. He can even be quite conventional and high-minded about it. You remember how shocked he was at Morgan leaving Tallis?"

"That was because he likes Tallis and dislikes Morgan."

"Well, he doesn't dislike you."

"I know. He's another ironical devil. But I am rather fond of him. Do you think that *ménage* will last?"

"Why not? It's lasted more than three years. I don't see why it shouldn't go on."

"Those queer friendships are so unstable."

"That's simply because they run more hazards of an external social kind, Hilda. Heterosexual relations would be just as unstable if it were not for the institution of marriage and the procreation of children. But if people suit each other why shouldn't they stay together?"

"Do you think you and I would have stayed together all these years if we hadn't had the blessing of society?"

"Yes, I do, my darling wife. Don't you?"

"Yes, I do, Rupert. *Angel!* But we're a special case, as we've already agreed, and we're so alike in some ways. Axel and Simon are so different. Axel must be a very difficult man to live with. He's so gloomy and morose. And Simon is so sensitive and childlike and sort of pleasure-loving. I don't mean this in a bad sense. And really, all queers do like trouble. I've never met one who didn't."

"Any sentence beginning 'All queers . . .' is pretty sure to be false! It's like 'All married men . . .' 'All married men over forty deceive their wives.'"

"Well, we know *that's* false! But I'm sure Axel bullies him."

"Some people like to be bullied."

"I suppose they do. And of course he is so much younger than Axel. Thank heavens our relationship is democratic. I suspect they quarrel bitterly every night."

"You've no reason to think so, Hilda. And they might quarrel bitterly every night and still love each other."

"We don't quarrel every night, thank God. And if we did I would take it as evidence against the view that we loved each other."

"There are all kinds of marriages."

"You are incurably compassionate, Rupert."

"I should have said the trouble with those two was almost the opposite. They're so wrapped up in each other they can hardly see the outside world at all."

"Talking about the institution of marriage and the procreation of children, I don't suppose our son will honour us with his presence tonight?"

"Naturally I asked him. Naturally he has not replied."

"He won't come."

"No."

"Oh dear, Rupert. Are you going to write to Cambridge again?"

"There's nothing new to tell them. I must say, they've been very patient so far about Peter's tantrums."

"How much does it matter, his not having done that first-year exam?"

"Not much—so long as he can be persuaded to go back in October."

"He knows he doesn't have to read classics. He could change to something else."

"It isn't the subject he objects to, it's the university!"

"You'd think at his age Cambridge would be heaven. Nineteen, first year at the university, lots of friends—"

"But there weren't lots of friends, Hilda. I think young people don't make friends nowadays the way we used to. Friendship's out of fashion. When I was his age at Oxford I had hundreds of friends."

"And you've still got most of them. I know. If only at least he'd shown signs of having a girl friend. I hope he isn't going to take after his uncle! Whatever made Cambridge go wrong for Peter? Well, we've asked ourselves that question often enough."

"I don't think it was anything specific. Just a quite different view of the world which you and I can scarcely begin to imagine."

"I just don't understand the modern young. I can't see any conceivable merit in this dropping out, can you?"

"They've got a sharper eye than we have for what's rotten in this society."

"Young people have always had that. But it usen't to affect their *joie de vivre*. We rejected society at his age, but it didn't stop us from going to commem balls!"

"We didn't really reject it, Hilda. And sometimes *joie de vivre* can amount to irresponsibility and compromise. These kids want to register some total protest against a set-up where they see so much that's bad. You must remember, Hilda, that Peter belongs to the first generation that can really envisage the end of the human race. And he belongs to the first generation that's grown up entirely without God."

"We disbelieved in God. It didn't turn us against the whole of creation."

"God was still around when we were young. It's different now."

"Then let him join the Communist Party. I think dropping out is cynicism."

"No, no. Cynicism is real vice. It's the vice of the age and it could be the end of us all. These young creatures are really consumed by a sort of incoherent love—"

"Sometimes you talk rot, Rupert darling, but I adore listening to you all the same. I do wish now we hadn't agreed to his going to stay with Tallis. Tallis is a sort of drop-out himself."

"Come, come, Hilda. But I agree it may have been a mistake to let Peter go to Notting Hill. I thought it might bring him back to some sense of reality. You know, after our relations with him became so—well, mine did anyway—"

"Peter was certainly keen to get away from us."

"And better living with Tallis than living all alone in digs."

"I know. I'm so terrified of his starting to take drugs. And he did want to stay with Tallis, and just then one was jolly glad that he *wanted* to do anything."

"And Tallis thought he could help him."

"That's the trouble. Poor old Tallis often thinks he can help people but really he's hopelessly incompetent. And that house, Rupert. It's never cleaned. It's littered with filthy junk of every sort. It smells like the zoo. And the old father making messes in corners. I wouldn't be surprised if there were lice, only of course Tallis would never notice. Peter needs discipline and order. Living on that stinking rubbish heap can't be good for his mind."

"You exaggerate, Hilda. When Tallis and Morgan were living together in Putney their house was pretty untidy too, as I remember."

"And I always took it as a bad sign. If people love each other they keep things neat."

"That's absurd. And surely there was no doubt that they *did* love each other?"

"Maybe. I was never so sure. Well, they *did*, but they were both such ninnies."

"If only they'd had a child."

"I doubt if Morgan wanted a child. She wanted to be free to take off. Of course, Tallis is a terribly odd man in a way. Losing his twin sister at the age of fourteen probably crazed him up for life."

"I think Tallis is one of the sanest men I know."

"I was just waiting for you to say that, darling. I could see that marriage would never work."

"But you shouldn't have said so quite so often! Sometimes the just prophet is not forgiven."

"Morgan would forgive me anything. I would forgive her anything."

"I know. You are very close."

"Yes. Closer perhaps than you've ever really realized."

"You're making me jealous!"

"Don't be silly, darling."

"Aren't you the tiniest bit possessive about your younger sister?"

"Certainly. I would never have thought *anyone* good enough for Morgan."

"Of course, the fact that you're beautiful and she's not—"

"Has nothing whatever to do with it. Morgan has an *interesting* face. And she's so clever. She could have married whoever she wanted. In a way, Tallis was the last thing she should have chosen. She needed someone with more dignity."

"Or possibly one of those bullies."

"No, no, Rupert. Morgan is a democrat too. If Tallis had even got himself a decent job, a university job, he could have done if he'd tried—"

"He only got a second, and—"

"Oh, all you dreary firsts with your built-in-for-life sense of superiority! Tallis is a perfectly self-respecting intellectual, or he could be if he'd only pull his socks up. What's happened to that book on Marx and de Tocqueville that he was writing?"

"I think he's abandoned it."

"There you are. His activities are all so wet and dilettante and disconnected. All that bitty adult education and dribs and drabs of social work and nothing ever achieved or finished. There's something *feeble* about it. And I wish he'd behave more normally about Morgan."

"You mean more jealously?"

"Yes. And don't tell me it's noble to overcome jealousy."

"I was about to do so."

"You can't cheat nature, you can't cheat biology."

"I personally find magnanimity very attractive. But in fact, my dear Hilda, we have no means of knowing how jealous or unjealous Tallis really is. Why should he tell us anything?"

"I know. But he's so spiritless. And such a muddler."

"He's damn tired at the moment is my impression."

"Tired? Of course he's tired. He takes on far too much and then he gets confused and overborne. And since Morgan left him he's begun to go to pieces anyway. He just can't cope."

"For us whose lives so pre-eminently work it may be hard to imagine. But I do think you're a little too down on people who can't cope, darling!"

"Well, I do think a reasonable amount of efficiency is an aspect of morals. There's a sort of ordered completeness of life and an intelligent use of one's talents which is the mark of a man. And Tallis is a peculiarly dangerous example to Peter just at this moment. Tallis never seems to know what he can manage and what he can't. Having his old papa to live with him is crazy. Then wanting to take on Peter as well. And do you know that Tallis calls Leonard 'Daddy'? A grown man who calls his father 'Daddy' is really out."

"Out, Hilda? Out of what?"

"Don't be so bolshy, Rupert. 'Yes, Dad.' 'Certainly, Daddy.' Oh, I suppose it's harmless but it's somehow a symptom of total ineptitude. Leonard is no fool, you know, though he's pretty peculiar too in some ways. I think I get on with Leonard now better than I do with Tallis."

"Leonard was very fond of Morgan."

"Yes. The break must have been a blow to him. I thought I'd go over there tomorrow. Have you got any matchboxes for Leonard?"

"I'll look. What are you going to say to Peter?"

"Nothing special. I can do nothing with Peter, dear heart. You know how it is. We both get emotional, and then Peter just withdraws into that awful unfeeling blankness. Oh God!"

"I blame myself—"

"For what? That's the trouble. For what? What mistake did we make with Peter? You must see him soon again, Rupert, you really must."

"When I see Peter I find myself play-acting the stern father. It's not what I feel at all. It's just mechanical."

"I know. We've both of us been rather mechanized about Peter, I'm afraid. We thought if he found Cambridge too luxurious he would automatically enjoy helping Tallis with Jamaicans. But he doesn't appear to like that either!"

"If only he wanted to go abroad. When I was his age—"

"Yes, yes. I suppose Tallis hadn't anything new to say when you last saw him? He never has."

"About Peter? He made one rather cryptic remark. He said Peter wasn't too strong on the mine and thine front."

"What on earth does that mean? He can't mean that Peter *steals* things?"

"I didn't pursue the matter. I'd just had a pretty grim half-hour with the boy. And a number of black children were screaming in the doorway."

"Darling, I suspect Tallis really irritates you just as much as he irritates me!"

"He lacks the concept of privacy."

"Anyway, Tallis always exaggerates. He likes everything to be awful."

"It's the characteristic of an unhappy man."

"Rupert, I think we should ask Tallis over here and discuss the whole matter and make some entirely new plan. Oh, damn, we can't if Morgan's here."

"I'm afraid Tallis has just rather lost his touch where Peter's concerned. He used to have some authority over him, but not any longer."

"The scales have fallen. People get over Tallis. I'm sure Morgan has. Anyway, I wish to God *someone* would persuade Peter to go back to Cambridge in October!"

"I thought perhaps a talk with Axel might—"

"Yes, I thought of that, but I rather suspect that Peter's gone off Axel. He used to like him. But recently— And you know how Peter's never really got on with Simon."

"The two things may be connected. There's still a good deal of time, you know, Hilda. And the college is being very decent about it."

"I know, we mustn't fret too much. I wonder if Morgan could help Peter."

"He used to be awfully attached to her, and he admires her, which is important with Peter."

"Of course he's grown up a lot since he last saw Aunty Morgan."

"Morgan may be in need of help herself."

"I know, Rupert. I suspect this whole thing has been a pretty severe shipwreck. Morgan treasures her self-esteem. And it must have taken a knock. What's that Latin tag you're always quoting about *dilig* something?"

"*Dilige et fac quod vis.* Love and do as you please."

"Yes. I think Morgan imagined she could live by that. And it's turned out a mess."

"I doubt if any human being can live by that. That we can't is a fundamental feature of this jumble."

"Did you say 'jungle' or 'jumble'?"

"Jumble. Human existence."

"Why are you always quoting the thing then, if it has no application?"

"It's—an attractive idea."

"Pouf! Yes, I do think Morgan will need help, and not only from me. Everyone must rally round. After all, she's very fond of you and Simon. We must all support her."

"When is Morgan arriving from America? She's coming by boat, isn't she?"

"Yes, it'll be another ten days at least. She didn't say the exact date."

"Julius may have moved on by then."

"That might be just as well. I wonder if Morgan has written to Peter."

"We'd have seen the letter."

"She might have written to college."

"You mean if she has, Peter will have told Tallis she's coming?"

"I doubt if she'll have written to him, actually. She's been so terribly depressed lately. She's probably forgotten Peter's existence. Anyway, she might have a go at him when she does arrive. At least she's an intellectual, not like me."

"Don't be silly, Hilda. Of course you're an intellectual. You—"

"I can't think of anything dottier than arguing about whether I'm an intellectual on our twentieth wedding anniversary! I mean I'm not one of your trained minds."

"Well, you could have been, only I snatched you up so early. You don't regret it, do you, darling, not having been to a university? You know it isn't important."

"Yet it's important that Tallis got a second. You mention it about once a month. All right, I'm only teasing you. I'm not an academic type. Morgan is, to her fingertips. You know, her being cleverer than Tallis was half the trouble. Tallis is a man without ideas, and Morgan lives by ideas. No wonder Julius turned out to be a pretty strong counter-attraction."

"Yes. She would be likely to be dazzled by Julius's cleverness. I'm afraid your sister is a bit of a cleverness-snob."

"Why snob? These are serious values. And cleverness can be sexual power. I must say Julius is terribly good-looking anyway, with that weird fair Jewishness. And Tallis is such a sort of *runt*."

"What a horrid word, Hilda. Surely that can't truthfully describe anybody."

"Why not, you high-minded old ass? Can 'sagacious open-faced and virile' truthfully describe someone?"

"Who are you trying to describe?"

"You, of course!"

"Hilda, you should have been a philosopher."

"I suppose Julius *will* ring up? I mean, I hope he won't feel he's *persona non grata* here after the story with Morgan."

"I think he'll ring up. Julius is a tremendously straightforward person."

"I must confess I'm curious to see how Julius will carry it off. Not that I know him particularly well, he's always been so much your friend. But he's a very interesting object."

"I'm curious too. But there'll be no excuses or undignified prevarications, that's certain. Julius may be clever, but he's also very truthful and sort of simple."

"If only Julius and Morgan had met years ago."

"Well, they've met now and it doesn't seem to have worked."

"We'll see, we'll see. Give me more champagne, will you, darling, and could you just tilt the umbrella a little more? Rupert, if only Peter would come, if only he'd come out through that door now. I said I was happy. And in everything to do with you I am, quite perfectly. But this other thing is such a cloud on the horizon. I can't help worrying the whole time with Peter in this awful mood." .

"I think it *is* a mood, my dear, and as moods pass, it will pass."

"I hope you're right. If we could only break down the mechanism. If I could only stop acting the emotional mother and you the stern father."

"I am sure that love tells in the end, Hilda. There are times when one's just got to go on loving somebody helplessly, with blank hope and blank faith. When love just *is* hope and faith in their most denuded form. Then love becomes almost impersonal and loses all its attractiveness and its ability to console. But it is just then that it may exert its greatest power. It is just then that it may really be able to redeem. Love has its own cunning beyond our conscious wiles. Peter is being difficult, but he knows that he has got a home in our love. He probably relies on it more than he realizes."

"*Amor vincit omnia.* That's one of the tags I do know."

"In some sense. Ultimately. In the end."

"You are such a wise person, Rupert. You have so much instinctive wisdom and goodness of heart. It sometimes worries me that you're putting it all into a book, if you see what I mean."

"You think I may damage my excellent instincts by analysing them! But I am not talking about myself in that book. The book is about real virtue, not instinct."

"I think you have real virtue. All right, I'm not being fulsome, it's quite an important remark. I think real virtue only comes in the instinctive kind, in your kind. It's connected with the heart, with natural responsibilities and real affections. Anything else is just cold—it's abstract—it's philosophy."

"Well, my book isn't philosophy either, Hilda. I'm a civil servant. I'm not a proper philosopher. I'm just a Sunday metaphysician."

"It looks like philosophy to me."

"If it was you wouldn't understand it."

"I don't understand it! I'm not against your book, darling. But I do wish you'd finish it. Oh, I know you'll miss it. But I keep worrying in case it gets burnt or lost or something. Eight years' work. All those precious pages of tiny writing and no carbon copy."

"I have very nearly finished it. Then we'll have a celebration. And it can be typed and you can stop worrying."

"Will it make you famous, Rupert?"

"I'm afraid not, dear. Do you want me to be famous? Hilda, you didn't really mind my refusing that title, did you?"

"No, that's different. Though 'Lady Foster' would have sounded rather well. I could have had some pink postcards printed with *From Lady Foster* on them. No, no, sweetheart, you must follow your judgement. Or what I called your instinct. I absolutely trust its absolute rightness. God bless you, my darling. Here's to the next happy twenty years."

✿ | TWO

"Penny for them."

"Julius King."

"Oh."

"What do you mean, 'oh'?"

"Just 'oh.' "

"You seem dismayed."

"I'm not dismayed."

"Perhaps you ought to be."

"Stop it, Axel."

"You are so teasable, Simon!"

Axel was edging the light blue Hillman Minx along through the closely packed rush-hour traffic in the Cromwell Road. It was a mystery to Simon, who could not drive, how all those cars could bustle along together without scraping each other. Simon, although he was so slim and graceful and handy in the house, was accident-prone, and Axel would not let him learn to drive. Simon pretended to have a sense of grievance about this. It might always come in useful to make Axel feel that he owed him a treat. In fact, being driven by Axel was a source of ecstasy which never dimmed. Simon felt this ecstasy now as he extended his arm along the seat behind his friend, the stuff of his sleeve just touching the collar of Axel's jacket.

"When's Julius arriving?"

"He's arrived."

"You didn't tell me."

"I only heard it this morning, Simon. He sent me a letter to the office."

"Why to the office?"

"Because he didn't know my address, fool."

"Oh."

Simon and Axel had lived in Axel's small flat in Bayswater during the first two years of their liaison. A year ago they had purchased a house in Barons Court. Simon was still happily engaged in interior decoration. Axel was indifferent to his surroundings. Simon felt the purchase of the house to be a deeply significant move. Axel had never professed to believe that their relationship would last. He still firmly refused to predict its future.

"When did you last see Julius, Axel?"

"Nearly four years ago. Before he went to South Carolina. And a bit before my momentous meeting with you in Athens, my dear. When did you last see him?"

"Oh, ages ago. It must be six years. I met him at Rupert's. But I've never really known Julius. He never paid any attention to me."

"Well, don't sound so aggrieved!"

"I'm not aggrieved. He was Rupert's friend anyway. Funny, he's never seen us together."

Axel was a coeval colleague of Rupert's in the civil service. He was a clever dry silent man. Through Rupert, Simon had known Axel slightly for some time without having any notion that he was homosexual. Simon suspected that Rupert had not known it either. He also suspected that Rupert was not altogether pleased when his old friend and colleague took up with his younger brother. But of course he could never discuss Axel with Rupert now. Axel had had love relationships with men when he was a student, and he had subsequently lived for some time with a dentist who later emigrated to New Zealand. At the time of the accidental and revelatory meeting in Athens, Axel had been living alone for several years and, he told Simon, was resigned to living alone forever. Axel never hunted. He once said, and it lightened Simon's life for many days, "You were a fantastic stroke of luck for me, kid."

"We're late again, Axel. You always make us late when we go to Rupert's. I suspect you do it on purpose."

"Possibly I do, little one."

Simon knew that Axel felt that it was rather bad form of Rupert to invite them to a wedding anniversary celebration. But nothing was said about this. Rupert and Axel remained close friends. Simon, though he was very fond of his elder brother, felt the association to be faintly menacing, just as he had in earlier years felt as menacing the association of Rupert and his father, even though it was so patently dedicated to Simon's welfare. He had deeply loved his mother, formerly an actress, who died when he was ten. Elder brother and Papa had brooded lovingly over his teens. Simon was grateful but oppressed. His father had died when Simon was twenty. Rupert was still instinctively paternal.

"Let's invite Julius to dinner," said Simon. This suggestion, unexpected to Simon himself, was the result of a very quick train of thought, beginning with a mental picture of Julius and Axel tête-à-tête at luncheon. Simon was a good cook. He liked to entertain in his own home. He was proud of his *ménage* with Axel and liked to show it off to selected friends.

"If you like. You think of a date and I'll drop Julius a note."

"Where's Julius staying?"

"At the Hilton Hotel. But he's looking round for a flat."

"Oh. He's going to stay some time?"

"Yes."

At the beginning of their association Axel had given Simon a lecture about jealousy. "We must trust each other and not be jealous." Simon had nodded his head, but he could no more control such feelings by acts of will than he could control the peristaltic movement of his gut. Whenever another man came close to Axel, Simon ached with jealousy. In fact, Axel was by nature a very jealous man himself, which perhaps accounted for the seriousness of the lecture.

"How was the day at the museum, dear boy?"

"Much as usual. That quarrel with the V. and A. is still going on. How was the day at the office?"

"Boring. The balance-of-payments meeting went on interminably. I do wish Rupert was still in the chair."

Axel had several times explained to Simon what the balance of payments was, but Simon had never understood. He felt he could not ask again.

"Did you have your swim today?"

"Yes, it was marvellous."

"You're quite an addict. Did you see Hilda?"

"Yes. Axel, Morgan is coming back."

"Really? When?"

"Oh, soon—in about ten days. I wonder if she knows Julius will be in London."

"I suppose she'll stay with Rupert and Hilda."

"I suppose so. By the way, Hilda said not to tell Tallis that Morgan was coming."

"Why ever not?"

"Well, Morgan might not want to see Tallis and there's no point in upsetting him, I imagine."

"I don't approve of these subterfuges."

Another subject upon which Axel had had occasion to lecture Simon at the beginning of their love was the subject of truthfulness. "Don't tell me lies, even trivial ones, and don't conceal things from me. Love should be without fear." Simon had found this injunction surprisingly difficult to follow. He concluded that he must have an exceptionally evasive temperament. Now that he had begun to notice it, he saw that he tended to tell small almost pointless lies almost all of the time and to embroider any tale in the telling. He confessed this once to Axel and was rewarded by an unusual demonstration of affection. The lies decreased in number and were almost always unimportant. The tendency persisted, however. Axel himself was an extremely truthful person. Perhaps in this case it was his early perception of Simon's frailty which accounted for the seriousness of the lecture.

"I think it's quite wrong to conceal this from Tallis," said Axel.

"Well, you argue it with Hilda." Oh dear, I hope it isn't going to be one of those evenings, thought Simon. Axel could be quite aggressive. "Let's ask Tallis over soon," he added. "We haven't seen him for ages."

"You suddenly want to see Tallis because you're *interested*."

"You are funny, Axel. You never want to see people when they're in trouble."

"One's interest is always base."

"But you know I like Tallis anyway, we both do. And what's wrong with being interested?"

"Any concern we have with that matter is bound to be vulgar. I think we'd much better leave Tallis alone for the present. We can't help him, we'd merely be tourists."

"You think he's in for a bad time?"

"Yes. Don't you?"

"I don't know," said Simon. He had been shaken by the news of Morgan's imminent return. He had been surprisingly shaken by her marriage to Tallis, though he was genuinely attached to Tallis and though he certainly did not want to marry Morgan himself. That had never been in question. Morgan, who was a year his senior, had always been like a delightful sister. He went to bed with her one night when he was a homosexually experienced twenty-one and she was a heterosexually experienced twenty-two. In spite of encouragement from Morgan nothing was able to occur, however. This was Simon's only experiment with the other sex. It preyed on his mind that he had never told Axel. Axel had never been to bed with a woman.

"You don't think Morgan will go back to Tallis?" said Simon.

"No, I don't, in fact. But it's not our affair." Axel was puritanical about gossip.

Simon did not know what he felt about Morgan going back to Tallis. He supposed he wanted it to happen because he supposed he wanted Tallis to be happy and he supposed that Tallis wanted Morgan back. Tallis could never be vindictive. All the same, would it not be more dignified of Morgan not to go back? Simon cared about Morgan's dignity. To go back: that smacked of penitence, humility, forgiveness, things which slightly made Simon shudder when he envisaged them for Morgan, though for himself in his relations with Axel they were an aspect of sex. Simon had been upset by Morgan's staying on in South Carolina and upset by the news of her love affair with Julius. Morgan was altogether a source of considerable upset.

"I suppose Tallis wants her back," said Simon.

"We've no evidence one way or the other."

"But I doubt if she'll go and I doubt if it would work if she did."

"Tallis is probably better off on his own," said Axel. "He's a natural solitary. I was surprised at his getting married at all and especially to Morgan."

"I think Morgan is awfully attractive," said Simon, and then wished he hadn't.

"Morgan means well but she's fundamentally a very silly person. Hilda is far more genuinely a rational being, though like so many women she preferred marriage to the development of her mind. Morgan's a lightweight."

Simon did not care for Axel's division of humanity into light and heavy weights. He had too clear a notion of which category he might be said to belong to himself. He could never quite understand Axel's hostility to Morgan. Of late he had very reluctantly suspected that Axel's old and deep attachment to Julius had been hurt by Julius's fling with Morgan. Simon was far too diffident to imagine that Axel disliked Morgan because Simon loved her. Yet that in fact was the origin of the dislike.

"I suppose Morgan and Julius have absolutely parted," said Simon. "Hilda seemed to think that that at least was certain."

"Haven't the faintest idea."

"Well, I suppose we'll soon know. It'll be nice to see Julius again." What a liar I am, thought Simon.

"I'm glad Julius gave up the germ warfare thing," said Axel. "I knew he would. I must say I do look forward to seeing him. Julius has *style*. He is the sort of man who could get away with wearing a monocle."

"He could get away with anything."

"He is a most amusing companion."

"More amusing than me?"

"Why do you make everything personal?"

"But this *is* personal."

"You don't have to amuse me, Simon. I love you."

"Thanks." Simon pressed his arm very slightly against Axel's back. The contact, which he had been saving up, caused deep joy.

"I've always been a bit afraid of Julius, really," said Simon. This was better, a nearer approach to the truth, a mitigation of the recent lie.

"He can be alarming."

"He would not be a man to have as an enemy."

"True. But he'll never be our enemy, so we needn't worry."

"I remember someone saying they thought he was a bit ruthless and cynical." I am going too far, thought Simon. And in fact I never heard anyone say that. These are my own impressions.

"He's certainly not cynical," said Axel. "He may seem so sometimes because he's exceptionally honest. Dostoevsky says that plain truth is so implausible that most people instinctively mix in a little falsehood. Julius just doesn't. And as for ruthlessness, a man of principle can seem ruthless to ordinary mortals. Julius isn't a compromiser."

Well, I am, thought Simon. "Yes, I see what you mean."

"Julius is a man with no nonsense about him."

I am a man with a lot of nonsense about me, thought Simon. Nonsense is indeed the element in which I live. "Yes, of course."

"Julius might read all your letters if you left him alone in your flat, but he'd be sure to tell you afterward. He can be tough, but there's something morally attractive about him."

I'm sure I have many attractions, thought Simon, but I doubt if moral attractiveness is one of them. "I can see that. Julius is awfully handsome, don't you think?"

"Yes. That fair look is so unusual in a Jew. He's Sephardic, of course."

"I'd quite forgotten he was a Jew." That was another thing. Axel had rather a penchant for Jews.

"Julius is a man almost entirely without vanity," said Axel. "It's rare."

"He always seemed rather proud to me," said Simon. Reflection on Julius was bringing back memories of being ignored by him.

"I said vanity," said Axel. "Not pride. The concepts are different."

Axel, who together with Rupert had read philosophy at Oxford, liked to argue about words. When he carried on these arguments with other Oxford-trained men Simon felt uneasy. Simon had read history of art at the Courtauld. But even about art Axel often contradicted him. And Axel was often right.

"I wonder if Julius will look up Rupert," said Simon, "or if he'll keep away."

"Of course he'll look up Rupert."

"Then he may run into Morgan."

"That's not our trouble," said Axel, pushing the Hillman Minx rapidly across the changing lights.

"Oh dear, we *are* late, Axel."

"They'll be perfectly happy drinking. By the way, for heavens sake don't let's stay too long. I simply couldn't get you away last time. Remember the signal. When I start fingering my lapel you make our excuses."

"Well, don't do it *too* soon!"

"You know I hate starting to drink so early in the evening."

It was never too early for Simon to start to drink. "All right."

"Rupert drinks too much," said Axel.

"Oh, I don't think so." Axel had sometimes shown signs of wanting to reduce Simon's ration of alcohol. Simon, who was fond of the stuff, was very anxious to avoid a conflict of wills on this front.

"Yes, he does," said Axel. "Rupert is so damned high-minded one tends to forget how unstable he is."

"I would never call Rupert unstable."

"He's a terribly emotional man. The rationality is superficial. On the other hand, he's lucky."

"You mean he hasn't been tried? But he's so intellectual, Axel. That book on philosophy—"

"We shall see, about that so-called book on philosophy. I suspect it will turn out to be a farrago of emotion."

"Don't tease Rupert about it, Axel."

"You're a kind thoughtful boy, and it was smart of you to remember to buy those flowers for Hilda, though I think you've bought an absurdly large bunch."

"It was meant to be an absurdly large bunch."

"Well, you can hand it over with a few well-chosen words. Don't do that, Simon, damn you, I've told you before!"

Simon had tilted the driving mirror so that it reflected his own face. "Sorry." What Simon saw in the mirror: a thin-faced pointed-nosed young man with a prominent rounded lower lip and anxious brown eyes. A lot of very slightly curly carefully kept hair of a darker hue than Rupert's and worn considerably longer. A delicate dandified head. The similarity of the two brothers resided rather in expression than in feature: a look of gentleness in Rupert and a similar look of diffidence in Simon. Axel, whose eye Simon could now apologetically catch in the readjusted mirror, was dark, although his surname was Nilsson and his ancestors were Swedish. Axel's hair was straight, the colour of rich dark earth, and also worn rather long. His eyebrows were bushy and his eyes a curious colour of light blue-grey. His mouth, though not unduly thin, was straight and rather hard. Some people found this face supercilious and forbidding. Simon thought it beautifully austere. He worshipped the traits of asceticism in one to whom, where love was concerned, nothing was denied.

"For God's sake, stop patting your hair, Simon."

"Sorry, darling."

"And I believe you're wearing that ghastly after-shave lotion again."

"I didn't put much on. You can only smell it because it's so hot in the car."

"Try to remember you're male not female, will you?"

"Sorry, sweetheart."

Axel hated the least suggestion of "camp." He banned homosexual jokes and indeed *risqué* jokes of any kind, nor would he tolerate upon Simon's lips the cant language of the homosexual world; although he was now prepared with misgivings to accept the word "queer," which Simon represented to him as being by this time a general usage and not a term of art. "Nothing," declared Axel, "is more boring than homosexuals who can talk about nothing but homosexuality." Simon, who almost always gave way to Axel, relinquished these trivia with a certain regret. It was a myth of their relationship that Simon's life before he met Axel had been depressing and even sordid, but this was only half true. It was indeed Simon's nature to seek to give his heart, and to want to give it entirely, and unresponsive and unfaithful partners, of whom he had had many, had caused him much unhappiness. Yet he had enjoyed some of his adventures and liked the jokey parochial atmosphere of the gay bars which he had been used to frequent in the old days before Athens and Axel. His philosophy had been: one offers oneself in various quarters and one hopes for love. The love he had hoped for was real love. But the search had had its lighter side.

In fact Axel did something extremely important for Simon. He made Simon understand for the first time that it was perfectly *ordinary* to be homosexual. Simon had never exactly felt guilty about his preference. But he had felt it as a peculiarity, something rather nice and even perhaps a bit funny, something rather like a game, but definitely odd, to be concealed, giggled about, and endlessly discussed and inspected in the private company of fellow oddities. He had never quite seen it as a fundamental and completely ordinary way of being a human being, which was how Axel saw it. Axel gloomily accepted a degree of discretion which the prejudices of society seemed still to make inevitable. But he refused to belong to a special homosexual "world," to what he called "that goddam secret organization."

Simon did his best to change his ways and to drop what Axel referred to as "tribal habits." But sometimes he felt that the change was only superficial and he was almost being guilty of insincerity. He felt uneasy about some of his instincts which he now judged to be frivolous. He speculated endlessly about what Axel really thought about him. He did not doubt Axel's love. But at the beginning Axel had certainly loved against his better judgement. Was he still doing so? How much did it matter not understanding about the balance of payments? Did Axel think he was stupid? Did he see him as a bit shallow, as a trifle corrupted, even worst of all, as rather vulgar?

A spiteful spectator of the early stages of Simon's romance had once said to him, "Axel says he just *adores* your particular brand of vulgarity." This reported remark tortured Simon until he suddenly realized that Axel could not possibly have made it. Why was this not obvious at once? Because it corresponded to a deep fear. In three years the fear had diminished but not departed. Simon remained diffident and uncertain. "You're a damn muddler, Simon," Axel had once said to him angrily. "It's a moral fault and it's not charming." Simon reflected and realized how much in the past he had traded on the charm of a certain fecklessness. ("Oh, you *flibbertigibbet,* you!" one of Axel's predecessors had been used to cry, while Simon hung his head coyly.) Would fecklessness and muddle one day lead him here to make a fatal mistake? Could there *be* a fatal mistake? He thought sometimes of asking Axel this question, but he knew that Axel would not answer it, any more than he would ever answer Simon's so often repeated cry of "Will you love me always?" "How on earth do I know?" said Axel.

"I will love you forever, Axel, to the end of the world. I give myself to you now and forever. I will be faithful to you always. I rejoice that you exist, that I have met you, that I can touch you, that we live in the same century. I will never cease to bless you for my good fortune." Simon could not prevent himself from saying such things constantly. They burst out of him as a paean of thanksgiving at his phenomenal luck in having discovered Axel and at finding that where he loved he also was loved. Axel smiled. Occasionally he said "Good" or "You do that" or "That's all right then," and pulled Simon's hair. Sometimes he said, "Oh, do shut up, Simon. It means nothing." Simon was not good at Axel's moods, whose principle he could not understand. Axel was often gloomy without explanation, and very occasionally made Simon distraught with tenderness and anxiety by bursting into tears. We *feel* life so differently, thought Simon. Oh, what agony it is, he thought, to love somebody so much and not to *be* him.

This difference of "feel" was sometimes the occasion of conflict. Simon was greedy for the surface texture of his life, whose substance he luxuriously munched second after second as if it were a fruit with a thin soft furry exterior and a firm sweet fleshy inside. Even unhappiness, if it were not terrible unhappiness, came to him like that. (Terrible unhappiness was different. It divorced him from his body.) Simon loved times of day, eating, drinking, looking, touching. All his experiences were ceremonies. He liked the slow savouring of moments of pleasure and he engineered his life to contain as many of these as possible. It sometimes seemed to him that all his enjoyments were similar in kind though not in degree, whether he was stroking a cat or a Chippendale chair or drinking a dry martini or looking at a picture by Titian or getting into bed with Axel. Whereas Axel had a much more petulant and withdrawn attitude to time and his life was much more layered and segmented. Simon felt sure that Axel's delight in *Don Giovanni* was quite different in kind from his delight in Simon. Axel had secret lives and hidden utterly un-Simon modes of experience. He had a passion for opera. Simon, who detested opera, had pretended for nearly a year to like it until a frenzy of excruciating boredom had wrung the truth from him screaming at last and exposed him to Axel's bitter reproaches, not for his lack of taste but for his failure to be honest. When they travelled abroad together Simon was an anxious busy greedy tourist while Axel was often maddeningly abstracted from the urgencies of the present. Axel was capable of sitting reading a novel in his hotel and ignoring a great monument at a hundred yards' distance. They quarrelled furiously once in Venice when Axel's dilatoriness made them arrive two days running at the Accademia just when it was shutting.

My love is never without anxiety, thought Simon, never without pain. Yet perhaps this piercing quality is inseparable from my happiness, from my own peculiar highest best happiness. Could it ever be otherwise? Was it not perhaps quite otherwise for hetero-sexual married people, for Hilda and Rupert for instance? He could not believe that they lived in this constant condition of ecstatic pain. For Axel not to hurt him terribly in the most ordinary pass-ages of their life together cost them both a kind of effort. There was at every moment total vulnerability. There was a dangerous thrilling trembling inner circuit of the soul. Simon had once tried to explain to Axel about this terrible vulnerability and Axel had not mocked him. Yet Axel had not said, "Yes, I feel like that too." Did love fill Axel's life in the way that it filled his own? There was peace sometimes at night. Sleeping with someone one loves one escapes from time. Yet there were early morning awakenings too when Simon wondered: what dreadful things lie ahead?

The light blue Hillman Minx swept into the Boltons. Feathery bushes and plump trees posed motionless with evening against white walls yellowed by a powdery sun. Pink roses clambered upon stucco balustrades and multi-coloured irises peered through painted lattices.

"Yes, I think Tallis is probably in for a bad time," said Axel thoughtfully.

"Why now especially?"

"Morgan will make—some ghastly muddle."

"Poor Tallis." And poor Morgan, thought Simon. Poor poor Morgan. Proud Morgan. I must try to help her, he thought. I shall go to her. I shall help her to pick up the pieces. And with the phrase "pick up the pieces" a curious thrill of pleasure shot through him. He would enjoy that somehow, helping Morgan to pick up the pieces.

The car turned into Priory Grove.

"Oh, do look at that poodle, Axel. Isn't he perfectly sweet?"

"Don't be soppy, dear boy. Yes, he is rather nice."

"I do wish we could have a cat, Axel. Don't you think we could?"

"It would be too much of a responsibility, Simon. We did agree about that before, you know. We're out all day. How would it get in and out?"

"We could have a cat-flap."

"A cat-flap! Sorry, no!"

"I would accept the responsibility. And think of the pleasure of a beastie in the house!"

"One beastie in the house is quite enough! We'd be enslaved by the animal."

"But I'd love that!"

" 'If you want to eat spaghetti you must use your teeth.' Wittgenstein."

"I don't think Wittgenstein really said any of those things you say he said!"

"Hell, there doesn't seem to be anywhere to park."

"When I first knew this road there wasn't a single car in it."

"You make that remark every time we go to Rupert's."

"Sorry to be such a bore, darling!"

"No, no, it's rather nice and cosy to hear these repetitions."

"Axel."

"Yes."

"The way your hair grows down the back of your neck drives me completely and absolutely crazy."

"Good show."

"Will you love me forever?"

"Haven't the faintest idea."

"I'll love you forever."

"Decent of you. Could we get in there, I wonder?"

"No, I don't think so. You're Apollo and I'm Marsyas. You'll end by flaying me."

"That's an image of love, actually, Apollo and Marsyas."

"How do you mean?"

"The agony of Marsyas is the inevitable agony of the human soul in its desire to achieve God."

"The things you know."

"The things you failed to learn at the Courtauld."

"I don't believe it though. Someone is flayed really. And there's only blood and pain and no love."

"You think our planet is like that?"

"I think our planet is like that."

"No redeeming grace?"

"None at all."

"None, Simon?"

"Well, only this kind."

"What do you mean, *only* this kind? Now, Simon, please, *not* just outside Rupert's house!"

❤ | THREE

"Oh, hello, my dears!" cried Hilda, jumping up.

Axel and Simon emerged through the french windows into the garden. Simon lifted his hand against the dazzle from the flickering blue pool.

"Sorry we're late, darling," said Simon. "Here, we've brought you a tiny bouquet with lots and lots of love. Let me kiss you. Hello, Rupert. Whoopee and all that."

"We congratulate you on the longevity of your married bliss," said Axel. "Evening, Rupert. We meet again."

"Oh Simon, what wonderful flowers and so *many* of them! I don't think anyone has ever given me such a huge bunch in my life. You're positively staggering under it!"

"Good, I hoped to break a record."

"Let me refresh them in the pool. Then I'll find a vase directly. Axel, could you open this bottle of champagne; you do it in such a masterly way and Rupert always smashes something. I'm afraid Rupert and I seem to have drunk nearly a whole bottle while we were waiting for you!"

"Very sensible of you," said Simon. "Now we must catch up. Gosh, it's hot. We expected to find you *in* the pool."

The cork flew out and plopped neatly into the water. Creamy champagne flowed into four glasses.

"Happiness, my pets!" cried Simon. "Happiness!"

"Happiness!" they all said and drank.

"I'll just put these in a vase," said Hilda. Carrying the flowers she moved across the hot flagstones and into the darkness of the house.

In the sudden coolness of the drawing-room she paused. After the bright sun the room was for a moment almost invisible, a matrix of dusky colour splashes and points of dim light. Hilda laid the flowers down on the table. She sighed, yielding herself to float lightly in a cool murk of rich colour, spreading out her hands as if to caress velvety colours about her in the air. She thought, I am a little drunk. It's nice.

After a few moments the room began to assemble itself, the cloudy colours to withdraw themselves into familiar surfaces. Hilda looked into the tall round-topped segmented gilt mirror which rose above the mantelpiece to see how her make-up was competing with the sun. A gilded Cupid with a ready bow, airborne at the apex, gazes silently down as Hilda burrows in a little brown silk woven vanity bag for lipstick and powder. She peers intently at the thrust-out face, radiantly perky, though now perhaps becoming just a little plump. If the head is not carefully carried there is a double chin. Dark natural curls frame the face and cascade in rings to the neck. The famous angel-look. Should not this hair be dyed before the grey becomes too apparent? Prominent grey-blue eyes scrutinize the image, behind which the trinkets of the room crowd and glitter. Moist pink lipstick is quickly dabbed, orange-brown powder light dusted onto shiny sunburnt nose and cheeks. Hilda approves herself.

She turned again to the garden. The sharp division between sun and shade made it seem far away, separated from her as if by a proscenium arch. Axel and Rupert were talking, just inaudibly, tilting their canvas chairs forward toward each other. Simon had taken off his socks and sandals and rolled up his trouser legs and was sitting on the edge of the pool with his legs plunged in the water almost to the knee. He had plucked some camomile and was smelling it luxuriously with his eyes closed. How crumpled his trousers will be, thought Hilda. She sighed again and felt a familiar ache which made her put her hand to her breast. I've been so lucky all my life, she thought. It would be unjust if I were not sometimes a little intimidated by my joy. She thought then of Peter and moved her hand as if to make a sign of blessing in the air. Peter will be all right, she thought, and felt certain of it in that moment. My bond with him has never been broken. All shall be well. But there was something more than that, and almost lazily she recognized what it was that had suddenly so caught and pleased her. Morgan was coming home. Morgan was coming home for refuge and comfort and help. Hilda would pick up the pieces.

Hilda took the flowers and went on into the little pantry where the flower vases were kept. It was so dark and cool in here that she nearly shivered. She found a big vase and filled it at the sink, letting the water overflow and run over her hot wrists. She did not trouble to undo the bouquet but just pushed up the paper a little and plunged the ends of the stems into the water. Then carrying the dripping vase she went back through the drawing-room and out into the dazzling garden.

"Let me give you some more champagne, darling," said Simon, jumping up and scattering drops of water.

Hilda put the vase down on the white cast-iron table beside the open bottle. "Phew. Yes, please. I think I'll follow your example." She sat down on the edge of the pool. The water, very faintly cool, encased foot, ankle, calf.

"You practically sizzle as you go in in this weather. Do you know my feet are dry already and the paving stones are burning them. Here you are, Hilda dear."

"Thank you, Simon. I wanted to ask your advice about the bathroom—"

"Yes, I know. I took the liberty of having a decko this morning. Now there's a very nice steam-proof paper I saw at Sanderson's, black with huge turquoise roses in big squares . . ."

"I wish we'd had you in the chair," Axel was saying. "Ogden Smith can't keep to the point himself let alone keep anyone else to it."

"I had to be at that thing on invisible earnings."

"I hear there's a parliamentary question about that coming up."

"It's up! In fact it's on my desk, for my sins."

"I'll bring you round a sample on Monday," said Simon, "and of the Marrakesh tiles, only they *are* rather expensive. And you *must* have a turquoise bathrobe to match."

"And towels I suppose."

"I thought perhaps emerald green towels."

"I can't understand a word they're saying, can you? Do you think they do it on purpose to put us in our place?"

"Probably! Move up, Hilda, I must get my feet back into the water. Hilda, isn't it wonderful that Morgan's coming back? I keep remembering it and feeling so glad."

"Yes. I'm glad she's coming *home*. I couldn't bear the thought of her being so unhappy so far away."

"We must stop her from being unhappy, mustn't we?"

"I hope you'll make a point of seeing her, Simon. She'll need old friends."

"By the way," said Axel's voice, faintly metallic, "I was saying to Simon, Hilda, don't you think Tallis ought to be told that Morgan's coming back? If he doesn't know already, that is."

"I thought it better not to tell him," said Hilda. She shifted round, drawing her dripping feet from the water and tucking them under the heat of her thighs. Axel and Rupert were still leaning forward, tilting the canvas and aluminum folding chairs beside the table and nursing replenished glasses of champagne. "I doubt if he knows. I'm sure Morgan hasn't written to him. I thought Morgan should be left free to decide what to do, whether to see him or not."

"What about Tallis's freedom?" said Axel. "Doesn't he have equal rights? Shouldn't he have the chance to decide whether to see *her* or not? I mean, I see your point, Hilda, but I do think Tallis—"

"Which of us knows Tallis best?" said Hilda.

After a pause Axel said, "I suppose I do."

"Well, do you know how Tallis is likely to behave if he hears Morgan's back?"

"I haven't the faintest idea."

"There you are. It's much better not to tell him. And it's kinder too. Morgan may be going straight on to somewhere else—"

"What Tallis may or may not do isn't our affair," said Axel. "And it's not for us to spare his feelings, it's an impertinence. Put yourself in his place. Suppose he finds out later she's been in London for ages, or else was in London for a short while, and we all conspired not to tell him. Don't you agree with me, Rupert?"

"Yes, I do,' said Rupert. "I agreed with Hilda before, now I'm convinced by your arguments. It would be a deception which Tallis would be quite right to resent." He put his glass down, wiping the sweat from his hot plump face back into his faded pale hair.

Hilda knew that Rupert was often nervy and argumentative when Axel and Simon were there, possibly to relieve a tension in himself caused by two-way jealousy of his brother and his friend. But this was not now her concern. Of course Axel was right in a way, it had only to be put clearly for one to see it, but all the same she did not want Tallis to be told. She wanted every possible weight and pressure to be taken off her sister; she wanted her to be left, for some time at any rate, in peace. Suppose Tallis were to come running round, demanding to see his wife, demanding her immediate return? Hilda had known Tallis longer than any of them: she it was who had introduced him to the family after she had made his acquaintance during a general election campaign. But she could not, any more than Axel, predict his reactions. He would not be deliberately unkind, but he could be extremely tactless. Hilda wanted Morgan here and wanted her unmolested and with time to assemble herself. She wanted Morgan alone. "I think we should just wait anyway until Morgan comes. After all, she's not due for at least ten days. And she may still decide to delay longer or not to come at all."

"Well, I vote for truth-telling. I hope your book deals with this sort of thing, Rupert. I'm most impatient to see it. I expect to be told how to live, my dear fellow. I shall take it as my guide to behaviour and follow it slavishly."

Hilda knew that Axel was sceptical about the value of Rupert's book. We'll show him, she thought.

"I'm afraid if you want a guide to behaviour you'll be disappointed, Axel," said Rupert smiling. He too was aware of Axel's views but appeared to be unresentful. "No philosopher ever did produce a guide to behaviour, even when he thought that that was what he was doing."

"So you admit to being a philosopher at last?"

"No, no, I mean even philosophers are ambiguous, so *a fortiori* I am. The thing is just a meditation on a few concepts."

"The relation of love to truth and justice and some small matters of that sort, I gather."

"Some small matters of that sort! But the application must remain for the individual to decide."

"Poor individual. No one ever really looks after him. Now what I want is a sort of case book of morals like a guide to etiquette."

"Well, I think we shouldn't tell Tallis," said Hilda, speaking at the same time. "What do you feel, Simon?"

"Morgan will need time to rest and think things out."

"Precisely. You *do* see my point. I don't want her *bothered.*"

"Ordinary people can't *apply* philosophy, anyway. I doubt if even philosophers can."

"People can *use* moral concepts, as you used the concept of truth just now to persuade me. Anyone can do this."

"Maybe. But I think moral philosophy is something hopelessly personal. It just can't be communicated. 'If a lion could talk we would not understand him.' Wittgenstein."

"Oh Hilda! Axel, look! There's a hedgehog. He's just peeping out from behind that delphinium, you can see his nose! A *hedgehog!*"

"Yes, Simon," said Rupert. "We meant to tell you about the hedgehog, since you're so fond of our dumb friends."

"Isn't he sweet? Can you see him, Axel?" Simon was kneeling on the flagstones beside the delphinium. The hedgehog was still, hunching its back, peering shortsightedly and wrinkling up its black moist nose. "Do you think he'd mind if I picked him up?"

"They're covered with fleas," said Axel.

"Just for a moment. He's got such a soft furry underside. Now he's trying to curl up, but they never really do it properly, they're such defenceless beasts. Ouf, he *is* prickly."

"Put him back behind the plants," said Axel. "You're frightening him."

Simon lifted the hedgehog carefully and put it down out of sight at the back of the flower bed.

"Mind my *galtonia candicans,* Simon."

"Oh Hilda, how marvellous to have a hedgehog. Do you often see him? Do you feed him?"

"We put out bread and milk and assume it's him who eats it, I'm terrified he'll fall into the pool."

"They're incredibly stupid animals," said Axel.

"I'm sure he'd have more sense," said Simon.

"Simon is so sentimental," said Axel, "he even feels himself bound to rebut a slur upon the intelligence of hedgehogs."

"Well, I'm *sure* he has more sense. You *are* lucky. I do wish we had a proper garden. You really should get a cat, Hilda. Think how happy a pussy would be here. Axel won't let us have a cat—"

"Please be exact, Simon! We *agreed* that it just wasn't practicable for us to have a cat."

"Well, all right. But I wish you'd have a cat, Hilda, and I could come and visit it. A Siamese perhaps."

"I think I'd prefer a plain tabby."

"Or perhaps a black-and-white cat. A black cat with white paws."

"And a white face and a white tip to its tail—"

"No, just white paws, and—"

"Good God!" said Rupert.

There was a moment's silence. Hilda turned to follow his look. A figure had emerged from the drawing-room and was standing regarding them across the pool. It was Morgan.

Hilda began to struggle to her feet.

"Morgan!" cried Simon, simultaneously with Hilda's cry.

Morgan was wearing a light grey macintosh and carrying a blue canvas travelling bag which she now slowly put down at her feet. She stared rather blankly across the pool.

Hilda reached her and uttering a low "Ooh!" threw her arms round her sister's neck. She drew Morgan against her and pressed her cheek against Morgan's, closing her eyes. "Oh, thank God you've come home—"

Morgan remained completely stiff, then jerked her head away. With a firm pressure of the hand she terminated Hilda's embrace.

"You've got a swimming pool."

"Yes, it's new." Tears flooded into Hilda's eyes.

"Morgan—*darling*," said Simon. He took hold of her hand which was hanging limply by her side. He seemed about to kiss her cheek but kissed her hand instead. He kissed it several times.

"My dear," said Rupert. "Welcome." He took hold of Morgan's other hand and pressed it.

"Hello, Morgan," said Axel. He was fingering the lapel of his jacket.

Morgan drew her hands away. She looked round at them all with vague eyes. She wore oval steel-rimmed spectacles which she now removed and began to clean with a rather dirty handkerchief.

"Let me give you some champagne," cried Simon. "Don't bother, Hilda, she can have my glass."

Morgan put the spectacles on again, still standing rather stiffly and frowning against the sun. She looked at the champagne, the flowers. "Something's going on. It's someone's birthday—"

"Our wedding anniversary, darling."

"I didn't expect—a lot of people—a party—"

"It's only us, Morgan," said Simon. "Here."

"No, thank you, Simon. I don't want any champagne. I think I'll take this coat—off." She twitched her shoulders and the grey macintosh fell to the ground. Simon hastened to pick it up.

Hilda, the sudden tears abating, gazed at her sister. Morgan was wearing a very brief very crumpled blue cotton dress. Her straight dark hair was cut boyishly but not very short. Narrow brown eyes and long nervous nose. Her face was bony gaunt and tired. Her figure long-legged and slim. In a sudden quick vision Hilda understood. They had reached an age where the years told. How that gaunt thin look became her. Even the tiredness was a grace. Even the steel-rimmed spectacles were an adornment. Morgan was the handsome one now. "Oh, my heart!" said Hilda. She hugged her sister for a moment about the shoulders.

"We weren't expecting you for another ten days," said Rupert. "Look, won't you sit down?"

"No, thanks. I know. I decided to fly after all and let the luggage follow. I've just come now straight from the airport. Once I decided to come it was agony to stay another hour."

"I can imagine that," said Hilda. "Thank God you *have* come, my darling. I was terrified you'd change your mind."

"Morgan, I do wish you'd have a drink," said Simon. "It would do you good. Let me get you some whisky."

"I hope you're going to stay with us a good long time," said Hilda. "You're not just going on somewhere else, are you? What are your plans?"

"I don't know what I'm doing," said Morgan. "I don't know where I'm going. I have no plans. I have no intentions. I have no thoughts. I have just got off a jet plane and I feel crazy." She turned around toward the drawing-room.

"Of course, of course!" cried Hilda. "Come upstairs this minute, you poor sweet. The spare room is all ready. You must rest at once. Rupert, carry her bag, would you. Give me the coat, Simon. Come along, my own darling girl, home at last."

✿ | F O U R

"Which room am I in?"

"Here—"

Hilda pushed open the door and Morgan went in followed by her sister and brother-in-law. Rupert put the bag down, hesitated, and then, obeying a signal from Hilda, withdrew. Hilda closed the door.

Morgan looked at the bed which was covered by a heavy green silk bedspread. She slowly pulled the bedspread off onto the floor. She took off her glasses, laid herself carefully face down upon the bed, buried her face in the pillows, and, just as Hilda started to say something, burst into streams of silent tears.

There was a soft dragging sound as Hilda moved a chair across the carpet to the edge of the bed. A moment later she laid her arm across Morgan's heaving shoulders.

"Sorry, Hilda, please don't touch me."

"Sorry, darling."

"Sorry."

"Shall I go away?"

"No. Just stay here and be quiet."

There was silence in the room, through the open window a sound of bird song and a murmur of voices where Rupert and Axel and Simon were still talking in the garden.

Hilda had got up and was walking about. Something was thrust against Morgan's hot cheek. It was a large clean handkerchief. Morgan fumbled to unfold it. More tears, more tears, more tears.

"Hilda."

"Yes, darling."

"Could I have a large scotch on the rocks?"

"On the—? Oh, yes, with ice. I'll get it at once."

"I couldn't drink—down there—with them."

"I won't be a moment. Would you like anything to eat with it? A little cold lamb? Or aspirins or anything?"

"No, no, nothing else. Bring the whole bottle, would you. And a jug of water. And two glasses."

"Yes, yes, I think some whisky would do me good too!"

As soon as the door closed Morgan sat up abruptly. She sat on the edge of the bed and mopped her face over with the cool handkerchief. The tears were less. She went over to the washbasin and soaked her burning eyes with cold water and dried her face on a crisp starchy embroidered face towel. She put on her glasses and went over to close the window. She returned and looked at herself for some time in the mirror above the basin. She would have liked to say something to herself, something apt, something bracing and encouraging, something witty perhaps; but she could not formulate it and she looked at herself in silence. Then when she heard Hilda's steps again upon the stair she returned quickly to her prostrate position upon the bed. That moment of self-regard had strengthened her, as she knew it would.

Hilda drew up a low table for the tray and sat down again upon the upright chair. Morgan pulled herself up, arranging pillows.

"Is this how you like it, sweetheart?"

"Yes, that's fine. No water, not at the moment. Just ice. Thanks."

"You're sure you don't want to rest, to be alone?"

"No, I want to talk to you. I feel *mad*, Hilda, *mad*."

"Take it easy, child."

"Whisky's good. Could you lend me a comb? Thanks."

"You're looking beautiful, Morgan."

"I feel a wreck. You're looking fine, Hilda. You've put on weight a bit. You don't mind my saying so? So has Rupert."

"We're getting old."

"Nonsense. So Simon and Axel are still together?"

"Yes."

"No sign of a crack? I wondered if that thing would last."

"They seem to be getting on all right."

"I'm rather sorry Simon went that way. I suspect Axel doesn't like me."

"He's just shy."

"I remember when we were children you would never admit that anyone disliked anyone! It does happen, you know. Do you have a cigarette?"

"Yes, I have. Here. Your luggage is following by boat?"

"Yes. It's mainly books. Well, some clothes and things. And notebooks and so on. I may not have mentioned it in my letters, but I did quite a lot of work at Dibbins."

"Good. Your letters weren't terribly informative, actually! They moved from the curt to the enigmatic to the frantic. I haven't really got a picture."

"Christ, do you think I have? I don't know who I am, Hilda. Maybe you'll have to tell me. It may take some time."

"Well, let us have that time, my darling. You will stay here, won't you, and not go away? Do feel that this is your home."

"I have no home. God, your house is elegant, Hilda. Just look at those black-and-white *toile de Jouy* cushions and that yellow china dog and that set of lustre jugs and that stripey French urn thing, I remember that, into which, if you had known I was coming, you would have put three perfect roses!"

"Darling, you're just the same! You always used to mock our domestic arrangements."

"Envy, Hilda, pure envy. I'd give my ears for a house like this and a husband like Rupert. A husband that *works*. Functions, I mean. Could I have some more whisky?"

"I'm afraid the ice is melting."

"Haven't you got a portable icebox? I must buy you one. Except, damn, I haven't any money."

"Don't worry about money, Morgan. I do want to tell you that. You've got enough troubles and it's *silly* to worry about money if it isn't necessary. Rupert and I have plenty and you can stay on here—"

"Well, I'm not totally destitute and if I pick up the old threads I expect I can get a job in England."

"I'm so relieved you're staying—"

"God, what's that noise outside?"

Hilda got up. "Simon has just upset the tray with the champagne glasses on it. I'm afraid they're all broken."

"Dear Simon. He hasn't changed. Except that he's better-looking than ever and more grown-up looking."

"Married life evidently suits him."

"Come back here, Hilda. Don't touch me, but I want you near. I want to look at you. Sometimes in America I've longed for you."

"I've longed for you. I've felt so happy since I knew you were coming back."

"You must think very ill of me."

"I love you, you fool."

"I don't think I could bear it if you really condemned me in your heart. I think I should die of it."

"I don't condemn you, *idiot*. Of course I don't understand. But when I do understand—I won't condemn you—ever."

"Ah, you think you *will* understand—I wonder—"

"Morgan, did you know that Julius—?"

"Yes. I saw it in the evening paper. I bought the *Standard* at London airport and there was Julius's picture."

"It's odd, isn't it."

"Uncanny. We might have travelled on the same plane. It was nice to see the old *Evening Standard* again, though I'm a bit out of date with the strip cartoons. Have they still got Modesty Blaise and Billy the Bee—?"

"Morgan, Morgan, Morgan—"

"Where's that bloody handkerchief?" Morgan took off her glasses and covered her face with the handkerchief. There was silence for a moment.

"You had no idea Julius was coming to London?"

"I didn't know where Julius was. I knew he'd left Dibbins."

"When did you last see him?"

"Oh, months and months ago. It seems like years ago. Absurd, isn't it. When I got onto that aeroplane I thought I was going away from Julius, away, away, away. And now here he is at the other end. Perhaps it's fate."

"Fate— Morgan, did you leave Julius or did he leave you?"

"I suppose that question has been much canvassed?"

"I'm afraid so, my darling."

"Well, literally I left Julius, but spiritually he left me. It was complicated and—awful. Awful, awful, awful."

"Have things entirely broken down between you?"

"Yes. Broken down, broken off. We haven't communicated since, oh, nearly the beginning of the year, when I just cleared out of Dibbins lock, stock, and barrel and abandoned all my students and all my classes and everything."

"I remember. You didn't write for some time. Then you wrote from that address in Vermont."

"Yes. I stayed with a nice old German philologist and his wife up there. They didn't understand a thing. Well, neither did I. I was practically insane. I still am. More whisky, please. Those damned ice cubes have all melted."

"I'll get some more."

"No, no, don't stir. I suppose Julius won't turn up here?"

"Rupert will head him off. Do you think Julius will try to see you?"

"No, he won't. But he won't try not to either. He'll do what he'd do anyway."

"Do you want to see him?"

"No."

"We'll see to it that you don't meet."

"It's hot, isn't it, Hilda. It's almost as hot as New York."

"It is hot."

There was silence. Morgan rearranged her pillows. The two women stared at each other. Morgan replaced her glasses and frowned, narrowing her eyes intently. "Yes, yes, I'm glad to see you, Hilda."

"I'm sure you should eat something."

"No. I've given up eating. I live on bourbon and aspirins. Now it'll have to be scotch and aspirins. Where's all my stuff, by the way?"

"Your stuff—you mean, clothes and books and—?"

"I was thinking mainly of the manuscripts. The stuff on theoretical linguistics which I was working on when I went to that extremely consequential conference in South Carolina."

"I'm afraid it's still with—"

"I rather hoped you'd have collected all my belongings."

"I tried to. But there was opposition."

"I see."

"What do you want me to do?"

"Nothing at the moment. I just want you to exist quietly near me while I discover who I am and what the purpose of life is. What is the purpose of life, Hilda?"

"I think loving people."

"Happy-marriage jazz?"

"No, I mean loving anybody, everybody."

"That's Rupert's line, isn't it. I think love's more difficult than he realizes. I love you. That's certain. But I sometimes wonder if I'm capable of any other love whatever."

"You're very tired, my darling. This isn't the moment to decide who you are and what life is about. You just stay here with me and everything will slowly sort itself out."

"I hope you're right. How's Tallis?"

"Well—he's—"

"Does he know I'm in England?"

"I don't think so. You didn't write to tell Peter?"

"Peter? Oh, yes, I couldn't think for a moment who you meant. No, I didn't."

"You see, Peter is living with Tallis. No, not like that, you ass! He's staying in Tallis's house. You knew Tallis had moved?"

"I know nothing about Tallis."

"He gave up the house in Putney just over a year ago."

"What did he do with the mortgage?"

"I don't know. Anyway, he moved to Notting Hill and he rents the lower half of a house there, and he has his old father living with him, and now Peter too."

"My God, he's got Leonard on his hands, has he. But why Peter?"

"Peter's been a bit peculiar lately. I told you some of this in a letter but I expect you've forgotten. He spent that year in Cambridge and then decided he wouldn't go back, and he didn't want to live here, and it seemed a good idea for him to stay with Tallis, and we hoped Tallis would persuade him to go back to Cambridge, only it hasn't worked so far."

"I see. How *is* Tallis?"

"He's all right. He—er—"

"Come on, Hilda, tell me. Do you know, I wasn't sure if I would be able to utter his name?"

"I know. It's hard to tell you, darling, not because there's anything special to tell, but really because there's nothing to tell. He's still giving those lectures on the trade-union movement, and he works part-time for the Notting Hill housing department and he's involved in some committee on race relations and of course there's the Labour Party and he does a lot of other odd jobs. Honestly, I haven't seen much of him lately, but he seems just as usual."

"What's happened to the book on Marx and de Tocqueville?"

"Rupert says he's abandoned it."

"I knew he would. It's all right, Hilda, I can still manage with this handkerchief. Oh Christ."

"Darling, I am sorry— I wonder if you *should* have more whisky."

"It's all right. I've been crying whisky for the last six months. I think I must have undergone a chemical change. Is he happy? Idiotic question. When was Tallis ever happy."

"When he got hold of you perhaps! Oh, he seems reasonably cheerful. But he's always terribly anxiety-ridden, as you know."

"Is there any woman hanging round him?"

"Not so far as I know. Morgan, what are you going to do about Tallis?"

"Do you mean am I going back to him?"

"Well, yes. I'm sure that he'd—welcome you back."

"Welcome me! I'm not so sure. I really don't know what Tallis would do if I proposed myself back."

"But are you going to?"

Morgan was silent for a moment, sniffing at her empty glass. "It seems ridiculous not to know, but it's not that I don't know, it's just that at the moment I can see nothing. I can't see myself, I can't see my marriage—"

"Over there, you just forgot it?"

"I couldn't! I arrived as Mrs. Browne and I had to stay Mrs. Browne. When Julius was displeased with me he used to call me 'Mrs. B.' "

"I mean, I imagine the thing with Julius must have rather effaced Tallis?"

"Oh, the thing with Julius was fantastic. But really, Tallis is ineffaceable. I used to see him, you know, all that time in America, I used to see those big light brown eyes looking at me, I used to see them at night in the dark when Julius was asleep—"

"It sounds eerie. Do you feel guilty about Tallis? You mustn't."

"Why not? I am guilty. No, it's deeper than guilt, Hilda. His consciousness binds mine, even now."

"It sounds like an obsession."

"Yes. It's something that I've always had about Tallis. And I must get rid of it. I thought at first that Julius would help me, but he didn't much want to talk about Tallis, and when I tried to tell him what Tallis was like it was—impossible."

"He is hard to describe. Darling, did you think of getting divorced and marrying Julius?"

"I thought about it. But you know, somehow, this is hard to explain—everything with Julius was so *high*—it was higher than anything like marriage. It was a heroic world. It was like living in ancient Greece or something. The light was so clear and everything was larger than life. Do you understand at all?"

"Yes, I think so. Julius is rather remarkable, isn't he."

"Julius is extraordinary. He is wonderful and awful. Well, no, he isn't awful. I'm awful. And I mustn't exaggerate about him. I was just terribly in love."

" 'Was'?"

"Oh, I don't know, I don't know. I can't think how I ever got away from him, how I got myself out of the house. It was torture. I felt he'd abandoned me in his heart and he was somehow willing me to go. Yet none of this appeared openly. Anyway, it's over now. And I've got this *job*, Hilda."

"Job?"

"To find out who I am and what life means. And to stop worrying about Tallis. You see, in a way I can't think about the real Tallis at all, and perhaps I never did. I've got to get rid of this blasted dream figure. I've got to go through—some ordeal—to set myself free—and then—"

"Will you go and see Tallis?"

"I don't know. I hope to God *he* won't turn up here?"

"No. He never drops in. And I think it's better if he just isn't told that you're here at all, for the present anyway."

"Yes, I agree. Oh, I'm probably exaggerating about Tallis too. As soon as I decided to come back I started having nightmares about him. Now that I'm actually here it may all just blow away. He's an unsolved problem, but in time one will see—"

"Do you think you still love Tallis?"

"Yes. No. In some curious way the question hardly arises."

"It must arise."

"You don't understand. Marrying Tallis was a sort of—action. Just an action. I know you were always against it, yes, you were. But I simply felt he was somebody I could not leave. Well, we've seen. Some crazy incoherent tenderness led me to marry that man. It was like animals—"

"Like animals?"

"Yes. My feeling about Tallis was like one's feeling about animals. I mean, that awful sort of naked pity and distress. Why is an animal's pain so piercing? Some music affects one like that too, it's awful. You remember when we were children we got so upset about stories about animals? We could quite cheerfully hear of human beings getting shot or starving to death, but if an animal was hurt we were in tears at once. Well, that's what it was like with Tallis. Everything about him wounded me. I mean, through him I was vulnerable to the whole world. It was like grieving over an animal. And it wasn't quite pity either, it was much more than that. Just by existing he tore my heartstrings."

"That sounds like love to me."

"I suppose it's a kind of love. Oh, I knew all along that he was inconceivably different from me. I just didn't foresee that I would ever feel that terrible—appetite. That I would ever *want* in the rapacious way that I wanted Julius."

"Of course Julius must have been dazzling—and I can imagine—different tastes."

"Oh, tastes. I think the only new taste I've acquired lately is a taste for big houses and money and drink. It's not that Julius is worldly. In a way he's very unworldly. But he's mythical. Men have mythical fates. But Tallis has no myth. Julius is almost all myth. That was what took me."

"Life with Julius was fun?"

"That's a weak word. Julius and I lived like gods. I can't convey it to you. You know, in some way Tallis is a sick man. He's perfectly sane, but his sanity is depressing, it lowers one's vitality. My love for him was always so sort of nervy, and he hadn't the instincts for making things easy and nice. Tallis has got no inner life, no real conception of himself, there's a sort of emptiness.

I used to think that Tallis was waiting for something but later on I decided that he wasn't. Sometimes his mode of being almost frightened me. He's obscure and yet somehow he's without mystery. Julius is so open and so *clear*, and yet he's mysterious and exciting too. I wonder if you see what I mean? Julius turned me into an angel. Julius is all soul, all inner life, all being, and he filled me with being and made me solid and compact and real."

"Oh Morgan. I do wish it could have been all right. Julius is so much more the kind of person—"

"I think we do live through each other's consciousness, even if painfully. There must be inwardness and spirit—and wit and grace and style—"

"I'm sure you ought to eat something, darling. We were going to have a cold supper—"

"Oh, do stop saying that. You eat if you want to. I know I'm drunk but it's doing me good. I have so much to *tell* you."

"When did you last write to Tallis?"

"Oh, ages ago. Near the start. I wrote saying I was going to stay with Julius."

"And Tallis replied?"

"He wrote a very kind understanding letter, as you can imagine, thanking me for being so frank, and if I changed my mind etc. etc. etc. God!"

"And did he write again?"

"Yes. He wrote several rather painstaking letters—they were like exercises really—just describing what he was doing and talking about the political situation. Christ! And mentioning in passing that he still loved me. The letters made me feel so sick I started tearing them up without even opening the envelopes. I didn't reply of course. Then he stopped writing. He never could write letters."

"There's something awfully flat about Tallis. I can imagine those letters."

"You know, it's a pity Tallis just missed being in the war. It might have given him a shot of ordinary natural toughness."

"He does rather tiptoe about."

"Sometimes he seemed to me almost like an apparition. And there's something fey about him, as if he attracts ghosts or something. Hilda, I must become free. It's not just Tallis."

"You must get over Julius."

"I'll probably never get over Julius; well, yes, I will, but I must learn to live. Oh Hilda, it was so terrible when his will just sent me away. I knew it was finished. And he put the burden of going onto me. Yet nothing was said. Sorry to *talk* so, Hilda. It's been all bottled up. I haven't *talked* properly to anyone, not since the last good days with Julius. And I haven't mentioned Tallis's name for a year. Hilda, have you got a picture of Tallis anywhere handy? I can see those eyes. I can see what you used to call his rosebud mouth. But I can't see his whole face, I've forgotten what he looks like."

"Wait a minute."

Left alone for a moment Morgan dabbled her hand in the bowl of melted ice cubes. The water was warm. She lifted her wet fingers and felt the pulse beating in her closed eyes. The great storms of tears, when would they cease?

"Here you are, Morgan. You remember, that's the one that Rupert took at the cottage."

Morgan reached out for the photo. She looked at it in silence for quite a long time. Then she tore the photograph into small pieces and handed the pieces to Hilda.

"Why did you do that?"

"I'd forgotten what he looked like."

"But why? Hate, love, fear—?"

"How should I know? I think I'll rest for a while. Well, no, I'll have a bath first. And if you could let me have a sandwich or something; no, nothing much, I should be sick. Why, it's getting darker, it must be evening. I've lost all sense of time."

"I'll bring you sandwiches and coffee. Have your bath. I think you should go to bed early. And don't worry about anything. Neither Julius nor Tallis will come to bother you. You must rest and feel quite safe."

"You always made me feel safe."

"You remember when we were in trouble when we were children we used to say, 'Hang out our banners on the outward wall'?"

"You always made me feel brave too. I'm afraid my banners are in tatters. How long is Julius staying in London?"

"I don't know, my dear."

"Hilda, it is inconceivable, isn't it, that those two should meet each other?"

"Julius and Tallis? I don't know about inconceivable, but it's extremely unlikely. I can't see anyone introducing them! And I don't imagine they'll look each other up!"

"Yes, yes, it is terribly unlikely, isn't it. Somehow I couldn't bear it if they met. It would be frightful, destructive, like some huge catastrophe in outer space."

"Don't fear it, sweetheart, it won't happen."

"Hilda, don't go yet. Oh Hilda darling, I do love you."

Morgan slid off the bed onto the floor and embraced Hilda's knees, putting her head into her lap. She began to sob again, wetting her sister's skirt with her tears. The fragments of the photograph were scattered round about as Hilda, her own tears rising, caressed the shuddering dark head.

❀ | FIVE

"What a rubbishy arrangement sex is," said Leonard Browne. "And I don't just mean the machinery of it, though that's stupid enough in all conscience. A projection upon one body is laboriously inserted into a hole in another. It's the invention of a mere mechanic, and a very fumbling and unimaginative one at that. I remember when someone told me about it at school I simply didn't believe him, I thought it couldn't turn out to be something so totally grotesque. Later on when I had more of a stake in it I persuaded myself otherwise. But now that it's all past and done with I can see it again for what it is, a pitiful, awkward, ugly, inefficient piece of fleshy mechanism. And consider flesh too, if it comes to that. Who could have dreamed up such stuff? It's flabby and it stinks as often as not or it bulges and develops knobs and is covered with horrible hair and blotches. The internal combustion engine is at least more efficient, or take the piston rods on a locomotive, and it's quite easy to oil them too. While keeping flesh in decent condition is almost impossible even leaving aside the obscene process of ageing and the fact that half the world starves. What a planet. And take eating, if you're lucky enough to do any. Stuffing pieces of dead animals into a hole in your face. Then munch, munch, munch. If there's anybody watching they must be dying of laughter. And the shape of the human body. Who but a thoroughly imcompetent craftsman or else some sort of practical joker could have invented this sort of moon on two sticks? Legs are a bad joke. Twinkle, twinkle, twinkle. However, as I was about to observe, sex is a rubbishy invention even apart from this absurd up it goes and in it goes. It's supposed to be something to do with love, at least that's the legend, but love is just a comforting myth and even if it wasn't it couldn't possibly have any connection with sex. We don't mix up love with eating, do we? Or with farting or hiccuping or blowing one's nose? Or with breathing? Or with the circulation of the blood or the operation of the liver? Then why connect it with our curious impulse to shove parts of ourselves inside other people, or with our in some ways equally curious impulse to thrust our damp evil-smelling mouths and decaying teeth up against other such unsavoury gluey orifices in other bodies? Answer me that, dear lady."

"Is Tallis at home?" said Hilda.

"I know not, dear lady, I know not and neither do I care. It would be difficult indeed to determine which is the stupider, your son or mine. Mine probably. He still imagines that his petty agitations and solemnities make some kind of difference to this stinking dung heap. He's eaten up with vanity, always busy making pronouncements, disapproving of this, condemning that. He can strut about and sit on his piffling committees and write his piffling manifestos, but the human kind is just an animal that lifts a sad eye and the plough goes over it. Just time to cast a glance upward and then crunch. It's not worth troubling about. Take me, for instance. I've been expendable all my life, what has my life been? I didn't love my parents, I didn't love my wife, I didn't like my job, I had no talents and no fun. I've got a son who's half-witted and hates my guts. When my wife left me for another man I couldn't stop worrying in case she was happier with him than she was with me. Well, she couldn't have been unhappier. I had no peace of mind about her until she was dead. Oh, that was splendid news. And even then I couldn't stop wishing her retrospective catastrophes. Does something like me deserve to exist? No. But that's not the point. I didn't ask to exist, did I? Why did this space in the universe have to be filled with a lump of smelly flesh attached to a guttering intelligence? You don't have to tell me it would be cleaner and more wholesome if it weren't. The point is, has the universe been just to me? No, it has not. If I was forced to exist I ought to have had something in return, oughtn't I? I don't mean anything vulgar like happiness. I dare say that's another myth anyhow. But a little grain of significance, as tiny as a pearl perhaps or a droplet of water or a mite of dust that you could hardly see as it settled on the tip of your finger—"

"You'll get psittacosis from feeding those pigeons," said Hilda.

"One gets psittacosis from parrots, dear lady."

"It was called psittacosis because people thought you could only get it from parrots, but in fact you can get it from any bird. Pigeons are notorious carriers of psittacosis."

"You don't say," said Leonard. "Well, well. I've got arthritis and cystitis and colitis and fibrositis and hay fever and chronic catarrh and varicose veins and Menière's disease, and now I shall have psittacosis as well. I suppose you are going to visit your loathsome idle spineless ill-mannered brat of an offspring. I imagine it is inconceivable that you should have covered the distance between your expensive and salubrious neighbourhood and this swinish sink of misery and vice with any idea of passing the time of day with me. I ask myself and I answer. Inconceivable."

Leonard was sitting on a wooden bench in the sun in the churchyard of St. Luke's church, his stick leaning against his thigh and a now almost empty bag containing fragments of bread clutched against his waistcoat. Round about him on the ground and on the seat a surging mass of blue pigeons scrambled and clawed, climbing upon each other's backs as they tussled without dignity for the crumbs. Soft wings beat fussily and hard little eyes peered and glittered. A pigeon perched on Leonard's knee was now eating out of the bag. A pigeon sat upon either shoulder and another one upon his head. Leonard, who did not resemble his son, was tall and thin with watery dark eyes, a large skull, and a small jaw. He still had quite a lot of stringy white hair round a bald spot. His face was flabby and pouchy, composed of little layers of flesh like pallid fungus, very lightly sketched over with wrinkles. He had no teeth and would not wear false ones, and this besides affecting his enunciation gave him a peculiar appearance when he spoke, since he used his lips very vigorously, thrusting them forward and then drawing them back to reveal tracts of moist red gum, as if his mouth were a sea anemone trying to turn itself inside out. He affected an old-fashioned mode of dress and always wore a stiff collar and a waistcoat and a watch and chain. His clothes, however, were filthy.

Hilda, who had witnessed the scene with the pigeons before, stood watching it with some amusement, though she was feeling in an odd frame of mind, worried about Peter and curiously exalted about Morgan. She hoped to avoid seeing Tallis and so to avoid the occasion of a sort of lie. Rupert had telephoned from the office to say that Axel had agreed not to mention Morgan's return for the present.

"I did come to see Peter," said Hilda, "but I didn't forget you. Here's a new matchbox for you. At least I hope it's a new one. Rupert brought it back from his last trip to Brussels."

Leonard accepted the matchbox with dignity and inspected it. "Yes. A good format dating from about nineteen hundred. A pretty one and in sound condition. Pray thank your noble husband for recalling the existence of this pitiful piece of flotsam and jetsam. My arthritis is bad today; I have a shooting pain at the base of my spine and a peculiarly insidious ache in my thigh. I am not long for this world."

"How has Peter been lately?" asked Hilda. "Anything special?"

"He rejects the universe. That at least we have in common. Only I reject it with screams of rage standing up on my two feet, while he rejects it by falling over backward onto his bed and lying there limp and stupefied."

"You don't think he's taking drugs, do you?"

"I don't know, dear lady. You must ask my idiot son. Incapable no doubt, quite apart from the fact that his wife has understandably left him for another, of procreating children of his own, he fusses round your bratling like an old hen."

"Well, Leonard, it's been nice to see you."

"Surely you exaggerate."

"And I must be getting on now to see Peter. Or are you coming back to the house and we could walk there together?"

"Never fear, never fear. I am fixed here until the hour of luncheon engaged in the burdensome task of passing the time. Ten minutes passed scarcely noticed as we conversed. The next ten will doubtless be correspondingly distended. And then the next ten. And thus laboriously we draw toward us the hour and moment of our death."

"I must go, Leonard dear."

"It's all a myth, dear lady. Love, happiness. They can't do it, they *can't* do it. It all went wrong from the start."

"I think a few people love each other, Leonard, and there are some pleasant moments. I've enjoyed talking to you and seeing you feed the pigeons."

"You lie. Don't forget to tell your husband it all went wrong *from the start*. He can put that in his book."

"I'll tell him. Cheerio then, Leonard."

Hilda turned away and hurried across the road. By the time she reached the opposite pavement she had forgotten Leonard's existence. The vague optimism which she had felt last night about Peter had entirely vanished. The impact of Morgan's return, more violent than anything that she had expected, had laid her soul open to fears. And when the prospect of meeting Peter was close it was now always rather alarming.

The door was still slightly off its hinges and lurched back, grinding along the floor. It only needed five minutes' work with a screwdriver. When Hilda had mentioned the door to Tallis once he had said that it was never locked at night as if this was an answer. Hilda went in, tugged and lifted the door back into its place, and found herself in semi-darkness. The indescribably horrible smell of the house assailed her. The smell was really mysteriously unpleasant. Hilda had never experienced anything quite like it. Old dirty lodging houses usually have a stale odour, stale sweat, stale food, stale urine, and the dark brooding smell of dirt. The smell in Tallis's house was fresh and bitter and at the same time nauseating. Hilda wondered if it were not caused by some extremely recherché form of dry rot. Or possibly by some insects too loathsome to think of. She shuddered and listened. Silence. She pushed open the kitchen door.

There was no one in the kitchen, which was a relief. When Tallis was at home he was usually in the kitchen during the day, where he worked at the big kitchen table. In fact an open notebook and several well-worn and learned-looking volumes from the London Library were lying about on the table together with stained newspapers, jam-smeared plates, brown-rimmed teacups and a milk bottle half-full of solidified sour milk. Hilda moved over to the table and looked at the notebook. At the top of the empty page in Tallis's rather large hand was written *In my last lecture I*

Hilda inspected the kitchen. It looked much as usual. The familiar group of empty beer bottles growing cobwebs. About twenty more unwashed milk bottles yellow with varying quantities of sour milk. A sagging wickerwork chair and two upright chairs with very slippery grey upholstered seats. The window, which gave onto a brick wall, was spotty with grime, admitting light but concealing the weather and the time of day. The sink was piled with leaning towers of dirty dishes. The draining board was littered with empty tins and open pots of jam full of dead or dying wasps. A bin, crammed to overflowing, stood open to reveal a rotting coagulated mass of organic material crawling with flies. The dresser was covered in a layer, about a foot high, of miscellaneous oddments: books, papers, string, letters, knives, scissors, elastic bands, blunt pencils, broken Biros, empty ink bottles, empty cigarette packets, and lumps of old hard stale cheese. The floor was not only filthy but greasy and sticky and made a sucking sound as Hilda lifted her feet. She resisted her usual impulse to start washing up straightaway. She did not want to dally in case Tallis returned. And the tap gave no hot water and the gas stove would take at least ten minutes to boil a kettle.

Hilda mounted the stairs feeling a bit sick inside and knocked on Peter's door. She entered on his murmur. Peter was reposing on his bed as usual, propped up against a grey mound of pillows, dressed in shirt and trousers, barefoot. His hands were clasped upon his breast and his eyes were dreamy. Peter was a good-looking boy, very blond like his father, and inclined to plumpness in the face. He had a good straight nose and long intelligent eyes of bright blue which gave him, possibly through some reminiscence of the youthful Napoleon, the look of a young soldier. He looks like a leader, Hilda thought, surveying the limp form of her son with tenderness and exasperation. He greeted his mother with a yawn and with an agitation of his fingers, his hands remaining clasped.

"Is Tallis in the house?" said Hilda.

"Tallis is doubtless somewhere if he is still alive. He is not here."

"You haven't any reason to think he's not still alive, have you?"

"None whatsoever."

"You got my note?"

"Yes."

"Peter, the scene in the kitchen is revolting. Why don't you at least wash up?"

"I'll think about it."

"And I think you ought to fix the front door. All you need is a screwdriver. Isn't there a screwdriver somewhere in the house? I thought I saw one on the dresser."

"You might have done."

"And I think you ought to lock that door at night."

"The people upstairs come in and out at all hours."

"Why can't they use latchkeys like ordinary Christians?"

"They aren't Christians, they're Moslems. And they would lose their latchkeys and knock us up."

Hilda sighed. She sat down rather carefully on the edge of the chair. The seat was a snare. Reflected sunshine lit up the room revealing its nakedness. Hilda shuddered. A stripped room is a place of fear. Apart from Peter's iron bedstead and the chair there was little furniture. There was a large cardboard box full of old shoes —not Peter's—and pieces of rope and what appeared to be leather belts. A dressing table, from which the mirror had been unscrewed, was littered with objects. The floor was of unstained wooden planks, grainy with dirt, and the whitish walls were scrawled over with spidery cracks and lightly festooned with cobwebs.

Hilda looked uneasily at the objects on the dressing table. They included two transistor sets, three silk handkerchiefs, obviously new, a camera, a shiny leather box which might have contained cuff links or jewellery, a rather expensive-looking electric torch, and an enamelled cigarette lighter. Hilda was about to ask Peter a question about these things when the door flew open.

A lot of white teeth and a hazy flurry of black hair came round the door.

"Cannayeh berroo yatipout aggen?"

"Sure, you know where it is."

The door closed.

"What was that?" said Hilda.

"A Moslem."

"What language was he speaking?"

"English."

"What did he want?"

"He wanted to borrow our teapot."

"Why doesn't he buy one of his own? They aren't expensive."

Peter reflected for a moment. "I don't know." He closed his eyes.

"Oh Peter, Peter!" said Hilda. "I wish you didn't live in such a *mess*. And by the way, where are all those books I brought you from home last time I came? I don't see them anywhere."

"I sold them."

"Peter! Your *art* books! You used to love them."

"I'm through with that sort of art. And the money was useful. I gave some to Tallis." Peter opened his eyes a little and surveyed his mother.

"There's no need to give money to Tallis. I pay for this room. And surely you can keep yourself on what your father gives you and what I give you extra?"

"I'm not complaining. In fact I'm grateful."

"And for heavens sake, don't tell anyone, not even Tallis, that I'm giving you that extra money, because I haven't told your father! He wouldn't stand for it, and I dare say quite rightly."

"I have already told Tallis, but Tallis never tells."

"Oh dear, I wish everything wasn't becoming so complicated. I'm afraid I'm just no good at being a parent."

"Don't start that again, Mother, please. We don't want any tears this time."

"But what are you going to do? You've got to make yourself into a going concern. You've got to fit into this society somehow. You can't spend your life in bed."

"Sssh, sssh, my darling mother. Give me your hand. That's right. No, just your hand. Yes, yes, there, there, you know I love you."

"But, Peter, you've got to *try*—"

"You mean compete. I'm not going to compete."

"And there's Cambridge and you'll have to decide—"

"I've decided. We see things differently, Mama. We see time differently. You worry about time, you strain against it. I just give myself up to it and it carries me quietly along. As for Cambridge, it incarnates that whole rotten set of beastly old class values. One simply mustn't touch it. It's no compromise and no surrender."

"Homer and Virgil and—Sophocles and—what's his name—Aeschylus don't represent the whole rotten set of beastly old class values."

"No, they're all right in themselves. But the whole set-up is corrupt. I can't explain to you, Mother darling. But I've got my own categorical imperatives. I've just got to reject the thing *in toto*."

"Peter, do try to *think*. You've got to earn money. Or do you expect us to support you all your life?"

"Of course not. Money isn't important though. I can easily earn a little if I want to."

"When you're older you'll want more money and you won't have the capacity to earn it!"

"This thing about more money as one grows older is precisely one of the assumptions of this lousy society which I refuse to accept. People spend their whole lives chasing money and chasing more of it and wanting more and more unnecessary things. They feel they've failed unless they're continually climbing up a sort of pyramid of material possessions. They sacrifice themselves to houses and refrigerators and washing machines and cars, and at the end they realize they haven't really lived at all. Their houses and their washing machines have lived their lives for them. I don't want to be like that. I want to live my own life, out in the open, outside the rat race, outside the capitalist dream. This room contains everything that a human being needs."

"No books," said Hilda. "What about your mind? You're clever. Don't you want to develop your talents?"

"Don't you worry about my mind, Mother dear. A great deal is happening in my mind. Probably more than ever happened in your mind in the whole of your life."

"Peter, you're taking drugs!"

"No, no. Well, I took some pot once or twice, harmless stuff. No, I'm not on drugs, I don't need them. I just wait quietly and the strangest and most wonderful things come. Just to wait, that's the secret. All this struggling and straining with conscious thought separates us from the real world. Look at that brass knob on the end of my bed. To you it's just a brass knob. To me it's a golden microcosm."

"Yes," said Hilda, "to me it's a brass knob and it's going to stay a brass knob! These are just moods and feelings, Peter—"

"Moods and feelings are very important, my old square angel of an aged parent. I want to be my moods, to live in the present. Feelings are life. Most people in this society just never live at all."

"I know your father thinks—"

"Please, Mama. We did agree."

"Oh, all right. Has Tallis been putting these dotty ideas into your head, I wonder?"

"Tallis! Really, Mama! Tallis is on your side!"

"Well, I think that if you reject this society, and you're quite right to do so in many ways, you ought to equip yourself to try to change it, and not lie on your bed having feelings, and that means—"

"That means the struggle for power. No. Power is just what I don't want, Mother. That's another false god. Gain power so that you can do good! That's another way to waste your life. Just look at Tallis. When did dear Tallis ever *live?*"

"He's a terribly anxious man, but—"

"Tallis is always somewhere else, he never really exists in the present at all. Can't you at least see how unanxious I am?"

"Ye—es. But I think one should try to help people—"

"Yes, but not anyhow. And if one's a real person oneself one can help more. I know you belong to the Socialist Old Guard, dear Mother, but that's not the sort of thing that's needed now, truly it isn't. Now be a darling and don't hustle me. I have to discover myself first of all."

"I can't understand you, Peter. When I'm with you, now, it sounds as if you've got some sort of real argument. But when I remember it later on it seems like nonsense, it's just faded away like the dream rushes in *Alice.*"

"True wisdom looks unsubstantial in the materialistic world. But really it's your life that's a dream."

"I can't agree, Peter, but I can't argue either. I don't know what to say to you. I must get Morgan to talk to you. Maybe she will be able to argue with you properly."

"Morgan?" Peter sat up. He swung his legs over the edge of the bed and fanned out his rather long golden hair. "Is there any prospect of Aunt Morgan?"

"Well, yes. Look, Peter, will you please keep this under your hat and not tell Tallis? Morgan is here, she's at our house at this moment. She arrived yesterday."

"Well, well, well," said Peter. He teased out his hair between his fingers, then smoothed it down and relaxed slowly, lifting his legs and burrowing his bare feet into a nest of blankets at the bottom of the bed. "That's good. I'd very much like to see Morgan again. Is she going to rejoin Tallis?"

"We don't know. And just for now, not a word to him, please, Peter. Morgan just wants a little peace and—"

"O.K., O.K. By the way, did you by any chance bring me a tiny cheque, dear Mother? That's fine. Just put it under the pillow, would you."

"You're telling me to go."

"I think it's wiser, my dear. This is just the stage where if you stay any longer you start to get upset. And then you upset me."

"And that spoils your communion with the brass knob. All right, all right. But, oh, Peter, I do so hate leaving you—"

"Now then, Mother, no love scene. Yes, yes, I love you very much. Now off you go, old dear, off you go."

⚙ | S I X

"Simon, I wish you wouldn't call everybody 'darling.' It's one of those damned tribal habits I wish I could cure you of. It's all right for you to call me 'darling.' If you feel like it. You probably don't at the moment. But if you use it on everyone you cheapen it and then it's no good to me. You ought to have the intelligence to see that."

"Sorry—darling."

"Don't simulate."

"I'm not simulating!"

"You must be annoyed with me."

"I'm not annoyed with you, Axel, damn you!"

"That sounds jolly convincing, doesn't it."

"I don't call everybody 'darling' anyway."

"You called Morgan 'darling' the other day—and Hilda."

"Well, they're special. I've always had a thing about them and—"

"What do you mean, a 'thing'? Must you talk basic English? Who were you trying to telephone when I came in, by the way?"

"I was just ringing Rupert's place."

"What about?"

"I—well—I just wanted to talk to Morgan. Only she wasn't in."

"You put the telephone down damn fast."

"Really, Axel— Don't you think the drawing-room's looking nice?"

"Not bad. I see you've bought another ridiculous paperweight. I wish you wouldn't keep buying trinkets. We've already got far too many possessions."

"It wasn't expensive."

"And for God's sake, Simon, don't drink too much tonight. Remember, when I start fingering the lobe of my ear it means I think you've had enough."

"I won't accept that signal, Axel."

"You'd better! You got tight that last time at Rupert's and I couldn't get you away and you broke all those glasses. I was quite ashamed of you."

"Sorry—sweetheart."

"I wish you wouldn't hum nervously when you're doing things. I wonder if you realize that you've been humming. You even hum when I'm talking."

"Sorry—"

"Do finish with those blasted flowers. You've been arranging them for twenty minutes. Why you want to mess around with dried flowers at this time of year is beyond me."

"Don't be so conventional, Axel."

"And surely you can't mix plastic bulrushes in with real flowers?"

"You can with dried ones. How do you know they're plastic, anyway?"

"I can see they are."

"I saw you touching them just now."

"Horrid fascination."

"You weren't sure they were plastic! And if they don't look—"

"That you should have plastic bulrushes in your possession

at all or introduce them into this house is a scandal. You're supposed to be the expert on interior decoration, but sometimes I think you have the taste of a suburban housewife."

"You only noticed it because Julius is coming."

"What is that idiotic remark supposed to mean?"

"You usually don't care tuppence what this place looks like."

"Perhaps I don't want your lapses in taste to be put on public show!"

"All right. You can arrange the bloody drawing-room yourself!"

Simon went down to the kitchen and slammed the door. For a second he felt hot about the eyes as if he were going to cry. But the next moment he felt better. Even the smallest quarrel with Axel upset him. But he knew by now that this was the sort of thing which usually blew away directly into the surrounding air. Axel had said to him at the start: absolute rule, one does not make tantrums with someone one loves. One never sulks. In fact Axel often snapped at him and sometimes said, even in public, rather accurate and wounding things. As on the occasion when Axel had let Simon hold forth for some time about the Titian *Pietà* in the Accademia before pointing out that it had been finished by Palma Giovane, a fact which Simon certainly ought to have known. In public, Simon suffered in silence. In private he sometimes hit back. But he knew that Axel was almost always sorry and a feud was not maintained. It was not really in Simon's nature to fight at all and he was incapable of sulking.

Two bottles of Puligny Montrachet and a bottle of Barsac had been uncorked and put in the fridge. They were going to start with a confection of cucumber and yoghurt with pepper which Simon had invented. After that there was a salmon trout with almonds, and new potatoes. Then pears stewed in white wine and served with a creamy egg custard. Then English cheese. Simon observed the salmon trout, wrapped in foil, through the glass front of the cooker. The cucumber and the pears were ready to serve. The potatoes would not take long and need not go on yet. Everything seemed to be under control. There was still nearly half an hour before Julius was due to arrive.

Simon was feeling nervous. He sometimes wondered if other people's minds were as hard for them to control as his was for him. It was not easy to find out such things. It was no use giving himself instructions and upbraiding himself for being irrational. Immense flights of fantasy were taking place. During the last few days he had lost Axel in any of a dozen different ways, all somehow connected with Julius. Simon tried hard to be generous in his thoughts. That at least he could usually manage. His temperament helped him to turn all conceivable blame onto himself. He did not seriously imagine that Julius would deliberately try to steal Axel. As far as he knew, Julius had no interests of that sort at all. He did not imagine that Julius would deliberately make trouble for him. He simply feared that the proximity of this very intelligent and high-powered old friend would open Axel's eyes. Axel would suddenly see how flimsy Simon was, how unsophisticated, how lacking in cleverness and wit, how hopelessly ignorant about important things such as Mozart and truth functions and the balance of payments. "There's just not much there," Axel had once damningly said of an acquaintance. And here, how much is there here? Simon wondered. And he sometimes despairingly felt, Not much. How could he, by what felicitous accident, have inspired Axel to love him? Simon had very little sense of his own identity and often it seemed to him that he only existed at all by virtue of Axel's love which was directed by what must be a mistake upon this almost-nothing.

Yet this was not the sum of his fear. He was afraid in some other way too, and even less rationally, afraid simply of Julius, as he remembered him, afraid of certain emanations from Julius which he had never quite been able to understand. Simon had poured himself out a glass of sherry, and as he now lifted it to his lips he noticed that his hand was trembling slightly. He wondered again if he ought not to have told Axel frankly everything that he had been feeling during the last few days. He knew that in concealing these thoughts and keeping everything on a casual "How nice to see Julius again" basis he was offending against an important canon of coexistence with his lover. Axel had adjured him to tell all dangerous thoughts and of course Axel was right. If he had told his thoughts Axel would probably have found some way to re-assure him absolutely. This often happened when he told his thoughts. But he had hesitated, and not only because he felt he was being foolish and did not want to "make too much of it." He had discerned in Axel too a counterpart of his own unease. Axel was quietly excited at the idea of seeing Julius again. And Axel was being equally disingenuous about it. I'll watch, thought Simon. I won't speak, I'll watch.

Axel had come into the kitchen. Simon did not turn round but continued to fiddle with the electric stove, turning on the ring to cook the potatoes. After a moment or two he felt his waist being encircled from behind. He had learnt from experience that Axel liked him to remain impassive on such occasions. He pushed the saucepan onto the glowing ring. Axel was beginning to pull him round.

Simon regarded him coldly.

" 'When I lie tangled in your hair and fettered to your eye, The birds that wanton in the air know no such liberty.' "

"Good show," said Simon.

Sometimes they exchanged roles.

The doorbell rang.

"I must say, Axel," said Julius, "when I heard that you had taken up with this brown-eyed beauty I did feel the tiniest bit jealous!" He beamed at Simon through his spectacles.

They were eating the cheese. The salmon trout and the pears had been excellent. There was something wrong with the cucumber and yoghurt, however. Not enough salt possibly.

The dining-room was lit only by six tall black candles in the two Sheffield plate candlesticks. Axel, in softened mood, had agreed to candlelight for once. Julius and Axel had talked without ceasing. It was the sort of conversation where a surfeit of interesting things to say and hear made the protagonists leap constantly to and fro. Every subject suggested six others, one or two of which might be rapidly pursued before a meticulous return was made to the starting point. There were no lacunae in the logical matrix. Nothing was dropped or left to the side. One or the other of them was constantly saying, "Yes, well *that* arose out of your saying so and so," and then they would turn back to deal with so and so. They hardly noticed when Simon removed the plates, and no one had praised the salmon trout.

Julius was plumper than Simon remembered him as being, but the plumpness suited him. He looked older and more benign. There had been a tigerish look, but that was gone. His curiously colourless hair, not exactly fair, seemed like a pale wig upon a dark man. The hair was fairly curly and fairly short, bringing into prominence the big long rather heavy face, bronzed by the sun and now a little flushed perhaps by argument. He had drunk very little wine. The eyes, of a dark colour hard to determine, a sort of purplish brown perhaps, were rimmed by heavy lids and much inclined to twinkle. At this moment, between two radiant candle flames, they appeared to be violet, but that must be an illusion. The nose was very slightly hooked and the mouth, which imparted a certain sweetness and sadness to the expression, long and very finely shaped. It was a face that was not noticeably Jewish except perhaps in a watchful heaviness about the eyes. Julius spoke with a faint Central European accent and a faint stammer.

Axel laughed. "Of course you've known Simon for ages. You probably met him before I did."

"When did we first meet, Simon?" said Julius. "It was at Rupert's, wasn't it?"

It was Simon's first direct entry into the conversation. He conjectured a year.

"Yes, that was just before I met him," said Axel.

"No, it wasn't," said Simon. "You met me before that only you didn't notice me."

"Well, he's noticed you now!" said Julius.

They all laughed, Simon a little uneasily.

"Have some more cheese," said Simon.

"Thank you. I can't tell you how glad I am to be away from American food."

"Weren't there any decent foreign restaurants?" asked Axel.

"Not in South Carolina! I've been in San Francisco actually for the last month and there are excellent Chinese restaurants there. I love Chinese food."

"We must take you to our local Chinese restaurant," said Axel. "I think it's good."

"I don't!" said Simon.

"Then you and I will go," said Julius to Axel.

"One never knows what to drink with Chinese food," said Simon.

"Lager," said Axel.

"Tea," said Julius.

"Even lager isn't strong enough for Simon," said Axel. "He's become quite a toper. I am going to have to take a strong line with his drinking habits!"

"Let me fill your glass, Julius," said Simon.

"No, thank you, I'm not much of a drinker. I have to watch my inside. Rupert's looking terribly fit, isn't he? No stomach ulcers for him!"

"Rupert thrives. I gather you had lunch with him at his club?"

"Yes. I adore English clubs and seeing Rupert putting on his English act. He is absurdly English, isn't he?"

"Why don't you join a club, Julius?" said Simon.

"He is a little tease, eh, Axel? Clubs are not for such as me. It would spoil the charm if I even thought they'd have me!"

"Are you still at the Hilton?" said Axel.

"No. Big hotels give me migraine. I meant to tell you, I've just moved into a most luxurious little flat in Brook Street. You must come and see it, both of you. Here, I'll write the address down."

"Have you seen Hilda?"

"No, Axel, I haven't. As they have Morgan at the house I haven't been invited and of course I'm keeping clear. Do you think I'm *mal vu* by Hilda at the moment?"

"No, no. I wouldn't say so, would you, Simon? Hilda is terribly rational. Much more so than Morgan, actually."

"I'd like to see Hilda, but I expect it's not the moment. *Port,*

Simon? No, certainly not. A little whisky with plenty of water in it."

"Did Rupert talk to you about his book?"

"He mentioned it. I think he wanted me to question him closely but I just didn't feel strong enough. I fear we shall all be rather embarrassed by that book!"

"Exactly what I think, my dear," said Axel.

Simon flushed and spilt some whisky. Then he felt Axel's foot pressing against his under the table. He retired to the kitchen to get a mopping-up cloth and in order to conceal an idiotic smile which he seemed to be unable to control. He must be getting a little tipsy. He took a quick drink from the secret bottle of whisky which he kept concealed in the kitchen cupboard. When he came back they were talking opera again.

"I doubt if you'll get into *Fidelio*," Axel was saying. "I'm going on Friday and I booked ages ago and couldn't get a decent seat then."

"What's on at Glyndebourne?"

"They're doing Purcell."

"How delicious! Could I get tickets? Let's go, all three!"

"I have some pull at Glyndebourne," said Axel. "I think I can get us in. Only Simon hates opera."

"Then once again, we two must go! I'm desperately hungry for opera. You can imagine how much decent opera I've seen in the last couple of years."

"I can't understand why anyone goes to Glyndebourne," said Simon. "It always rains and you have to picnic in the car, and if it's not raining you're certain to meet some ghastly person you know beside the lake and have to give him half of your champagne and chicken pie."

"There *is* music involved, dear boy," said Axel. "Glyndebourne isn't just champagne and chicken pie."

"Remember when we went on your birthday," said Simon, "and there was a thunderstorm and the car was leaking and we got a flat tyre on the way home?"

"You deserved to suffer," said Axel, "for reasons which you know of."

"Why did he deserve to suffer?" asked Julius, twinkling.

"Oh, just a little *suppressio veri*. A little *suggestio falsi*."

"I think I'll cook salmon trout and almonds again for your birthday dinner this year which, thank God, we'll have at home. And we'll try that hock with it instead of the white burgundy."

"Have you an imminent birthday, Axel?" asked Julius.

"Yes. I wish Simon wouldn't fuss about it. I'm not ten years old."

"I love birthdays," said Simon, "and anniversaries and celebrations of all kinds."

"Any excuse to get drunk, in fact!" said Axel. He began to finger the lobe of his right ear.

Simon poured himself out another stiff whisky.

"When is your birthday?" asked Julius.

"The twentieth."

"So you're under Cancer. I'm Leo. What are you, Simon?"

"Sagittarius."

"So you know all that stuff too, do you? Simon always knows everybody's sign. He's a great believer in the stars."

"Morgan's Gemini," said Simon, "Rupert's Cancer, Hilda's Virgo, Tallis is Capricorn, Peter is Aquarius—"

"Oh, I'm a great believer in the stars too," said Julius. "I'm terribly superstitious. I believe in the iron hand of destiny. I wouldn't *dare* to have my horoscope cast."

"I don't believe in destiny," said Axel. "I just believe in trying."

"Trying for what? What do you want out of life, Axel?"

"I want to do my work and have innocent friendships with gentle intelligent people."

"You are delightfully unambitious. Isn't he, Simon?"

"I think it's a lot to ask from life," said Simon. Axel's foot touched his again.

"I think I want a good deal more than that," said Julius.

"What? Fun? Power?"

"Not fun. Power perhaps. And what are these friendships of yours to be like, eh, Axel?"

"Just friendships. 'Love which can't be classified is best.' Wittgenstein."

"Have a chocolate peppermint cream," said Simon.

The doorbell rang.

"Who the devil can that be," said Axel, "calling on us so late at night. Go and tell them to go to hell, Simon." Axel detested droppers in.

Simon got up and left the dining-room, half closing the door after him. The light was on in the hall revealing the highly polished oak chest, on which Simon had placed a copper bowl of white roses, and the big mirror with the marquetry frame which had belonged to Axel's family. Simon quickly adjusted his hair at the mirror and went to open the door. He peered out.

The visitor was Tallis.

Simon's immediate instinct was to shut the door, then to come outside himself and close it behind him. He hesitated, began to push the door to, then darted out through the crack, holding the handle on the outside and making Tallis step back.

"Sssh!" said Simon.

"What's the matter?" said Tallis in his ordinary voice.

"Sssh! We've got Julius King here, and—"

"What's going on?" said Axel's voice behind him. "Who are you whispering to in this conspiratorial way?" Axel pulled the door open. "Oh!"

Tallis began to explain. "I'm very sorry to call so late, Axel; I know you hate late callers, but the fact is—"

"The fact is, Julius is here," said Axel.

"Oh, that's what you were saying," said Tallis to Simon. "I couldn't hear what you were saying. I think I must be getting a bit deaf."

"You'd better come in and meet him," said Axel. "I don't approve of whispering on doorsteps."

"Tallis wasn't whispering," said Simon.

"Well, I didn't hear what you said," said Tallis.

"Come on then," said Axel. "Unless you'd rather not?"

"No, no, of course I'll come in, I quite see, I quite understand—"

Tallis followed Axel and Simon into the hall, blinking against the light. Tallis was a rather short man with short jagged ginger hair and bushy orange eyebrows. He had a shiny bumpy forehead and very wide apart very light brown eyes and a short shiny nose and a small and slightly prissy mouth. He stood awkwardly in the hall, half took off his shabby macintosh and then pulled it on again, until Axel took him by the arm and propelled him in through the door into the candlelit dining-room where Julius was sitting alone on the other side of the table.

"Julius, we've got a visitor. This is Tallis Browne. Julius King."

Julius rose. He was considerably taller than Tallis.

Tallis stared at Julius and visibly shuddered. Then he took a step forward and held out his hand. "Hello."

With a marked raising of the eyebrows Julius took the proffered hand. "Good evening." Julius sat down.

"Have a drink, Tallis," said Simon desperately. He liked Tallis, whom he had never regarded as a menace. He felt terrible embarrassment on his behalf.

"Do sit down," said Axel. "Or must you rush away?"

Tallis sat down in Simon's place opposite to Julius and Simon drew up another chair. "What'll you drink, Tallis?"

"I'll have some beer," said Tallis. "Oh, sorry, you don't keep beer, I remember. Anything will do. Sherry. Yes, some white wine is fine, thank you, Simon."

Simon and Axel sat down, Simon sitting a little away from the table behind Tallis, his arm on the back of Tallis's chair. Julius, who had pushed his chair back as if to have a better view, was regarding Tallis with a slightly sardonic and yet friendly air, the corners of his long mouth quivering very slightly and turning upward. Axel was frowning and showing his teeth as he did when he was anxious. Tallis drank some of the wine out of Simon's glass as if this were a grave almost ritualistic action, his eyes lowered and his attention fixed upon the glass. He had long orange eyelashes. There was a short silence which Julius was very evidently enjoying.

Simon and Axel spoke simultaneously. Simon said, "How did you get here, by bus or by tube?"

Axel said, "What did you want to see us about?"

Tallis said to Simon, "By tube," and to Axel, "About Morgan."

Axel said "Oh" and began fussing with the whisky bottle. Julius was raising his triangular eyebrows once again. Simon said, "Oh Tallis—"

"Is Morgan in England?" said Tallis. He looked first at Axel and then at Julius.

After a moment's silence Julius answered him. "Yes. She arrived several days ago. She is staying with Rupert and Hilda."

"Thank you," said Tallis. He rose to his feet. "Sorry to have barged in, Axel."

"How did you know or suspect she was here?" said Axel.

"Peter kept dropping hints. But he wouldn't tell me anything outright."

"We ought to have told you," said Axel. "I apologize, Tallis."

"Don't worry."

"Hilda persuaded us not to," said Simon. "She wanted Morgan to have time to recover sort of."

"I understand—I won't go round there— If she doesn't—" Tallis stopped for a moment. Simon put a hand on his sleeve. "I won't go round." With a wave of farewell which vaguely embraced the room Tallis disappeared into the hall and opened the front door.

Simon ran after him and followed him down the steps into the street. "Tallis, she isn't with Julius. They came separately. She's not seeing Julius. Can I give her a message from you?"

The lamp-post was distant and it was hard to see Tallis's face. "No, thank you, Simon. But thank you for thinking of it. Good night."

Simon ran back again into the dining-room.

Axel had covered his face with his hands. Julius was smiling and tilting his chair back. "Well, well, well," said Julius.

"Oh God!" said Axel, running his hands back through his hair. "What a very strange little person," said Julius. "He ought to be sitting on a toadstool."

"He ought not to have taken your hand," said Simon. He felt suddenly very upset, filled with pity for Tallis.

"I agree," said Axel.

"And I agree too," said Julius. "In fact, it was he who offered the hand and I think he didn't really intend to. He stretched it out instinctively. He's obviously an extremely nervous man."

"Tallis is a marvellous person," said Simon. He poured himself out some more whisky.

"I have no doubt," said Julius. "I have only first impressions which I am not likely to improve upon. Well, Axel, I think I must be going. I'm an early bedder, as you'll probably remember. I have my newly hired car outside so I won't be running the risk of meeting your orange-haired friend at the railway station."

Julius rose and they moved out into the hall. "Your coat's upstairs, isn't it," said Axel. "Stay there, I'll get it." Simon and Julius were left standing together.

Julius smiled down at Simon. Then he leaned forward and put a hand upon Simon's shoulder. Simon shivered, unable for a moment to interpret the gesture. He said in a whisper into Simon's ear, "Come round to my flat next Friday evening at eight. Don't tell Axel."

The door closed upstairs and Axel reappeared with Julius's coat.

"Well. Thank you, Axel, very much, and thank you too, Simon. There, you see my car is just outside. A British car, you'll be glad to see. Rupert would approve! Good night, my friends, good night."

Simon closed the door and followed Axel up to the drawing-room. He was completely stunned by Julius's invitation. What could it mean? "Don't tell Axel." Why? Should he not tell Axel at once?

Axel had sat down beside the gas fire and was taking off his shoes. Simon began automatically to collect up the ash trays. What ought he to do? It was extremely odd.

"Well, that *was* unfortunate," said Axel.

"Tallis didn't seem to mind," said Simon.

"Who knows what Tallis minds and what he doesn't mind?" said Axel. "He looked pretty sick when he clapped eyes on Julius."

It then occurred to Simon what the meaning of Julius's words must be. Friday was a few days before Axel's birthday. Axel would be at *Fidelio*. Julius was wanting Simon to help him to plan some pleasant surprise for Axel. That was what it was, it must be. And in that case, of course it was quite all right not to tell. Simon felt a curious thrill of excitement and uneasiness.

He paused in front of Axel, looking down at him. The lamp beside the fire-place shed a bright diffused light upon his friend's face which was looking stern and tired and rather sad. Behind Axel's head upon the wall hung the photo of the tall slim long-nosed Greek *kouros* from the National Museum at Athens, the tutelary deity of their love.

"Apart from the finale, I think the evening went quite well, don't you?" said Axel. "Julius didn't eat you! I could see you were nervous beforehand."

"I've been nervous for days, actually."

"Why didn't you tell me, you little ass!"

"I know, I should have done. Somehow the *idea* of Julius is a bit frightening. But now that I've seen him it'll be all right. He is so awfully nice. Isn't that stammer charming?"

"Yes. I must confess, I was a little nervous too."

"Why didn't you tell me?"

"I have my dignity to keep up."

"Have I no dignity?"

"None. Come here. On your knees. No, I'm not going to beat you, even though you did ignore my signal; I just want to put my arms round your neck. Good heavens, I see you've removed those plastic bulrushes."

"Well, you said you didn't like them."

"You mustn't let me influence you so much, dear boy. I can be wrong too."

🐚 | SEVEN

"Morgan, you look a different person."

"I'm feeling so much better, Rupert. So rested. You and Hilda have been angelic."

Morgan and Rupert were sitting in Rupert's study. The evening sun was shining in and making the room tingle with soft lustrous light. There was a smell of tobacco and roses. Rupert was sitting at his desk and Morgan in an arm-chair, with her feet propped up on another chair. She was rolling her dark boyish head about, smelling the glazed cretonne of the chair and gently agitating some whisky in a cut-glass tumbler. She looked indeed much better and, Rupert thought, distinctly handsome in a short silk shirt-looking dress with blue-and-white stripes and little blue flowers on the white stripes which she had bought that day in the sale at Marshall and Snelgrove. Her face was lean and sunburnt, with dark roses in her cheeks. She was, Rupert thought, wearing no make-up.

"Rupert, are these chair covers new? I don't remember them."

"Yes, they're just new."

"They have that lovely fresh furnishing material smell. Mmm. I love smells. Where did you say Hilda was this evening?"

"She's at a meeting of the Chelsea Preservation Society."

"Hilda has so much energy. I feel I have enough to do to preserve myself without preserving Chelsea. Did Simon come for his swim?"

"Yes. He and Hilda had another set-to about the new bathroom plan. He was very sorry to miss you. He keeps missing you."

"There will be a time for Simon. I'm only just beginning to feel human again."

"More whisky?"

"Yes, please, Rupert, I depend terribly on this stuff. Is it wrong?"

"You keep asking me that question about all sorts of things! Well, you'd better watch it. I must say, I depend on it too."

"What a bloody wreck my life is."

"Don't be foolish, Morgan. If you use your mind and your heart you can put everything together again."

"My mind is bedlam and my heart's dead."

"That's not true and it's treachery to say so."

"Treachery—to whom, to what? There isn't a God."

"You know quite well what I mean."

"Oddly enough I do. How's your book getting on, Rupert? Could I read part of it? Do you explain about treachery?"

"I try to explain. You'll see it when it's finished."

"Is that it over there, that huge pile of yellow notebooks?"

"Yes."

"Oh God, there's all that stuff of mine over at Tallis's place. At least I hope it's there. I don't imagine he'll have torn it up in a rage. All that stuff on language theory. I wish Hilda had managed to get it away."

"Tallis wouldn't give it up."

"I know. Hell."

"Morgan, what are you going to do about Tallis?"

"I knew you'd ask me that. When you asked me to come in this evening I knew you were going to tell me off, to put me through it."

"Morgan, don't be ridiculous."

"Well, why not? In a way, Rupert, you're really the only person who can help me. I'm too close to Hilda. And there isn't anyone else I really respect."

"You know I'd love to help you, Morgan. But there are things you've got to do for yourself."

"Do have another drink, Rupert. I hate drinking alone. It makes me feel even more immoral."

Rupert poured himself out some more sherry. He tried to keep off spirits until late in the evening, but did not always succeed. He sighed. He had had a long tiring day at the office, including an extremely exhausting session with the Computer Forecast Working Party. He felt weary now but fairly satisfied with himself and his tired body was filled with compassion for his sister-in-law. Without at the moment being able to think very clearly, he wished for her sake that he could become wise and good.

"You'll have to go and see Tallis, you know," said Rupert.

"Yes. But I can't even think about it yet. Thank God he doesn't know I'm here."

Rupert frowned uneasily. He had heard from both Simon and Axel of the curious encounter between Julius and Tallis, and how Tallis had been told of Morgan's arrival. He had informed Hilda, who had persuaded him to say nothing to Morgan. Hilda did not want Morgan rattled. And she seemed to think that Morgan would detest the idea that Tallis and Julius had met. "Spare her feelings for a little while longer," she pleaded with her husband. Rupert did not fancy the deception and could not understand or picture Morgan's state of mind, but he agreed. If he had been in Morgan's place he would have been incapable of recuperating in someone else's house while the person whom he had offended was kept waiting in ignorance. To have delayed the meeting would have been torment.

"Have you seen Julius again?" said Morgan.

"No." Rupert was to see Julius for lunch tomorrow, but he saw no reason to tell Morgan that.

"I do wish Julius would move on. I expect he will soon. Someone from Dibbins told me he was on his way to a job in Germany. I don't want to run into him in Oxford Street."

"Have you got over him, Morgan?" Rupert asked. He felt intensely curious about the mind and heart to which he had just so confidently alluded, but he was much less good than Hilda at asking the right questions.

"I don't know. I don't want to see him. I want a clear head."

"You'll need one."

"Yes, yes, yes. Keep me to it, Rupert. I feel such a bloody coward at the moment. How's Peter, by the way? Are you going to see him?"

"I've asked him over here. Perhaps he'll come, perhaps he won't." Rupert shrank from the possibility of encountering Tallis.

"I'd like to see Peter. I wish he wasn't living—over there."

"So do we, now."

"He must look so different. Have you got a recent picture of him?"

Rupert leaned over to forage in the drawer of his desk. Hilda kept the fat family photograph album meticulously up-to-date. "Here."

"Good heavens. He's a man. He looks like you."

"Handsomer."

"No, you're handsomer. But he must be taller. You both look awfully *noble*, actually. I love those big blond commanding faces. You look awfully young, you know, Rupert; with that floppy fair hair and that shy smile you look just like a boy."

"Sounds more like an ass. I've put on weight, I'm afraid. So has Hilda."

"It suits you. Let me look at some of the earlier ones. Being with you and Hilda makes me feel continuous again. One ought to feel continuous, oughtn't one? Lately I've just felt like a sort of stump. Why, there's Hilda and me. That must be ages ago. How stunning Hilda looks, she's got her angel-look. Of course, Hilda looked marvellous in those days. Well, she still does."

"You've changed," said Rupert. He looked at the photo. A much slimmer Hilda with the dark hyacinthine locks and the radiant brave face. Morgan looking shrunken and sulky, shoulders hunched and hands stiffly in pockets. "You're—in flower—now."

"Marriage and adultery have evidently done me good. Hilda—yes—"

"Do persuade Hilda to dye her hair. She can't make up her mind."

"Dye her hair? Is it going grey? I didn't notice."

"A little. I don't see why she shouldn't dye it. That sort of dark hair dyes quite successfully."

"You amaze me, Rupert. I would have expected you to view hair-dyeing as a falsification! Remember that great lecture you read me about smuggling that time I smuggled the camera from Switzerland."

"Smuggling involves lying."

"Rupert, I do admire you so much!"

"Stop teasing!"

"I'm not teasing, I mean it. And, oh God, I envy you. I envy you and Hilda. You've got what I need. Order, order, order. I told Hilda I envied her having a husband that functioned. As a spouse poor old Tallis was just a broken spring."

"I can't imagine Tallis providing order! But he has other qualities."

"Living with Tallis was like living in a gipsy encampment. At first it all seemed very unworldly and spiritual and free. Later it was depressing. Later still it was frightening. It made me lose my sense of identity. I resented the muddle but I couldn't dominate it. The trouble was that Tallis didn't expect me to, he didn't expect the right things of me. With Tallis there were no forms and limits, things had no boundaries. Oh, it's hard to explain. In the end everything about him began to irritate me terribly, even his freckles."

"Why *even* his freckles?"

"I adore it when you're a little catty, Rupert. You're so confoundedly charitable most of the time."

"What did Julius expect of you?"

"To respond to his magic. To be predictable. To be gay at the right times, quiet at the right times. To live to his timetable. To cook. Julius is quite a good cook himself, actually."

"I can see it was different."

"And yet not easy either. With Julius everything was ritual. Oh Rupert, there are people who communicate with the deep abysses of one's mind and these people are frightening."

"Julius did this."

"Yes. And Tallis too. Why couldn't I have found an ordinary man?"

"Like me."

"You aren't ordinary, silly. Tell me, Rupert, what did Julius do during the war? I asked him once and he wouldn't tell me."

"I don't know either."

"I suspect he was doing something absolutely *beastly* for the Americans. Some awful biological thing."

"He said to me once, 'I had a cosy war.' I expect he was doing research of some kind."

"I'm sure it was something horrible. Do you mind if I help myself to some more whisky?"

Morgan got up and began to prowl around the room swinging her glass. She stretched her long legs. She stood on her toes. She was wearing navy blue stockings and blue sandals. She went to look out of the window, pushing the open sash a little bit farther up. Rupert watched her. He felt that his tiredness was making him stupid. Morgan was in an electrical mood. She needed to be questioned, cornered, pinned. She wanted to be, to use her own words, put through it, told off. Rupert wished that he could be swift, accurate, compassionate, and stern instead of clumsy and vague and somehow sentimental.

"How strange these summer twilights are," said Morgan. It was darker in the room. "The light becomes so intense and yet it dissolves forms instead of revealing them. Your garden looks so odd. There's such a peculiar bluish lustre on the pool. It's a light for seeing ghosts in. One could easily imagine—it looks as if— You know, Rupert, I think Tallis used to see things, things he didn't tell me about. It was rather alarming sometimes."

"Tallis never hit the bottle much, did he?"

"Oh, no, nothing like that. How luminous your roses are. And the air gets heavy and you can smell the dark. Oh Rupert, Rupert, Rupert—"

"I know, my dear. I wish I could help. I feel a dolt with you this evening. Shall I turn the light on?"

"No, no light! There speaks a guilty voice. Tell me what I need, Rupert. Do I need an ordeal, punishment or something? What will make me stop feeling like a piece of filthy screwed-up newspaper?"

"Do you really want me to talk to you, Morgan?"

"I'm screaming for it! I need your help, Rupert, *absolutely.*"

"Is it clear that Julius is over?"

"For the sake of argument, yes."

"Do you still in any way love Tallis?"

"I suppose I must do. He obsesses me."

"You *did* love him?"

"There was a terrible *fatal* tenderness. He was so unutterably touching—before he started to annoy me."

"Suppose someone were to say: Why not try going back to Tallis?"

"I love the way you say, 'Suppose someone were to say X,' instead of just saying X! I expect it's your philosophical training. I don't know, Rupert. Perhaps I just want to get away from Tallis, to *escape*. Oh God, if only it were simple."

"Suppose someone— Well, what about divorce?"

"You are right to administer shocks."

"Yes, but what about it?"

"Everything about divorce is ugly and destructive and horrible."

"Try to think clearly, Morgan. If you really want to get away from Tallis—which I doubt, actually—you must be fair to him too. His life is passing as well as yours. And he's put up with a pretty unclear situation in a very patient way."

"Yes, yes. I want to be honest and just. How's it done, Rupert?"

"Ultimately through love, my dear. Love is the last and secret name of all the virtues."

"That's pretty. Do you say that in your book? But how can an obsession be changed into love? I can't *see* Tallis any more. He's just something hung round my neck. I think love in your sense is too hard, Rupert. Give me an intermediate goal. What can I try to do that I might conceivably manage to do?"

"Be calm. Calm of mind is so terribly important. Be quiet and let yourself sink. Sink into the depths of your own spirit and lose your fretful ego there."

"Rupert, you are marvellous. I'm dying to read your book. But how can I be calm when I'm living with the prospect of seeing Tallis?"

"Go and see him and get it over."

"Oh, not yet, not yet. Rupert—"

"Yes, child?"

"I did a very caddish thing to Tallis. I don't mean carrying on with Julius, that was a catastrophe but not caddish. I took some of Tallis's money."

"How do you mean?"

"We had a joint bank account. Idiotic thing to have of course. It was rather more my money than his. But when I decided to stay in America I pretty well cleaned it out."

"How much do you owe him?"

"About four hundred pounds."

"You must pay it."

"I haven't got it, Rupert. I saved quite a lot at Dibbins but I spent it all dillydallying on the West Coast and in Vermont trying to make up my mind to come home. And I had to pay for—oh, various things—and—"

"I'll lend it to you."

"Rupert, I didn't really mean to bring this up—"

"Look, Morgan, don't worry about *money*, for Christ's sake. I mean, don't worry about borrowing it from me. I've got plenty. And I am your brother."

"You're my angel. I'm sorry, I feel awful—"

"If you want to be able to *think*, you must pay the debt. Any trouble to do with money confuses the mind."

"You're right. I didn't really reflect about it in America. Since I got back it's been tormenting me more and more. But it seems—"

"Oh, don't be silly, Morgan! Look, I'll write you a cheque straightaway. Do you want any more money? I can easily let you have more."

"No, Rupert, just that. I will pay you back. And I'm very very grateful. I won't say more. You must know how I feel. And there's one other thing, Rupert."

"What?"

"Would you mind not telling Hilda?"

"Not telling her—"

"About the loan. You see, I never told her about the original thing. Oh, I *will* tell her. But I felt so damned ashamed—and you know I've always—all my life—been afraid of Hilda's disapproval."

"You should tell her. But, all right, I won't."

"Thank you, Rupert. You see, she'd hate *this* much more than the love affair. But I will tell." Morgan had put her glass down and drawn an upright chair close up against the desk, staring at Rupert in the half light. "So you doubt if I really want to get away from Tallis? And you think I must see him?"

"Yes. And soon. And not here. On his territory. Write to him, Morgan. You needn't say much in the letter. Say you'll come. You know he'll be very gentle."

"Don't, Rupert, *don't, don't—*"

"You've got to decide what sort of person you want to be—"

"The thought of even writing to him makes me feel giddy. And the thought of his gentleness makes me want to vomit. And the idea of going into his house—Tallis oughtn't to have a house —sorry, I'm talking nonsense. Leonard's there now too, isn't he? God, I don't want to see Leonard either. I couldn't stand the relation between Leonard and Tallis. It's so unnatural for a man to love his father. Sorry, Rupert, I'm just crazed. You're quite right to reproach me but I'm afraid I simply enjoy your reproaches. They comfort me. They don't connect with any real possibility of change at all. How very peculiar one's mind is. There's no foothold in it, no leverage, no way of changing oneself into a responsible just being. One's lost in one's own psyche. It stretches away and away to the ends of the world and it's soft and sticky and warm. There's nothing real, no hard parts, no centre. The only reality is just—immediate things—like—oh, like what—like this." Morgan stretched out her hand. She picked up a green oblong paperweight off the desk and laid it against her brow. There was a moment's silence. She lowered her hand and began examining the paperweight. "How pretty this is. It's some kind of mineral, isn't it. Such a marvellous swirly grain."

"It's malachite. Keep it. It's yours."

"Oh Rupert—dear—you mustn't—"

"I've had it since I was a child. I'd like to give it to you."

"It must be so precious—I—thank you, Rupert, I'll keep it. You are inconceivably good to me, my dear—you have been so good to me, you and Hilda. Perhaps we should put the light on, Rupert." Morgan got up.

There was a sound behind them and the door began to open slowly. A tall pale-clad figure was seen standing in the gloom in the doorway. Morgan gave a little shriek and retreated to the window. "Switch on the light, please," said Rupert in a sharp voice. A number of lamps went on and the room sprang into brightness. It was Julius.

Rupert leapt up. Morgan stood with her hands at her throat and the darkened sky behind her. Smiling, Julius closed the door. He said, "Hello, Rupert. Good evening, Mrs. Browne."

Rupert said, "Look here, Julius, I asked you—"

Julius was still smiling, his eyes glistening. "I'm sorry, Rupert. I see I've come at an inconvenient moment and I'm disturbing a tête-à-tête. I was passing near by and I thought I might manage to catch you alone. It was not an unreasonable idea. I want to change our arrangement for tomorrow. But perhaps I had better go. Forgive me." He did not look at Morgan.

"I'll see you out," said Rupert. He felt very angry. He followed Julius down the stairs, closing the study door behind him.

At the front door the evening light seemed brighter, still intense and not yet quite dark. The garden smelt almost unbearably of limes and honeysuckle. A blackbird was singing. Rupert took Julius's arm and propelled him to the gate. He said in a low voice, "Damn you."

Julius murmured, "Sorry. About tomorrow. I'll telephone. Good night." He turned quickly away in the direction of Gilston Road. Rupert ran back into the house.

Morgan was standing by the window in the same attitude. She lowered her hands and stared at Rupert with a blank expression. Then she said, "More scotch please." Rupert picked up her glass. Then she said, "Oh *God*, why did that have to happen."

Rupert poured out the whisky. He said, "Look, Morgan, you must make a serious effort—"

She said, "Rupert, hold onto me, tie me down—" Then she said, "Sorry." She moved, gave a short "Oh!" and for a moment Rupert thought she was going to faint. But as he stretched out his hand to her she darted past. The study door flew open and he heard her running feet on the stairs. The front door opened.

Rupert hurried out onto the landing. He saw Morgan reach the gate, look both ways, and then run away along the road to the right.

Rupert returned to his study and put the tumbler on the desk. The piece of green malachite was lying where Morgan had laid it down. He put it away in a drawer. Then he sighed deeply and began to drink the whisky.

🎗 | EIGHT

When Morgan reached the gate she knew Julius must have turned to the right, otherwise he would still be in view. She ran to the corner of Gilston Road and looked both ways but could see no sign of him. The whole area suddenly seemed to be portentously empty, lines of parked motor-cars, still trees, silent houses.

The street lamps had come on but the twilit sky of luminous rich blue could still contain their light. The Boltons was nearer than the Fulham Road. She turned right again and the heels of her sandals clacked upon the warm pavement. She reached Tregunter Road and looked along it, crossed to the other side and looked again. There was no one to be seen, only the desolate road full of ominous empty cars and the globes of street lamps fuzzy and bright in the glowing darkening air. Now the uncertain light was baffling her eyes. Gasping already with breathlessness and fear she began to run along the left-hand curve of the Boltons. When she had reached about half-way she had to stop and lean against a wall. She was sobbing for breath and choking with incoherent emotion. Then she began to walk quickly on, touching the creamy stucco balustrades for support. When she had nearly reached the end of the curve she saw a pale figure materializing ahead of her. It was Julius, who had walked up the other side of the oval and was now nearing the intersection with the Old Brompton Road.

"Julius!" But the sound she made was like a dream sound, a soft voiceless croak, and he continued to recede, walking rapidly.

Morgan began to run again. She caught him up on the corner of the Old Brompton Road where he had paused and was looking both ways, evidently hoping for a taxi.

"Julius, it's me."

He turned toward her, not surprised, faintly irritated and preoccupied. Then looked again along the road in both directions.

"Julius—"

"You should not have run."

"What can I do but run," she said desperately, "run, run, run—"

Julius was still looking for his taxi. The lamplight was reflected on his glasses. He was wearing a yellowish linen jacket and an open-necked shirt. He said, "I am very sorry to be in a hurry but I have an appointment."

"Why did you come to Priory Grove?" said Morgan. "You must have known you'd see me. You did it on purpose. Why, why?"

"A not very felicitous impulse. I apologize. Now please excuse me." He began to walk away from her along the Old Brompton Road in the direction of South Kensington.

Morgan began to hurry along beside him. There were a number of people on the pavements now and she had to keep falling behind. She found herself gasping again. The sheer physical authority of his presence almost reft her of breath. If only he would be quiet with her, stop somewhere and be quiet and let her experience that presence. She cried, "Julius, don't walk so fast, please, I must talk to you."

"What about? There is nothing more to say, is there?"

"Oh, why did you come. Julius, I'm in despair, please help me, it's all because of you, you're the only person who can help me now."

"I do not like melodramatic speeches in public places. And what you say is hardly true. And I am in a hurry to be somewhere else. I am sorry."

"Please stop walking for a moment, only a moment, and then I promise I'll go away."

They stopped and faced each other at the corner of Drayton Gardens. There was a pub on the corner with golden windows and a friendly hubbub coming from within. The sky was almost dark now.

"Please come into the pub for a moment," said Morgan. She felt that if she could only sit down she would be able to think.

"You know I detest pubs."

"Julius, *help me.*"

"You are a grown-up person and you must help yourself. Or if you must burden somebody with your troubles then burden your sister and her husband who will undoubtedly enjoy it. I am not a nurse."

"I know I went away from you, Julius. But you made me leave you. You know you did."

"This is a profitless and rather metaphysical discussion. I don't want to seem hard-hearted, but you are merely upsetting us both and as far as I am concerned the episode you refer to is over."

"Perhaps you feel hurt and resentful—"

"I feel neither. I merely wish you to recognize that you are a person endowed with free will and reason. And to go and exercise these faculties elsewhere."

"But I still love you."

"You must deal with that problem yourself. There are various well-known methods of extinguishing love."

"But I don't want to extinguish it. Oh Julius, don't you love me at all any more?"

"Please keep your voice down. As you will recall, I never once promised you love or said that I loved you."

"Oh God, that's true," said Morgan. She gave a raucous tearless sob.

"I thought we understood each other."

"I could never accept it," she said. "Oh, my dear—"

"Come, come. Remember we are in the public street. I dislike scenes and I dislike excitable muddled women, as you know. You once seemed to me not to be one. You once seemed to me, in this respect, exceptional. That was my mistake and I apologize for it. I told you clearly that I could not offer love. I made it plain to you what I could offer. You seemed to agree. But you took the liberty of assuming that I felt exactly what you wanted me to feel all the same."

"I know I did," said Morgan. "But I couldn't not. I loved you so much. And you were *there*. Oh Christ—"

"Please. I am sorry, as I say, to sound so cold. Possibly I am as upset as you are. But I should be of very little service to you if I became sentimental. You are an intelligent woman. Try to see this."

"I see it," she said, "I see it. And it's *hell*. Oh Julius, out of so much, can we not salvage a little? This was the greatest thing of my life. Even a little would help me now. I know you never deceived me, never, never, never. I deceived myself. But please, can you not give me something?"

"What do you want?"

"Friendship, support, understanding—"

"Either that is a great deal or else it is nursemaid's work. In any case I cannot give it. How can you so misconceive my character? I thought then that you knew me."

"I am stupid and emotional now, but please will you see me later? Just say you will and it will keep me going. I'll be very calm and sensible."

"It is pointless. You admit to being sick. And I certainly cannot cure you since I am the cause of the sickness."

"You are responsible," she said. "It is *your fault.*"

"You are becoming hysterical. I am in a hurry and I must leave you."

"Are you saying that you won't see me?"

"No. That sort of pronouncement belongs to a kind of drama which no longer exists here except in your mind. Mortal things finish and this has finished. I am saying that I no longer want to see you. And that if you will reflect when you are feeling less emotional you will realize that any further meetings would be likely to be just as fruitless and upsetting as this one. Now please let us separate. Good night to you."

He began to walk quickly away, crossing Drayton Gardens and continuing along the road. It was quite dark now and Julius seemed at once to disappear, absorbed into a bobbing darkness of hurrying figures. Morgan ran after him. She caught him up again and plucked at the linen sleeve.

"Julius, let me just walk with you until you get your taxi."

"As you wish."

"Julius, what am I to do?"

"Why not go back to your husband? He seemed to me to be quite a nice man."

"*What?*" Morgan stopped and Julius paused a pace or two ahead of her, looking back.

"What's the matter now?"

"Wait a moment," said Morgan. "Seemed to you— But you haven't ever met Tallis."

"I met him a day or two ago at Axel's. Didn't anybody tell you?"

Morgan began to walk automatically and they walked on to-gether, now more slowly.

"At Axel's," she said. "You met Tallis. Oh my God."

"Well, why not? He didn't hit me. He even offered me his hand. Why are you so upset?"

"He offered you his hand." Tears rose into Morgan's eyes and she rubbed them away with her knuckles.

"You should be pleased that we've met amicably. As I say, he seemed a decent chap."

"This is—somehow—the end. I'm sorry, I don't know what I'm saying—"

"I wonder why no one told you? Rupert must have known."

"I'm sorry. I think I'll turn back now. Does Tallis know I'm here?"

"Yes."

"Who told him?"

"Axel," said Julius, after a moment. "Don't cry then. Well, good night."

"One moment," said Morgan. They were standing on the corner of Cranley Gardens.

"What is it this time?"

"Listen," she said. Her mouth seemed filled with bitterness and pain. "There's something you don't know. When I left you—when you made me leave you—in South Carolina I took away a little memento with me."

"What do you mean?"

"I found I was pregnant."

Julius drew in a shuddering breath. He moved stiffly away from her and took several paces down Cranley Gardens. She followed, trying to see his face.

"And what happened?"

"I had an abortion of course. It was very expensive. But I wasn't going to ask you for money."

The traffic rumbled on beyond the moving frieze of darkened people. After a moment Julius said, "You regard the destruction of a child as a financial transaction."

"It certainly seemed like one at the time." She felt an awful premonitory pang of grief.

"And it did not occur to you to consult me about the continued existence of my own child?"

"I didn't think you'd care." She had not, not for a second, thought so.

Julius was silent. Then he murmured, "Again," and began to move back toward the main road. Then he said, "Was it a boy?"

"I didn't ask," said Morgan. "I didn't think of it as having a sex. As far as I was concerned it was a disease."

A lighted taxi appeared moving slowly up toward the traffic lights. Julius hailed it and it drew in toward the kerb. He said to the driver "Brook Street" and to Morgan "Good night." The taxi door slammed. The lights changed and the taxi drew away.

Morgan stood there, brushed and jostled by passersby. Then she took a few steps and leaned her head against a brick wall and began to sob hysterically.

🐠 | NINE

"What are they for after all but to kiss the foot that kicks them in the teeth? And when they've had the boils and the cattle have died and the children have died and they're scraping themselves with potsherds or whatever, though what that's like and why I've never been able to make out, I suppose if one hadn't any soap one might try to scrape the dirt off like when you scrape the mud off an old boot, not that there's any point in talking about soap to you, or potsherds either if it comes to that, since you never wash and go around like an old sheep with a filthy tail, and after all that and the damned irrelevant rubbish about the elephants and the whales and the morning stars and so on, there they are still whining and grovelling and enjoying being booted in the face— My toes are itching like hell. What do you think that's a symptom of?"

"Itching toes," said Tallis.

He was sitting at the kitchen table. He had been trying to write a lecture entitled *The Trade Union Movement and the Russian Revolution.* He had started a sentence: During these years Lloyd George played an ambiguous role, he—when Leonard had entered the kitchen. That was half an hour ago.

Although it was late in the evening it was still hot in the kitchen. The window was wide open and the electric light revealed a square segment of caked and crumbling brick wall just outside. The kitchen smelt of old frying fat and the general bitter smell of the house. The sink smelt of urine. Tallis had pushed some dirty plates into a pile to make room on the table for his notebooks. Leonard was sitting in the wickerwork chair, swaying himself to and fro so that the chair emitted a squealing sound. The Pakistanis were playing jazz music upstairs. Somewhere out in the street a woman was screaming. Tallis fidgeted, half got up, and then as the sound receded fell back on his chair. He found it difficult to focus his eyes on the page. Leonard talking had the effect of emptying his mind of thoughts.

"Furthermore," said Leonard. He leaned forward, brushing the loose pendant strands of his chin to and fro across the top of the stick which he was holding between his legs. "Furthermore, it's no good their talking about progress. If they get hold of one thing they lose another. It's automatic. They can't win. Now they are prating of happiness. But what is it? They don't even know. If they had it they'd keep their coal in it. And there's another thing. They crave for change, at any price, and they'll always crave for it, at any price, and that's why they'll always have wars, wars upon wars upon wars, until this globe's got nothing on it but old bones and plastic bags and a seething mass of spiders. Spiders will survive longest. And plastic is indestructible. That's what this place is like. What a planet."

"Oh, go to bed, Daddy," said Tallis.

"Of course it all went wrong from the start."

"Oh, fuck off, Daddy, I'm trying to work."

"What did you have for supper?"

"Baked beans."

"What did I have?"

"Chicken something or other."

"I'm hungry."

"Well, make youself some toast."

"Will you poach me an egg?"

"No."

"Where's Peter?"

"I don't know."

"The spiders will eat each other."

"I expect they will. Look, Daddy—"

"So they'll be all right."

"It's nearly midnight—"

"They can live in the plastic bags."

"I've got to finish this lecture—"

"Did you know that your wife was in England?"

"Yes."

"Are you going to see her?"

"No."

"What did I do to have a wet as a son?"

"The point is—"

"I wonder if you know what your mouth looks like when you talk. You ought to look in a mirror sometime. Only I doubt if you'd survive the shock."

"How did you know she was?"

"Peter told me. He told me not to tell you."

"You and Peter are a jolly discreet pair."

"Why aren't you?"

"If she doesn't want to see me I don't want to bother her. Not yet anyway."

"So you've got a plan?"

"No. I just know I'm unstable. I don't know what I'll do. I mean, I can't predict it."

"The only real and beautiful thing you ever did in your life was to marry that girl."

"We can agree about that."

"You could have knocked me down with a feather."

"Me too."

"It's a bloody mystery why she ever looked at you twice."

"Agreed, agreed—"

"And then you let a bloody Jew take her away from you."

"She's free—"

" 'Free'! That's gibberish. You haven't mentioned her name for a year. I thought you'd forgotten her."

"Well, I haven't forgotten her."

"If I had my way all the bloody Jews would be deported to Palestine and all the bloody nig nogs would be sent back to wherever they came from and all the Welfare State scroungers would be sent to Australia. Do them good to do a little work for a change. They could clear the bush."

"The bush is desert. There's nothing to clear."

"Let them die of thirst then. And all Americans would be shot on sight."

"Do stop squeaking the chair, Daddy, it's getting on my nerves."

"You never gave her any fun. You've got to give a woman fun."

"Did you give my mother fun?"

"Don't you dare to speak to me of your mother!"

"Well, did you?"

"No. But that's because I never had any blasted money."

"Fun—" said Tallis. He pushed his notebooks away from him and several plates went over the side with a crash. "Oh, hell—"

"Are you daring to insinuate that I behaved badly to your mother?"

"I've no idea. We were— I was only five when she cleared off."

"I wish you were five again, I'd give you something. Not that beating ever did you any good. But my God I enjoyed it."

"Do go to bed, Daddy."

"Couldn't get a woman all those years. Had to have some erotic satisfaction. Whacking your bottom was something."

"Do go to bed, I'm tired—"

"You're always tired. You make me sick with your bloody tiredness. You had every bloody advantage and look what you've done with your life. Just look at you."

"Another time, if you don't mind."

"I've had a bloody awful life and what's more it's nearly over."

"Nonsense, Daddy."

"I've nothing to hope for. What's the best I've got to hope for? That same lady who visits old-age pensioners will come and see me and lend me a book. Christ, I'd even be glad. That's what I've come to. You went to a university. I slaved for you."

"I had a government grant."

"Spiritually speaking, I slaved. God, what a rotten life. Started work at fourteen. Fifty years of sodding boredom. Wife left me, the bitch. You as an offspring. I often wonder why I didn't end it all long ago."

"Well, why didn't you?"

"So now you're trying to drive your old father into his grave—"

"No, Daddy, of course I—"

"I know you hate my guts."

"Daddy, don't talk *rubbish*."

"God, as if it wasn't enough punishment living in this shit-house and seeing your face every day I've got this blasted pain all the time in my hip. Can you imagine what that's like? No, you can't, and you don't even try to. You've got no physical sympathy. All you care about is your precious nig nogs and lay-abouts."

"The doctor wanted you to go to hospital for a test—"

"You come out of those places feet first. They're swarming with bugs. They don't even bother to sterilize things any more. They know it's no use."

"They can operate for arthritis now, Daddy. They can give you a new hip joint."

"I don't want their bloody machinery rusting away inside me!"

"It won't rust. Things only rust if they're exposed to the air."

"Fat lot you know about it. I doubt if you know a single true fact."

"It's after eleven-thirty p.m."

"It isn't in Australia. It isn't on the moon. So it can't be true here."

"Oh, all right. But do let someone help you or else stop complaining. The doctor said—"

"The doctor's a fool. They don't teach them properly nowadays. Did you know that your hair goes on growing after you're dead?"

"No."

"They have to shave corpses. There's a man at the hospital who does nothing else."

"O.K., O.K.—"

"Must you talk like a bloody American? You needn't bother to shave me. You'll be too busy celebrating anyway."

"Daddy, please—"

"And I'll tell you another thing you weren't able to give your wife—"

"Shut up, Dad, and clear off. I've got to work."

"Work he calls it. You live in a dream world. You clear off. I'm sick of the sight and the smell of you."

Tallis stood up and gathered his notebooks together. He picked the pieces of the broken plates up off the floor and put them on top of a pile of old newspapers underneath the sink. He resisted the familiar impulse to slam the door and began to go slowly up the stairs. The jazz music from up above became louder. Tallis pulled himself up by the banisters and went into his own bedroom and shut the door. He pulled the blind down. There were no curtains. He sat down on the divan bed and began to pick his nose.

The room was small and narrow and the bed, which stretched along the wall, took up most of it. There were no sheets, but a mound of thin blankets underneath which Tallis slept in winter and on top of which he slept in summer. Books were piled against the other wall. Tallis pulled his legs up and leaned back. He could not think without a table. Better give up and sleep now. Get up early and finish lecture. Better not thoughts now. Sleep. Unbeing. No point in kneeling down, folding hands, muttering. Self-abasement, prostration, licking the ground and wriggling through. Tears and sex. God, what a muck-heap my mind is, thought Tallis. He closed his eyes and tried to breathe slowly and regularly. Words came without volition, sinking very slowly through his mind like pebbles. Words out of some lost and ancient past. Lighten my darkness. Tiddy pom tiddy pom tiddy pom from up above. The perils and dangers of this night. With his eyes still closed he uncurled his legs and turned over to lie prone upon the bed, burying his face in the pillow. That peace which the world cannot give. There was light somewhere, cool precious light, some-where quite else. The pillow smelt of dust and age and grief. It was an old old pillow. It had attended upon life and death and birth and was tired of them all. It had no pillow slip on and it tickled Tallis's nose. Get undressed and turn out light. Idiotic go sleep like this.

His sister was standing at the foot of the bed dressed in a long dress. There were visitants from another world by whose presence he was sometimes troubled and perplexed and more rarely de-lighted. These he knew were minor presences, riff-raff of con-sciousness. This was different. She came with a vividness which was not that of dream, yet always at these still moments and at night. Sometimes he felt she cheated him of other things. She interposed. Was it a protection? She wore a long robe of a pale colour. She must have altered with the years, growing older with him, but he could not clearly remember. She was silent and yet seemed to speak. Perhaps she spoke to some part of him of which he knew nothing. She looked and yet he could not see her eyes.

He was always very quiet when she came, pinned down, heavy, glad, and yet a little frightened too.

He jerked over with a fast-beating heart. The room was empty. The electric light was on. It was too bright. His mouth had moistened the pillow. He sat up. The room was filled with the appalling thought of Morgan. While she had been inconceivably far away the thing had been bearable. Now he felt crippled with pain at the knowledge that she had returned to England and had not come straight to him. Yet why should he have expected this? He had not really expected anything, he thought, during the time that she was away. He had tried not to think of it as an interim, though he had never for a second told himself: It is finished. It was as if she had been translated to another planet. There was no spatial tug any more between them. Yet he must all the time have retained his hope and thought of himself still as being her home and the natural ground of her being.

Now that she was back, every day and every hour of her silence turned that hope into torture. She was no longer outside the world. The distance between them was the familiar traversable distance between W.11 and S.W.10. They could reach each other by bus. No, he had no plan. He did not even wonder whether it was pride which made him idle when every tormented nerve yearned to cry out: Come back! He did not look so deep. He knew that for the moment he could do nothing. He just thought about her and about the past. They had known it would be difficult. The tender humble consciousness of difficulty, of distance, had always been a part of their love. Yet it had seemed like the beginning of a great enterprise. They had never quarrelled.

He sat on the bed rubbing his eyes. His eyes itched with tiredness and dust. His body was warm and restless with sexual desire. He had not made love since the last time with her. The Pakistanis' wireless played "God Save the Queen" and became silent. Good night, good night. There were distant cars and the intermittent night cries of the neighbourhood. There was almost always to be heard some sound of human trouble, shouting people, quarrelling people, weeping people, drunks. Tallis wondered where Peter was now. Although he tried, he communicated less and less with the boy. Tallis's Peter was a very different person from Rupert's Peter or even Hilda's Peter. Tallis knew that. With his parents Peter acted a part. Tallis had thought this was something bad but was just now beginning to believe that it might be an element of salvation. The separation from which so much had been hoped had conceivably stripped the boy of his last defence, the imperative need to keep up appearances. With Tallis, Peter had no role and lived in a state of vulnerability and nakedness which was not too far from despair.

They had also begun to get on each other's nerves. Tallis was clumsy, Peter was surly. Tallis had hoped that his protégé would have eyes for the unfortunates about him, who even if they could not always inspire compassion might appear interesting or at the very least picturesque to a boy nurtured in a world where money and good breeding precluded screams and blows. Here the causes of human misery, though they were infinitely complex, were shadowily visible and one could see the machine. Tallis had trusted that a glimpse of the machine might make Peter understand something, might make him see that revolt may be itself mechanical, and that human ills need thought and work which are disciplines of the imagination. Even if Notting Hill had made Peter want Cambridge that would have been something. But now these calculations seemed merely stupid. Peter was shut up inside a world of private mythology and personal adventure and the picturesque ministered merely to that. Tallis knew of all the dangers. There was crime, there was heroin, there was despair and unbalance of the mind. Peter no longer told him with whom he spent his time. The objects which appeared at intervals in Peter's room were doubtless not acquired by the old-fashioned method of handing money across a shop counter. Tallis had so far failed to make Peter discuss this seriously. He had imagined that Peter needed love and for the moment not parental love. Now he was not far from thinking that perhaps what the boy needed was professional psychiatric help. The idea was detestable.

All Morgan's things were still in the locked room downstairs.

Would she come for them? No. She would send Hilda. And this time he would not be able to say no. Then I'll let the room, he thought. At any rate that would bring in four pounds a week. Hilda paid him for Peter's room, of course, but she seemed quite unaware how much London rents had gone up, and only paid him thirty shillings a week, though it was the best room in the house. The bank manager was getting nasty about the overdraft. The problem of how to run an ordinary life seemed to be getting more and more insoluble. How can I be responsible for Peter, thought Tallis, when I can't organize myself? I must find more lecturing, he thought, another class. Why on earth did I agree to write that report for the housing committee? Would this muddle just go on and on or would it end in some sort of final catastrophe? Sometimes he wished for that catastrophe, wished that someone would come and just cart him away. Yet he knew his own toughness and knew that in all probability while he lived the muddle would simply go on and on and on.

Tallis got up and began to take off his trousers. He stood in his shirt vaguely scratching his back. He felt depressed and amorous and very tired.

There was a soft padding sound on the stairs and a tap at the door. It was Peter. His plump face and tassels of blond hair leaned round the door. "Hello, Tallis. I'm starving. Is there anything to eat? I can't see anything."

"There's a tin of tongue in the cupboard," said Tallis. "The tin opener's somewhere. On the dresser. Where have you been?"

Peter had vanished. Tallis pulled off his shirt. He always slept in his vest. He pulled back the top blanket and turned off the light. He sat upright in bed with his back against the wall, looking at the red night sky outlining the blind. He saw Morgan's face alight with tenderness and humour. He deliberately blotted it out. He thought of quite other things. He began vaguely to caress himself.

"Tallis, are you asleep?"

Damn. "No, Peter, what is it?"

"Can I talk to you?"

"Oh, all right. Where have you been?"

"Walking."

Peter sat down on the end of Tallis's bed, his big head outlined against the reddish light.

"Peter, I looked into your room today and what did I see? I saw two transistor sets, two cameras, two electric torches, three electric razors, two silk scarves, and a cigarette lighter."

"Really?"

"Did you steal these things?"

"Not the smaller electric torch. Mother brought that over ages ago. I've had it since I was ten. I think she felt it might cheer me up, like an old teddy bear or something."

"Peter, you know you mustn't steal."

"So you said before. But you were unable to tell me why."

"To begin with it's wrong. And secondly you might get into serious trouble."

"I'm indifferent to secondly and I don't understand to begin with. What does it mean to say stealing is wrong? I only take things from big shops. No one is hurt. What's wrong with that?"

"It's *wrong*."

"But what does that mean?"

"Oh, hell," said Tallis. He felt very weary and aching with unsatisfied desire. Right and wrong were as shadowy as bats. "It's undignified."

"Suppose I reject dignity as a value?"

"You should respect other people's property."

"I'm prepared to respect other people. But under capitalism these things are not the property of people, they're the property of big impersonal combines which are already making far too much money."

"It involves concealment and lying."

"Not even much concealment. I just pick the stuff up. And no lying. If someone asks me what I'm doing I shall say I'm stealing. And I'm not lying to you."

"Your parents would be very unhappy if you were arrested."

"Possibly, but that's nothing to do with *stealing*. And parents must take their chance."

"You haven't joined any kind of gang, have you?"

"No, I'm on my own. I'm free. I'm just experimenting with myself. You mustn't worry so."

"It's all so bad for you, Peter. God, I wish you were back at Priory Grove."

"Well, I'm not going back there! If you chuck me out I'll find another room around here by myself."

"I'm not going to chuck you out. But can't you see that your whole mode of existence is crazy, that you live in a wretched muddle?"

"You live in a muddle too. And you believe your muddle is superior to my parents' order. And you're right."

"I don't think it!"

"Yes, you do. Morality, *their* morality, is all superstition and self-interest. You know that."

"I don't know what I know or think. Go to bed, Peter. I'm bloody tired."

"Tallis, don't be cross with me. But could you sleep with me tonight? I'm feeling awfully eerie. I think I shall get miserable if I sleep alone."

Tallis was used to these changes of mood and now to this request. "Oh, all right. But make it snappy, will you."

"I feel there are demons around."

Tallis began to get out of bed. They used Peter's bed when they slept together, since it was wider. Tallis's interesting fantasy was still unfinished, but it would be a pity to sacrifice what vague inadequate satisfaction there might be in holding Peter in his arms. Holding another human body does sometimes help. He followed Peter across the landing.

Tallis blinked in the electric light. Peter was putting on striped pyjamas. There was a bitter smell. Tallis felt nervy and unsympathetic and weary of his consciousness. He wanted darkness. "Come on, Peter, let's sleep, for God's sake."

He straightened Peter's bed a little and got in. The light went out. The bed sagged and creaked. They lay down together, bumping about, adjusting arms and knees in the cramped space and then were still, Peter with his face pressed into Tallis's shoulder and Tallis looking over the light cool hair into the dimness of the room. Peter could feel the demons. Tallis could see them. They were not the dangerous kind. Holding the sleeping boy in his arms, with the rudiments of an erection, Tallis watched the demons play.

🏵 | T E N

Morgan pushed the door. It reeled back, attached by only one hinge, scraped noisily along the floor and then stuck. She stepped inside into darkness. A door opposite to her opened. "Oh Christ," said Tallis.

He stepped quickly back into the sunny kitchen, and she followed him in, closing the door behind her. She wanted to say something immediately about the untidy littered scene which she could see so clearly. She could not see Tallis. But all that came was an inarticulate sound which she turned into a cough. She coughed again, putting her hand to her mouth. Tallis offered her the chair on which he had been sitting and moved hastily to the other side of the table. Morgan sat down. Tallis said "Oh Christ" again. It was five o'clock in the evening.

"Were you having tea?" said Morgan. She could still not see him.

"No. I was working."

"There was silence. Tallis leaned back against the dresser knocking some things off it.

Morgan said, "I'm sorry not to have given you any warning. I only decided to come this morning."

"Would you like some tea?" said Tallis.

"No, thank you. Have you any whisky?"

"No, I've only got beer. Would you like some?"

"No, thank you."

"I can go out and get whisky."

"No, no, it doesn't matter."

Ever since she had learnt that Tallis knew of her presence and had met Julius she had felt an agonizing almost humiliating need to see her husband. He haunted her and drew her. Not till she was walking down the road, however, had she really reflected that she had no idea how Tallis would behave. Would he be angry? Would he be cold? Would he weep? She had managed to get through the door without fainting and now she was sitting down and had said something, she did not know what.

"Why didn't you come to see me, Tallis?" said Morgan. Her eyes seemed to be paralysed, fixed upon a corner of the dresser where a tangle of string was trailing over the edge, but her voice seemed to be steady. "You knew I was here."

"I didn't want—to see you—if you didn't want—"

"How do I know what I want? What a horrible smell there is here. What is it?"

"Various things."

"It's rather like the smell we had at Putney. Where's Leonard, Peter?"

"Out."

"Pity."

Tallis said, "But you came to see me—?"

Morgan blinked hard and managed to focus her gaze upon him. He was looking at her, but she tried not to see his eyes. He was clutching the dresser behind him with both hands. He had turned pale behind his freckles and his face looked diseased. The undefended face, older, bumpier. She thought, He has less hair.

"I came to get my manuscripts."

As Tallis simply continued to stare at her she added, "I hope you've still got them." She coughed again and patted her hair. She had managed several minutes and it must get easier. If only she could breathe more deeply. And not to look into his eyes.

"Yes—all your stuff here—I locked it up. Would you like to look?"

"Yes, please. Tallis, I want us to be very quiet and businesslike. No emotional talk. Do you understand?"

"Yes. The stuff's here, in the room opposite."

"Could I see it at once, please? I have an engagement at six."

Tallis made an inarticulate noise which sounded half laugh half moan. Then he said, "I don't know where the key is." He turned and began scrabbling among the things piled on the dresser. Something fell and broke. He uttered a long "Ooooh—" He dragged out a bunch of keys and opened the kitchen door with his head still turned away from her, but she could see that his face was screwed up. She looked at his back and at his flapping bedroom slippers with the trodden-down heels. She said to herself, No tenderness, no pity, nothing. I must see him as a puppet. I must go through this like a machine. She felt sick and breathless but dry-eyed.

Tallis unlocked a door. "I'm afraid there's an awful jumble in here. I just put it all in here when we moved. I kept meaning to— I think the manuscripts are all there in the corner. But perhaps you'd like to look at the rest. There's—clothes and things—"

"You might have kept the place dusted." A cloud of dust seemed to hang in the doorway like a curtain. Morgan sneezed.

"Dusted!" Again the laugh and the moan.

"Would you mind leaving me to look round?" said Morgan. "I'll be about ten minutes."

"Shall I shut the door?"

"No, leave it open. I don't want to stifle. Could you open that window, if you can get to it."

"It's stuck, won't open."

"Well, never mind, thank you, thank you."

Tallis vanished, the kitchen door closed. Morgan half closed the door of the room and sat down upon a trunk and covered her face.

At any rate I've *seen* him, she thought. Something of the worst is over. That particular shock can never happen again. I've managed to stay upright. She had been feeling so sick all day, like an examination sickness. She had made herself wait until five o'clock to be more sure of finding him in. She did not want to have to walk down that street twice. Her imagination could not beforehand frame the moment of meeting. It was as if at that anticipation, her deepest faculties swooned. What she could imagine, and hung onto desperately, was the idea that there would come a moment later on in the day, when she *had seen* Tallis. When she had seen him and come away. When she would be having a drink with Hilda and telling her about it. Morgan drank a lot of whisky before she left the house. She told no one of her intention.

She had now no memory of what had been said, only of that terrible air of suffering. She tried to remember how much it had irritated her once. Tallis was framed for suffering. Let him suffer. She must remain cold and hard and purposeful and vile. She must keep sharp and rigid her intent to survive, whatever cries were heard, whatever blood was shed. So long as I can keep it all completely dismembered, she thought. Keep everything small and separate and manageable. Frame no general picture. Do not wonder what he is doing now in the kitchen. She thought, and her consciousness seemed to reel at the effort, I simply *must not* give way to that ghastly heartbreaking tenderness, that *animal* feeling. For this moment, I must have no heart-strings and no heart. She felt giddy. It was as if love or terror or something were trying to thrust itself through into her mind. She felt a pain which was curiously like sexual desire. She knew that in a moment she would be in tears.

Morgan got up. Detail, detail, detail, keep everything small and separate. She closed the door. She breathed in the hot dusty air, expelling it slowly through her mouth. The sun was slanting along the grimy window and the cluttered room was bright and curiously attentive and still, as if all the things in it were watchful and alive. She made herself scan it. The floor was entirely covered. There were three trunks and several suitcases, a lot of cardboard boxes with shop labels on them, several half-collapsed heaps of books, and a number of tins. The manuscript notebooks, tied together with string, were in the corner on top of a suitcase. Coats and jackets and jumpers, thick with dust, lay strewn about, together with odd books and pamphlets and offprints. Morgan kicked a few things aside to clear a space, scuffing up sheets of yellow newspaper which had been laid down as a covering upon the bare floor boards.

She clambered across to the notebooks and slipped the string off. She checked them quickly. Her embryonic articles, the backbone of her book. They looked almost weird to her now. *Language, Form or Substance. Association Theory and Homonyms. From De Saussure to Chomsky. The Prague Circle and After. The Real Definition of Phonemes. Towards an Algebra of Language.* She tied them up again. There was nothing missing. She would be able to carry them away. She began to look around her at the other things and felt with a sick jerk the appalling reality of the past. All those tins of pâté and jellied chicken and dressed crab and cocktail sausages and lambs' tongues from Fortnum's which she had once suddenly decided to stock the larder with. Why hadn't they been eaten long ago? Why were they lying here, a little rusty, among these old jerseys which she could now see were moth-eaten? And those awful nightmarish cardboard boxes. During the last period with Tallis, just before, out of her restlessness, she had taken off for that ludicrous philologists' conference, she had had a bout of frenzied clothes-buying. She always spent money when she was depressed. Dresses, skirts, shoes, even hats, although she hardly ever wore hats. These purchases, which she could not afford, which she had never worn, some of them not even unwrapped, were in those cardboard boxes. They reminded her of what she now knew she had forgotten: the special smell of her unhappiness with Tallis before she even knew that Julius existed.

But had it really been unhappiness? There had been some strange frame of mind which the cardboard boxes now exuded into the thick warm dusty air. She had loved Tallis once. He had utterly pierced her with that agony of protective tenderness, with his quite peculiar unleavableness. And he had exalted her somehow, made her feel that she loved him with the best of herself. She remembered this exaltation and thought now how hopelessly misleading, how *fatal* that strange idea had been. She simply could not live with that part of herself, it was not operational, it was too small. That love was crippled from the start. Could it have changed in time and did she then believe that it would? Perhaps she had imagined that the rough and tumble of married life would make them both more ordinary with each other, more like warm unreflecting animals sharing a hutch. There had been too much consciousness. Would it all have become easier and better if there had been no Julius? Or would her restlessness have, whatever happened, invented a Julius? He expected too much of me, she thought. No, that wasn't it, how could it be? He really had so few claims and expectations, perhaps too few. It was as if he bored me, except that it wasn't boredom. We are made of different material.

"Can I help?" said Tallis. He had thrust the door open a little.

"No, thank you. Well, take these out, could you." She thrust the pile of notebooks toward him with her foot. No risking a contact of fingers. Tallis took them away, but was back at the door a moment later as Morgan opened one of the cardboard boxes. To avoid a silence she said, "This dress, I've never worn it. And it's too long now." She held the dress of dark blue terelyne up against herself.

"You could shorten it," said Tallis.

Morgan felt the tears away behind her eyes, gathered, present. She threw the dress down. "What a jumble here."

"I'm sorry. If I'd known—"

"Well, you did know."

"Yes. I should have—"

"The moths have got into all these woollies."

"I did mean to spray or something—"

"Why didn't you eat these tins of pâté and chicken and so on? They've probably gone bad by now."

"They were your special stuff and I thought—"

"There was nothing special about them. They were just for eating. Why, there's my old necklace of amber beads. I wondered where it was."

"I'm afraid it's still broken," said Tallis. He was leaning in the doorway looking down. The tail of the necklace emerged from under some yellowed tissue paper.

Morgan stooped to pull it out. She remembered the clasp had broken and Tallis had said he'd mend it. He liked mending things for her. She recalled the scene in the kitchen, Tallis's pleased look as he examined the clasp. He hung the necklace on a hook on the dresser and said he would get some araldite at the ironmonger's and mend it. That must have been the evening when she told him she was going to America. The necklace was somehow associated with her departure. She had been a little defiant, Tallis rather silent. They must have both known it was an important step. She left England soon after. And he had not mended the necklace. She avoided looking at him now, knowing that his head was still bent. She glanced at her watch but the dial was hazy. "I must keep an eye on the time."

"Come into the kitchen for a minute," said Tallis.

Morgan blinked hard, dropped the necklace into the mess of moth-eaten woollies, and followed him. Only when she had entered the kitchen and heard the door close behind her did she suddenly feel menaced. She tried the little cough again, but this time it made her feel she was going to be sick. Bitterness rose in her throat.

Tallis very deliberately set the table between them once more. He was looking less pale now and Morgan saw how tired and how dirty he looked. The scanty ginger hair was jagged and uncombed. He wore a shapeless light blue jersey with a crumpled collar and a lot of stains down the front, and rather limp damp-looking grey trousers, baggy at the knees. The big light brown eyes stared at her, not accusingly, but with a kind of amazement. He seemed to be trembling slightly. Morgan avoided looking at the eyes or the mouth. She turned her head, feeling his gaze like a physical ray beating upon her cheek. She leaned back against the dresser. "Well?"

"I think I should be saying 'Well?' " said Tallis. "Are you coming back to me, or are you just visiting?"

Morgan swallowed the bitterness. Some darkness seemed to be hovering just above her head. She said, "I didn't imagine you'd want me to come back." She concentrated her attention upon some dirty milk bottles upon the window sill.

"Of course I want you to come back."

"Why 'of course'? It's not simple. It's certainly not simple for me."

"You're not still with——?"

"No, that's over."

"Then it's over, it's past."

"You mean you don't care?" she said.

Tallis was silent for a moment. "Don't be a bloody idiot, Morgan. Here you are back again. That's the main thing, isn't it?"

"I don't understand you," said Morgan. Then she felt, I am not only vile, I'm vulgar. Of course I understand him. He is talking beautiful plain sense and, suddenly, it could be simple. But I won't let it be. I must act a part, play a scene, to preserve myself, I've got to. I ought to show some genuine emotion now, I feel sick enough. I ought to cry. But I won't. God, I'm a hollow thing.

"Please don't—just argue," said Tallis. "It doesn't matter about the argument. There is no argument."

"I can't simply come back," said Morgan. "It doesn't make any sense to me."

"You mean something else has got to happen first?"

"No, no——"

"I know this house is ghastly. But we could soon clean it up. With you back I'd want to. Everything would be different."

Morgan imagined herself scrubbing the kitchen floor. Well, why not? "Oh, don't be so *irrelevant*," she said. She took a quick glance at him and saw the small mouth quivering. She thought, I must get away, enough, enough, enough.

"Morgan, *think*."

"I am thinking. There's no use in my coming back. I should only run away again. It would all end in tears."

"We are in tears anyway." The voice was firm enough.

"You may be," said Morgan. She felt exasperated, stronger. "But I'm not. I've had a wonderful adventurous time these last two years. I've really lived. And I'm going to go on having a wonderful adventurous time. I'm not going into any more cages. We ought never to have got married, you and I, as you very well know. We are totally unsuited to each other. I can't imagine how or why it ever happened. It was a mistake. We never shared our deepest thoughts. I realize that, now that I know myself a good deal better. I imagined I loved you. I didn't really. Least said soonest mended."

"Of course you loved me. And you love me. And I—"

"Oh, stop it, please. Could you lend me a bag to put those notebooks into? A paper bag will do so long as it's a fairly strong one."

Tallis grubbed about under the sink and produced a crumpled paper bag with a string handle. He took the notebooks from the table and put them into the bag. He said, "Morgan, I beg you—"

"And there's another thing," she said hastily. "I took all that money out of the bank."

He stared at her and she looked away.

"I took the money, your money as well as my money, out of the bank. Or didn't you notice?"

"Yes, I noticed."

"I'd like to pay you something now. You'll accept it? Well, why shouldn't you, it's your money." She fumbled with her hand-bag. When the cheque book was in her hand she hesitated. She wrote a cheque for a hundred pounds and sighed deeply. "Here's a hundred pounds. I'll pay you the rest later on." She threw the cheque onto the table.

Tallis picked it up and thrust it unfolded into his trousers' pocket. "Thanks."

He stood staring at her and now she could not avoid those eyes. No accusation, but the look was hard to bear. She thought, Tallis is like radium. Too much exposure to him damages the tissues. She became aware of a faint strange booming sound. Perhaps it was just the eternal torment of London's traffic which she had just become aware of. Perhaps it was the blood beating in her ears. Perhaps—

"Aunt Morgan!"

Peter had pushed open the kitchen door.

"Oh Peter, *Peter!*" Morgan's relief was intense.

Peter was wearing tight black trousers and a clean open-necked white shirt. He had the air of a young commander.

"How marvellous, you're back, you're back!" He rushed at her and they embraced higgledy-piggledy, laughing and jostling.

"Peter, you've so grown up, so handsome, so *tall.* I'm terribly glad to see you!"

"Gosh, Aunt Morgan, you look stunning! I say, I'm sorry to butt in."

Peter was a good head taller than Tallis. Morgan found herself confusedly delighted by his sheer tallness, mingled with her relief at the ending of her tête-à-tête with her husband. Peter's plump face was rosy and shiny, his long abundant blond hair glowed in the sunshiny air, he shone with health and youth. He was trying to apologize while laughing with pleasure.

"That's all right, I was just going," said Morgan. She picked up the paper bag. "Will you see me along the road, Peter? I'd love to hear all about you."

Peter opened the kitchen door for her, still laughing and exclaiming. He took the bag out of her hand. "Here, let me carry that."

"Good—day," said Morgan. She had intended to say "Goodbye" but choked upon it. She attempted a smile.

Tallis said nothing. He nodded his head. His face had become harder and more remote. The light brown eyes gazed in her direction without seeming to focus upon her.

Morgan raised a hand in vague salute and quickly followed Peter out of the door. With relief and now almost with joy she breathed the sunny stale air of the shabby street, she looked in wonder at the houses and the blue sky. She thought, I've seen him, I've done it, it's over, it's over, it's over. I shall tell Hilda all about it over a drink. Oh God, the relief! Whatever the future might hold, whatever, when she came to have intentions and purposes again, she might intend and purpose, the primal shock was over and everything was going to be ever so much easier and nicer. A sudden sense of freedom made her feel light and unconfined as a dancing shadow. She turned, looking up into Peter's still laughing eyes. They began to chatter incoherently to each other.

🎋 | E L E V E N

"What a baby Simon is!" said Rupert.

He and Axel with glasses in their hands were standing at the window of Rupert's study, looking down at the sunlit scene in the garden. Axel stared gloomily at the slim figure of his young lover who was just climbing out of the pool. He said nothing. Hilda, dressed in a pink towelling shift, was stretched out on a blue rug on the flagstones, rubbing a sunburn lotion into her shiny brown legs. Simon looked up and waved. Rupert waved back. Axel almost imperceptibly raised his glass.

"My God," said Rupert, "look who's here!"

Peter and Morgan had just marched out through the french windows.

Hilda began hastily to get up, upsetting the sunburn lotion onto the rug. Simon gave a joyous cry and opened his arms. Axel moved away from the window.

"Come on, Axel, let's go down."

"I just thought I'd bring him along with me!" said Morgan.

"Morgan, how marvellous to see you, I've kept missing you. Hello, Peter," cried Simon.

"Evening, Peter. Nice to see you here," said Rupert.

"Where from?" said Hilda.

"From Tallis's," said Morgan with a careless air. "Give me a drink, will you, someone."

"At once, at once," cried Simon. "I'll get more glasses. What a bit of luck we dropped in."

"You saw Tallis, good, good," said Rupert. He smiled approvingly at Morgan, but she was not looking at him.

"My dear—" said Hilda, kissing Peter, who moved stiffly away, then patted her at arm's length.

"Drinks for all, drinks for all."

"Thank you, Simon, but do dry yourself a little before you embrace me! Boy, could I use a drink!"

"Sorry, Morgan darling."

"Peter, could I have a word with you?"

"Certainly, Father."

"Then let's sit over here away from the others."

"Morgan, what happened at Tallis's?"

"Nothing, Hilda. I collected my notebooks."

"But you saw him?"

"Yes. What's that orange muck on the rug?"

"Suntan lotion."

"I thought somebody'd been sick. Hadn't you better clean it up?"

"Oh, later, later. And you tell me that nothing happened!"

"Of course nothing happened. There was nothing *to* happen, was there? What a big handsome boy your son has grown into."

"Morgan, I am going to weave you a wreath of roses. May I pick some of the roses, Hilda, to weave a wreath for Morgan?"

"Certainly, Simon, but you can't pick them like that, you'll need secateurs. You'll find them in the kitchen drawer."

"I know, I know. Oh Axel, I'm terribly sorry, I haven't given you a drink."

"Sit down, Morgan, for heavens sake, over here. Peter and Rupert are quite wrapped up in talk. What did you *say* to Tallis?"

"Nothing."

"Oh, stop it. You didn't say anything about coming back to him?"

"I said I'd come for the notebooks and I took the notebooks and I left."

"Was he upset?"

"Not specially. I didn't really notice."

"Would you like pink or white roses for your wreath, Morgan, or a mixture of the two?"

"A mixture, please, Simon."

"I think the pink and the white go so well together, don't you? Did you plant these ones, Hilda?"

"No, they were here when we came."

"And are the white ones *really* called Little White Pet?"

"Yes, they are."

"What a sweet name. I thought you'd invented it!"

"It is pretty, isn't it? Were *you* upset?"

"Not specially."

"I don't believe you. How did Tallis seem to you?"

"Smaller."

"Let me fill your glass again, darling, before I start on your wreath."

"Thank you, Simon."

"You see, Peter, I'm getting a bit tired of writing evasive letters to your tutor."

"They're called supervisors in Cambridge."

"All right, supervisor. You profess to despise the place but you think it worthwhile to correct me!"

"I didn't ask you to correspond with my supervisor. As far as I'm concerned the Cambridge business is over."

"But why? That's what I can't make out."

"All those values are false ones."

"What you need, my boy, is a little philosophical training. What do you mean by 'those values' and 'false'?"

"All those values you're writing that big book about."

"Come, come, be more precise. And let's be more careful with our terminology, shall we? Propositions are true or false. Values are real or apparent. Now education is something which is genuinely valuable. Training your mind—"

"That's all hocus-pocus. It's a sort of conspiracy. People read a lot of old authors without understanding them or even liking them, they learn a lot of facts without feeling anything about them or connecting them with anything that's present and real, and they call that training their minds."

"But that's just what education is about, connecting the past with the present."

"Then it isn't going on at Cambridge."

"Now let's start again, Morgan, and have the whole thing from the beginning. Simon and Axel aren't listening. Axel's sulking and Simon's much too busy with the roses."

"What do you want to know? I've told you."

"You went down the street, you knocked at the door. Then what happened?"

"I didn't knock at the door. The door was sort of open, so I pushed it, and there was Tallis."

"And who said what?"

"He said 'Christ' or something. There was a lot of stuff on the kitchen table so I asked if he was having tea."

"You just don't know how to tell a story! You're in the kitchen already. How did you get to the kitchen?"

"Walked. Hilda, do lay off. I'll tell you later. Yes, Simon, those ones are lovely. Why don't you fill Axel's glass and offer him some of those funny-looking olives?"

"For heavens sake, don't prompt Simon to look after Axel. You won't be thanked."

"Oh Hilda, do stop being so damn sensitive. You're getting on my nerves."

"So you *are* upset."

"Do you want me in tears?"

"And if some people don't understand and like what they read so much the worse for them. I understood and liked what I read at Oxford. It has travelled with me ever since."

"Has it? When did you last open a volume of Homer or Virgil?"

"Well, I must confess, not for several years."

"So it's not a part of your ordinary life at all."

"Yes, it is, it's been absorbed. It's all part of a scale of values."

"What's a scale of values?"

"Knowing that one thing's better than another."

"What's better than what, for example?"

"Shakespeare's better than Swinburne."

"You just say that because everybody says it. You don't know it in your own experience, you don't really feel it. You stopped *experiencing* things long ago. When did you ever really compare Shakespeare with Swinburne? When did you last read a play by Shakespeare, if it comes to that?"

"I admit, not for some time."

"I bet you've never even read the whole of Shakespeare."

"There are one or two minor plays possibly—"

"I say, your roses are fearfully prickly, Hilda. Axel, could you lend me your handkerchief? Messing around with roses when practically naked is quite a hazard."

"Get dressed then!"

"I think I will, Axel. Don't disturb the roses. May I pinch some string from the kitchen, Hilda?"

"Of course. So he was quiet and negative?"

"He mumbled."

"And you were cold and businesslike?"

"Yes."

"Were you afraid you'd suddenly weep and throw your arms round him?"

"Beforehand, yes. When I was there, not."

"Why not?"

"I suddenly saw him as unimpressive. You know, Hilda, Tallis used to remind me of blessed are the poor in spirit, but now he just reminds me of from him that hath not shall be taken away even that which he hath."

"I've often felt, my dear, that there isn't such a great distance after all between those two texts!"

"It was the memories that were awful really, not anything present."

"I wonder if you can be sure of that. Are you really out of it?"

"Of course not. I'm just whistling in the dark."

"I'm afraid nowadays it's you young people who are cynical and we middle-aged ones who are idealistic."

"We aren't cynical. And you aren't idealistic. You're just a lot of self-centred habit-ridden hedonists."

"Well, maybe. But I'm inclined to think that it's decent self-centred habit-ridden hedonists who keep this society going!"

"Why should this society be kept going? The trouble is, you can't see our morality as a morality."

"I confess I see it as a form of lunacy!"

"Your morality is static. Ours is dynamic. What this age needs is a dynamic morality."

"Morality is static by definition. A dynamic morality is a contradiction in terms."

"Nothing is real unless it's felt and present. Your world is all elsewhere."

"Hello, Simon, you were quick. What a super shirt. I like the way the light pink stripes contrast with the dark blue and the green."

"Thank you, Morgan, it's Indian. I think it does rather suit me. The pink matches Hilda, doesn't it? Got drinks, everybody? Why, Peter, you haven't got a drink."

"Nothing for me, thank you."

"But you must drink something!"

"I'll have some water. There's some in that jug, isn't there?"

"Here you are, you abstemious boy. You put us all to shame. Isn't it funny how the young don't drink nowadays. It makes one quite uneasy."

"It's not the only thing about them that does that!"

"But of course you'll see Tallis again soon?"

"I don't know. It seems possible, likely. But I have no intentions at the moment. Thinking Tallis through is going to take a long time. And there's something else I've got to do, something rather urgent, before I can even start on that thinking."

"Hilda dear, isn't this a happy scene? Wouldn't you say, dear?"

"Yes, Simon, I hope so!"

"So long as Peter and Rupert aren't quarrelling. Can you hear what they're talking about, Hilda?"

"No, Morgan, but at least they're *talking*. Peter hasn't set foot here for ages. We have you to thank for this visitation."

"Morgan, I've finished your wreath. It's a work of art. Look, everybody, I've finished Morgan's wreath. I'm going to crown her Queen of Priory Grove."

Everyone stopped talking. Peter and Rupert, who had been sitting on the teak seat just outside the drawing-room windows, rose and joined the group beside the pool. Hilda and Morgan were sitting on the flagstones. Axel, in shirt sleeves, was sitting in a canvas chair beside the white cast-iron table. Simon, dressed in light blue trousers and his striped Indian shirt, pirouetted about with the wreath and then with an elaborate gesture of obeisance laid it lightly upon Morgan's dark hair.

"Charming!" cried Hilda. "Darling, you could wear that to Ascot!"

The wreath, densely woven out of profusely flowering branchlets of Albertine and Little White Pet, formed a rather high pink-and-white crown, laced with glossy apple-green leaves and translucent red stems. It gave Morgan a curiously formal and dressed-up appearance, as if she were indeed bound for Ascot or a garden party at Buckingham Palace.

"You must see yourself!" cried Simon. "I'll get a mirror."

"Here's one in my bag," said Hilda.

Morgan surveyed herself. There were smiles, some of them a little forced.

"Simon, you really are an artist."

"Now you're Queen of the May, darling, except that it's July, and—"

"And I hardly qualify technically as a May Queen. Ooh, it's rather prickly, Simon."

"Odd thought," observed Axel to himself. "The original crown of thorns might have been a crown of roses."

"I think Peter ought to wear it," said Morgan. "That would be much more suitable. I'm not guessing about your sex life, Peter! But you're obviously the youngest and least corrupted person present! Come here." She began to scramble to her feet.

A little sulkily Peter bowed his large blond head and let Morgan perch the pink-and-white confection on the top of it. It was too small for him and looked extremely absurd. It was suddenly evident how very big Peter was, plump and burly, broad-shouldered, larger than his father. Everybody laughed.

"Oh Peter, you do look a scream!" said Hilda. "You make it look like a pre-Raphaelite bird's nest! All it needs is an enormous white dove sitting on top to complete it!"

"I think it looks lovely on him," cried Simon. "Peter, you look enchanting. Like a young woodland god. A sort of male Flora."

"In that case I think you should wear it," said Peter. He pulled it off rather roughly and gave it to Simon.

"You've scratched your forehead, Peter," said Morgan. She touched his brow and her hand came away with a smear of blood.

Simon had put the wreath on. It fitted him perfectly. The tall crown of roses extended the thin lines of his features and lent a sudden ambiguous elfin beauty to his now rather flushed and laughing face. "Oh Hilda, I must see myself. I do look rather marvellous, don't I, Axel? Who am I? Puck? Ariel? Peaseblossom? Mustardseed?" He began to dance lightly about on the hot flagstones.

"I understood that even they were males," said Peter.

"Don't be so nasty, Peter," said Hilda, laughing.

"I must be going," said Peter.

Simon stopped dancing.

"Please don't go yet, Peter," said Morgan. "Stay here for dinner. There'd be plenty, wouldn't there, Hilda."

"Of course there would."

"Oh, let him go if he wants to," said Axel. "Look, I think we must be going too. We've got a dinner engagement."

"No we haven't!" said Simon. "We're entirely free— Oh, yes, I'd forgotten, of course, we have a dinner engagement."

"Simon and I must go, Hilda."

"Well, you needn't offer me a lift," said Peter.

"I wasn't going to," said Axel. He began to put on his jacket.

"Do let's all have one more drink," said Simon. "Peter, do drink *something*, not just water. It would do you good."

"What sort of good? You people all drink in order to escape from reality. I happen to like reality. I'm staying with it, not taking off for the land of make-believe."

"Don't be so censorious, Peter!" said Rupert.

"You *are* hard on us!" said Simon.

"Well, I'm going to have another drink anyway," said Morgan. "What about you, Hilda?"

"Come on, Simon," said Axel. "Get moving."

"Oh, please not yet, Axel. We were all so much enjoying ourselves a moment ago."

"Pity you all have to get drunk to enjoy yourselves, isn't it," said Peter. "I suppose that's the result of higher education."

"A little higher education in good manners would do you no harm," said Axel.

"What you people call good manners is just hypocrisy and buttering each other up. I happen to prefer the truth."

"The truth is the reward of a hard discipline," said Rupert. "You'll understand that when you're older. It can't be just snatched up with a careless gesture."

"Peter, please don't pick a quarrel with us," said Hilda. "It's been such a joy to see you here."

"You all drink every day, don't you?" said Peter. "You drink at lunch-time and you drink all the evening. You never go to bed sober. It's an addiction. You couldn't do without it. How many drinks do you have a day, Mother?"

"Peter!"

"Civilization, Peter, is based on not saying what you think," said Axel. "It's based on inhibiting one's impulses. You'll learn that in time. Come now, and don't be so cross with us."

"Peter, please don't spoil things," said Simon.

"Well, you started it. I think you're a lot of hypocrites."

"Peter, Peter," said Hilda. "That's just silly abuse and doesn't mean a thing."

"Doesn't it? You all pretend to like each other but you don't really. You say the most spiteful things behind each other's backs. You pretend to admire my father but you say his book is rotten. You don't say that to him of course, oh no! I at least—"

"Peter, *please*—" said Hilda.

"Enough, enough!" said Rupert.

Peter, who was still holding his glass of water, had retreated as far as the drawing-room windows. Hilda hovered near him, making little impulsive movements as if she would have liked to dash and seize him, perhaps to hustle him away before worse happened. Axel, beside the white table, was going through the ritual of imminent departure in slow motion, with a bored expression on his face. Simon, still wearing the rose crown, was looking distractedly from Peter to Axel and even more distractedly into his empty glass. Rupert, standing by the wall, was nervously adjusting a spray of pink roses which Simon had pulled out of place. Showers of pale petals fell suddenly onto the stiff spires of dark blue delphiniums. Rupert seemed apart from the scene. Simon quickly filled his glass with gin. Morgan, feet wide apart, was watching it all with amusement. "At 'em, Peter, at 'em!" she cried.

"Oh God, it's so *hot*," Hilda moaned.

"Simon and I are going," said Axel. "I think this little drama can proceed better without us." He removed the glass from Simon's hand and began to move toward the drawing-room door.

"And why don't *you* tell the truth!" said Peter. He pointed a long arm at Axel, who stopped in his tracks.

"What do you mean?"

"You keep your relationship with Simon a dark secret, don't you! Oh, you let *us* know because we're your so-called dear friends and we're discreet. You can rely on us to tell lies on your behalf. But you'd die if everyone knew. You'd be ashamed!"

"I would not be ashamed!" said Axel, in a voice electric with anger.

"Peter, please come inside, come with me!" cried Hilda.

"Why do you lie about it then? Why don't you tell everyone in Whitehall that you live with another man? Are you afraid of losing your precious job? Afraid of being called a pansy? Why don't you tell the truth to the world?"

"Peter, *stop that!*" cried Rupert. He tore himself away from the wall, opening his arms helplessly.

Axel was silent for a moment. Then he said in a cold voice, "My private life is my own affair. And would be if I were heterosexual. Why should I tell Whitehall whom I sleep with? I don't reject this society. I live and work in it and make my own judgements about how this is best to be done. You accuse us of hypocrisy. All right. Very few human beings are innocent of that. But I think you should also consider your own case. Let me suggest this. Why do you refuse to continue your education? Not for the reasons which you so loudly profess. But because you are afraid to compete intellectually with your peers, you are afraid of measuring yourself against other people, you are afraid of turning out to be third-rate. So you decide not to compete at all. You retire into a dream world of drugs and layabouts and fuzzy fragments of Eastern philosophy about which you really understand nothing, and you call that reality. If you want to change our society, and I agree it needs changing, you must first learn how to think, and that requires a kind of humility which you show no signs of possessing. You imagine you've stepped out of society. You haven't and you can't. You're nothing but a symptom of corruption, a miserable little scab upon the body politic. You're a part of the thing and you seem to prefer to be a powerless and unconscious part. If you really want to get out of it you'd better emigrate or commit suicide."

There was a loud crash and a wail from Hilda. Peter had hurled his glass across the pool where it broke into fragments against the farther edge. Peter turned and disappeared through the drawing-room doors, banging them behind him. Hilda struggled with the doors and followed him in. Morgan poured herself out another drink. She said, "Well, well, well."

Rupert walked round the pool and started picking up pieces of glass from the flagstones.

"I'm very sorry, Rupert," said Axel.

"That's all right," said Rupert. "It was Peter's fault. I simply don't understand that boy."

"Have a drink, Rupert," said Morgan. "You need one."

"Thanks."

"It wasn't Peter's fault," said Axel. "At least not entirely. And I ought not to have lost my temper. The fact is he said something that was true and it upset me extremely."

"You don't mean—" said Morgan.

"I probably ought to tell everyone in Whitehall. Only I'm not going to. Simon, we're leaving. I do apologize, Rupert."

Axel marched away and through the french windows. Simon said, "Oh dear, oh dear," and was about to follow him when Morgan said, "Wait." She turned him round by the shoulders and very carefully took off the crown of roses and laid it down on the table. Then she kissed him lingeringly upon the cheek. "Don't worry, Simon." Simon said, "Darling!" fluttered his hands, and ran after Axel. Rupert sat down.

"Cheer up, Rupert," said Morgan. She touched his hair. "Young people are terribly cruel. But it's because they don't know. I think young people *really* don't know how wretched and vulnerable every human heart really is."

"Hilda and I have failed," said Rupert.

"Nonsense. It's just that you're probably the last people who can help Peter just at the moment."

"Will you have a try, Morgan?" said Rupert. "Will you really have a try, really take him on? I'm sure you could get through to him."

"Of course I'll try," said Morgan. "After all, I'm a professional tamer of adolescents! I should be able to communicate with young Peter."

"Bless you—"

"I think I'll just see what's going on inside, if you don't mind. I'm afraid I was rather disgracefully fascinated by the whole scene. I adore violence!" She left him and went catlike into the house, her lips moist, her eyes bright with interest.

Rupert put his head in his hands. His open eyes could see through his fingers glittering fragments of glass upon the bottom of the pool. He felt ready to weep. The violence had hurt him, Peter's words, Axel's words. Perhaps Axel was right about Peter's refusal to compete. In any case, Rupert felt deeply, it was somehow all his own fault. Calm of mind, he thought, calm of mind. If only he could be wise. He had been far too stiff with Peter all along. He ought not to have tried to admonish him this evening. He should have embraced his son, nothing else really mattered except an indubitable show of love. But a show of love was something for which Rupert was entirely untrained. He did not even know how to lay his hand on Peter's arm without the gesture's seeming artificial. How could he possibly convey to his son the tenderness with which his heart was now so overbrimming that it stretched his bosom with a physical pain? Love, love was the key. Suppose he were to write Peter a letter. Yet what kind of letter would serve his turn and would not his pen just stiffen in his hand? "My dear Peter, I should like you to know—" Love was the key. But Rupert knew too that his whole training, the whole of the society which kept him so stiffly upright and so patently and pre-eminently successful, had deprived him gradually of the direct language of love. When he needed gestures, strong impetuous movements to overturn barriers, he found himself paralysed and cold. There is a path, he said to himself, because for love there is always one. But for him it was a mountain path with many many twists and turns.

樕 | T W E L V E

"Mrs. Browne!" said Julius.

He opened the door a little wider and Morgan walked into the flat.

"I'm sorry to arrive unannounced," she said. "I hoped I'd find you in. So this is where you live?"

She began to look around. The flat was small but richly furnished. A tiny bedroom and bathroom, a rather larger sitting-room, a well-appointed kitchen with a huge refrigerator. The sitting-room had a very thick dark yellow Indian carpet. Low fitted bookshelves on either side of the electric fire supported a pair of greeny yellowy Chinese horses which looked as if they were genuine T'ang. Sofa and chairs were covered in fine light-brown velvet and scattered with petit-point rose-embroidered cushions. Modern abstract paintings of orange shapes adorned the walls. A glass-topped table with a green marble cigarette box and a neat pile of scientific periodicals. The sun glowed in a veil of white nylon at the window between great looped back folds of darker stuff. Double glazing muted the roar of Brook Street.

"Mmm. Posh," said Morgan. She turned to survey Julius.

Julius was unsmiling. He was not frowning. His face expressed a slightly distracted weariness. He looked at his watch. "What did you want, Mrs. Browne?"

"To see you. Is that strange?"

"Your unexpected arrival does not move me to speculation. I
have to go out very shortly, I am afraid."

"Well, let me stay until you go. Won't you offer me a drink?"
Julius reflected. "No."

"You aren't very polite, Professor King. In that case I shall have
to find one for myself."

Morgan went into the kitchen. She looked into several cup-
boards and then into the refrigerator. There were some bottles
of Danish lager. Further search revealed nothing stronger, so she
took a bottle opener from the dresser and poured herself out a
glass of lager. She tasted it. It was unfriendly and very cold. She
hated lager. She went back to the sitting-room where Julius, who
had not followed her, was sitting on the sofa reading *The Times*.

"May I give you some lager, Julius?"

"No, thank you."

"Haven't you got any whisky in the house?"

"No."

"You always used to have bourbon."

He looked at her in silence and then tossed *The Times* aside.
"You presumably had some special purpose in coming here, something you wished to say perhaps? Could you say it, please?"

She stood before him holding her glass. She looked at the long
mouth and the violet-brown eyes and the weird pallid hair. "My
God, Julius, you are beautiful!"

He got up and went to the window. "Did you come here to
tell me so?"

"Yes. Why not? Mayn't I tell you?"

Julius turned back to her. "If you knew, my dear Mrs. Browne,
how extremely repellent I find the simpering coy manner which
you have thought fit to put on, you would doubtless select some
other act."

Morgan put her glass down on the table. "I am incapable of
simpering!"

"I have little time. Say what you want to say, please."

"I love you, Julius."

He sighed and looked at his watch again. "Is that all?"

"Isn't it a great deal? Oh Julius, please listen to me. Since I left you I've been lost and crazy. But I haven't stopped thinking about you for a single second. I've breathed you and eaten you and drunk you and wept you. Perhaps I needed to leave you for a while just to find out how much you meant to me. You drove me away, you know you did. You were trying to test me, and I seemed to fail. But, Julius, I haven't really failed. Oh, if you only knew how I've suffered, how I've cried and cried in awful hotel bedrooms and talked to you endlessly in my heart. Your absence has clung to my side like an animal devouring my entrails. I've wanted you minute after minute half-way across the world. And I've come to realize it now, that you're the most important thing that has ever happened to me, you're the *only* important thing that has ever happened to me, and if I'm to live with the truth I must live with *this* for the rest of my days even if it burns me, even if it kills me!"

Morgan was shaking the table. The tumbler of lager jumped and rattled upon the glass surface. Julius took it off the table and placed it carefully on top of the bookshelves beside one of the horses. "Well?"

"What do you mean 'Well?' Julius, I love you and I need you. I thought that I loved you over there in South Carolina. I was completely carried away, I was laid low by that love, you saw that, you had the evidence of all your senses. I was yours, yours, yours. But now it seems to me that that was just a beginning, a shadow. I love you now a thousand times more, a thousand times better. Julius, I could be your slave."

"I don't want a slave."

"Julius, please. I only ask you not to drive me away. I *must* see you. Just let me see you. We could learn about each other again. And if you want me to suffer I could suffer. Only let me do so with you, in your sight, and not alone, not alone any more—"

"I don't want you to suffer. Your sensations no longer interest me."

"You must want me to suffer or you wouldn't behave in this way."

"Please try to think more clearly." He spoke in a quiet precise voice, not looking at her, pulling aside the pearly nylon curtains and looking down at the moving lines of cars in sunny Brook Street below. "I did not ask you to come here. I did not ask you to come and torment yourself in front of me. If you reflect you will see that you have acted wrongly. I really do not want to see you any more. The *interest* has gone. I'm afraid you must just attempt to face this fact, however unpleasant you find it."

"I would do anything you wanted, perform any penance. Oh Julius, let me find the way back to you, show me the way back, help me, help me."

"You deceive yourself. Suffering is amusing and may even do work in a situation where two people are connected with each other. Where there is no mutual connection it is undignified, grotesque, and ugly. It is seen to be something totally pointless and unnecessary, like all the rest of the suffering human beings do every day. There is now no relationship between us and I find your contortions merely embarrassing."

Morgan was silent for a moment, still leaning on the table. "Is it because of the child?" she said.

"You ask a rather elliptical question. No, I am not taking revenge on you because of that, if that is what you imply."

"But you—blame me—about the child."

"That is not a concept which I employ."

"Yes, you do. Oh Julius, I can't bear your disapproval—"

"These are quaint words. You surprised me, that is all. A woman who is fortunate enough to have a child and who then murders it seems to me a rather odd phenomenon."

"Please don't use that horrible word. You must be very hurt really. I'm sorry."

"You are beginning to annoy me. It seems to me that you have asked your question and you can be in little doubt about the answer."

"You started it all—over there in America. You were mad keen to get me."

"I find your language rather lacking in taste. As I recall, you were not particularly difficult to get. I'm sorry to be so unpleasant. You are forcing me to be rude and I assure you I am not enjoying it. Now will you please go? I have to change."

"Well, change then. I've seen you in your underclothes. Oh, Julius, don't you see that you *can't* get rid of me? You'll have to do something about me. At least now we're talking to each other and it relieves the pain even to hear you curse me."

"I haven't cursed you. The strong emotions are all yours."

"We could talk about all kinds of things like we used to. You could tell me about DNA—"

"You don't want to know about DNA. Like so many academic women you want to use superficial intellectual chat as an instrument of seduction."

"Let me seduce you then. Let's make a new start. I'm going to leave Rupert and Hilda's. I've found a little flat in Fulham—"

"You will not have me as a visitor."

"Julius, see it as a *problem*. Couldn't it even interest you? You are the most important thing that has ever happened to me—"

"So you observed before. But what about your husband? Was it not important that you once undertook some solemn obligations toward him?"

"You didn't care much about those solemn obligations when you wanted me in bed!"

"True but irrelevant. I don't care about them now. But as I no longer want you in bed I commend them to your consideration."

"I find that rather funny."

"I am not trying to amuse you. As you know, I detest the spectacle of self-deception of any kind. You are pretending to an exclusive passion when there is no such thing in question. You can easily get over me. You can easily interest yourself in your husband. I suggest you attempt both these things."

"Why are you on his side?"

"I am not on his side. I am tired of hearing you tell lies and I think you could be profitably occupied elsewhere."

"I can't stand the idea that you two met. What did you think of him?"

"I formed no impression. I only saw him for a minute. He was at a disadvantage."

"Then you did form an impression. You thought he was—what was it you once said of someone on the staff at Dibbins?—'a negligible wisp.'"

"That appears to be what you think."

"No. Tallis is somebody. At least he's something. I'm not sure that he's quite a person."

"Well, these un-persons are no concern of mine."

"He was hopeless in bed. Everything happened all at once."

"I have no desire to discuss your husband's sexual performances."

"Julius, I really am through with Tallis. You may have been wondering—"

"I haven't."

"Well, it *is* at an end."

"If you are relying on me to help you with your divorce I'm afraid you must look elsewhere."

"I hadn't even thought of that! I am relying on you for much more important things."

"Well, don't. I appreciate that you want some sort of drama, and you desire me to enact a part. You feel guilty and mixed up and you want to go through some sort of ritual of purification or even punishment. But I cannot assist you, my dear Mrs. Browne. I am no actor. I always told you the truth. I told you my feelings were probably temporary and should not be called by serious names."

"Every moment you go on talking to me gives me more hope."

"You drive me to tell you that I now realize that you are fundamentally stupid. And I cannot care for what is stupid. Will you now go?"

"Julius, do you remember this dress?"

Morgan was wearing a sleeveless white dress with a little-girl collar and navy blue spots, rather unfashionably long.

"Yes. You were wearing it on the first occasion that we met."

"Ah, you remember!"

"An involuntary matter."

"You said it was a sexy dress."

"The fashion has changed."

"And this handbag and these shoes—"

"You remind me fruitlessly of things which are old and stale and dead."

"And do you remember *this?*" Morgan picked up the copy of *The Times* from the sofa and laid it on the table. She shook the outer pages of the paper free and began to fold them. She produced a pair of scissors from her handbag. "You taught me to make those extraordinary chains of paper just by folding and cutting."

"And you seem to have forgotten what I taught you. You are not reducing me to tears by your reminiscences."

"Yes, I was folding it wrong. That's better. Do you remember what happened on that other evening? We were sitting in your office after walking round the campus. I'd written you a letter only you'd said nothing about it. It was terribly hot. And you started very quietly folding the newspaper, not saying anything. Then when you started to cut it you kept looking at me and I realized suddenly that this was a sort of love scene—"

"I don't want *The Times* cut up. I have not read it yet."

"You do remember. You can't deny the past. And we're still talking. You must forgive me if I believe in magic. Most women do. And it's need need need that makes people turn to it. You said you adored the dress. Don't you like it any more?"

"Please go away."

"All right then, I'll take it off."

Morgan stepped quickly away from the table. She unzipped the dress down the back and let it fall and stepped out of it, revealing a very pretty black lace petticoat. Julius, who had half turned to the window, playing with the curtain, turned to look. He studied her.

"You *are* still interested," said Morgan in a soft voice. "You must forgive this rather shameless device. But I do love you, you see, I do."

"A youngish and moderately good-looking woman half undressed attracts the attention," said Julius. "Now put your dress on and *get out.*"

"No!" Holding her dress, Morgan darted to the door. She ran into Julius's bedroom and kicked off her high-heeled shoes. She took off her glasses. She began to pull the rest of her clothes off. She dragged back the pale green silk bedspread and undid the bed. More leisurely, she took her stockings off last, now watched by Julius from the doorway. She seated herself in the nest of crisp pale green sheets, her long legs tucked sideways under her, and waited. Her eyes grew big and dazed.

"I'm sorry," said Julius. "I appreciate your device, which has a certain elementary picturesqueness. But I am fundamentally bored. Now if you will excuse me I will follow your advice and change. I am already late."

He opened a white door in the wall to reveal a long wardrobe, and took out his evening clothes which he laid upon a chair. He found white evening shirt and tie in a drawer. Without haste he began to change. He put his day clothes with clean shirts and socks into a small suitcase. He pulled on the black evening trousers and began to adjust the tie at the mirror. Morgan watched. At one point she groaned.

"And now, Mrs. B., as I am going away for the week-end without returning here, and as I do not want to leave a naked woman in possession of my flat, I must request you to dress and go. I think I have been very patient with an extremely rude and thoughtless intrusion."

"I'll write you a letter of apology!"

"Come along." Julius picked up Morgan's bundle of clothes and threw them onto the bed. He fetched her handbag and shoes and the pair of scissors from the sitting-room. "I shall retire to the bathroom and not embarrass you by watching you dress. We leave in three minutes."

"You look wonderful in evening clothes," said Morgan. "I love your mouth and I should like to kiss it, but I'd be content to kiss your feet if that was all you would allow."

"Will you please start to get dressed?"

"No," said Morgan. "I like it here. And I don't believe that you're going away for the week-end. No one goes away for the week-end directly after a dinner party. I shall wait here until you come back. And if you don't come back till Monday I shall wait till Monday."

"Are you trying to provoke me to violence," said Julius, "in the hope that if I touch you I shall find your charms irresistible? I might even be tempted to disillusion you."

"Yes, yes, touch me, Julius, seize me, be rough to me. Hold me and subdue me. Come, let us start it all again at the beginning. Let us cut up the paper again. Remember how I was holding the scissors and you put your hand on top of mine in order to guide it? And we had been laughing. And then we stopped laughing—"

While she was speaking, Julius had picked up the scissors. Morgan's voice trailed away into silence.

He stood holding the scissors and staring down at her intently. She became rigid, putting her hand to her breast, to her throat. She remained quite still as he now moved toward the bed.

Julius picked up the white nylon dress with the navy blue spots and the little-girl collar. He sat down on a chair, drawing the dress across his knee. He began very carefully to fold it. Morgan released a sighing breath. She watched him, fascinated. When at last the scissors bit into the material she shuddered slightly. But she watched in silence until the entire dress had been cut through, first one way and then the other. Julius shook the thick pad of folded nylon and what had been the dress fluttered out in a long chain of white spotted links, each link evenly cut in a zigzag pattern. He gave the chain a light tug and it parted and he let it fall in a heap on the floor. He rose to his feet and kicked it aside.

"You love me," said Morgan.

Julius picked up the black lacy petticoat and began to cut it straight across into narrow black strips, pulling the material tight and letting the flashing scissors rip through it. After that he cut the black brassière and matching pants into ribbons. The suspender belt was rather harder to cut, and Julius contented himself with dividing it into four pieces. The stockings he folded two ways and cut briskly through, tossing the fragments away with the point of the scissors.

"Oh my God," said Morgan. "You are wonderful."

Julius stooped and gathered together the ribbony silky pieces of white dress and black underclothes and threw them into a heap in the hall. He put the scissors back into Morgan's bag and threw the bag onto the bed.

"Who but you," said Morgan, "would think of cutting a girl's clothes into ribbons."

Julius opened the wardrobe and took out a light raincoat and threw it over his arm. He picked up the small suitcase.

"That was even better than cutting the paper," she said.

Julius went out of the bedroom into the sitting-room. Morgan pulled herself out of the bed and followed him through, excited, swaggering, happily naked.

"After that you can't possibly go, Julius. Don't you see you've given in, you really have?"

Julius was putting the scattered pages of *The Times* together again. He folded the paper and thrust it into his suitcase.

"Dear dear Julius—"

He passed her by and went to the bedroom door. He closed the bedroom door and turned the key in the lock. He thrust the key into his pocket and went to the front door.

"Julius—"

He opened the front door and went out, closing it quietly behind him. His footsteps receded down the stairs.

His departure was so sudden, the transition from presence to absence so fast, that Morgan was quite stunned. She stood in the middle of the room in a state of shock, one arm outstretched, surrounded by a sudden silence behind which, outside the double-glazed windows, murmured the interminable traffic of Brook Street. She said, "Oh!" Then she ran to the window just in time to see Julius getting into a taxi. She said, "Good God!"

When Morgan had told Julius that she had wept for him in hotel rooms and thought about him ceaselessly ever since their parting she had told the truth. She had not begun to "get over" him, except perhaps in the rudimentary but not unimportant sense of having survived a certain number of days without seeing him. What she did not tell him was that she had despaired. Morgan had seen something in those later days with Julius which had seemed like a deep truth. It had been like a mystical vision into the heart of reality, as if one were to be promised the secret of the universe and then, with all the sense of significance and finality fully preserved, be shown a few mouldering chicken bones lying in a dark corner covered with dust and filth.

Morgan had loved Julius with her whole nature and in the first shock of that love she had found it impossible not to believe that Julius loved her. Such is the natural illusion of a lover. She had heard Julius's faintly accented, faintly stammering voice saying over and over again, "I am not in love with you. I have nothing to offer you except completely superficial emotions. Such emotions do not endure. These will not." But the sound throbbed in her ears like the ceaseless cooing of a dove which said, "I love you, I love you, I love you." What she had, through some strange agency, perceived at the very end was that Julius did not in fact love her. She had perceived an immense coldness from which she had recoiled shuddering and it was to save herself from that icy contact that she had at last fled from the house, packing feverishly, throwing her things together and weeping with haste, on one afternoon when Julius was absent at a conference. How she had been able to sense that deep cold she did not later know, and could not recall any definite change in Julius's behaviour. Surely he had been as ardent as before. Yet it had seemed to her that she had been driven away, even discarded.

Later it all looked different again. There was simpler suffering, tearful self-pitying misery in those hotels, the horrible business of the abortion through which she had passed in a coma of grief, the dead time in Vermont. Morgan forgot the details and no longer wondered why or what. She simply felt that she had suffered an inevitable loss which had almost completely crushed her but which possibly she might survive. It scarcely mattered whether she did or not. Each day just had to be got through somehow.

Then she began to feel a faint interest, and at last an urgent need to go home to England. She began to need to see Hilda.

Morgan's relationship with Hilda was probably the only thing in her life which was so deeply buried that it had never been subjected to any strain or touched by any critical doubt. Of course their relations had sometimes been stormy, especially when they were younger. But Morgan since infancy had accepted Hilda as her shield, the more unquestioningly as it became clear that Morgan was "the clever one." Hilda had never resented that. It was known between them that Hilda had a kind of human strength and a kind of authority to which Morgan did not aspire. It was Hilda who was the deeply rooted tree. Morgan had indeed drawn a picture of this tree, the Hilda-tree, when she was six years old and had drawn a little bird in the branches which she announced to be herself. The girls were from the first bound to each other more closely than to their parents. Morgan saw later on how much this had hurt their mother, from whom most of all they drew away into the secret society of each other's company. With their father, a vague rather sybaritic man, an unambitious solicitor, they played the parts of merry affectionate little girls, pretending to be little children in the knowing way that little children pretend. The parts were simple and the need they met was simple too. The more complex hunger of their mother they were unable to satisfy. She died fairly young. Their father, who died many years later, never knew that his wife had yearned so grievously for the love and trust of her two daughters. She had watched the secretive little faces timidly and in vain. Hilda and Morgan had spoken of this much later. It was something about which they both thought for many years before, at what seemed to be the proper moment, revealing their thoughts to each other. The deferred confession, the emotional discussion not without the shedding of tears, consoled them both and mitigated a sense of guilt.

The cosmic explosion of falling in love with Julius interrupted Morgan's converse with Hilda as it interrupted everything else in her life. Morgan's marriage had not touched the deep bond with her sister. It remained, often seeming like a conspiracy, unaltered in the midst of change. Julius of course did not really damage it either. But it was for a long time impossible for Morgan, as she lingered on miserably in America, to think of seeing Hilda or of writing to her frankly. Trying to analyse why this was, Morgan concluded that she felt ashamed. Defeated and discredited certainly, and also ashamed. She had always been terrifyingly vulnerable to Hilda's opinion of her. "Be gentle. You can wound me with your little finger." That Hilda disliked her relationship with Tallis had seemed to Morgan to operate at one stage as a motive in its favour. Had she married Tallis as an act of defiance against Hilda and was her marriage nothing but an incident in the long drama of her relations with her sister? Of course this was absurd. Later and more soberly she felt that Hilda's opposition had probably undermined her marriage. After the débâcle in South Carolina, as one day after another was lived through somehow, the need for Hilda began gradually to reassert itself, the old magnetism made itself felt in the deepest places of the heart. Hilda, destroyer and preserver. It was here that defeat must be acknowledged and shame overcome. What had been done amiss could here, and only here, be looked at steadily.

Yet oddly enough, the glare and violence which had, for a time, blotted out Hilda's image had not obscured Tallis's. While she lived with Julius, Morgan thought about Tallis every day, but she did so in an odd way. She had told Hilda about seeing his face at night, those great wide-open light brown eyes, radiant, not accusing. It occurred to Morgan that she did not then, and scarcely even later, *connect* her immediate sense of guilt with Tallis personally. There was some general situation in which Morgan had failed. Hilda had been right to say that some very stiff pride, some extremely precious sense of herself, of her dignity and her integrity, had been damaged by the adventure with Julius. But her relationship with Tallis, and this was something she had noticed about it much earlier, was in some way temporally strange. It was as if she had known Tallis for a very long time, as if he were something which was diffused and general in her life. This sense of his not being quite temporally located had once seemed, though later she could not see why, an argument for his importance. She had more lately decided that this lack of location was simply something to do with Tallis's own peculiar vagueness, something almost physical about him. Whatever it was, one effect of it was to make her sense of guilt in relation to him less than urgent. If she had offended Tallis, she had offended him years ago, years before she knew him, years before either of them was born.

Of course coming home had brought Tallis more into focus. But still she could think about him constantly, and much more than she ever admitted to Hilda, without feeling any need to act. So it was that she had been able to sit, in the way which so much puzzled Rupert, in S.W.10, thinking about her husband in W.11, and deferring any plan to go and see him. What made that situation suddenly intolerable for Morgan was the fact that Tallis had met Julius. Why that was so awful, even more awful than Tallis's knowing that she had returned without telling him, she was not entirely sure. It was as if the whole hideous *mess* represented by Tallis had been in an instant potentiated by the appalling power of the resuscitation, in as it seemed to her an even more violent form, of her love for Julius.

She had known perfectly well that she had not got over Julius. She had known it with sickening violence when she had seen his picture in the *Evening Standard* on the evening of her arrival, and had found herself the next second hoping and then believing that he had come to England to see her. She had tried, and tried very hard, to steady herself, to go on behaving as a convalescent. She had attempted to go quietly on with Hilda's view of the situation. But all the while she had been secretly vibrating with a dark excitement which she had known to be unhealthy and possibly evil. She surrendered herself at last to destiny, that wicked and consoling force, the destiny which made it certain that her path would cross again with that of Julius. When he had come, in order to find her, there could be no doubt at all about that, to Priory Grove, she had felt herself indeed to be in the hands of gods.

The conversation in the Old Brompton Road was more like an experience of the inferno, but lovers are accustomed to fire. The fate of the child, the child whom she had mentioned to no one, not even to Hilda, and which she had never for a second thought about as a human individual, burdened her suddenly, an indissoluble lump in her inside like a second pregnancy. She had indeed treated the child, as she had told Julius, as a disease to be got rid of, as a growth. That Julius might have cared about the child and wanted it, that the child might have reunited them, that everything might have become unimaginably different and better, these were thoughts which she simply dared not now permit herself to think if she wished to retain her sanity. Mercifully perhaps, the other shock, of the encounter between Julius and Tallis, distracted her from this peculiar pain and made it urgent that she should see her husband. She felt a strange impulse to defend Tallis against Julius, against Julius's belittling contempt, against the rays of sheer personal power which emanated from her former lover. She also felt, with the fearful renewal of her love for Julius, the need somehow to settle with Tallis, to deal with him, to put him, for the moment at any rate, somehow or other out of the way. Of Julius's other words, his coldness and his apparent unwillingness to see her, she made and thought very little.

With Tallis she had been determined to be cool. There was, she felt, no action now of gentleness or love which could genuinely profit her, or even him. All kindness must mislead. What she feared most of all was a renewal of that fatal gushing tenderness, that pitiful "animal" feeling which she had described to Hilda, and which had made it seem to her long ago that Tallis was the one man whom it was impossible to leave, the being whom it would be her happiness to render happy. How much joy his happiness, his amazed humble sense of his luck, had given her once. But that way pity lay, and dangerous and tender tears. Morgan had realized, as soon as she was inside the door, how hard it was going to be not to weaken and to make him, even for a moment, happy once again. She had at the same time realized what it was that could save her: contempt. That which was at the opposite extreme from love: the cynicism of a deliberate contemptuous diminution of another person. As she profited by it she thought, I am seeing him as Julius sees him.

Of course Tallis was not "settled." But he was for the moment put aside. The road away from Notting Hill was the road back to Julius. Come what may, she would try again. Julius: the second adventure. And let the gods decide. Now as she watched Julius's taxi recede and vanish she felt shock, but rather joyful shock. Julius had said terrible things, but his tongue had always been terrible. What gave her hope was his assault on her clothes. This act of violence did not belong to the conduct of a man who did not care. Julius cared. It was such a deeply characteristic action, and indifference does not produce such actions. She had seen Julius in this mood before when he had carefully and ruthlessly dissected a hat of hers which she had gleefully reported to have been much admired at a garden party at Dibbins by a colleague who had been making tentative advances. Julius's reaction had thrilled her with alarm and joy. After the destruction of the hat, it is true, they had gone to bed.

Standing, still rather dazed, upon the thick tawny Indian carpet beside the window in Julius's sitting-room, Morgan became aware of another curious feature of her situation. She was completely naked. She went to the bedroom door and shook the handle. Locked. She leaned against the door and pushed. Well and truly locked. She paused for thought. She was beginning to feel the tiniest bit cold. The telephone: but the telephone was in the bedroom. Then she began to search the rest of the flat. No garment of any kind was to be found. No friendly macintosh hanging behind the door, no capacious bathrobe in the bathroom, no odd jacket and trousers tossed down in a corner. Julius was a fanatically neat man. Of course all his clothes would be hanging on hangers in that inaccessible and now so highly desirable wardrobe. What was more, not only were there no garments, there seemed to be no loose textiles of any description, except for one rather exiguous washing-up cloth and a very damp towel in the bathroom. There weren't even any rugs, and the bath mat was made of cork.

There were the sitting-room curtains, of course. The kitchen and bathroom had frosted glass and were curtainless.

Alert but not yet anxious, she surveyed the curtains. Inner curtains semi-transparent nylon. Outer curtains thick blue velvet stiffly embroidered with golden threads. The windows were tall and the tops of the curtains well out of reach, even if she were to stand on any available piece of furniture. Of course a stout pair of scissors would soon make two half-curtains available to her. But could she find a stout pair of scissors? Her own scissors were incarcerated in the bedroom. A search of the kitchen revealed nothing handier than a carving knife, and armed with this Morgan advanced upon the curtains, only to become instantly aware of two things. It is practically impossible to cut through thick velvet curtains stiffly embroidered with gold thread with a bluntish carving knife. And in any case the curtains would be useless to her except possibly for purposes of keeping warm. She had vaguely intended to fashion them into a makeshift dress, but they were so *very* stiff and thick, and would be extremely difficult to sew, even if, which she was not, she were able to cut them up, and even if, which there were not, there were any sewing materials available in the flat. I could probably get the curtains down by just hauling the rail out of the wall, she thought, but what's the use? Well, I may yet need them as bed clothes if I have to stay here till Monday!

It really was rather a peculiar situation. She went to examine the pile of lacerated clothing in the hall. Julius had cut everything into hopelessly small pieces. She hurled herself against the bedroom door. It resisted stoutly. There were no tools with which she could try to force the lock. She began to search again. No chair with a loose cover. No cushion larger than one foot square. No spare table linen. The central heating appeared not to be turned on and by now she was beginning to feel very distinctly cold. Though the sun was still shining, the air seemed to be darkening outside. What *shall* I do? thought Morgan. I suppose Julius will come back. And yet will he? He had taken his suitcase away. He was perfectly capable of not coming back. He would be interested to see what she would do.

Of course she could shout for help from the window. Or she could issue from the flat clad in the washing-up cloth and knock on the neighbouring doors hoping to find a sympathetic woman. But what explanation could she offer of her extraordinary predicament? There must be some idea I haven't had, she told herself, some possibility that I haven't thought of. She sat down on the sofa and tried to pile the petit-point cushions on top of herself. They were small and fat and they kept falling off. She tried to reflect. After a while she began to cry.

✿ | THIRTEEN

Simon was feeling very disturbed. He could not quite make out what was the matter with him. Perhaps it was the heat. Like most Englishmen, Simon pretended to like hot weather but really didn't. London in July with the sun for once continually shining had become a mad place, stifling, enclosed, dry, whose rows of unreal and shimmering houses seemed to conceal something quite else, some more than Saharan desolation. Ought to get out of town, he muttered to himself. But it was not so easy. He might have got leave, but Axel, who was working very hard, probably too hard, at one of those things that Simon could not understand, would certainly not agree to taking a holiday at the moment. And to get away for a week-end demanded a degree of will and organization which the very inertness from which he wanted to flee made Simon quite incapable of. Anyway, Axel now worked all Saturday.

Axel was in a bad mood too. It was not that he was out of temper with Simon. That would in some ways have been easier to
bear. He was thoroughly out of temper with himself. He was going
through one of those periods of black self-depreciation and gloom
which had been so frequent when Simon first knew him. Axel was
very upset that he had lost his temper with Peter. He explained to
Simon that when one feels shame at having offended someone
it is the damage to one's own pride that really hurts and not the
distress of the other person. This philosophical observation seemed
to be of no assistance however. He brooded upon his pride. He
wrote a long letter to Rupert. He wrote, Simon knew from finding
the fragments in the wastepaper basket, several letters to Peter.
Simon did not think that one was posted. Axel also went off into
long speeches about the unfairness of an older person imposing
love upon a younger person. He speculated about whether he had
not blighted Simon's life. He wondered whether Simon might not
really be heterosexual after all. He pictured Simon happily married
to some charming long-legged twenty-two-year-old girl. He provided Simon with several splendid children. He gave a favourable
estimate of Simon's possibilities as a father. Almost in tears, Simon
threw his arms round his friend's neck. Axel gloomily conjectured
that the whole thing was, in the crudest possible sense, nothing
but sex after all.

Axel was also tormented by what Peter had said about concealment and hypocrisy. This torment was not new. Simon had often
heard Axel say, with various accents of bitterness, how much he
detested the necessity for discretion. Sometimes in such moods
he blamed the rottenness of a society who still looked askance
at such a harmless and natural phenomenon. Sometimes he
blamed himself for lacking the courage to be frank about his pref-
erences. Someone has to make a start, said Axel. This was not a
matter which had ever worried Simon. In his wilder pre-Axel days
the secrecy had seemed something rather amusing, connected with
his sense of it all as a sort of vast romp. Even when his great love
for Axel had made Simon so much more serious and so much
happier, he still could not quite share Axel's scruples. The instinc-

tive prevarications, the euphemisms, "My friend Nilsson, with whom I share a house" and so on, seemed to him more like a protective fence, a useful barrier behind which he and Axel hid the marvellous secret of their love. It made everything somehow cosier and more enclosed. He could not see it, as Axel undoubtedly did, as something potentially corrupting. "Oh, well, why don't you write to *The Times* about it!" said Simon flippantly at last. "Maybe I ought to," replied Axel morosely, and then relapsed into frowning preoccupied silence, consuming without comment an excellent cheese soufflé which Simon had just concocted.

Another source of unease, of course, was Julius. Simon was not at all sure what he thought about Julius. Julius aroused, in relation to Axel, a very deep jealousy fear in Simon. Simon knew these fears. He had often talked about them to Axel and Axel had helped him to fight them. He had attempted, with Axel's help, to see how base and how fruitless and how damaging these black instincts really were. However, they *were* instincts and not at all easy to suppress. Simon had not in fact talked to Axel, since Julius's visit, about this particular manifestation of the demon. This was partly because Axel had of late been struggling with demons of his own. Partly it was for another reason which Simon shifted about uneasily in his mind. Julius disturbed him. Simon had been upset too, in a confused way, by Peter's attack. He had been hurt by that tone of contempt, though he felt no impulse to blame Peter, who was clearly in some sort of bad way himself. What puzzled Simon was that the distress occasioned by Peter seemed now somehow to be attaching itself to Julius, as if Julius were its real source. Was it that Simon sensed that Julius despised him? Did Julius see him as a flimsy effeminate *poseur*? Yet Julius had been perfectly friendly and had not said anything which could suggest this belittling vision.

Everything is getting on my nerves, thought Simon, as he walked along Bond Street in the hot bright evening. The shops were shut and the street was full of well-dressed strollers, some of them in evening clothes. London felt idle and languid and wicked. I feel as if something were going to happen, he thought, and something not at all nice. His heart winced and his thoughts flew protectively to Axel. Suppose something happened to Axel, suppose Axel were run over or developed cancer or— Stop it, he told himself. He paused deliberately and gazed into the window of a very select man's outfitter's. He concentrated his attention on a royal blue cravat with emerald green acanthus leaves upon it. Would it suit him? Would it not! He craned his neck to see the price ticket, digested the shock, pictured himself looking stunning in royal blue with emerald green, and decided to return the next day to buy it. He began to walk slowly on. He turned into Brook Street.

Axel was at *Fidelio*. Simon had not told Axel of Julius's extraordinary invitation. "Come on Friday. Don't tell Axel." He was about to share a secret with Julius. What sort of secret would it turn out to be? Simon felt guilt, alarm, excitement. It occurred to him for the first time that he found Julius physically attractive. At any rate, the idea of now confronting him was producing certain sorts of familiar tremors and symptoms. But then, thought Simon, I have never really been able to distinguish between fear and sexual desire. His nervousness increased. He stopped at a shop window and adjusted his tie and inspected his appearance. He had dressed with care. He was wearing a plain purple shirt and a plain pink tie, with the light black terelyne summer suit which he had bought in Milan. He pushed back his slightly curly dark locks and gave them a careful pat. He gave a keen-eyed glance at his thin face. A trifle foxy? His nose was undoubtedly too long. A narrow clever face? Do I look clever? he wondered. Am I clever? he wondered. He walked on trying to look keen-eyed. When he reached Julius's number his heart was beating rather hard.

It will be about Axel's birthday, Simon said to himself, for sure. After all it was only this belief which made it right not to tell Axel. Indeed, what else *could* it be about? Julius wanted to plan some jolly surprise for Axel, and he wanted Simon's assistance. Very nice of him too, thought Simon, very nice indeed. Nothing to get excited about. He began to mount the stairs. When he got to the door of the flat he took a deep breath and rang the bell.

There was silence within. Then there was a faint cautious

flurrying sound. Simon thrust his head nearer to the door and listened. A voice from very close to him said through the door, "Who is that, please?"

The voice sounded familiar. It was a woman's voice. Startled, Simon said, "It's Mr. Foster, Simon Foster, I wanted to see—"

"Simon!"

"Morgan!"

"Wait a minute, Simon."

Simon felt confusion, shock. Whatever was Morgan doing there? Distress.

The door opened and Simon went in from the sunny landing to the dimmer light of the little hall. He blinked. He blinked again. The door closed.

"Morgan—whatever—?"

Morgan was dressed in nothing but a small piece of coloured cloth which she had wound about her waist.

"Simon, how marvellous! The gods must have sent you! You're an answer to prayer."

"But, Morgan, what on *earth*—?"

"Come in, come in. Oh God, but this is funny!" Morgan was laughing wildly. She turned, revealing the limitations of the small loincloth. "Come on in, Simon, welcome, welcome!"

He followed her into the sitting-room which glowed shadowily with reflected light from the declining sun. The room looked as if it had been hit by a bomb. Cushions were scattered over the floor together with the fragments of some sort of Chinese ornament. Over one window there were jagged holes where a great deal of plaster seemed to have come out of the wall. A long brass curtain rod and a chaotic pile of velvet curtain lay on the floor below. Another curtain rod hung down diagonally across the window, supporting a swirl of white nylon material from its lower end.

"Darling Simon," cried Morgan, "thank God you've arrived! I was just beginning to get desperate! I suppose I ought to drape myself in the curtains, only what the hell. You've seen me naked before."

"I haven't, actually," said Simon. "If you remember we never turned the light on."

Morgan stopped laughing. She looked at him for a long moment, and then said, "Dear Simon, dear dear Simon—" She twined her arms round his neck.

"Where's Julius?" said Simon, drawing himself nervously back.

"Gone away for the week-end!" said Morgan. She began to laugh again. "Oh God! I pulled the curtains down because I felt I had to do *something*. And then they fell on this blasted Chinese thing. Could you look at the bits? Is it genuine?"

Simon picked up a fragment or two. "Yes, I'm afraid so. T'ang."

"Oh Lord. Would it be expensive?"

"Yes. But look here, Morgan, have I gone mad or have you? What on earth *is* all this? Why did you pull the curtains down? Why have you got no clothes on? Why—?"

"You see, Julius cut up my clothes."

"Cut up your clothes?"

"Yes, darling. You see, I leapt into his bed."

"Oh."

"Nothing happened, nothing happened at all, except that he cut up my clothes, that is, so you see I had none. Look—" She darted into the hall and came back with a pile of silky ribbony stuff smelling faintly of face powder which she threw into Simon's arms and which he promptly dropped onto the floor. He felt extremely upset and alarmed.

"But why ever did he do that? What was—?"

"He was a bit cross with me. I don't know why he did it. It must have amused him. Why does Julius do things? Don't you think it's rather marvellous though? Who ever else would slash one's clothes to pieces?"

"Morgan, I simply don't understand—"

"Do I trouble you like this? Would you like me to get underneath the curtains?"

"No, no. But aren't you cold?"

"No. I was getting cold and I thought I might have to spend

the night here so I hauled the curtains down for bed clothes. But now you've come I am simply glowing with relief!"

"Why don't you put on some of Julius's clothes?"

"That's just the joke! He locked the bedroom door. And there isn't a cloth or a clothe in the whole of the rest of the flat, except this dish clout which I've twined about me, quite unnecessarily really as you're such an old friend." Morgan twitched the cloth off her and cast it away. She began to laugh again. She began to prance friskily about the room.

"Well, well, well," said Simon. He sat down on the sofa and watched her. It occurred to him that apart from one rather upsetting guilty evening at a strip joint in Paris he had never seen a woman entirely undressed. He had certainly never seen a woman whom he knew dancing naked in a flat in central London, her breasts quivering with laughter and velocity. He did not find it enjoyable.

"Morgan, *please*. We must do something. Suppose Julius comes back."

"He won't," said Morgan, stopping her dance. "He's gone to Market Harborough."

"Market Harborough?"

"Well, he's gone *somewhere*. Yes, we must certainly do something. But just at present I am feeling that this is one of the great moments of life."

"I'm not!" said Simon.

"Simon, you're frightened of me!" said Morgan. "That's rather beautiful." She came and knelt in front of him, gravely placing her elbows upon his knees. Then she very gently took one of his hands and laid it on one of her breasts. She closed her eyes. "Oh dear," said Simon. He left his hand where it was, holding the moist soft warm heavy thing.

Morgan without her clothes was a completely different being, scarcely recognizable to him. Her bronzed sharp-featured face looked birdlike and ambiguous and old. The human traits of humour and sweetness seemed to have withdrawn from it. Without the glasses her eyes looked blind and insentient. The long neck descended to hard bony shoulders and prominent collarbones. White flesh still faintly outlined upon her body the pattern of a bathing costume. The rounded breasts were slightly pendent and the dark damp channel between them smelt of sweat. The flesh was layered a little, coiled below the waist, the hips curved, recessed and curved again, the tensed knees shiny. Simon, looking yet not looking, felt alarm and pity and disgust. He also felt physically agitated and upset. "Please, Morgan, *please*—"

"All right. Do something. Yes." She sprang up.

Simon got up too. "Look, I'll go and get you some clothes. I can get to Rupert's in a taxi in fifteen minutes, well, twenty. Hilda will show me where to find your things."

"No," said Morgan. "I've got a better idea."

"What?"

"I'll take your clothes."

"*What?*"

"Only for a little while, silly. Just to fetch my own. I'll come back again at once."

"But, Morgan—"

"Don't be an ass, Simon, nobody's going to see you. You can wrap yourself in the curtains if you like. I'll only be half an hour away. I'd buy something in Bond Street, only all the shops are shut."

"Morgan, isn't it much more sensible if I go? After all—"

"You know quite well it doesn't matter what women wear nowadays. No one will even look at me. It isn't as if I were going into the bar at Claridges."

"But what about me? I mean, I shall be— Really, Morgan, I'd much rather not. It wouldn't take a minute to—"

"Simon, I don't want Hilda to know about this little drama. And if you went and asked for my clothes you'd have to tell her *something*. Do understand and be a sport. And whatever would Rupert think? He'd be *shocked*."

"I could tell them that you'd—I don't know—fallen in the river."

"Now, Simon, don't be *silly*. Off with them, dear. I'm tired of having nothing on, and honestly I'm beginning to get claustrophobia in this flat."

"So am I!"

"You'll have to lend me some money though. My handbag is in the bedroom. Damn, my glasses are in there too. Come on, let me undo your tie."

Simon stood helplessly as Morgan undid his tie and began to unbutton his shirt. Then he groaned and began to take off his jacket.

"That's right. Dear Simon, you really must forgive me. I'm just suddenly cram full of purpose. I told you it was one of my great moments. You see, the test was to get out of here somehow. And your coming was such luck, and now I just can't wait to be out. I couldn't bear it if Julius came back and found me, even if help was on the way."

"Came back! But you said he'd gone away for the week-end. Is he likely to come back?"

"Well, he might. And I wouldn't want him to find me here all naked and shivering."

"I wouldn't want him to find *me* here all naked and shivering!"

"You needn't shiver. I pulled the curtains down just to spite him actually, but you'll find them handy if you're cold. I'm sorry about that T'ang thing. I won't be long away. What a lovely colour your shirt is. Does it suit me?"

Groaning again, Simon stepped out of his trousers.

"You can keep your underpants. But I'll need your socks and your shoes. I think our feet are about the same size."

Morgan began to pull the black trousers on, tucking in the purple shirt. She zipped them up. She fumbled with the tie. "Could you do this for me? I've never tied a tie."

"You can't do it on someone else," said Simon. He was shivering. "You can do without it."

"No, I can't. I want to be properly dressed. I *must* have the tie as well. Do please try."

Simon tied the tie rather clumsily and Morgan slipped into the jacket. "My God, Morgan, you look just like a chap!"

"I feel I look *terrific*. Your trousers fit me marvellously. And look, so do your shoes. Let me look at myself in the bathroom. Oh Simon, I look so smart in a tie! I must wear one always!"

It was getting dark outside now and Morgan had turned the light on in the bathroom. Shuddering a little, his bare feet chilled by the tiles, he looked over her shoulder into the mirror. Morgan was transformed again. The bony face, the dark cropped hair, the narrow eyes, sentient now, seemed to belong to a clever boy, not even raffish, not even a dandy, just hard and clever. Morgan put on a stern stare and tightened her lips. Simon, feeling vulnerable and frail, saw his own white naked shoulder behind the square shoulder of the black jacket. He was only very slightly taller.

"We resemble each other a little," she said. "I've often thought it. Only your hair is flowerier. If your hair were straight—"

She turned to Simon and began to strain his locks back behind his ears.

"Morgan, you make a lovely lovely boy." He clasped his hands together in the small of her back and drew her up against his body. They were silent for a moment.

"I must go." Her lips warmed his skin. "The sooner I go the sooner I'll be back. I don't want to see anybody but you this evening. Thank you for your clothes." She slipped from his embrace. "Where do you keep your money?"

"In that pocket."

"It'll seem strange without a handbag. *Au revoir.*"

The front door opened and closed and Simon was alone. He surveyed himself for a while in the mirror and ran his hand up and down the narrow band of curly black hair which ran from his chest to his navel. His navel was absurd and always caused him shame. His body was horribly pale and in this light looked faintly bluish like watery milk. His collarbones jutted out grotesquely. He was distinctly *skinny* and he looked a good deal less keen-eyed without his clothes. He was beginning to feel seriously cold. He went into the kitchen hoping to find some gin or whisky, but could discover nothing except refrigerated Danish lager. He went back into the sitting-room, where it was now rather dark.

Simon could not decide whether he thought the whole thing amusing or whether it were not thoroughly frightening, the beginning perhaps of those horrors of which he had felt the cold premonition in Bond Street. He imagined himself telling the story to a lot of people who were shrieking with laughter. "And there I was left all alone in my underpants . . ." It would certainly sound madly funny. Except that I won't want to tell anyone, he felt suddenly.

The twilight was a little eerie and the room looked different. He moved to turn on the light, but then realized that he would be visible through the denuded window. He went to the sofa and piled up a few cushions. He reclined, and dragged one of the velvet curtains up to cover himself.

There were distant sounds from the street. But the room had an encapsulated silence of its own, a slightly dramatic silence as if a clock had only just stopped ticking. It grew darker. The walls seemed to be changing into huge hanging shadows charged with positive obscurity. They became menacing and deep, tall mahogany bookcases that reached to the ceiling, immense carved wardrobes with open doors and soft furry interiors of dark suspended clothes. Places where a child might get lost. A very long time seemed to be passing.

Simon was moving through a dark twilit garden underneath huge plane trees through whose leaves a luminous but darkening sky could intermittently be seen. There was different light under the trees, strange light, dark and yet lurid. He was following his mother who was walking some ten paces ahead of him and guiding him. He felt terrible choking anxiety and had difficulty in walking. His mother moved onward like a dog, turning every now and then to look back at him, and when she turned the luminosity under the trees was reflected in the steel-rimmed spectacles which she was wearing, and her eyes gleamed cold like those of a nocturnal animal caught in a ray of light. Simon knew that she was going to show him something appalling. The garden seemed to go on and on and the plane trees grew thicker and darker overhead. At last his mother stopped and pointed at something on the ground. In the illuminated darkness Simon saw a long mound of ashes, like the ashes of a bonfire. There were sticks and fragments of branches and withered flowers lying all about as if they had been part of the bonfire but had not been consumed. He felt an urge to touch the ashes and leaned down. Then he saw, only a few inches from his hand, a piece of brown tweed. It was a trouser leg. He saw the turn-ups of the trouser, and then a protruding leg with a dark sock and a shoe. He withdrew his hand with horror, thinking instantly, This is my father's grave. My mother has led me to my father's grave. Yet that cannot be. My father was cremated. Would he be lying like this in his clothes underneath a pile of ashes? Is that what happens to people when they are cremated? He began to stir the ashes with his foot. The material of the brown suit, filthy with ash, began to emerge from the mound. Simon fell on his knees and dug. He dug his way up the recumbent body, clawing the cold sticky ash away frantically with his hands. He dreaded to uncover the face which his digging fingers were now touching. He brushed the ash aside. The dead face was that of Rupert. Suddenly there was a great deal of light.

Simon woke with a gasp. The terror of the dream made him breathless and his heart was beating violently. He panted for breath, struggling against a great weight upon his chest. He saw his bare arm and his hand clasped upon some heavy blue-and-gold material. He thrust the stuff away, trying desperately to sit up.

The light had been switched on in the sitting-room and Julius was standing in the middle of the room regarding him. Simon had the impression that Julius had been there for some time. He was in evening dress, looking grave and thoughtful as if by now he was really looking at something else. Simon remembered, succeeded in sitting up, then pulled the curtain back about him. He looked at Julius with appalled staring eyes.

"This is certainly a day of surprises," said Julius. He went out of the room and Simon could hear him turning the key in the bedroom door.

"Julius! Julius! I'm sorry—" Simon began to stagger up. He tried to lift the curtain to wrap it round him, but it was too heavy. He ran after Julius.

Julius was opening a cupboard in the bedroom and taking out a bottle of bourbon whisky.

"Julius, I must explain—"

"Get two glasses from the kitchen, there's a good boy."

Simon ran to the kitchen. He looked at his watch. It was midnight. What on earth could have happened to Morgan?

"I'm most terribly sorry—"

"Would you like to borrow my dressing gown? You are shivering in a most unbecoming manner and you do look a trifle quaint with nothing on but those open-work pants. You really should try to put on a little weight. I see somebody has destroyed my curtaining, and you must be plainly visible from across the street."

"It wasn't me— I mean—" Simon pulled on Julius's dressing gown of quilted dark red silk.

"And I see one of my T'ang horses has been broken. A pity."

"Morgan pulled the curtains down because she hadn't any— she was very sorry—and about the horse— I can't think what can have happened to her."

"I leave a naked girl and I return to find a naked boy."

"You see, I arrived—"

"All right, I can reconstruct it. Morgan took your clothes and fled. She would, of course."

"You mean she won't come back?"

"I have no idea whether she'll come back or not. Have some whisky. You seem to be in a rather disturbed state."

"She said she'd just get her own clothes at Rupert's and come back here. But that was hours ago."

"The point that puzzles me is what you are doing here. *Why* did you arrive?"

"But you asked me to!"

"Did I?"

"Don't you remember? When you came to dinner with us.

You whispered to me in the hall, 'Come on Friday. Don't tell Axel.' "

"Did I? Well, I may have done. Oh, yes, I do recall it now. I'm afraid it had entirely slipped my mind. Did you tell Axel?"

"No. I couldn't think what you wanted. I thought you might be planning something for Axel's birthday; you know, some treat or something."

"I wasn't, actually. When is Axel's birthday?"

"The twentieth."

"Well, I must try and give him a treat!"

"But, Julius, if it wasn't that what was it? Why did you ask me to come and not to tell Axel?"

"Oh, I forget. I expect I just wanted to see if you would."

"If I would—?"

"If you would come. And not tell Axel. And you have come. And not told Axel. Would you like some water in your whisky?"

"I just can't understand—"

"Where is Axel this evening, by the way?"

"At *Fidelio*."

"Will he be missing you?"

"No. He's going on to a sort of supper party afterward. But I must get back— I can't— But— Oh dear, oh *dear*—"

"Don't fret, child. All manner of thing shall be well. Drink your whisky and then we'll decide what to do next. You can have some clothes of mine. I'm rather larger than you but I expect we can fit you out."

The front doorbell rang. Julius got up and went to the door, leaving Simon standing distractedly in the middle of the floor with his glass. Morgan entered slowly. She glanced at Julius, passed him, and came on into the room. She was wearing a dress and her grey macintosh and carrying a small suitcase. She turned and looked very coolly at Julius.

Julius began to laugh. Simon gave a sickly smile. Morgan looked detached, dignified. Then in a moment she began to laugh too. She and Julius laughed, falling about the room, swaying weakly with ever renewed paroxysms of helpless mirth. Simon sat down and drank some neat whisky. He surveyed them morosely.

"Oh Julius," said Morgan at last, reeling to the sofa, "you really are a *god!*"

"Have a drink," said Julius. "Simon, get another glass and also a jug of water."

Simon padded gloomily out to the kitchen.

"So you were holding out on me, you had some bourbon after all! Oh gosh, I'm so sorry about the T'ang horse. I'll pay for it."

"You couldn't afford to," said Julius.

"Why were you so long?" said Simon accusingly to Morgan, bringing the glass and the jug. "I thought you were never coming. And what about my clothes?"

"Poor Simon, oh, *poor* Simon—" More laughter.

"I want to go home," said Simon.

"Yes, yes, your clothes are here, in the case, I'm terribly sorry—"

Simon took the suitcase into the bathroom and began to dress rapidly. He could hear Morgan explaining to Julius. "You see, everything went wrong, you know, like it does in dreams, first I couldn't get a taxi, then when I got to Priory Grove no one was in and I remembered Hilda and Rupert were out to dinner and I couldn't remember where, and you know usually they leave the back door unlocked, only this time they hadn't, and I spent ages trying to get in but I couldn't, and I fell off a window sill and thought I'd twisted my ankle, I'm afraid I tore your trousers, Simon, I'm terribly sorry, and then I decided I'd go to another friend's place and borrow her things, only she wasn't in either and it took ages getting there and getting back and there were just *no* taxis, and then I waited at Priory Grove and at last Hilda and Rupert turned up and I got the clothes and do you know all they said when they saw me was 'What a frightfully smart trouser suit you've got yourself, it does suit you'!"

Simon emerged. "*Good night!*"

"Oh Simon, don't be cross with me!"

"One moment, Simon," said Julius. "Wait just a moment. Morgan will be going with you."

Morgan looked at his face and raised her eyebrows. "All right, Julius. Still God."

"Simon," said Julius, and he was very serious now, almost grim. "I advise you not to tell Axel about this evening's little farce."

"Oh Simon, you *can't* tell Axel," cried Morgan. "I couldn't bear it. He wouldn't think it funny."

"It isn't funny!" said Simon.

"You know how dignified Axel is," said Julius. "He hates the absurd."

"Whereas you have a genius for it, Simon darling," said Morgan.

"He would feel you had let him down," said Julius.

"Besides it wouldn't be fair to me," said Morgan. "Just think, Simon. Suppose Axel were to tell Rupert? This must be our secret, no one else must know."

"Morgan is right," said Julius.

"All right," said Simon. He felt that fear again, a feeling as of taking a first step in under a dark canopy. "But suppose Axel is home when I get there—"

"Then invent something, you fool," said Morgan.

"Careless talk costs loves, my Simon," said Julius. "A necessary ingredient in a happy marriage is the ability to tell soothing lies to your partner."

"All right then," said Simon. He looked from one to the other of them. They were still glowing with laughter and they looked authoritative, strong.

A few minutes later he and Morgan were out in Brook Street looking for a taxi. Simon arrived home before Axel.

🙢 | FOURTEEN

"You'd better go fairly soon, darling," said Hilda to Morgan, "if you don't want to run into Tallis."

"Are you two going to *court martial* Tallis?" said Morgan.

"No, of course not."

"You're going to ask him if his intentions about me are honourable!" Morgan went off into wild laughter.

Hilda looked at her sister anxiously. For the last two days Morgan had displayed a sort of desperate feverish cheerfulness which Hilda was at a loss to understand. She had not succeeded in making Morgan talk. Something was being concealed.

"I do wish you weren't moving into that flat," said Hilda. "I hate the idea of your being all alone there. I can't think why you won't stay on here, you know we love having you."

"I've got to think things out by myself, Hilda. I know you're worried. But it will be better in the long run, I do assure you."

"I wish you'd let me give you some money."

"Oh, I will, I will! I'll borrow some anyway, a bit later on."

"Morgan, you really must *think* about Tallis."

"I assure you, Hilda, Tallis is a permanent feature of all my thoughts. Even if I'm thinking about what there'll be for dinner, Tallis is there, like a little brown picture stuck up in the corner!" More wild laughter.

"I wish you'd be serious, sweetheart."

"Oh, but I am serious. Deadly serious. *Deadly* serious."

"Tallis will expect us to know what you propose to do."

"Anyone who knew that would know more than I do. Perhaps a little bird knows it. Or God. I certainly don't."

"But you must make up your mind. It's something you've got to *do*. You can't expect to wake up one morning and find it's been done for you!"

"That's exactly what I do expect, Hilda. Exactly. I'll wake up one morning and I'll say to myself—"

"Oh Morgan, Morgan! What *is* the matter?"

"Nothing's the matter. Except that I've gone mad. When is poor Tallis coming to be court martialled?"

"About six."

"Well, I've got an hour."

"Do you want to borrow the car?"

"No, I probably wouldn't be able to park it. I've got enough for tonight and I'll fetch the rest of my stuff tomorrow by taxi."

"I hope you'll be warm enough over there in the evenings. Did you air the bed properly?"

"Oh Hilda, do stop worrying! I'll be perfectly all right."

"By the way, are you seeing Peter again?"

"I hope so. Fingers crossed, but I *think* I've persuaded him to go and see his supervisor! The idea of my driving him to Cambridge seemed to be attractive!"

"Oh Morgan, if only you could! You really are our last hope with Peter. I suppose that's one advantage of your living somewhere else. You might see a little of the wretched boy."

"I've asked him round for a drink. Better lay in buns and ginger pop!"

"Oh dear, Peter was unspeakable the other day. One would think that at least good manners could be absolutely bred into somebody."

"I thought Axel was pretty unspeakable too, Hilda."

"Axel wrote a long emotional letter to Rupert, castigating himself!"

"Much good that does. I wish Simon wasn't living with Axel."

"I respect Axel. Simon was leading a pretty crazy sort of life before Axel turned up."

"Well, I expect he was happier, and I'm not sure that a crazy sort of life isn't the best kind of life to lead."

"Morgan, have you seen Julius again, since that time he turned up here and you ran after him?"

"No."

"You're lying—"

"Quite right, I'm lying. Oh, I'll tell you all about it later, Hilda. Whatever happens, you won't think too ill of me, will you? I think if I absolutely lost your good opinion it would kill me."

"Darling, you're always attributing harsh moral judgements to me, but I'm not making any! I just want you to be happy! I *couldn't* condemn you!"

"People like you and Rupert make harsh moral judgements just by existing."

"You make us sound awful!"

"No, no, it's wonderful. I worship you both. But I may have to vote for craziness in the end. Maybe that's something I have in common with Peter!"

"I'm worried about what you're going to *do* when you're all alone in that flat."

"I'm going to enjoy life, Hilda. I shall give wild parties and be the talk of the neighbourhood!"

"Darling, I do hope—"

"No, no, I'm not serious. I *will* enjoy myself, but ever so quietly and intelligently. I shall cultivate Peter, I shall get drunk with Simon, I shall go to theatres and concerts, I shall visit every art gallery in London—"

"I know, you always used to be a great gallery hound. But you must come here *often*. You won't neglect us, will you, sweetheart? Now I do think you should go. Shall I telephone for a taxi?"

"No, of course not, I'll walk. I've only got this little case and the basket. Don't worry, Hilda. And don't forget. Love me."

"I couldn't forget that."

"Give my love to Tallis!"

"Don't be flippant, darling!"

Hilda smiled and waved out of the window as Morgan disappeared down Priory Grove. Then she turned back into the bedroom and sat down in front of her mirror. If she dyed her hair would it give it a sort of dead appearance? Deciding to dye one's hair did seem like a final farewell to youth. She looked terribly tired around the eyes again today. She could still see her younger face, perky, pert, angelic. But could anybody else see it now? How radiant Morgan was looking, but somehow unhealthily excited. Perhaps she ought to have pressed her about Julius.

Hilda ran a comb through the longish darkish greyish locks and they fell back into their handsome layers of curls. She put a little powder onto her nose and a little lipstick onto her lips. The lipstick gave her a dated look. Perhaps it was the wrong colour. It was years since she had *thought* about cosmetics. She was not at all looking forward to the interview with Tallis. It had been Rupert's idea. Rupert got so anxious and felt so responsible for other people's welfare and he wanted to get things *clear*. Men so often did.

Hilda herself was feeling increasingly distressed. She did not like the mood that Morgan was in, and though she had denied making moral judgements it did hurt her to see her sister behaving in an unworthy way. She felt sure that nothing but further insanity would result from Morgan's playing around with Julius. Her own feelings about Julius had hardened, and when Rupert had suggested that now that Morgan was leaving them they might invite Julius to dinner Hilda had been unenthusiastic. Hilda felt an increasing pity for Tallis, and she realized too that her irritation with the whole situation was partly caused by guilt. She ought never to have let it be seen that she was disappointed in Morgan's marriage. She had made her own contribution to the gradual shrinking of Tallis. She hoped Rupert, who had been heard to condemn Tallis for irresolution and vagueness, would not try to play the stern inquisitor. It would be so out of place. It was they who should be begging Tallis's pardon.

Hilda crossed the landing to Rupert's study. "I got Morgan off all right. She thinks she may manage to take Peter to Cambridge."

"So she told me. I'm very relieved. The more she can see of him the better."

"How's the book?" Hilda leaned over her husband, running her fingers through the loose faded blond hair, dry and cool.

Rupert thrust away a yellow notebook in which he had been writing in his neat tiny hand. "Quite alarmingly nearly finished!"

"We must have that celebration dinner."

"We must indeed. You don't mind if I invite Julius? He has always taken such an interest in the book."

"All right. But if we invite Julius we can't invite Tallis."

"I suppose that does follow."

"Well, Julius is your friend. Where shall we see Tallis, here or downstairs?"

"Downstairs is more friendly."

"I'm glad you're feeling friendly! I put the drinks out down there. What are you going to say?"

They began to walk down the stairs, Hilda walking behind with her hands on her husband's shoulders.

"I want to see what *he* says," said Rupert.

"You think he ought to have a showdown with Morgan?"

"Frankly, yes."

"Tallis is incapable of violence of any sort."

"It's not a question of violence. It's a question of responsible firmness."

"Morgan has seen Julius again."

"What's the situation?"

"She wouldn't say."

"I think Morgan is behaving badly."

"So do I. You know, Rupert, I sometimes think Morgan really does love Tallis still. I didn't understand this before. But she's terribly obsessed with him. If only the picture could change a bit, if only Tallis could *surprise* her in some way, if only she could suddenly see him in a different light—"

"A change of *gestalt*, yes. But that's just why I favour the showdown."

"Maybe. But not like you think. Not 'Look here I want to know where I stand.' "

"Well, *you* talk to him, Hilda. There's the front doorbell. That'll be him."

Hilda quickly arranged the cushions in the drawing-room and checked her face in the glass as Rupert's and Tallis's voices were heard in the hall. The curtains had been pulled a little against the sun and the room was dim. She drew the curtains back and revealed the quiet blazing garden and the blue pool so still now that its sleek surface gave not a flicker of light.

Tallis came in.

"Hello, Tallis dear." She shook his hand and rather hesitantly kissed him.

"Hello, Hilda." They were always a little constrained with each other.

"Do sit here."

"How lovely your garden is," said Tallis, sitting down.

Tallis sat in a small arm-chair sideways to the garden. He was wearing a dark blue jacket and trousers, rather old and spotty and mysteriously tinged with green and far too heavy for the season, and a clean blue-and-white-striped shirt which needed but had not got a detachable collar.

Hilda and Rupert sat side by side on the sofa facing the garden. They looked at Tallis and Tallis looked out of the window. There was a moment's silence.

"It's so quiet over here," said Tallis. "It's like a visit to the country."

"We hear the aeroplanes more than you do," said Hilda.

"I rather like the aeroplanes," said Tallis. "It's a sort of going home sound. There's one now."

Hilda was about to tell him to take off his jacket when she got a hint of braces. "What'll you drink, Tallis? Some sherry? A little gin and French? Gin and tonic?"

"Yes, please. I mean, yes, some sherry. Thank you."

"I expect you're very busy," said Hilda. "I heard your name in connection with that new housing project in Notting Hill."

"Yes. It's in an awful muddle at the moment, I'm afraid."

Hilda thought, Wherever Tallis is there's always a muddle! Then she thought, This is unjust. Wherever there is a muddle, there Tallis is.

"Tallis, we did rather want to talk to you, to talk to you frankly," said Rupert. "Yes, thank you, dear, some gin."

How different these two are, thought Hilda, as she saw the dear familiar puzzled obstinate look in her husband's blue eyes. Rupert is so strong and firm, so typically masculine and so marvellously honest. He wants complete information and straight answers and unambiguous positions. He wants clarifications and rational policies. Tallis is so much more indefinite and feminine. If he wasn't so nice one might call him sly. And he looks so small beside Rupert.

"Yes," said Tallis. "You must be worried stiff about Peter. So am I."

"Oh," said Rupert. "Well, it wasn't— Naturally we are worried. But just now it seems he may be persuaded to go back to Cambridge."

"I think he should see a psychiatrist," said Tallis.

"*Tallis!*" cried Hilda. "You've always been so much against them!"

"Ordinary human affection is the best healing power," said Rupert.

"Except that it doesn't always work," said Tallis. He was still squinting out at the sunlight in the garden.

"Peter needs love," said Hilda. "Of course he's a bit rebellious. All young people are nowadays."

"And I think he ought to stop living with me," said Tallis. "Though I'm hanged if I can think where he should go to. He needs professional help."

"I'm amazed at you, Tallis," said Rupert. "Most psychiatry is bunk, as you quite well know."

"What an admission of failure!" said Hilda.

"Well, I have failed," said Tallis. He turned back toward the room, blinked, frowned, and took an absent-minded gulp of sherry.

Hilda, feeling a bit upset and annoyed, said in her calmest

tone to Rupert, "We must think about somewhere for Peter to live, mustn't we, dear, if Tallis thinks he should move. After all, Tallis is very busy and he's been most patient with Peter."

"Why shouldn't Peter go and stay with Morgan?" said Rupert.

"That's not a bad idea!"

"You know, of course," said Rupert to Tallis, "that Morgan has moved out of this house."

"No, I didn't know."

How should he know, after all, thought Hilda, since nobody bothered to tell him. No one tells him anything. And serve him right, she thought the next moment.

Rupert was saying to her, "Yes, let Morgan take over Peter, why not?"

"Where's she moved to?" said Tallis.

"A flat in Fulham," said Hilda.

"Is she living alone?"

"Yes, of course," said Ruppert.

"Why 'of course'?" said Tallis.

"Do you want her address?" said Hilda.

"No, thank you. She's got mine." Tallis was peering intently into his glass. He thrust in a little finger to rescue a struggling fly, then got up and walked across the room to a bowl of roses. He coaxed the fly off onto a leaf. Then he resumed his seat.

Hilda watched him with exasperation. "Oh Tallis, why don't you try to *win* her," she cried. "Morgan just doesn't know who she is or what she's doing at the moment, she's simply drifting along. Use some initiative. Use some imagination. Do something to startle her. You do still love her, don't you?"

"Yes," said Tallis. He gave Hilda a quick glance and then lowered his eyes again. The skin seemed extra taut over the polished knobs of his brow.

"Well, then for God's sake *do* something about it!"

Tallis put his glass down rather abruptly on the carpet, spilled a little sherry, and remained leaning forward staring at the faint round stain. He was silent. Rupert, who had been looking impatient, raised his eyebrows to Hilda.

"Look here, Tallis," began Rupert.

"It's not so easy," said Tallis. "She knows all about me. There's nothing much to know and there's nothing more to know."

"Nonsense," said Rupert. "All human beings are mysterious."

"There's no point in my forcing myself upon her or putting on some kind of show. She'd see through it anyway. She doesn't appear to want me. She appears to want somebody else. It's in her nature to—"

"People don't have 'natures' in that sense," said Rupert.

"Morgan certainly hasn't," said Hilda. "She's terribly unstable. The one thing that's certain is that the girl is obsessed with you. Tallis, don't you see that you've got *power* over her? You could shake that girl to her foundations." Hilda had got up in her agitation and was standing behind the sofa.

Tallis raised his head. He said in a matter-of-fact voice, "I know. I know. But what on earth use would that be? *That* isn't it."

"Oh Tallis—you—you *ninny!*"

He smiled faintly. His face now had the relaxed luminous look which Hilda had sometimes noticed when he was most serious. Faintly comical, she thought, but rather moving. What ridiculous gingery eyebrows and such a short and *shiny* nose and such a little mouth. But the eyes, yes, the eyes.

"I assure you," said Tallis, "I am fully aware of the situation and I am not enjoying it. When I see what to do I'll do it."

"Listen, Tallis," said Rupert. "I hope you will forgive me if I am slightly critical. We are all worried about Morgan. She's in an absurd state of mind and, as Hilda says, she's drifting. As her sister and brother-in-law we have a responsibility. But you have a much more direct and obvious responsibility. You are her husband. In a more primitive society it would have been your duty to fetch her back to your house by force if necessary. It should be possible to find some enlightened equivalent for this. At any rate, you should try. I know how intensely scrupulous you are about forcing her in any way. But if I may say so, I think you should ask yourself whether this scrupulosity does not originate in pride. You have been deeply hurt: and very reticent behaviour can be a kind of revenge. You are preserving your dignity by refusing to show your feelings. But there are moments when love ought to be undignified, extravagant, even violent. For make no mistake about it, only love can really alter this situation and really heal these dreadful wounds. Both you and Morgan are wounded people. She is the more wounded because she is the more guilty, and for that reason too she is probably the more proud. So it is all the more important for you to be brave and positive. In a situation like this one, genuine humility is active and takes risks. Don't let two prides paralyse two loves. Show her how much you care, not abjectly but ardently. True love is something impressive, something beautiful. Morgan has been living in a sordid and wretched world, a world of prevarication and muddle and shabby thinking. She needs the vision of a life of trust and truth and mutual devotion. You must use authority. The authority of a husband. The authority of a *loving* husband."

Tallis was leaning back in his chair and listening intently, his eyes very wide open and his small mouth pursed. He said thoughtfully, "Authority." Then he said in a reasoning and unemotional voice, "But suppose she loves Julius King?"

"She doesn't!" cried Hilda. "*She doesn't!*"

"I agree with Hilda," said Rupert. "But you can only try. And you ought at least to try."

Tallis rose to his feet. "I love Peter. Fat lot of good that's done," he said in a ruminative tone.

"Oh Tallis, you drive me mad!" cried Hilda.

"I'm sorry," said Tallis. He smiled again. "I am grateful to you for talking to me, both of you. I assure you I will think very carefully about what you've said. And now I think I must be off. Rupert, could I just ask you one question?"

"Yes, certainly. What?"

"Why is stealing wrong?"

Rupert, who had not had a philosophical training for nothing, was never startled by any question, however bizarre, and was ready at once to give it his undivided attention. He reflected now for a while, staring at Tallis. Then he said, "Of course the concept of stealing is linked to the concept of property. Where there are no property rights there is no wrongful appropriation of the goods of another. In completely primitive situations where there is no society—if any such situations exist or existed—it could be argued that there are no property rights and so no stealing. Also in certain kinds of community, such as a monastery or conceivably a family, there could be mutual voluntary renunciation of property rights, so that within the community stealing would not exist by definition. Though even in these two cases what a man customarily uses, such as his clothes or his tools, might be thought of as natural property and *ergo* as deserving of respect. Indeed one might argue that it could never be right under any circumstances to remove a man's toothbrush against his will. However, in state and society as we know it there is no prospect of any universal voluntary surrender of the concept of property, and extremely complicated property rights, extending far beyond the area of clothes and tools, appear to exist and are upheld by law. Doubtless many of these complex arrangements can be argued to be economically and politically necessary to the well-being and continuance of the state, and in a healthy open society the details of these arrangements are properly a matter for continual discussion and adjustment in the light of both expediency and morality. Acceptance of any society, and even a bad society gives its members many benefits, does seem to suggest a certain duty to respect property. In a bad undemocratic society there might of course exist specialized duties to disregard particular alleged property rights, or even to break the law as a matter of protest, though it should be kept in mind that there are always *prima facie* utilitarian arguments against stealing, in so far as people may be distressed by the removal of their goods. But in a democratic society stealing is surely always wrong not only for utilitarian reasons but because property is an important part of a structure generally agreed to be good and whose alteration in detail can be freely sought."

When Rupert had finished speaking Tallis waited as if there might be something more to come. He looked puzzled. Then he said, "Thank you very much, Rupert." And to Hilda, "Please forgive me, I must go. Don't bother to see me to the door. Oh, how kind of you. Thank you, good-bye, good-bye." He went away smiling and waving.

Hilda and Rupert walked back into the drawing-room. They picked up their drinks. They stared at each other in complete bafflement.

❀ | FIFTEEN

"I want a pee," said Peter.

"Well, let's stop here," said Morgan. "It seems a nice place."

She stopped the car. They were on their way back from Cambridge, where Peter, all docility and common sense all of a sudden, had conversed with his supervisor.

Peter, perspiring in white shirt and rolled-up sleeves, jumped out and disappeared through a screen of tall pale yellow grasses into some sort of gulley. Morgan sat at the wheel of Hilda's car, dreamily looking up into the blue sky. It was suddenly very silent now that the engine of the car was switched off. No, one could hear insects, a quiet incessant buzzing, not peaceful, rather frenzied really, but happy. There was an intense summery sense of the present moment. A dry smell of grass tickled in the nose. The flowers of the grass were mostly dried up and baked to a brittle tawniness, but there were a few feathery mauve globes here and there, and also some plump red poppies.

The world is crazy but good, she thought. That seemed to be the right formulation. It had all become so much clearer in the last few days. It had been right to go to Julius. When one has such a deep instinctive need to do something then it cannot be wrong to do it. Julius always *shows* me things, she thought, he is a great world-revealer. I have no idea what is going to happen, but I feel whole for it now, whole in madness. Madness can be a kind of spiritual strength. I will see Julius again. We have not yet done with each other and we are in the hands of the gods. Yes, that is it. With Julius one is in the hands of the gods, one has *fallen* into their hands. That is frightening but life-giving. To be *deep* in life: not to creep by or tremble on verges. She looked up. A strange regular metallic sound was coming down out of the sky. She saw three swans flying, their whiteness kindled and almost invisible against the pale sun-brimming sky. The rustling whistling sound of their wings passed on over her head and faded.

"Morgan, do come and look. It's such a marvellous place. It's an abandoned railway line."

Morgan got out of the car and parted the screen of yellow grass. Ahead of her Peter was plunging down a steep slope through a tangle of grass and milky white flowering cow parsley. The place was a railway cutting. Only the rails and sleepers had been taken away and the floor of the cutting was a green level where shorter finer grass now almost entirely concealed the stony bed of the vanished railway line. Morgan slid and scrambled down, pulling up the skirt of her dress, until she reached the level. It was hotter here and rather stifling with the drowsy honey smells of flowers and the smell of green. The banks were tall and very wild, narrowing the sky. She thought, It is a place, a human place, and yet not any more; it has been taken over, lost to us, taken by, yes, by *them*.

"Isn't it wonderful?" said Peter. He spoke quietly, not raising his voice. "I'm just going to walk along a bit."

She nodded.

She stood staring up at the sloping walls of grass and flowers on either side of her. She began to see more detail, more and different flowers hidden in the grassy jungle. Flowers which the scientific farmer had long banished from his fields lingered here in secret, dazing with their variety the drunken bees who crawled laboriously among the stems, buzzing as they walked with sheer exhausted joy. Small wild-rose bushes scattered the slope with circles of papery luminous pink. Deeper pink of willow herb and white of flowering nettle and purple of selfheal, trailed over by bryony and latticed by stiff networks of radiant blue vetch. Their names came back to Morgan from very far away, out of childhood, out of distant classroom innocence. Tufted vetch, wood vetch, wood bitter vetch. And wild mint with its woolly flowers of creamy blotting-papery rose. She plucked a leaf and crushed it and smelt the cool quick odour on her hand.

Peter had disappeared. She saw that the cutting curved a little and a bulky shoulder of sun-baked grass and flowers hid the next part of the line. She began to walk slowly along the level grassy floor. She could feel the perspiration quietly running down her back. She pulled at her light blue cotton dress, detaching it here and there from her body. She ran a hand round her damp hot neck, lifting up the ring of her hair. She ought to have brought a hat and dark glasses. The flowers were beginning to quiver in front of her eyes. How extraordinary flowers are, she thought. Out of these dry cardboardy rods these complex fragile heads come out, skin-thin and moist, like nothing else in the world. People from a planet without flowers would think we must be mad with joy the whole time to have such things about us. She now saw that what she had taken for flowering nettle was white comfrey, a plant which she had not seen since she had found it long ago in rivery meadows in Oxfordshire on holidays in childhood. She leaned forward to caress the drooping flower heads and touch the strong slightly hairy stems.

The next moment she was lying full length in the long grass and there was a great deal too much light. Light was vibrating inside her eyes and she could see nothing but dazzling and pale shadows as if the whole scene had been bleached and then half blotted out by a deluge of light. Her body seemed to be weighted and pinned to the sloping bank by a potentiated force of gravity. Rays from very far away were being focused through her flesh. Her head fell down into deep grass and she fought for breath.

The blazing light was rhythmically changing into luminous flashes of black, tugging the visible world away from her, tugging her out of consciousness. The earth was pressing upward against her. As she resisted it with her hands and rolled her head about, trying to breathe, the sky above her through the dome of grass was lurid and brilliant and dark.

Morgan pushed the earth away and rolled down the slope onto the level of the shorter grass. She lay there prone and struggled with giddiness and nausea and unconsciousness. She told herself, and hung desperately onto the thought, I have got sunstroke, that is what it is, it must be. She got herself onto her knees, panting, gasping, keeping her head down. She did not know whether her eyes were closed or not. She seemed to see the expanse of green floor between the high flowering banks and it was alive with movement and huge forms. The great ray from afar was pinning her between the shoulder blades and trying to force her down again. Was it giddiness she was feeling now, a dazzled sensation of spinning drunkenness, or was it something else, disgust, fear, horror as at some dreadfulness, some unspeakable filth of the universe? Saliva was dripping from her mouth. The loathsomeness at the centre of it all. She let herself fall forward again and the stones pressed into her face. She spread her hands upon the grass, upon the stones, and attempted to lift her head. She felt the sun burning into the back of her neck as if it was directed through a prism. She thought, *I have got to get up.* Gasping and sobbing for breath she got to her feet and as if still blind and yet seeing began to run as fast as she could along the level floor of the cutting.

"Isn't it a magic place?" said Peter. "Why, Morgan, what's the matter? Whatever is the matter?"

Her body gave way again and she sat down abruptly with legs outstretched, leaning back against the longer grass. Her heart was pounding violently but her vision seemed to have returned and the awful light was gone. She wiped her mouth.

"What is it, Morgan?"

"Just a case of panic," she said.

Peter was silent. Then he said gravely, "Yes, Pan might be here."

"I don't know what his name is," said Morgan, "but he was certainly here just now."

"Or it might be a touch of the sun," said Peter.

"Or it might be a touch of the sun!" She laughed weakly. "Are you feeling sick?"

She breathed deeply. Her head was spinning but the nausea was gone. Just breathe quietly, deeply. "No, I feel odd, but not sick now."

"Rest a bit," said Peter. "Then we'll go back to the car. You're not frightened now?"

"No. It's strange. I *was* frightened, terribly. One can have these open-air nightmares, meet open-air ghosts, in summer. But now it's quite gone."

"Lie back in the grass."

"No, it's better to sit up. I feel all right."

The scene was there before her again, the yellow grass of the slopes alive with flowers, the green grass of the track, wiry and short as if it had been cut, as if the place were a garden, as if it were still a road, but a road not trodden by human feet. The hot air was thick with flowery scents and subtle dry emanations. The insects were hissing and murmuring in the honeyed forest of the grass. But now it was suddenly more beautiful to her, more intensely coloured and more absolutely here, under a sky which had resumed its blue. It was as if she had passed through a screen into some more primitive and lovely world, as if she were millenia away in the past or in the future in some paradise of undimmed experience and unblurred vision. "How beautiful it all is," she said. "How infinitely beautiful. I worship it."

"It's certainly an enchanted place," said Peter. He sat down beside her on the grass. He was still looking at her in a puzzled and anxious way.

"I don't mean this place," said Morgan. "I mean the world, the universe, everything that is. All is good, all is beautiful. Heaven is round about us."

"Morgan, are you really feeling all right?" said Peter.

Morgan turned to him. She had to prove it to him now. If she could only *prove* it. "Things are good, Peter."

He stared at her, wondering how to take her words. They were close together now, their hands almost touching on the grass. Peter's plump face was flushed and reddened by the sun, his eyes clear and blue, his long floppy hair bleached and glinting. He looked at her, serious, puzzled. "I think things aren't good," he said in an obstinate voice. "There's war, and hunger, and terrible injustice. I think things are bad."

"No, good, good," she said. "What seems bad is just apparent. If one thing is good then all things are, if one thing is intact and precious and absolutely beautiful then everything is. That's it. One simply needs a starting point."

"Well, nothing in the world," said Peter, "is intact and precious and absolutely beautiful. Everything is contaminated and muddled and nasty and slimed over and cracked."

"Something is good," she said. "Something is. This is." She lifted up a feather-leaved stem covered with tiny vetch flowers. Each flower was purple above and blue beneath and very faintly striped as if the colour had been drawn in by repeated strokes of a very fine pen.

"Oh, *nature*," said Peter. "I don't count that. That's just stuff. I mean *our* things. Find me one of those and I'll be impressed."

"What about," she said, "what about, what about . . . What about this?

> "Full fathom five thy father lies,
> Of his bones are coral made.
> Those are pearls that were his eyes,
> Nothing of him that doth fade,
> But doth suffer a sea change
> Into something rich and strange.
> Mermaids hourly ring his knell.
> Hark now I hear them,
> Ding dong bell."

There was silence. The insects buzzed and whispered and behind their small patient frenzy the hot stifling air sighed with its own stillness.

Peter and Morgan were staring at each other.

"Yes," said Peter very softly. "Yes. That is—perfect. And— Oh Morgan—"

Morgan took off her glasses. The next moment she and Peter were locked in each other's arms.

Morgan shifted her knees, drawing the boy's body close up against her own. She could feel the firm sweaty flesh through the flimsy shirt. Her arms were locked behind his shoulders and her lips quested over his hot cheek. His hands moved upon her back, gentle at first, now suddenly violent. Their heads, pressed bone to bone, struggled for space and their lips met and remained joined.

After some time Morgan opened her eyes and began feebly to thrust him away. After that they kissed slowly and deliberately, eyes open, several times. Morgan sighed, Peter groaned. Their bodies parted a little.

"Oh heavens—" said Morgan.

"I'm awfully sorry," said Peter.

"Don't be sorry. I think it's one of the nicest surprises I've ever had in my life."

"I didn't expect it either. But you know—you've always been for me—someone very special."

"That's good."

Morgan knelt now, pulling down her cotton dress. Peter tucked his shirt into his trousers, half got up, and then sat cross-legged. They were not touching each other. They stared luminous-eyed.

"Morgan, I am sorry— But you see— Please let this mean something."

"It does mean something," she said.

"It's not just part of that—vision—or whatever it was you had just now? It is a real thing in the ordinary world?"

"Yes, Peter, it is a real thing in the ordinary world. Perhaps we're both a little—suffering from shock. But it is real, my dear, and it's good. It's part of the good that I saw—only this isn't just an apparition."

"Then kiss me again."

She kissed him slowly, more gently. "Dear, dear child."

"You see me as a child?"

"Inevitably in a way. I've known you as a child. And yet also of course you're not. You are so big, so tall. You are a stranger to me. And a man."

"I've never been in love, Morgan. Oh, I've had girls, that's different. But I've never really been in love."

"You will be."

"I think I am now." He took her by the shoulder, frowning, not letting her draw away.

"No, no. This is something else. It—"

"Why not? I've always loved you. I could never tell you before. I didn't in that sense know before. But now I've grown up, and my love for you has grown up too."

"That's how it seems to you, but—"

"I want you terribly. Would you let me make love to you? Morgan, please, here, now, in this magic place. It's obviously *meant*. And you said this was part of the other thing, its real part. We must make love, please, please. It would be a crime not to."

Morgan felt her head spinning again. She desired Peter, she wanted intensely to let him make love to her, here, now, in this magic place. But she felt with equal intensity, though entirely without clarity, the imposition of a veto. "No."

"Why not? We aren't conventional people. No one would ever know. And it needn't ever happen again if you don't want. But it *must* happen, now, it *must*."

Morgan held her head in her hands. She thought, Is that awful giddiness going to begin again? If only she could speak to him clearly, it was so important, what she wanted at that moment to try to say. "Wait, wait—

"Peter, listen," she said at last. "I love you. That's the essential thing, the thing that's revealed. I won't stop loving you. But if we make love it will all be different, there'll be a story, a drama—"

"Well, why not? I'm mad about you, Morgan."

"You mustn't be."

"Why ever not? You're not so much older than me, and even if you were— You're my mother's sister, but that's what's so marvellous. You're like my mother and yet you're quite different. That makes you perfect."

"Oh Peter, Peter—"

"I know about all that old stuff. But what matters is whether there's real deep love, love that comes from the whole person. I love you in this whole way. Morgan, darling, let's make love, I know you want to, I *know*."

"Peter, please, let's *think*." She stared at him, her two hands clutching her head, moving her head a little to and fro as if it were an alien object. "Yes, I do want you. You're beautiful and young and dear. But there's something much more important at stake here. There's something to *win*." If only she could find the eloquence, if only she could *see*, and that would bring the eloquence.

"I *am* in love. And you're the special one, the real one. With the others it was just casual and rotten. Now I feel—"

"Stop it, Peter. Listen. You're thinking of yourself. Think about me. You may not feel any gap between us, but I feel it. I feel responsible—oh, all right, but I was going to say it isn't that. It's something very much deeper that I need and that you, and possibly only you, can give me."

"What is it, Morgan? If I can give it I'll give it."

"Innocent love."

Peter was silent, frowning at her against the sun. "Does that mean not going to bed?"

Morgan burst into sudden peals of laughter. Peter continued to frown.

"Oh Peter, you make me so happy. Don't you see that? Don't you see that *that's* the essential thing? Love-making seems so vital to you because you haven't done much of it. I've probably done too much. No, I know it is important, but just now I feel so selfish, so intelligently selfish. I couldn't see clearly before but now I see. Peter, I've been so terribly unhappy and so terribly muddled.

Well, you know. I feel that if I could only have someone to love innocently, someone to look after a little, someone for whom I was a bit responsible in a natural sort of way, it would do me so much good. You said just now that I was 'perfect.' Well, for me, you're perfect too, you just fit, you see, you fit the role, you're exactly what I need. When I came home I thought, Hilda, family, to be looked after, but it wasn't enough. I just felt excluded, however kind you all were, I felt I was on the outside of your real concerns. But now *you* can let me in. We'll love each other, innocently, with a *happy* love. Oh Peter, I've never in my life had a happy love. Let me have it here. Please understand. *Please.*"

She reached out and tried to grasp him, but Peter's hand was unresponsive. He was still frowning. "You haven't answered my question, Morgan. Does this plan of yours mean not going to bed?"

"Yes."

Peter's frown gradually cleared. He began to look rueful. He said, "Oh dear."

Morgan began to laugh again, and found that she was suddenly shedding tears, happy tears. "Oh, darling Peter, don't be angry. You'll find wonderful girls. But I'll always be special. And you'll always be special for me."

"You do mean that 'always'?" he said. "You said you'd go on loving me. You will, won't you? I feel now I couldn't bear it if you ever stopped."

"Of course I'll go on loving you, sweet dear child. No, no, don't be angry. This must be a *good* place, an invulnerable place. Something not threatened by time and change. Don't you see how important this could be for both of us?"

"I think you could help me—a lot."

"I think you could help me too. You have helped me."

"Morgan, you're crying."

"It's odd, I feel suddenly released. It's so moving. I've felt shut in for such a long time—shut in by nightmares and shut in by sort of—excitement. But this isn't nightmares or excitement, it's real, it's something *free.*"

"Free. I suppose if it's free it must be good."

"Of course, that's just what I mean. Let us be good to each other, Peter. Human beings are so mechanical, certain relations, certain situations, inevitably make one behave rottenly. This one can do the opposite. We can be a blessing to each other. We're *framed* to do each other good. You do see now?"

"Yes," he said, still a little dubiously.

"Then you agree? It's a compact?"

"I hope it's not in the compact that I can't even kiss you." Morgan seized him round the neck.

A few minutes later they were walking back hand in hand along the green grassy track toward the car.

Morgan's tears of joy were dry upon her cheek. She thought, *This* is happiness, *this*. I'd forgotten what it felt like. Happiness is free innocent love. It's so different from everything else that I've been up to almost all of my life. The rest remains, tangled, awful, the decisions to be made, the pain to be caused and suffered, the unpredictable edicts of the gods, the machine. But this is outside the machine. This is felicity, blessing, luck, sheer wonderful utterly undeserved luck. It can come to me after all. Oh, *good!*

🕂 | S I X T E E N

"I don't think you can *quite* wear that with that, dear," said Simon to Morgan.

Morgan had called in unexpectedly. She rang up from Barons Court station and then came round. She had been at a cocktail party near by, she said, but got bored and wanted to see Simon. It was half past six and Axel was not yet home. Simon was delighted.

Morgan was sitting beside him on the yellow sofa in the diminutive drawing-room. She was rapidly consuming a glass of gin. She was flushed and perhaps faintly tipsy. She seemed to be rather elated.

She fingered the necklace of dark amber beads. She was wearing a silk dress of a dark blue and scarlet zigzag pattern. A small tasselled blue velvet cap sat, a little awry, on the back of her head, making her steel-rimmed spectacles and her clever face seem to belong to some handsome learned Jewish boy.

"The beads? I thought they'd go all right with the dress."

"With a strongly patterned dress like that you shouldn't really wear any jewellery, darling. It just confuses the effect."

"Dearest Simon, you were always on at me about my clothes in the old days, remember? And you were always quite right of course. I haven't really got the faintest idea how to dress."

"Let me plan your wardrobe!"

"I'd love that! You are so clever at making things pretty. Look at the way you've arranged those artificial flowers on the mantelpiece."

"They aren't artificial, they're dried."

"Well, look at them anyway. And those yellow roses in the black vase with eucalyptus and iris leaves or whatever they are. Who would have thought of that?"

"Montbretia, actually. I got them from Rupert's garden. It's a fallacy that roses have to be by themselves."

"Darling Simon, you always make me want to laugh so. I am so glad to see you. How happy you make me feel!" Thrusting out the hand containing the glass and spilling a little upon the carpet she leaned forward and kissed his cheek. Simon hastened to kiss her back. More gin got spilt.

"I hear you took Peter to Cambridge yesterday."

"Yes. He saw his supervisor. He's going to be good."

"You mean he'll go back in October?"

"Yes, of course he will. I don't think he was ever serious about not going back."

"I think he was. I think you're a miracle worker."

"No, no. Just a little sense and a little affection. I'm afraid Peter was very naughty to you the other day, wasn't he?"

"Oh, I've forgotten all about that."

"I doubt if you have, Simon. I wouldn't if I were you. Shall I make Peter apologize to you? I can make him do anything I want these days."

"Oh, heavens no, Morgan, let it drift. I'll make my own peace with Peter. And I'm not such a sensitive plant as you imagine. I've had plenty of experience of being sneered at!"

"Poor Simon."

"I'm all right. I'm fine."

"How does married bliss really suit you, Simon? Do you never yearn for the mad old hunting days? The strange adventures you used to tell me about?"

"No, I'm happy now." It was true. The old days had their charm, but only in memory. Simon felt, as he so often felt when he thought suddenly and intensely about Axel, a sort of lifting supporting tide of love. He smiled at Morgan.

"Do you think you're really monogamous, Simon?"

"With Axel, yes."

"Ah well. Time will show. Come, I don't mean anything by that. Give me some more gin, my dear."

"You're looking so marvellous, darling, as if something divine had happened to you."

"I feel better," she said. "Of course there's still so much— But I feel better. I can cope. Perhaps something divine has happened to me."

"What?"

"I've made a discovery."

"Tell me! Or is it a secret?"

"It is possible to love people."

"Oh. I knew that already, actually."

"No, but I mean really, securely, in innocence. Falling in love is something different, it's a form of madness. I think I just didn't realize that at this moment in time I was really capable of noticing other people at all or that I could come to care for people in a new way, in an unselfish unfrantic sort of way. I feel I've won a victory and I'm rather pleased with myself. There are good surprises after all."

"I'm not sure that I understand you," said Simon, "but it sounds splendid. I only hope that you love *me*. And I don't even mind if you're selfish or frantic!"

"Of course I love you, darling. It was to tell you that that I left that stupid party."

"Oh Morgan—how marvellous—how terribly sweet of you. I must kiss you for that." Simon put his glass down on the carpet. He took Morgan's glass carefully out of her hand and put it beside his own. Then he took her in his arms and kissed her, first laughingly. Then they both looked at each other and kissed again, gravely.

"Dear Simon, I've always been terribly fond of you, you know that."

"And I of you. I so much wanted you to come home. Let's love each other and look after each other a bit."

"How strange that you should say just that. Yes, let's. The world is so full of violence. It's good to find a love that's gentle."

"Let's meet often. No, let me keep on holding this hand. Here's your glass."

"I doubt if Axel— Ah, well. I've moved into digs of my own, by the way, in Fulham. I'm not with Hilda and Rupert any longer. I felt I must have a separate place where I can see people. It will do me good, it may even help me to think. You'll come and see me in my new place?"

"Of course I will!"

"That's good. Simon, I feel I've got to get to know you all over again. You know how one suddenly feels one must *explore* one's old friends? Tell me about yourself, about your new self. I don't even know how you got fixed up with Axel. I can't recall your being friendly with him in the old days. I suppose you met him at Rupert's? I remember Axel used to come to dinner occasionally. I met him there myself."

Simon reached behind Morgan and pushed the black Wedgwood vase of roses and eucalyptus a little farther away and put his glass down on the polished surface of the table, first smoothing it across the dark blue sleeve of his jacket to make sure that there was no gin on the bottom of it. He settled himself, still holding Morgan's hand, in the shaded warm quiet of the room. The window was open upon the sunny evening, but there was no sound from the road; only at times came the drone of an aeroplane homing to London airport. It gave Simon an intimate happy feeling to be talking to Morgan about Axel.

"Yes, I met Axel quite often at Rupert's, but I didn't really take him in. Axel is so terribly reserved. I can imagine people not liking him, thinking he's proud or conceited or even unkind. I admired him rather, I must say, he's so fearfully clever, but he made me feel uncomfortable. And of course I hadn't the faintest idea that he was queer. I don't think Rupert had either."

"But he might have known that you were queer," said Morgan. She squeezed his hand. "That is, if you *are* queer, dearest Simon!"

Simon thought for a moment and then smiled. "I won't ask you if you think I look it. I know I look it. Whereas Axel doesn't. Oh yes, he knew. But he thought that I—"

"Was hopelessly promiscuous? Forgive me!"

"Yes," said Simon. "That was it." He had talked this through with Axel a hundred times. There was always a strange pain and a strange pleasure involved. Of course he had been promiscuous. It had taken a long time to persuade Axel that he had changed. How easily he might have missed Axel altogether. It was Simon's great luck that Axel, absolutely against his own judgement, fell in love. Axel in the bonds of love waited, had to wait, to listen to Simon's explanations, to hear Simon's vows. Oh, Simon had been eloquent. But it had taken a long time. And Simon had been very frightened.

"Well, what suddenly brought you together?" said Morgan.

"He did." Simon pointed to the photograph which hung beside the fire-place, the photograph of a Greek statue of a youth.

"He? How ever? What is he, some Greek thing?"

"A *kouros,* a youth, an Apollo as they sometimes call them. Archaic, fifth century B.C. National Museum at Athens."

"Let me look at him," said Morgan. She returned to the sofa and slid her hand back into Simon's. "Yes, go on."

"I was in Athens," said Simon, "by myself . . ." That was pure chance too. He had intended to have a companion. But the companion developed stomach trouble and had to be left behind in Rome. Simon did not reveal this absentee's existence to Axel until very late in proceedings. It cost him a scene.

On his first day in Athens, Simon, who had never visited the city before, went to the National Museum and noticed the *kouros.* Something happened at once. It is not impossible to fall in love with a statue. The *kouros* stood alone in a deep alcove and once inside the alcove one could be out of sight of the attendants, unless one of them should come to the corner and look in. There were, as it happened, very few other visitors. Simon had the *kouros* to himself. He could not resist touching it. With a fearful backward glance he drew his hand rapidly down the calf of the leg. Then he walked nonchalantly out of the alcove. But he knew even then that he was caught. He walked round the museum, looking with ostentatious seriousness and blind eyes at the other things. Then he went back to the *kouros.* He returned that afternoon. He returned the next morning and the next afternoon.

The marble was warm and golden and very slightly rough. The modelling of the figure had an exquisiteness of sensitive detail which gave itself voluptuously to the questing fingertips. The *kouros,* which was about six feet high, stood on a pedestal with its navel just about level with Simon's eyes. His hands could reach up as far as the shoulders and could just touch the serrated line of stiff curls at the back. He could not caress the face. But, coming back day after day, he caressed everything else. His fingers explored the bones of the long straight legs, the hollow of the thigh, the heavenly curve of the narrow buttocks, the flat stomach and the noble pattern of the rib cage, the pretty eye-shaped navel, the nipples of the breasts, the runnel of the back, the shoulder blades. He lightly stroked the feet, probing between the long separated toes; he reverently touched the penis. He looked up into the serene divine countenance: huge-eyed, long-nosed, so enigmatically smiling. After a while fingers were not enough. He had to worship the statue with his lips, with his tongue. He kissed the buttocks, the thighs, the hands, the penis, first hastily and then with slow adoration.

He grew bolder and bolder. One of the attendants began to be suspicious. Simon was spending so much time in with the *kouros*. The attendant would come and peep suddenly round the corner. But some sixth sense always told Simon when this was going to happen and he relinquished his contact and was found staring innocently into his guide-book. The relinquishment was pain. When other visitors came to see the *kouros* he would walk round the rest of the gallery, hastening back soon in the hope that they had gone away. In the evening when the gallery was closed he went to the Acropolis or walked dreamily in the garden near to the figure of Byron expiring in the arms of Greece. He felt blissfully happy.

On the fifth morning he had been in the museum for some time. It was very hot. He had just been on his routine circuit of the other rooms. He came back and to his joy found the *kouros* alone again. He walked round to the side of the statue and laid his hand lightly in the small of the back. Then he drew it downward very slowly, outlining the curve of the buttock, and led his fingers gently in onto the interior of the thigh. At that moment he realized that someone was watching him. It was Axel.

Axel had just come round the corner of the alcove and was regarding the little love scene with gravity. Simon recognized his intruder at once and felt an immediate pang of alarm. But for some reason he stood there paralysed and did not remove his hand from its exquisite position. After a moment Axel moved forward and with great deliberation and absolute solemnity laid his hand on top of Simon's.

Half an hour later they were sitting in a café drinking ouzo. Axel, after that first gesture, had retired into formality. But a faint humorous gleam in his eye declared both that he realized the magnitude of his indiscretion and that he did not care. "It could never have happened in the British Museum, dear boy," he told Simon later. They sat in the café and talked about Greek politics, about Byron, about hotels, about Axel's journey (it was his first morning in Athens), about food and drink, about an excursion to Delphi and about the appalling rate of exchange, so unfavourable to the pound. Each casually elicited the information that the other was alone.

From that first moment of contact Simon had known that something quite amazing had occurred. He gazed and gazed at Axel in the café. Axel looked quite different, he looked strange, he looked glorified. Simon ached to touch him. He was already in an agony of calculation about his chances. He felt sick with joy and terror. He thanked the gods that he really was alone. He prayed with the humility of true love to be favoured far far beyond his desserts. He prayed to Apollo, he prostrated himself in thought before the figure with which he had taken such strange liberties. Axel continued to talk about antiquities and Greek wine, but the humorous look remained in his eye and filled Simon with wild wild hope. They separated before lunch at Axel's decree. Axel shook hands and departed to his hotel: but it had been agreed that they should meet in the evening. They met and drank a great deal too much retsina. Simon went back with Axel to Axel's hotel room. Axel, still formal and distant, brought out some whisky. Simon took the bottle and the glass out of his hand. They stared at each other. Then Simon slowly slid his arms round Axel's waist. It was his greatest moment of relief when he felt that his embrace was being returned. Then the argument started.

Axel had lived alone for years. He hated trouble, he hated emotions. He admitted to being captivated, but he blamed himself for having shown it. He blamed the sun, the city, even the *kouros* which he had already visited that morning and which he had known from photographs but never seen before. He blamed the ouzo and the retsina and the whisky, which by this time they were both drinking freely. He explained lucidly to Simon, and he did not spare Simon in his explanations, that they were homosexuals of completely different types. He, Axel, was a naturally monogamous person. He wanted to live with someone in absolute fidelity and truthfulness and trust. He had done so once and he knew that it was possible. But that had been long ago and he had for years been resigned to doing without what he now regarded as, for him, an impossible blessing. He dwelt on his great age (forty-two) and on Simon's extreme youth (twenty-nine). He analysed the weaknesses of Simon's character. Simon was by nature frivolous, inconstant, evasive, impulsive, irrational, shallow. "Then how can you love me?" cried Simon. "Love has nothing to do with *merit*," said Axel irritably. "Then you *do* love me, Axel, you've just admitted it!" According to Axel, however, nothing followed from that. "But we can't just *leave* each other, Axel!" "Why not? I don't want to be cut in pieces by this thing. I've had enough. I'm too old to suffer." "Why should you suffer, my darling? I love you." "So you imagine, but you would soon be unfaithful. And you would tell me lies. I would look into your eyes and I would know that you were lying and I would be in hell. Better to leave it here."

But that proved to be impossible. They were both by now too much in love. They returned to England and Axel, with loud professions of misgiving and disapproval, took the shallow frivolous inconstant irrational boy into his bed. The argument continued. "You'll leave me." "I won't, I'll never leave you." "You'll lie to me." "I swear I won't." Simon used all the force of his great love to persuade his friend of his fidelity. At last Axel was convinced, almost.

"So that was how it happened," said Morgan, as Simon's story came at last to its end. "How extremely romantic! So a god really brought you together."

Simon had been quite excited and elated by telling her the story. His face was flushed and his heart was racing. He squeezed Morgan's hand. "Yes, we were blessed."

"What a priceless story. I never knew, Rupert never said—"

"I've never told Rupert, for heaven's sake!"

"Really. Have you ever told anyone else?"

"No, of course not. I haven't told anyone except you."

"That pleases me very much," said Morgan. "Simon—"

"Yes, dear?"

"Did you tell Axel about what happened that day at Julius's flat?"

"No," said Simon. He felt suddenly cold, as if the sun had gone in.

Simon had felt unhappy, at moments very unhappy, about not having told Axel. But he had had little difficulty in not telling him. Axel, very overwhelmed by *Fidelio*, had made only the most cursory inquiries about Simon's evening. And afterward it would somehow have seemed unbearably artificial to raise the matter apropos of nothing. Simon thought, It's over, it will now drift without consequences into the past, it is after all completely trivial and it doesn't matter. He found himself worrying about it all the same, partly because the incident itself had been distressing and in some way nasty, partly because he was afraid that Axel would discover that he had concealed it, and partly because he could not now quite make out why he *had* concealed it. He had been struck by Julius's saying that Axel was dignified and would feel let down. That was undoubtedly true. And could one tell such a story about a girl, especially if she asked you not to? Yet were these reasons good enough and were they the real reasons?

Simon had an uneasy feeling that in keeping silent he was protecting himself rather than sparing Axel or Morgan. Axel must never see him in a certain light. Yet surely it was all unimportant, he told himself, and not worth worrying about.

"Good. I was sure you wouldn't," said Morgan. "I rather wanted to ask you though. Let that be a little secret between us." She kissed his cheek and rubbed her own cheek against his. "Let me decorate you!" She took off the necklace of dark amber beads and put it round Simon's neck. "There! It suits *you* all right.

Though I think it would improve the effect if you took off your jacket."

Simon laughed and pulled his jacket off. He was wearing a duck-egg blue cotton shirt today. Oh, the soft caress of very fine cotton after the slippery touch of nylon! It meant he had to iron it, though. He lifted the beads a little, surveying them against the blue background. The effect was delightful. "You see what I mean, Morgan? You should wear these beads with a plain dress, preferably a blue dress."

"They quite transform you, Simon dear!"

"How pretty they are. I think I remember them; you've had them for years."

"Yes. They got broken. Tallis mended them just now. He sent them through the post."

"Oh."

"Simon, don't ask me about Tallis."

"I wasn't going to, darling."

"You've got so much more tact than your brother. I've decided that time will arrange everything for the best. I'm just not going to worry about it. You don't feel you have to take sides, do you?"

"No. But if I did I'd be on your side."

"There's a good boy. You look so sweet, Simon. Let me complete the effect." Morgan took off the blue velvet cap and set it upon Simon's head, adjusting it on the dark slightly curly hair.

They were both laughing and Simon was just getting up to look at himself in the mirror when Axel came in through the door.

Simon exclaimed and hastily pulled the cap off. He got entangled with the necklace and took a moment to drag it with clumsy frantic fingers over his head. Morgan rose to her feet. Simon thrust the cap and the necklace at her rather unceremoniously and she put them into her handbag. Axel stared expressionlessly.

"Hello, Axel," said Morgan. She looked bland.

"Good evening."

"I just called on Simon. I'm so sorry I've got to go now."

"Ah, yes," said Axel.

"Well, good-bye, Simon darling. Don't forget about what we

said. And you will come and see me, won't you?" She patted
Simon's cheek. "Good-bye, Axel. Simon's been telling me all
about how you both flirted with a statue in Athens. It sounded
most amusing. Bye-bye."

Axel stood aside and Morgan went down the stairs. Simon hesitated, fluttered, ran down after Morgan, and waved her out of the
front door. She kissed her hand to him and then put her finger
on her lips. He ran upstairs to Axel.

Axel was leaning against the mantelpiece. His face was cold
and hard. "You told that woman all about those sacred things."

"Oh Axel," cried Simon, "I'm sorry, I see now I shouldn't have
done, I'm terribly sorry. She asked and I—"

"She *asked?*"

"She asked about how we met, and then I just enjoyed remembering it and—"

"I shall never forgive you."

"Axel, *please* don't say that!"

"Can't you see that she's completely malevolent, that she enjoys destroying things?"

"I don't think so. Really, she—"

"Well, she has destroyed this thing anyway."

"Axel, you don't—"

"You can take that photograph down, I don't want to see it
any more, it's spoilt."

"Axel, I know I shouldn't have talked, *please*—"

"And letting her dress you up like a pet monkey!"

"Axel—"

"She's vulgar and horrible."

"Just let me say—"

"I'm going out to dinner. Alone."

"But I've cooked an Irish stew!"

"You can eat it yourself."

"Axel, please forgive me."

Axel turned to go to the door. Still protesting, Simon shrank
away to give him room. Axel paused in the doorway. "You'd better
keep Friday night free. I suppose we may as well keep up appear-

ances for the moment anyway. Julius rang up and said he wanted to meet Tallis again."

"But will Tallis come?"

"Yes. I've fixed for us to dine at the Chinese restaurant."

"But couldn't we dine here? I'd love to cook—"

"What you'd love to is of little consequence. Julius likes Chinese food."

"Axel, please don't leave me like this. Don't be angry with me, I can't bear it."

"I shall never forgive you for having babbled to that bloody woman."

Axel shut the door sharply and marched away down the stairs. A moment later the front door banged.

Simon dissolved into tears. How could he have been so inconceivably foolish? He saw it all now, the vile indiscretion, the betrayal. Why had he not seen it earlier? He did not in his deepest heart believe that Axel would reject him utterly for this. But he knew that the wounds which he had inflicted upon them both would take long to heal and he wept bitterly over his own folly.

☙ | S E V E N T E E N

"You're late," said Morgan to Tallis, opening the door of the house in Seymour Walk. It was ten in the morning.

"Sorry."

"And what's that there?"

"A handcart. Or barrow."

"Good God, are those my things on it?"

"Yes. I thought you wanted them brought."

"Of course I did, but I imagined you'd bring them in a car."

"I haven't got a car," said Tallis.

"Well, you must know people with cars. Even you. Do you mean to say you pushed that cart all the way from Notting Hill through all that traffic?"

"It's downhill," said Tallis.

"That's just the sort of thing you would do to upset people and put them in the wrong. It's not funny."

"I didn't mean—"

"If I'd known I'd have borrowed Hilda's car."

"Sorry."

"Better get the stuff upstairs anyway. I'm on the first floor."

"Those cardboard boxes with the books in may bust. Better unload them a bit."

"You are a fool, you've brought all those tins. I don't want the tins."

"Leave them on the cart then."

"No, I'll have them. They may come in handy. And they seem to be mixed in with all the rest."

They began to carry cardboard boxes up the stairs, boxes of books, boxes of clothes, boxes containing hairy jumbles of brushes and combs and tins of asparagus and dried-up cosmetics and old handbags. The boxes, propped crazily on top of each other, splitting apart at the edges and giving way at the bottom, covered the floor of Morgan's sitting-room.

"You might have sorted out the junk first," said Morgan.

"I didn't know which was junk."

"I don't want all this stuff. Half of it will have to be thrown away. Look at those old moth-eaten jumpers. I don't want moths here."

"I didn't know— I didn't look properly."

Tallis felt sick with emotion and aching with tiredness. He had not slept. It was partly nervous anticipation of seeing Morgan. He had wanted to be alert and decisive. He had spent the first part of the night lying rigid and telling himself how important it was that he should sleep. Later there had been familiar and wearying phenomena: the booming sound, the sense of imminent light which never quite became light. He was restless, physically exasperated, his nerves ringing with awareness and expectancy. Was he supposed to be pleased? His body took on a peculiar quality at these times, a sense of his feet not touching the ground. He knew that this was an illusion, but the sensation was very definite and persistent. If he lay down he seemed to float. If he knelt down he seemed to fly. Had this been ecstasy when he was younger? He could not remember. Now it just tired him out.

In a mechanical and repetitious way these exhausting manifestations were accompanied by the idea of love. The connection was mechanical and puzzling and Tallis seemed to know merely by some sort of external association or semi-conscious memory, and not by direct experience, that this concept was somehow involved. He accepted the connection, since he had by now almost entirely given up speculation. He felt a bond at such moments not with anything personal but with the world, possibly the universe, which became a sort of extension of his being. Occasionally the extension was gentle and warm, like the feeling of a river reaching the sea. More often it was uncomfortable or even horrible, as if he had immense dusty itching limbs which he could not scratch. Sometimes he felt it as an awful crippling weight, as if a steam-hammer were very slowly coming down on top of his head. On two extraordinary occasions the steam-hammer phenomenon had been immediately combined with the feet-off-the-ground phenomenon and Tallis had lost consciousness.

He never spoke to anybody about these matters. It was, he believed, from some quite other region that his sister visited him. Or the phantasm that seemed to be his sister. There were principalities and powers, tall cool detached things. Her visitations were enigmatic and often even menacing, yet perhaps she shielded him from what was other and worse. Perhaps because of her he did not suffer certain temptations. He suspected this because of a deep sense of lack of merit in certain regions where he was blameless. Can one being shield another from evil and if so must the shield itself grow dark? But about this too he had long ceased to speculate. She came only in those clear and vivid night appearances. Yet at times increasingly he had seemed to feel her presence in the house and had opened doors with fearful expectation upon empty rooms. The demons were other again. They were minor presences, riff-raff of creation, debris, and had merely a nuisance value. Occasionally they were even diverting. When there were other visitations they kept away, but annoyed him the more on their return. The great perils of his soul were formless.

"Well, that seems to be the lot," said Morgan. "Thanks."

They stared at each other across the boxes.

"What a nice flat."

"It's quite cheap," she said defensively.

"I mean, how nice you've made it."

"I can't get over that handcart."

"Sorry."

"If you say 'sorry' again I shall be sick."

It had seemed to Tallis quite natural to cart the stuff by hand. It was more than an ordinary car-load. And he often pushed people's furniture round the streets. But he ought to have thought how it would look to Morgan. Had he really done it to embarrass her or to make her feel compassionate or ashamed?

"Well, what have you been up to, Tallis, since we last met?"

"Nothing special. Usual stuff. This and that."

"Same old things? Tell me what you're doing during the rest of today, for instance."

"There's a meeting of student volunteers, they're going to paint houses. Then there's someone just out of jug I've got to see. Then there's a United Churchmen's Committee on prostitution. Then I've got a class. Then there's a probation officers' study group I promised I'd talk to. Then I've got to write a—"

"All right, all right. I can't think how you stand it. The boredom must be lethal. And it isn't as if it did much good anyway. You take on too many things and you don't do any of them properly. Isn't that so?"

"Yes."

"I see you're all spruced up. Is that for me or for the United Churchmen?"

"For you." Tallis was wearing a cleanish shirt and a tie of sorts.

"You even look as if you've had a shave for once. Your hands are filthy, however."

"Sor— I was cleaning out your room. There was an awful lot of dust. I meant to wash."

"My room?"

"I mean the room where your stuff was. I've let it from tomorrow." God, that was another thing. He would have to find time to dash round the junk shops and find something for furniture, since the room was supposed to be being let furnished.

"Haven't lost much time, have you?"

"I need the money," said Tallis.

"Are you getting at me again?"

"No," he said in exasperation. "I'm just damn tired. I'll wash my hands now, if you don't mind."

He went into the bathroom and shut the door and pressed his hands into his eyes. This sort of nervy aggressive non-communicative conversation was worse than no talk at all. If only he could be calm and gentle and eloquent and firm and all the excellent things he had resolved to be. And now there was the distracting irrelevancy of physical desire, whose promptings all seemed to have gone crazy. Even his physical love for Morgan was becoming unhinged and getting all mixed up with the muck-heap of his mind. If only it could be simple and tender once again. He tried to look at himself seriously in the mirror but his image looked stupid and mad. He dashed a good deal of cold water into his face and remembered to wash his hands. A lot of dirt came off on the towel. He went back to the sitting-room.

The flat was simple but pretty with small Victorian chairs, gay flowery cushions matching the design of the curtains but a different colour, clean rush matting, a small roll-top desk, and an elegant writing table beside the window with a square of worn red leather upon it. Morgan's letters were neatly piled under a paperweight of grainy green stone. There was a vase of freesias upon the white bookshelf.

"Have a drink, Tallis."

"No, thanks, I've got to— Yes, maybe I will."

"Gin? Nothing else in stock and nothing to dilute it with except water, I'm afraid. Here."

Tallis stood in the middle of the room holding his glass and surrounded by boxes. He tried to shift one of them a little with his foot, but a lot of very funny-looking stuff started to come out of the bottom. Morgan had seated herself upon the writing table and was swinging her legs. She was wearing a plain blue cotton dress and the necklace of amber beads. Tallis looked at the beads.

"Oh, thanks for sending the necklace, by the way. I meant to acknowledge it but I've been so busy with the move."

"Uh-huh."

"Say something, Tallis."

"What are you going to do?" said Tallis.

"Nothing."

"That's one thing you can't do," he said, "in this situation."

"I mean a glorious nothing. I propose to give myself to the the situation like a swimmer to the sea."

"I'm in no mood for metaphors," said Tallis. "Do you want a divorce?"

"Not particularly."

"Do you want to come back to me?"

"Not particularly. Things aren't going to be like that. I think I'm going to live quite differently. Why not, after all, there are plenty of ways of living. Did you have anybody while I was away?"

"No. Only fantasies."

"No one special living in the house?"

"Only Daddy and Peter."

"You know I took Peter to Cambridge?"

"Yes."

"And all's well. Peter eats out of my hand."

"So I gather," said Tallis, "but be careful."

"Peter just needs a little love."

"No. Peter needs a great deal of love. Don't mess around with Peter unless you've got a great deal to give."

"Well, I seem to have succeeded where you all failed. And don't look so sullen."

"Don't mess around with Peter," Tallis repeated, "unless you're really prepared to commit yourself to him in some serious and sensible sort of way. Peter needs permanencies."

"Why shouldn't I be serious and sensible? I'm going to love people. That's what I mean by living differently. That'll be my new way of life. I'm going to be free and love people."

"Oh, don't talk such sickening rot, Morgan!" said Tallis. He kicked the nearest box and several old powder compacts and a jar of cold cream came out of the bottom. He moved back to put his glass on the bookcase. He wanted to stop all this talk and take her in his arms but if only he could *think*. He sat down on one of the pretty but extremely hard arm-chairs.

"I thought you'd approve!" said Morgan, and she laughed self-consciously. "You were always one for love."

"You're mixing me up with Rupert. How does marriage fit in with this new policy of freedom and love?"

"I'm not sure that it does. Marriage is so old-fashioned and ex-clusive. But I don't at all mean that I don't want to see you."

"Do you or don't you want a divorce?"

"You haven't understood. It's just not important. Let it drift."

"I see. You might even love me too, in your free way, along with the rest?"

"Yes. Why not? If you're generous enough to accept my love. Or are you worrying about your property rights?"

"I'm worrying about not being able to bear it."

"Oughtn't you to try?"

"What about Julius?"

"Julius is my godfather. My father in god with a small g. He has shown me myself."

"I mean do you want to marry Julius or go on living with him or something?"

"I have a free relationship with Julius. He understands about these things. Have you any objection?"

"No," said Tallis, "but that's not the proper question. There's something absolutely wrong here. I mean it's the wrong policy, you can't do it, you don't understand the meaning of the words you use—" How could he explain it? He got up and went to the window and looked out at the rows of parked cars like fat multi-coloured pigs and the white wall and neat black well-painted woodwork of the expensive little house opposite. Or should he just seize hold of her and shout? Would that work?

"Sorry, Tallis, but I think I do understand at last. When I married you I was childish and half asleep."

"Maybe. But all the same—" He concentrated on the cars.

"Well, now I'm wideawake. Julius woke me. Tallis, I thought you were my virtue. But I realized you were really my vice."

"I'm your husband."

"That ugly heavy word. That cannot name anything here."

"It names an important fact, Morgan. I think you are mistaken about your nature. You need deep belongingness and connections and stability."

"And why shouldn't I have them all over the place? Or are you trying to use your authority?"

"Funny. Rupert talked about authority. But it's nothing to do with authority or property rights. What can I do or ask for in the ridiculous position I am in now? I am sure that you love me. I just want that love to have a decent chance."

"You think I'm not telling the truth?"

"I think you're hopelessly theory-ridden." He turned to look at her. "You're chasing empty abstractions. What *happens* will be quite different."

"You have power, Tallis," she said. "You have power, I don't deny it. But I'm not going to undergo you again. You always somehow made me feel ashamed. You and your false simplicity."

Tallis was silent.

"Sorry, Tallis, I don't want to be unkind. But the path for me is away from guilt and shame. I think I wanted to sink down into some deep deep sea with you. When I married you I felt I was killing myself. It seemed somehow wonderful at the time. But I couldn't kill myself. I couldn't even love in the end, down in that deep sea. I have to be outside, in the open, in the clear air, on the high places, free, free, free. It's only out in that clear fresh air that I can really love people. I have to follow the kind of love that I am capable of. Everybody must be guided by that."

"It sounds like sense," he said, "but somehow— Oh, how stupid you make me feel. Perhaps I am stupid, especially about you."

"No. It's just that I'm a much more complicated person than you are."

"You see, I feel that we're related, as if we were blood relations. I could as soon think of abandoning you as I'd think of abandoning Daddy."

"Really, Tallis, what a comparison! It's hardly flattering to me! Surely nothing but the grimmest sense of duty ties you to that dear old bore!"

"Sorry, I'm putting it terribly badly. Marriage is a symbolic blood-relationship, it's the creation of a new family bond."

"Well, I don't care for bonds, family or otherwise."

"I don't mean constraint. I mean real connection."

"Don't be sentimental, Tallis, I can't bear it. And don't talk about marriage as if it were a *condition*."

"It is a condition. All kinds of things are conditions and it's one. It relates the past to the present."

"As far as I'm concerned it was an arrangement. And as far as I'm concerned the past is finished, done for, gone."

"Morgan, please. I've searched— Let it not have been in vain."

"Now you really are going to pieces, Tallis. Come, how deeply have I hurt you? I'm interested!"

"Don't speak so."

"Tallis dear, don't appeal to my pity. If you want to impress me you must appeal to my moral nature and not to my compassion. Only you can't. You're not on the wave-length, you don't understand what I'm saying half the time. Oh Tallis, if you could only change a bit, just a little bit, be a little bit different from yourself! But it's no good, you'll never change."

"You do love me still."

"Of course I do, silly. We can talk to each other. I'll hope to meet you a lot in the future. We can have a more adult relationship."

"It doesn't make sense, kid."

"And don't call me 'kid' like that or I shall cry. Oh Tallis, you can make yourself look so beautiful sometimes. I wish you wouldn't. You're doing it on purpose. Come over here." He came to her slowly. "Tallis, let's be quiet for a minute."

"That's a good idea at last."

Tallis sighed very deeply. Morgan was still sitting on the writing table. He stood in front of her, studying her. Then he leaned against her knees and drew one hand down her leg. He took off one shoe and held the warm foot in his hand. He leaned closer until his cheek touched hers.

He felt a warm touch. Morgan had slipped the necklace of dark amber beads over his head and round his neck.

"What's that, Morgan? A charm?"

"An experiment. I don't want to do without you, Tallis. I want to have everything and you as well. I want to keep you on a lead."

"I love you," said Tallis.

"If you kneel down now I shall kick you in the face."

"I'm not going to kneel down, damn you." The shoe clattered to the floor. Tallis slipped his arms round her waist and pulled her off the table.

"Yoo hoo, Morgan!" There was a loud knock on the door.

Tallis released his wife.

Peter bounded in.

"Oh Morgan, darling! Hello, Tallis. Morgan, I just got your letter and came straight round; the char let me in. I've got the stuff. I've got a screwdriver and a hammer and those picture hooks and string and the light plugs and all the things you said. I got them all at the ironmonger's just here, and I've got you lots of things for your kitchen as well, drying-up cloths and pan-scrubbers and cleaning stuff and a *mop!* Look!"

Peter emptied out the contents of two shopping bags onto the floor in between the cardboard boxes.

"Peter, you're super!" She kissed him. "Have a drink. Tallis, don't go. I asked Peter to come and help me put everything in order. Lord, what a mess. Just look at it all."

"I must go," said Tallis.

"Oh, must you?"

"I've got to see those students." He moved to the door.

"Peter, you're a hero! Good-bye, Tallis dear, *see you.* Don't forget what I said."

He went down the stairs hearing their laughter.

Once out in the street he quickly began to push the handcart down into the Fulham Road and then up Hollywood Road. He pushed it into the side of the kerb and paused. The dark brown amber beads were still hanging round his neck. He took his tie off and tucked them down inside the collar of his shirt. A little later as he was pushing the cart across Redcliffe Square he stopped again and took his jacket off. The mounting sun shone down out of a sky of unflecked light blue. Sweat was pouring down his chest. The handcart was empty, but it was uphill all the way back.

❧ | EIGHTEEN

"Good heavens, Julius, you made me jump!"

Julius had suddenly materialized in the half light in Rupert's house. It was about nine o'clock in the evening.

"Sorry, Rupert. I couldn't find anybody so I went to the lavatory."

"I was in the garden."

"Do you always leave your front door open like that? Anyone could walk in and steal the Cézanne reproductions."

"Hilda must have left it open. She's just gone out to a meeting about the abatement of aeroplane noise."

"Hilda is so altruistic. Always busy serving others."

"She has a social conscience. And that's partly self-interest, after all."

"Well, could I trespass on *your* altruism, social conscience, and self-interest to the extent of a glass of whisky?"

"Of course, I was just going to offer it. Come on up to my study. Have you dined?"

"Yes. I was at a dinner party. But there were no attractive women. So I came away early. You said you wanted to see me?"

"Yes, but I didn't mean urgently. I'm so glad you've come now, though, it's a good moment."

Rupert turned the lights on in his study and pulled the curtains against the blue darkening evening. "Let's be shut in, shall we?" He produced whisky and glasses. Rupert sat at his big desk in the middle of the room. Julius pulled up an upright chair and sat at the other side of the desk. He stretched his feet out underneath the desk so that Rupert had to withdraw his. He yawned and stretched elaborately.

"No water, thanks, Rupert, I'll have it neat. I need some strong clean stuff after that ghastly dinner. Why are English hostesses so pretentiously inefficient? I've scarcely had a proper meal since I reached England."

"You need a holiday across the Channel."

"Even Paris couldn't feed me decently last time. Everything seems to be getting worse. Or else I'm getting intolerably old and finicky."

"Hilda and I discovered an excellent restaurant last time we were in Paris, quite cheap too. It's called A la Ville de Tours. In the Rue Jacob."

"*La cuisine Tourangelle.* I shall try it if I'm over. What are your holiday plans?"

"Oh, we're holidaying in England this year. I feel we should with the pound so rocky. We'll spend the second half of September at our cottage in Pembrokeshire."

"Nature, the country-side. How I hate all that. And no more small-town life for me either. From now on I want great big European cities. That was why I left Dibbins."

"Surely there were other reasons for that decision."

"Well, I was bored with that detestable squawky little campus and that unspeakably insipid main street. I can't think how I stood it for so long."

"You're the only man I know who enjoys presenting himself in an unfavourable light."

"Yes, I got fed up with the research too, but not for the reasons you think. In the end it was aesthetically unpleasing."

"I can imagine that one's general respect for the human race—"

"I have no general respect for the human race. They are a loathsome crew and don't deserve to survive. But they are destroying themselves quite fast enough without my assistance."

"You always profess cynicism, Julius. I wonder how many people you take in."

"It isn't cynicism. These little games will end civilization and probably end human life on this paltry planet in the not too distant future. Why are people ill now so much of the time with mysterious virus ailments? Little escapes from establishments like Dibbins—and there are such establishments all over the place and there will be more of them and more and more and more— filter into the outside world at regular intervals. It's practically impossible to prevent it, though of course these accidents are always hushed up. One day some really sensational virus, the absolute pet of some biochemical hack like myself, will get out and all human life will cease in a matter of months. This isn't science fiction, Rupert. Of course you won't believe me. A truth like that can't be believed. That's why the whole thing will go merrily on until it brings the whole rotten human experiment to an end for good and all."

Rupert was silent for a moment, studying his friend. Julius's face was calm and rather inward. It might have been the face of a man listening to music. The heavy-lidded violet-brown eyes were drowsy and unfocused, the long mouth serene and faintly smiling.

"I hope you're wrong," said Rupert. "Meanwhile we have to work on the assumption that there's a future. And of course there are plenty of things which we as free responsible citizens can do to make our leaders realize—"

"Rupert, Rupert, Rupert, your voice comes to me out of the past, out of some old history book, millennia away."

"I don't understand you, Julius."

"You just don't see what makes things happen in this locality. Never mind. You'll be accusing me of cynicism again. What was it you wanted to talk to me about?"

"Oh well," said Rupert, shifting his chair. "I just wanted to see you. And to be quite honest I'm rather worried about Morgan."

"Aha," said Julius, his attention now keenly on Rupert. "So you summoned me. The action of a free responsible citizen, of a free responsible brother-in-law. If you intend to horsewhip me you haven't got off to a very convincing start."

"Don't be an ass, Julius. I want your help. Hilda and I saw Tallis on Tuesday and he's obviously not going to make any move, and I thought—"

"Rupert, confess that you *despise* Tallis."

"Of course I don't," said Rupert irritably. "I think he's completely spineless—"

"But you don't despise him. All right, all right. Now where do I come in?" Julius took off his glasses and leaned forward with an air of enjoyment, his dark eyes aglitter with a benign twinkle.

"I should have thought you *are* in!" said Rupert.

"Ah. In a moment you will say, 'We are men of the world' and 'What are your intentions?' How wonderfully you illustrate the unreality of time!"

"We are not men of the world," said Rupert. "Let us pay ourselves that compliment. As for your intentions—well, what are they?"

"None, none, my dear Rupert. I have never been more innocent of intentions in my life!"

"Come, come," said Rupert. "You know how unstable Morgan is. And as far as I can see she's still in love with you."

"So?"

"So, to be extremely crude and blunt, I think you ought either to come to her and at least help her to decide whether she wants to divorce Tallis, or else you should clear off altogether."

"You mean leave London?"

"Yes, for the time being."

"Oh, but Rupert, I *adore* London. I've just decided to buy a house in the Boltons."

"*Have* you?" The thought of having Julius living two hundred yards away down the road struck Rupert as surprisingly alarming. Not exactly unpleasant, but alarming.

"Well, it's an idea. Perhaps I shall change my mind."

"You must be a rich man," said Rupert rather sourly.

"But it is *the* place to live. Don't you agree?"

"Yes, yes. But about Morgan— She can't make balanced decisions while you're sort of here and not here. You obviously paralyse her."

"Why don't you persuade *her* to go away?"

"She has duties here," said Rupert. "Surely you see—"

"Tormenting her husband? Of course. Poor old hubby."

"Have you seen her lately, by the way?"

"Not since a rather curious encounter some days ago. But I've had a long letter from her."

"What sort of thing did she say, if that's not an indiscreet question?"

"Not at all. I'll show you the letter. Oh dear, I haven't got it on me, I must have thrown it away. It was rather ecstatic. All about some new era of love and freedom which she proposed to inaugurate. She is such an intense girl."

"Morgan's a fool," said Rupert. "She's always lived in one dream world after another."

"Don't we all?"

"Tallis was one of Morgan's dreams. Tallis represented holy poverty or some such stuff. Then she woke up one morning and saw she just had a weak and unsuccessful man for a husband. That hurt her pride."

"So you don't blame me too much?"

"No. You were an efficient but not a formal cause."

"You relieve my mind! Tell me something about Tallis. Do you think he's epileptic?"

"Epileptic?" said Rupert, surprised. "No. That's never been suggested. As far as I know Tallis enjoys perfect health. He's tough as nails. Whatever put that idea into your head?"

"A passing thought, never mind. May I say that I think you are worrying too much about Morgan?"

"I just want the girl to be happy."

"Few people *just* want other people to be happy, dear Rupert. Most of us prefer our friends in tears. If by any unusual chance anyone does want others to be happy, he invariably wants them to be so as a result of his own busybodying."

"Possibly. But at my age, Julius, I don't worry too much about my motives. It's enough for me if I can see the right thing to do and do it."

"That's beautiful. I hope it comes in your book. Is that your book over there on the table, all those fat yellow notebooks? May I look at it?"

"Yes, certainly. It's pretty well finished now. Hilda wants us to celebrate. She'll be sending you an invitation."

"How charming. Shall we all have to make philosophical speeches like in the *Symposium?* I should enjoy that."

Rupert watched uneasily while Julius adjusted his spectacles and leaned over the table, opening the notebooks at random and tilting them toward the light of the nearest lamp, blinking and smiling his sly coy smile.

"You are well defended against pessimism, Rupert. All this cosy Platonic uplift. You ought to have been a parson."

"I hope it doesn't sound too high-minded. It's supposed to be philosophy, of a sort."

"Philosophy, philosophy," said Julius, returning toward his chair. "All human beings fly from consciousness. Drink, love, art are methods of flight. Philosophy is another one, perhaps the subtlest of all. Even subtler than theology."

"One can at least attempt to be truthful, Julius. The attempt has meaning."

"About these things, no. The Venerable Bede observed that human life was like a sparrow that flies through a lighted hall, in one door and out the other. What can that poor sparrow know? Nothing. These attempted truths are tissues of illusions. *Theories.*"

Rupert was silent for a moment. He knew that Julius was trying to upset him and he was determined not to be upset. He smiled at Julius, who was still standing, staring very intently, leaning a little on the back of his chair, and Julius smiled back with a flicker of his coy eyelids.

"I think you are the theorist," said Rupert. "You seem to hold some general view which makes you blind to obvious immediate things in human life. We *experience* the difference between good and evil, the dreariness of wickedness, the life-givingness of good. We experience the pure joys of art and nature. We are not pitiful sparrows and it is theological romanticism to say that we

are. All right, we are without guarantees, but we do know some
things for certain."

"Such as what?"

"That Tintoretto is a better painter than Puvis de Chavannes."

"*Touché!* You know my passion for the Venetian masters!
But we talk a lot of nonsense about art really, dear Rupert. What
we actually experience is minute and completely ambiguous compared with the great long tale we tell ourselves about it."

"I agree up to a point," said Rupert, "but—"

"No 'buts,' my dear fellow. Kant showed us conclusively that
we cannot know reality—yet we go on obstinately imagining
that we can."

"Kant thought we had inklings! That was indeed his point!"

"Kant was stupidly Christian. So are you, though you deny it.
Christianity is one of the most gorgeous and glittering sources
of illusion the human race has ever invented."

"Surely, Julius, you don't take the old-fashioned view that it is
merely a tissue of fabrications? Is it not, in its own way, a vehicle
of spirit?"

"Possibly. But what is that? Nothing could be more ambiguous."

"Spirit may be ambiguous," said Rupert, "but goodness isn't.
And if we—"

"As for evil being dreary, that's an old story too. Have you ever
noticed how naturally small children accept the doctrine of the
Trinity, which is after all one of the most peculiar of all human
conceptual inventions? Grown men show an equal facility for
making completely absurd metaphysical assumptions which they
feel instinctively to be comforting—for instance the assumption that good is bright and beautiful and evil is shabby, dreary,
or at least dark. In fact experience entirely contradicts this assumption. Good is dull. What novelist ever succeeded in making
a good man interesting? It is characteristic of this planet that the
path of virtue is so unutterably depressing that it can be guaran-
teed to break the spirit and quench the vision of anybody who
consistently attempts to tread it. Evil, on the contrary, is exciting

and fascinating and alive. It is also very much more mysterious than good. Good can be seen through. Evil is opaque."

"I would like to say exactly the opposite—" began Rupert.

"That is because you fancy something to be present which in fact is not present at all except as a shadowy dream. What passes for human goodness is in reality a tiny phenomenon, messy, limited, truncated, and as I say, dull. Whereas evil (only I would prefer some less emotive name for it) reaches far far away into the depths of the human spirit and is connected with the deepest springs of human vitality."

"I am interested that you want to change the word!" said Rupert. "I fancy you will soon try to substitute some more neutral term, such as 'life force' or some such nonsense, only I won't let you!"

" 'Life force'! Really, Rupert, I've got past that stage!"

"All right, evil has depths, though I don't think that nowadays they are all that unfathomable, but why not admit that good has heights? I don't even mind if you reverse the metaphor, so long as you allow the distance!"

"The distance is just what I don't allow, in the case of good. Let's keep your up and down picture, it's convenient and traditional. My point is that the top of the structure is *completely empty*. The thing is truncated. Human beings have often *dreamed* of the extension of goodness beyond the pitiful level at which they muck along, but it is precisely a dream, and a totally vague one at that. It is not just that human nature absolutely precludes goodness, it is that goodness, in that extended sense, is not even a coherent concept; it is unimaginable for human beings, like certain things in physics. Only unlike physics there isn't even any notation with which to indicate it, since it simply isn't there at all!"

"There have been saints—"

"Come, come, Rupert—with the knowledge which modern psychology has put at our disposal! Of course people have sacrificed themselves, but that has nothing to do with goodness. Most so-called saints really interest us because they are artists, or because they have been portrayed by artists, or else because they are men of power."

"But you admit there *is* goodness, even though it is limited and dull?"

"There is helping other people and letting oneself be imposed upon. This isn't very interesting and as you know it can proceed from all sorts of motives. And anything of this sort which does not proceed from self-interested motives is rare to the point where I take leave to doubt whether it exists at all! To be really gentle and selfless with moral impunity one would have to be God, and we know *He* isn't there!"

"On your view it seems far from clear why human beings ever conceived of the idea of goodness or thought it important at all!"

"My dear Rupert, you know as well as I do that there are hundreds of reasons for that! Ask any Marxist. Social reasons, psychological reasons. These ideas always help the powers that be. And they are very deeply consoling too."

"You make human beings sound like puppets."

"But they *are* puppets, Rupert. And we didn't need modern psychology to tell us that. Your friend Plato knew all about it in his old age, when he wrote *The Laws*, after he had given up those dreams of the high places which so captivate you."

"But if goodness isn't important, what is important, according to you? Though if we're all puppets I suppose 'important' is the wrong word too!"

"Precisely! Well, we know what moves people, dear Rupert. Fears, passions of all kinds. The desire for power, for instance. Few questions are more important than: who is the boss?"

"Though of course some people prefer to be bossed!"

"Yes, yes. It's all a question of choosing one's technique. The moral superstition is part of the consolation."

"Because people who are unhappy like to feel virtuous?"

"Well, that's one thing. And not just unhappy people either. You, for instance, Rupert. You may deny this too, but you feel very deeply persuaded that you are a virtuous man. You like to picture yourself as involved in a significant battle with self. You feel that you are upright and noble and generous, your life is orderly. You gain satisfaction from comparing yourself with others."

Rupert laughed. "I won't rise to that one, Julius," he said.

"That is why, forgive me, dearest Rupert, your big book will be no damn good. You do not even conceive of, let alone face or consider, the possibility that your world of good and evil is simply a consoling superstition."

"I agree that a sense of virtue consoles. But a sense of being justly judged consoles too."

"Why do you say 'but'?" said Julius. He had been staring intently at Rupert. Now he pushed his chair away and began to walk up and down the room. "That is what consoles most of all, most of all, most of all."

Rupert watched him for a moment. "Would it console you?"

Julius stopped in front of his friend. "Listen, Rupert. If there were a perfectly just judge I would kiss his feet and accept his punishments upon my knees. But these are merely words and feelings. There is no such being and even the concept of one is empty and senseless. I tell you, Rupert, it's an illusion, an *illusion*."

"I don't believe in a judge," said Rupert, "but I believe in justice. And I suspect you do too, or you wouldn't be getting so excited!"

"No, no, if there is no judge there is no justice, and there is no one, I tell you, *no one*."

"All right, all right. Have some more whisky."

Julius was staring down at Rupert. Now he was smiling and drooping his eyelids. "Well, well— I've enjoyed our talk. No thank you, Rupert. And now I think I must really go. I hope I haven't bored you. No more to drink, I have to look after my inside. Is life worth living? It depends on the liver. Freud's favourite joke. Good night, my dear fellow."

After Julius's departure Rupert sat for a long time thinking about what had been said. Was Julius wholly serious, half serious, or not serious at all? It was very hard to say and perhaps Julius himself did not really know. Rupert looked over at the pile of yellow notebooks, their neat order destroyed by Julius's inquisitive hand. Was it true that he had never, in all those tens of thousands of words, really questioned certain assumptions at all? His mind felt tired and hazy. Was it true that he believed himself to be virtuous? Well, why should he not believe that he had certain qualities of truthfulness and generosity and certain standards of decent behaviour? His life was orderly and open. To see this much was not to romance about saintliness. There *was* a difference between orderly lives and disorderly lives. Rupert drank some more whisky. He felt confused and uneasy. As he got up at last to take himself to bed he reflected, The trouble with poor old Julius is that he has had no philosophical training. When scientists talk philosophy they always tend to oversimplify.

Waiting for Hilda he went to bed and read Proust.

🕸 | NINETEEN

"Why, hello, Julius," said Morgan. "Are we on speaking terms?"

"Why not? How nice to see you, Mrs. Browne."

They had just met by accident in the Tate Gallery, at an exhibition of modern sculpture. Morgan had felt a violent shock which she seemed only a moment later to identify as having been caused by a glimpse of Julius's shoulders and pallid hair seen through a break in the crowd.

"Have you been here long?" said Morgan, fanning herself with her catalogue. "It's all very interesting, don't you think?"

"Interesting! When people don't understand something they

feel they have to say that! It's so conveniently non-committal!"

"Well, will you commit yourself?"

"Yes. This stuff is pure and absolute junk. And just look at all those asses staring at it with reverence! The human race is incurably stupid."

Morgan laughed. "All right. I'm not going to do battle for those objects. What a mob! I can hardly breathe. Let's get out and look at some real art."

They pushed their way out and emerged into the space and air of the long gallery. "I suppose it's too early for a drink?" said Morgan.

"Yes."

"Then let's go and look at the Turners. I want to talk to you."

"As you will."

There was no one with the Turners. Morgan sat down opposite one of the Petworth interiors and after a bit of wandering round Julius came and sat beside her.

"How *calm* great pictures make one feel," said Morgan. "I love these late Turners. Passionate turmoil held in perfect immobility. Elemental energy mysteriously constructed into space and light."

"Um."

"Don't you care for Turner?"

"Not much. A hopelessly derivative painter. Always copycatting somebody, Poussin, Rembrandt, Claude. Never finished a picture without ruining it. And he had far too high an opinion of himself. He should have remained a minor genre painter, that's about his level. I'm afraid his painting resembles his poetry."

"I didn't know he wrote poetry."

"He wrote pretentious doggerel."

"But you do like some painting, don't you, Julius? I remember when we went to Washington—"

"There is a characteristic pleasure in looking at certain pictures. But the whole thing is ephemeral."

"How do you mean, the whole thing?"

"Oh, this great legend of European art and literature. That rubbish we saw in the other room is a clear enough announcement that the show is over. In a hundred years or so nobody will have heard of Titian or Tintoretto."

"I hope you're wrong. Did you get my letter, Julius?"

"Yes. I'm afraid I didn't understand it. Was I meant to? It was rather long. I'm not quite sure that I finished reading it."

"I'm beginning to see myself clearly at last."

"A remarkable feat, if true."

"Ever since I've been grown-up I've been some sort of slave. I was always stupidly in love. Then there was that *idea* with Tallis. Then you—"

"I gathered there was to be some kind of new era."

"Yes. I suddenly got a vision of what it would be like to be free."

"Congratulations."

"Don't be tiresome, Julius. I suddenly saw how marvellous it would be to have free affections. And do you know who somehow made me see it? Peter."

"Who is Peter?"

"Peter Foster, Hilda and Rupert's son. You know."

"Oh, yes, of course."

"He's a very interesting boy."

"Very. He appears to live on nothing and do nothing."

"Hilda gives him quite a big allowance, only don't tell Rupert, it's a secret. Peter's going back to Cambridge in October. I persuaded him to."

"Really. I am afraid that I find young people rather boring."

"Peter's fallen quite madly in love with me. It's awful!"

"Don't pretend you aren't delighted."

"Well, of course I am in a way, though it's a bit embarrassing. But anyhow, I suddenly saw how wonderful it would be to love a whole lot of people, not in a frenzy, but freely, in *innocence*. That's what I felt with Peter—a sense of *innocence*. I've never before felt innocent as an adult."

There was silence. Julius looked at his watch. Morgan fidgeted with an incoherent desire to touch him. She wanted to pull roughly at his sleeve, pinch his arm, kick him. But by now some other people had come into the room.

"Well, Julius?"

"I don't know what you want me to say. You are always wanting other people to act in some drama which you have invented. I think you are in a silly emotional frame of mind. Why don't you try to do some *work?* You managed to work at Dibbins in spite of your thrilling sex life."

"Work will come. I've got to sort myself out first. I've got to find out how to love people with *my* kind of love. I've never really done that before."

"You'd better explain this to Rupert. It's more up his street than mine."

"I gather you had quite an argument with Rupert. He pretended not to be, but I think he was rather upset."

"I can't stand that sort of facile optimistic High Church Platonism. These sensitive people are so terribly absorbed in their own reactions."

"I know what you mean. Of course Rupert's always had a quiet easy life, even during the war. But I do think he'd be splendid in an emergency. When the Gatling's jammed and the Colonel's dead."

"I don't know what you are quoting. Presumably some dreary panegyric of British Imperialism. I have no idea what Rupert would do when the Gatling was jammed and the Colonel was dead. I was referring to his somewhat high-minded theorizing."

"Rupert is a bit pleased with himself. Of course he's got plenty to be pleased about, successful man, successful husband. I only wish he and Hilda wouldn't put it on display quite so much."

"I hate exhibitions of family life," said Julius.

"Yet you did enjoy living with me, didn't you, Julius, in that house in the woods? That was a sort of family life."

"Of course I enjoyed it."

"Then why are you so changed?"

"People get bored with things. I am bored with this conversation."

"I don't think you ever really loved me at all."

"That is the sort of remark which women make which makes

men sick, and which shows that women really are inferior. What's the matter now?"

Morgan had stiffened, half risen, and then sunk back again with an exclamation. "It's all right. I thought I saw Tallis. That man just going out. He's not really like him at all. I'm haunted by Tallis. I keep thinking I see him everywhere. Do you know, Tallis brought my books and things round to Seymour Walk on a *handcart!* That was typical. And his idea of a compliment was to tell me he'd as soon abandon me as he'd abandon his old papa!"

"What are his relations with his father?"

"I don't know. They quarrel endlessly."

"It could be a significant remark."

"Really, Julius! But hardly gallant. I feel rather especially bothered about Tallis at the moment, so no wonder I see these apparitions! I've just swindled him out of three hundred pounds!"

"How?"

"I owed Tallis four hundred and Rupert gave it me to pay him and I gave him a hundred and kept three hundred. Don't you think that's caddish?"

"Yes."

"Not a word, by the way, as Hilda doesn't know Rupert lent me the money. I never told her I owed Tallis anything."

"How does hubby fit into the new scene of free innocent loving?"

"He'll get his share."

"We'll all play ring-a-ring-a-roses?"

"Julius, we will be friends, won't we, you and I? It's terribly important. Your *thoughts* about me are so important. You know how someone else's consciousness could drive one mad? Yours could drive me mad. You must be merciful. I'm terribly connected with you, I always will be. I love you and I'll always love you."

Morgan had not meant to say this. Her thoughts about her new life had not really comprehended Julius any more than they had really comprehended Tallis. She felt a fierce determination to change herself. But she felt too, with a sort of relaxed despair, how in these two relationships she was not yet changed. Her own men-

tion of the house in the woods had brought it all back. Breakfast
on the terrace with the hot resiny smell of azaleas, the marzipan
smell of magnolias. Julius singing arias as he fries eggs and ba-
nanas. Scarlet wings of cardinal birds in live-oak trees. Chipmunks
and red squirrels and mysterious pendent possums. Alligators
with jewelled backs and huge-eyed dragon flies in swampy steamy
creeks. Long breathless silent evening walks beneath the canopies
of Spanish moss, Julius's hand caressing her shoulders, plucking
at her dress where perspiration had glued it to her body. Cascades
of clematis and trumpet vines and bougainvillea, a paradise. Julius's face a brilliant mask of tenderness after love-making. The
secret house with its huge windows full of luminous green pine
branches and radiant blue sky. The house in the woods had unmade London for her, unmade Europe.

It can't all have gone, she thought, gone away, vanished into
nothing. Julius is *in* me. I haven't solved Julius. All my moods
have been modes of consciousness of him. First ecstasy, then
misery, then cynicism. Now this new sense of a possible enlarge-
ment. In which he *must* help me. This can only be done *with*
him. We shall never be finished with each other, *never*. This is
only the beginning of a drama which will last the whole of our
lives. The thought was deeply consoling.

Julius now turned to look at her. Before, he had been gazing
vaguely around the room, twitching his shoulders, glancing
at his watch.

"*Please*," said Morgan. She laid her hand lightly upon his sleeve.

Julius looked at her as one might look at a child. "I am afraid
you attach too much importance to personal relationships."

Morgan twisted the stuff of the jacket savagely and let it go.
"You are a monster. You are the sort of man who really would
prefer the destruction of the world to the scratching of his finger!"

"No, no, I'm serious. These things are not as important as you
think, Morgan. They are flimsy and unreal. You want some sort of
drama now, you want an ordeal of some kind, you don't want
to suffer in a dull way, and you want me to help you. But these
are merely superficial agitations. Human beings are roughly con-

structed entities, full of indeterminacies and vaguenesses and empty spaces. Driven along by their own private needs they latch blindly onto each other, then pull away, then clutch again. Their little sadisms and their little masochisms are surface phenomena. Anyone will do to play the roles. They never really see each other at all. There is no relationship, dear Morgan, which cannot quite easily be broken and there is none the breaking of which is a matter of any genuine seriousness. Human beings are essentially finders of substitutes."

Morgan glared at him. She was delighted that he had used her name. It was a moment for argument. With a physical thrill, she felt the sudden immediacy, the directness of connection, the old current once more at last flowing between them.

"I don't agree. There are some relations which can't be broken."

"None, none. All human beings have staggeringly great faults which can easily be exploited by a clever observer."

"What do you mean?"

"I could divide anybody from anybody. Even you could. Play sufficiently on a person's vanity, sow a little mistrust, hint at the contempt which every human being deeply, secretly feels for every other one. Every man loves himself so astronomically more than he loves his neighbour. Anyone can be made to drop anyone."

"In some cases maybe—in the very long run—"

"No, no, quickly, in ten days! Don't you believe me? Would you like a demonstration?"

Morgan stared at him. Then she laughed. She felt the quivering of a physical bond between them and her eyes kindled at his eyes. Julius's face had the clever delighted look which she had loved, which she had kissed, once.

"My dear! You really are— All right, why not? But you'll fail. I'll bet you—ten guineas. But who can you try it on?"

"Ten guineas. Done!"

"And I'll be generous and make it three weeks. Four if you like. You're completely mad, of course. But whoever could you try it on? It must be people we both know. You really are a mischief-maker!"

"Let me see, let me see!" Julius was now in high spirits. "What about—what about the little Foster?"

"Simon? Oh, no! You mean—what?"

"I wouldn't do him any harm. I would simply detach him quite painlessly from Axel. I would rather like to have the little Foster for my squire."

"It seems so unkind now it's real people!"

"But no one would really suffer, that's part of my point. I'd do it in the most *angelic* manner."

"Oh Julius— You know, in a way I really think it might be good for Simon. I do feel Axel rather forced it on him. And I doubt if they're really happy. I'm sure they torment each other."

"You make it sound as if it'll be too easy! Would you like some other test case?"

"No, no, that one will be fine. I shall be absolutely riveted! Julius, you really are the most fantastical person I have ever met!"

"Well, I think it's time for a martini. Let's go and clinch our wager."

As they rose and turned to go Morgan drew her fingertips along his sleeve and lifted her hand up into the air. Her body felt alive and light. She was suddenly blindingly happy. She looked round upon the Turners. She could see now how limited and amateurish they really were.

🎠 | TWENTY

The Chinese restaurant was in a basement. One reached it by going down a flight of steep crumbling rather fungoid steps, holding carefully onto a handrail. The evening was warm and a little overcast.

Simon was early. He hoped to settle in and get himself a drink before the others arrived. He felt thoroughly irritated by the prospect of Chinese food. Axel would insist that one must drink lager. Simon would fight for white wine. In any case, neither drink really went properly with that mess of anaemic bean shoots and nameless fragments of fried stuff. Oh God, Julius would want to drink *tea!* That would be the last straw.

Simon was not in any case looking forward to the evening, though he felt a little interested to see how Tallis and Julius would behave. He thought it odd of Tallis to come. Could Tallis be moved by anything as vulgar as curiosity? Relations with Axel were still strained. Axel had never been quite like this before. He was polite and kindly but in some scarcely definable way still distant. Had some condemnation been made, some decision been taken, in a secret department of Axel's mind? Had there perhaps been some cold and final act of writing-off? Simon woke and slept with fear. He knew his friend too well to attempt any sort of emotional showdown while Axel was in this kind of mood. Any desperate appeal would be treated merely with raised eyebrows and slight frowns. Simon would have to wait for the right moment. But the right moment did not come, and meanwhile Simon's own apparently calm response to Axel's treatment of him widened the gap between them.

The curious incident at Julius's flat was refusing to recede into the past and mix itself with oblivion. If only he had told Axel about it at once! It was impossible to tell him now. This secretiveness not only constituted, what Axel had always adjured him against, a lie, it also made the incident itself curiously potent with psychological consequences. Consequences which concerned Julius, and consequences which concerned Morgan. Simon had several times dreamt about Julius. He had had a version of a dream which had been a familiar visitant over many years. When he was at his prep school, the boys' letters were set out in a big set of black pigeon-holes, one hole for each letter of the alphabet. F was rather high up and, when he was an exceptionally small new boy, Simon had not quite been able to reach it. He longed for letters from his mother. These came regularly, but to obtain them became an early morning ordeal. Simon would stand shyly near the pigeon-holes, hoping that someone fairly tall who knew him and was also nice would come along and could be casually asked if he could see if there was anything for Foster. Sometimes the older boys laughed at him. Once, a big boy, with a cry of "Letter from Mummy!" lifted Simon up to the top pigeon-holes. Simon wept with shame afterward in the lavatories.

These pigeon-holes, mercifully forgotten in his adolescence, began to haunt his dreams in his early twenties. Very greatly enlarged and deepened, they became portentous windows out of the deeply recessed interiors of which Simon was always wanting to look at some brightly coloured scene of intense interest. Only the hole through which he wanted to look was always just out of his reach. He would climb up toward it, mounting on piles of crumbling collapsing boxes or precarious scaffolding, or sometimes climbing endless stairs. The scene itself, when, now and then, he managed to glimpse it through the long shaft of the pigeon-hole, was always strangely separated from the rest of the dream, a weird landscape perhaps, or strange animals at play. It inspired painful excitement. But awful anxiety attached to the clambering up. Very occasionally in the dreams someone actually lifted him up, and this feeling of powerful hands gripping him about the waist revived the old terrible sensation of shame. In so far as he could identify the lifter-up it was usually his father or Rupert. In his most recent pigeon-hole dreams Simon had realized on waking with extreme distress that the person who had lifted him up had been Julius.

Simon had thought a good deal about Morgan too and wanted very much to go round and see her. He felt a kind of laceration which talk with her, talk about anything, would have soothed. But he knew that if he went to see her at the moment he would have to conceal this from Axel. Any mention of Morgan would increase the aloofness and the coldness which even now were just as much as Simon could bear. Sometimes he felt that it would not matter too much if he did see Morgan and said nothing about it. This concealment would be merely an extension of the first one. The "compact" of which Morgan had spoken seemed to have begun on that evening at Julius's flat, though it had been given its substance later. At other times Simon knew that this was muddled thinking and that the best way to encourage the first lie to shrivel right away was to be guilty of no more. He wrote a long affectionate letter to Morgan and then did not send it. He had the pigeon-hole dream again, once more with Julius. What he saw through the dark shaft was Morgan walking in a garden with no clothes on.

The restaurant was lit by neon strip lighting and made a bright cold rather sickly impression after the blue misty light outside. Simon blinked. He wondered if Axel had booked a table. The place appeared to be empty. He looked around, searching for the most protected place to sit. No, there were some people in the far corner, standing round a table in a group. Simon chose a table fairly near the door and against the wall. He picked up a menu and began gloomily to study it. Chow this and chow that. He would have a decent drink to start with anyway. Where were the waiters?

There was something a little odd about the atmosphere. Simon looked up and his eyes were now a little more accustomed to the bright gloomy greenish light. The light seemed to be flickering very faintly. The people in the far corner, who had looked round when he came in, were now intent again on something else. Five of them were standing, one sitting at the table. The five who were standing were, he saw, burly youths of about eighteen. The man who was sitting down appeared to be a dark man, perhaps a Jamaican. There was a curious silence. As Simon watched he saw the Jamaican slowly raise his table napkin to his face. The white napkin came away stained with something dark. Blood.

There's been some sort of accident, Simon thought. Something has happened. The man is hurt. He felt a sudden tension in the chest. Then, as he watched, one of the youths reached out and cuffed the coloured man on the side of the head and then drew his hand roughly down over his face, pushing him backward. The chair rocked and grated on the floor. The youth then ostentatiously wiped his stained fingers across the front of the Jamaican's shirt. The other four laughed. The Jamaican put the napkin back in front of his eyes and nose. Another of the group reached forward and snatched it away from him. They leaned over him.

Simon sat rigid with fear and horror. He both detested and feared violence of any description. He had never experienced it and scarcely ever glimpsed it. His immediate instinct was to keep absolutely still. He moved his eyes cautiously toward the door which led into the kitchen. The door had a little glass window in it and through the window he could see the faces of two Chinese waiters observing the scene. The Chinese had their own troubles. They lived there. This part of Fulham had its petty criminals, or so Simon had read in the paper. The Chinese waiters probably knew this lot already. One could not blame them for not intervening. Five violent men can paralyse a much larger group of ordinary citizens, and behind the kitchen door there were only the two waiters and the elderly cook. The rest were women. They'll have telephoned for the police, thought Simon. There is absolutely nothing that I can do. With a trembling hand he quietly lifted the menu up again in front of him, peering surreptitiously over it.

"Rotten nigger!" said one of the youths. The Jamaican had lifted his two hands to protect his face. One of the group moved behind the chair and pinioned the man's arms from behind, while another struck him again casually and began to press his knuckles into his eye. The Jamaican's head went back. The blood was trickling from his nose. Why doesn't he cry out? thought Simon in anguish. How can he be silent like that? "Rotten lousy nigger." There was the sound of another blow.

Simon rose to his feet. He felt near to fainting. Cold anger kept him conscious and kept him upright. His trembling legs functioned. He walked over to the group, who turned their heads lazily toward him. The man behind the chair did not release his victim.

"Stop that," said Simon. "You can't do that." He was almost too breathless with fear and anger to be able to speak properly. He noticed that the two youths nearest to him were armed, one with a piece of iron piping and the other with a bicycle chain.

"We're doing it!" said the leader of the group, a huge fair lout with fluffy hair. He still had his fist pressed onto the Jamaican's face, forcing the head back. "Any objections?"

"You stop," said Simon, gasping for breath.

"Look who's here," said another of them. "A fucking queer. Listen to his squeaky little voice."

"Want those pretty looks spoilt, mister?" said the youth with the bicycle chain. "We don't like pooves. Want to have this wrapped round your head, do you?" He swung the chain suggestively.

"Give him the treatment, Sid."

Simon tried to step back, but one of the louts had already laid a large steely hand upon his arm. The grip was tightened, the arm was slowly twisted. Simon stood gazing at them, his eyes wide with fright. He knew now why the Jamaican had not cried out. He could not have uttered a sound. He waited for the blow.

There was a faint noise behind him. Never had anything been more welcome to Simon's ears. Someone had opened the door of the restaurant and entered from the street. There was a moment's silence. Then Axel's voice said, "What on earth is going on here?"

Simon was released and he stepped quickly backward. Axel, Julius, and Tallis had just come into the restaurant. Axel advanced. "What's this?"

The fluffy-haired youth, who seemed to be the leader, pulled the Jamaican round chair and all and let him go with another resounding cuff on the side of the head. "We're operating on this nig nog. You want to be operated on too?"

Simon edged away. He could see Julius's face alight with thrilled fascinated interest, his gaze now fixed on Axel.

"Listen, my man," said Axel, "in this country—"

"Want your face smashed, or what? Lend me the chain, Bert."

"People like you—" Axel was continuing, raising his voice.

Julius's eyes were gleaming with pleasure, his moist lips slightly parted.

The fluffy-haired youth moved toward Axel. The next moment something happened very quickly. Tallis moved in from behind Julius and before anyone could shift or cry out he had struck the youth very hard across the side of the face. He struck him with the flat of his hand but with such violence that the boy staggered back against his companions and almost fell to the floor.

Simon clenched his fists. If there were a general fight now he felt he was ready for it. Axel was staring at Tallis with an air of puzzlement. Julius was smiling with irrepressible delight. Tallis stood hunched like an animal.

"Fucking hell," said the fluffy-haired youth, his hand to his face.

"Come on," said one of his companions.

The next moment they were all trooping off. The restaurant door slammed behind them.

"Thank you, gentlemen," said the Jamaican.

Tallis sat down on a chair.

"That blow was *terrific!*" said Julius.

He was drinking whisky with Simon and Axel at their house.

They were all in a state of high excitement. It was two hours later.

"My God, it was impressive!" said Axel. "Do you know, we all acted characteristically. Simon intervened incompetently, I talked, you watched, and Tallis acted."

"It was perfect," said Julius.

By mutual consent the Chinese meal had been abandoned. Then it seemed wiser to leave the area before the louts changed their minds or returned with reinforcements. They had put the Jamaican into a taxi to return to his hotel. He had turned out to be a secretary attached to a visiting delegation. Tallis had set off for the police station where a statement had to be made. He had refused to come to Barons Court afterward for a drink.

"How awfully nice that man was and so jolly dignified."

"What a first impression of England!"

"I do wish we could have persuaded him to come round."

"He was rather shaken, poor chap."

"Tallis was rather shaken too. He was trembling afterward, did you see?"

And I am trembling now, thought Simon. He was still reliving those awful moments of violence. Suppose they hadn't arrived in time? He quickly drank some more whisky.

"Well, I must say I did enjoy that," said Julius. "I was looking forward to this evening. I didn't know it would be quite so glorious."

"Yes, Tallis was quite upset," said Simon.

"If we'd hit someone like that we'd be upset too," said Axel.

"I don't think I could ever hit anyone," said Simon.

"Nor could I," said Julius.

"You surprise me, Julius," said Axel. "I think I might be able to."

"Whom and when?"

"Well— I dare say I could hit Simon under certain circumstances!"

Axel and Julius laughed.

"Under *what* circumstances?" said Julius.

They both laughed again.

Simon thought, Quite soon I am probably going to be sick or to burst into tears. I had better get out of the room first. He got up and began to make quietly for the door.

As he passed behind Axel's chair Axel reached up a hand and gripped Simon's jacket. "Simon."

"Yes." Simon shuddered.

"I think you were very brave, my darling." Axel's hand fumbled for his arm and squeezed it.

All is well now between us, thought Simon.

Axel's head was turned toward him. Over Axel's head Simon could see Julius's face, still radiant with delight. The radiant face compulsively drew Simon's glance. As he now turned to the door Julius slowly and deliberately winked at him.

Simon got as far as the kitchen. He thought, I am a rotten swine. He put his head down on the kitchen table and wept.

PART *Two*

✿ | ONE

As Big Ben was chiming ten o'clock Rupert Foster entered his room in Whitehall. Give or take a minute or two, this was his invariable time of arrival. The big square window showed him St. James's Park, feathery with high summer, the curving lake pale blue enamel under a clear sky, and the Palace as hazy and tree-blurred as any gentleman's residence in the deepest country. Rupert sighed with satisfaction.

He laid his copy of *The Times* down on the desk. He had almost finished the crossword in the train. He hoped one day to create a record by finishing it. The room was businesslike and pleasant. Some of Rupert's colleagues introduced knick-knacks, coloured photos of the family, even flowers. Rupert could not approve of that. He had gone so far as to adorn the white walls with a set of eighteenth-century architectural drawings which he had bought at a sale. For the rest, there was government furniture of no outstanding ugliness. The carpet was thick, the desk immense. Rupert's papers were set out in neat piles. Papers in neat piles calm the mind. They were weighted down by water-smooth stones brought back by Rupert and his wife from rivers and seas all over Europe.

Rupert opened the window and leaned on the ledge looking out. He was not really a man for holidays and he would have been quite happy not to have any. He liked these ordinary days when he felt the orderly rhythm of his life as a physical pulse of well-being. He liked his job and he knew that he did it well. He was never in a hurry. When he travelled it was more to please his family than to please himself. And the cottage in Pembrokeshire was his wife's toy. Hilda enjoyed scrubbing the tables and drying people's wet clothes and catering for a week at a time. She undoubtedly had, as he often told her, a Robinson Crusoe complex.

Rupert now woke up every morning with a relieved sense of something nice having happened, and then recalled that his son Peter had decided to return to Cambridge in October after all. Peter's decision to reject society had been happily short-lived. Hilda's sister had somehow done the trick, capturing the boy's affections and making him docile. Peter had even visited his home on two occasions, and had had a long talk with Hilda. It is true that he had chosen times when Rupert would be absent. But Rupert was not unduly worried about Peter's hostility to himself. It was a phase which would pass. He could remember feeling like that about his own father, with whom he had nevertheless been on perfectly good terms generally. Of course he and his father had tended to make a common cause of looking after brother Simon, especially after Rupert's mother had died.

It was so important to have innocent affections and people to look after. There had always been Simon. Then Hilda, Peter. Now Morgan too. His dear sister-in-law certainly needed looking after. She was a strange case. He had so often discussed her with Hilda, worrying away at the matter with affectionate puzzlement. Morgan had left her husband in order to live with Julius King. Now she had left Julius too. Or had Julius left her? No one seemed to be quite clear about that. Hilda now professed to think that Morgan would end up by going back home again to Tallis Browne. "She loves him, she's married to him, Tallis is her fate." Hilda had not always thought that. It was not plain to Rupert why she thought it now. Hilda was very emotional about her sister and Rupert suspected that this new view was simply the outcome of an increasing hostility to Julius. Rupert could understand how people, especially women, might dislike Julius, always assuming they were not in love with him. Julius was so outrageously honest. He never mixed into his behaviour that hazy little bit of falsehood which most people find necessary for the general easing of social intercourse.

No, Rupert did not think that his sister-in-law would return to her husband. As he saw it, Morgan was traversing a serious crisis of identity. Morgan posed as an independent and liberated woman, but she had really led a very sheltered life. She had grown up in the shadow of Hilda. Although Morgan was so much cleverer than her sister she had always been both cherished and dominated by Hilda's simpler gentler less problematic nature. School and university studies had absorbed the ferocious energy of Morgan's youth. There had been a few scrappy love affairs. "These men are just no *match* for her!" he had heard Hilda complaining. Certainly nothing flimsy would do for Morgan. Then there had been what Hilda called "the Tallis fantasy. Morgan's living in Malory or something." Rupert could not quite envisage Tallis as an Arthurian knight. But he could see that the poor fellow could do with a little fantastical refurbishing. "Morgan thinks that with Tallis she can combine marriage with giving up the world. There's a fanatical nun tied up inside that girl." Rupert could not quite understand.

All these goings-on, thought Rupert, had merely postponed Morgan's growing up. It was happening now. She has got to decide what sort of person she is and what human life is about. I cannot see her returning to Tallis. And I cannot see her staying with Julius either. Julius has done her no harm, he has shaken her, probably educated her. But Julius is not a marrier. He is a man who has to strip himself bare at regular intervals. Morgan will have to be alone for the time being. There is a lot of violence in her and she will have to suffer, more perhaps than she yet realizes. She is still trying to be on holiday from her problems. She is trying to be on holiday from herself.

He thought of her as he had last seen her, helping Hilda to arrange roses in the kitchen at Priory Grove, Morgan in tight mauve pants and blue cotton sweater, clowning around, throwing flowers about, putting pink and white petals into her hair, into her mouth, down Hilda's neck, pricking herself, screaming, laughing. While Hilda, smiling, placid, plump, her greying hair bunched up inside a scarf, wearing a huge butcher's apron over her dress, went on clipping off the leaves and arranging the blooms in a pretended disregard of the cries and the capers. She might have been Morgan's mother.

She must confront life, he thought, with a twinge of warm preoccupied concern for the younger woman. I must talk to her, help her if possible. She must see that there is *a way*. Rupert's mind swerved in a natural and familiar manner toward the book on morals which he had now so nearly finished, and he wondered to himself if that book would ever help anybody who had, like Morgan, lost his bearings. Would his words ever bring comfort to another, help ever to check a bad resolve or stiffen a good one? It was a presumptuous thought. Rupert did not imagine that he was a great philosopher. He was a clear-headed and experienced man and he knew how to write. But there were plenty of men like that. What Rupert had extra, he often told himself, was simply a confident sense of moral direction and the nerve to speak about it. He knew where good lived. Moralists are far too timid, he thought, especially now when they feel they have to placate the logical positivists and the psychologists and the sociologists and the computerologists and God knows who else. They fill their pages with apologies and write everybody's language but their own. Whatever his book was, it was not apologetic. When it was in typescript he must let Morgan look at it. He would be interested to have her opinion.

Rupert smoothed down his blond hair. It had become bleached and unruly and dry from the sun, which had also given his face a smooth bloom of reddish bronze, making him look, he was well aware, even more juvenile than usual. Today he would have to be mature and impressive at a meeting of government economists. He would not find it difficult. Rupert knew the meeting game. And he had long since stopped feeling nervous of these latter-day panjandrums, or imagining that they had secret expertise of which he was ignorant. He had seen too much of their bungling and privately believed that he could do their jobs better than they did. However they were ministers' darlings and had to be soft-soaped. He would be deferential, dignified, not quite imperceptibly sceptical.

Rupert returned to his desk leaving the window wide open. The air from the park was light and fresh and seemed to smell faintly of flowers. There was that strange lucid light-weight atmosphere of early mornings in summery London, when the sun seems for a time to rinse the city and make it silvery and hollow and clean. Only, as Rupert now reminded himself, it was not in fact all that early and he must stop dreaming and get on with his work.

His well-trained personal assistant, a charming girl with a passion for potted plants which Rupert only just managed to keep confined to the outer office, had set out his papers, including such of the confidential ones as he allowed her to handle. Briefing copies of ministerial committee papers were fanned out in folders of blue, yellow, and green. Something unpleasantly familiar with a red flag on it had been weighted down by a piece of pitted volcanic stone from Sicily, and today's letters, all opened and sorted, were neatly held in place by a lump of pinkish Aberdeen granite. No, one of the letters had not been opened. A typewritten envelope marked *Personal*. Rupert looked at it with faint puzzlement. He never received personal letters at the office, though he knew that, for various peculiar reasons, many of his colleagues did. As he reached for the letter the telephone rang and Rupert's day began with a conversation with an anxious man who was being pursued by an irate man who was extremely exercised about what a certain minister would think about the thing with the red flag on it which was now lying upon Rupert's desk. After nearly an hour of telephone calls Rupert wrote a tiny minute and sent the dangerous file away to burn a hole in somebody else's desk. He noticed the letter again and began with one hand to prise it open, skimming through a memorandum on *Notional Promotion in Absentia* at the same time. He saw out of the corner of his eye that the communication inside was from Morgan.

Rupert felt a curious shock as he saw the familiar handwriting.

He dropped the memorandum, pulled the letter out, and unfolded it. It was rather long. It showed signs of having been written hastily and there were many crossings out. It ran as follows.

My dear. Listen. You have been extremely kind to me. You have given me your time, you have given me your company. I have been guided, philosophized at, befriended, and have enjoyed every moment of it. You talked such superb sense to me the other day. I suspect you are the wisest person I have ever met. You not only steady my nerves, you make me feel that I am a rational being after all and able to thread the mazes of the world. I am grateful to you for the big things and for the little things: for your help in all the immediacies of my situation, for your so evident and sweet concern.

Now. What will you say and what will you think when you hear what comes next? I swear to you that I did not expect this and I am as surprised and alarmed as you could possibly be. Since I arrived in this country I have, as you know, had many and various preoccupations. I did not expect this *too!* Even the last time I saw you I did not really divine it, though I have known for some time that you were becoming important to me and that, oh God, I rather needed you. Now it appears that, quite suddenly, I have fallen as deeply and foolishly in love with you as a child of seventeen. And I feel I have no choice but to put the matter before you. I am a married woman. And you—I dread to imagine what you will think of me for having forced just *this* problem upon you! You with your orderly and busy life and your quite special commitments! Have pity on me, I am inclined to say: yet I know that your pity might lead us straight into the kind of confusion which I know you detest. I am in a complete muddle, my darling. My own life is full of problems and emotional needs about which you know a little. But that scarcely excuses my making you a present of this embarrassing and unrequested love. I dread your judgement upon me. But I ask you *at least* to believe in the tragic seriousness of the deep and, alas, *passionate* feeling which you have inspired in me. Please please don't do anything hastily about this. I need the coolness and rationality of which you are so pre-eminently the master. I have never needed it more. When I see you I will speak with calmness and I beg you to do the same. But I *must* see you soon, and not in any of our usual haunts for obvious reasons. My flat is too public. I will suggest a place. Please, my darling, *help* me now and forgive me for loving you.

Morgan

At the bottom of the page, in a hand so hasty and scrawled as to be almost illegible, was written:

Don't reply or speak of this letter even to me. I die of shame. A new start must be made. Meet me on Wednesday at 10:30 at the Prince Regent Museum, Room 14.

Rupert read the letter through carefully twice. Then he lifted the telephone and asked his personal assistant to see that he was not disturbed during the next hour. Then he went to the window once more and surveyed, with a very different eye, the hazy bosky vista of St. James's Park. Later, Rupert was to tell himself censoriously, though it was by no means so clear to him at the time, that his very first feeling had been one of mad elation. Human beings crave for novelty and welcome even wars. Who opens the morning paper without the wild hope of huge headlines announcing some great disaster? Provided of course that it affects other people and not oneself. Rupert liked order. But there is no man who likes order who does not give houseroom to a man who dreams of disorder. The sudden wrecking of the accustomed scenery, so long as one can be fairly sure of a ringside seat, stimulates the bloodstream. And the instinctive need to feel protected and superior ensures, for most of the catastrophes of mankind, the shedding by those not immediately involved of but the most crocodile of tears.

Yet this was only a momentary leap of the consciousness. Rupert was not in any way inclined to discount what lay before him. He might have been if not wiser at least luckier if he had decided at once to laugh it off. But Rupert was not a laugher-off. He took the letter seriously and settled down to study the situation. He thought: Poor Morgan. Then he thought, and this was less pleasant, We are all endangered. Things can never be quite the same again. Our quiet world, our *happy* world, has been disturbed. Life will be anxious, uncomfortable, unpredictable.

Rupert returned to his desk and sat there rigid while nearly an hour went by. He cared for Morgan. He grieved deeply that this strange aberration had damaged, perhaps fatally, a friendship whose warmth had been so easily carried by the sweet casualness of family life. How much warmth there really had been he now felt with an almost elegiac sadness. The impetuous girl had brought all to consciousness and landed them both with a really frightful problem. Morgan had spoken of quite special commitments. Yes! If Rupert were married to anyone else in the world but Hilda it would all matter much less. Rupert drew in his breath. He began gradually to see the whole hideousness of what had happened.

Rupert thought, Of course the girl is in a thoroughly unbalanced state. Tallis, Julius, me. No one must know, for the present not even Hilda. Morgan must be persuaded to go away. And yet, poor child, where could she go to? She had come to England, she had come, it was now suddenly clear, to *him*, as to a last refuge. To drive her out now would be to drive her into a life of desperation and perhaps into a mental shipwreck. I've got to enclose this thing, thought Rupert, I've got to contain it, I've got to live it through. I can't just send her off. This has got to be dealt with by love. How would I feel if I told her to go and she committed suicide? Morgan was someone who could commit suicide. She must not feel rejected, he thought. I must keep her with me.

Rupert got up and began to pace the room. He saw now with a coldness which really did chill his heart what the difficulties were likely to be. He was, in a way which ordinarily would not matter at all, damn fond of Morgan. What he had said to Julius once had been true: he had come not so much to despise as simply to ignore the drama of his motives. He sought simply for truthful vision, which in turn imposed right action. The shadow play of motive was a bottomless ambiguity, insidiously interesting but not really very important. Could he do it here, latch himself onto the machinery of virtue and decent decision, and simply slide past

the warm treacherous area of confusing attachment? For there
was no doubt that he was extremely attached to his sister-in-law.

The more reason, he then thought, to be absolutely coolly responsible. He would, he could, say nothing to Hilda. It's just a
matter of steadying her through, he thought. In extremities human beings need love and nothing else will do. Morgan was hungry for steady unviolent unpossessive love which neither Tallis
nor Julius could give her. I cannot refuse this challenge, Rupert
told himself. All my life as a thinking man has led me to believe in
the power of love. Love really does solve problems. To adopt a
mean safe casual solution here would be unjust to both myself
and Morgan. She has called me wise: let me attempt to be so. True
love is calm temperate rational and just: and it is not a shadow
or a dream. The top of the structure is not empty.

❧ | T W O

"Naturally," said Julius, "you felt you had to have a flat of your
own. This can be important."

"Rupert and Hilda were very kind—"

"But you felt you had to move out. Of course. Other people's
family life can be so oppressive."

"Hilda found me this place—"

"What ghastly pictures. Oh dear, are they yours?"

"Yes."

"Sorry. I'm allergic to reproductions. I don't imagine it's cheap
here? This part of London is becoming fashionable I'm told."

"It's not bad. Are you really going to buy a house in the Boltons?"

"I might. One must have a little place somewhere to stow one's kit, don't you think?"

"I can't imagine you staying anywhere permanently."

"I'm a great home-lover really. Are you still living on that three hundred pounds you swindled your husband out of? You honest middle-class English people are full of surprises."

"I have a little money. I thought perhaps—"

"I'm terribly sorry I'm not in a position to lend you any. My income-tax position is most peculiar at the moment."

"I wasn't going to ask you!" said Morgan, exasperated.

For once she was in no mood to talk to Julius, who had appeared at her flat unannounced half an hour ago. Morgan wanted to be alone just now to think about a letter which she had received that morning. Julius's humorous malicious probing, which she remembered that she used quite to enjoy, was now causing pain and annoyance. Masochism has strict rules. Acceptable pain is on the inside of love. Of course Morgan was not disenchanted. But for the moment the circuit seemed to be switched off.

"Have to find a job, won't you," said Julius. "It won't be easy. Oughtn't you to be looking out for something?"

"I am looking," she said. "I get the *Times Educational Supplement—*"

"Your old job at London University folded up, didn't it?"

"Yes. But I'll find something else."

"I suppose you'll have to be prepared to teach in a school. You could teach French or German, couldn't you, or Latin?"

"I don't want to teach in a school!" said Morgan. "I'll get a university job somewhere."

She was sitting on the writing table. Beside her was a letter half concealed by the green malachite paperweight. She had put it down hastily with its envelope on top of it as soon as she had heard feet on the stairs. Julius had been prowling the room, examining books and papers. He had even opened her desk.

"I hope you're not being too optimistic. The trouble with your subject is that it isn't one."

"I think we've had this argument before."

"It's not an argument. You have nothing to say. You just get cross."

"I don't get cross. You just haven't got that sort of mind."

"A talent for languages— Aren't you going to offer me a drink? It's after eleven."

Morgan left the table with reluctance. She left the door ajar, darted into the kitchen, and came back in a minute or two with a bottle of whisky and a soda siphon and glasses. Julius was still standing in the same place. "My fridge isn't working. I'm afraid there's no ice."

"That's all right. I find I don't want ice in England. Such is the power of environment. I'm even beginning to prefer scotch. No, no soda. Thank you. As I was saying, a talent for languages is a handy though not terribly elevated piece of mental equipment. And I personally am extremely grateful for being quadrilingual by circumstance. Knowledge of languages is something simple but of course useful and for what it's worth, it is genuine empirical knowledge. But the attempt to find general structures or deep patterns or abstract systems beyond the rickety jumbled façade of a natural language is exactly like the attempt of the metaphysical philosopher to rest the muddle of the ordinary world upon some rational and purified original: idle, misguided, vain."

"You don't deny causality in language—" said Morgan. She was determined not to get cross this time. She wished heartily that he would go.

Julius sat down in one of the arm-chairs, banished a cushion, and made himself comfortable. "Causality, yes. If you mean something like Grimm's law or Verner's law. But these are the merest observations of surface regularities and are ultimately extremely boring. Language is a reasonably useful jumble with an in-built capacity to manoeuvre itself. These manoeuvrings can be watched, I don't deny. But they are merely what they are. There is nothing behind them. To imagine that there is is the familiar childishness of the metaphysician here rather gracelessly masquerading as a science."

"You seem singularly uninterested in the facts," said Morgan.

"Linguistics is not an *a priori* system, it is a natural extension of philology. It derives from empirical studies of just those 'manoeuvrings' you spoke of so lightly. Why should language be a mountain of accidents? Nothing else in the world is. Any theory tries to explain, or at least to display, multiplicity by conjecturing deep pattern. Of course linguistic theories are hypotheses, but they are hypotheses in the scientific sense."

"I doubt if your fellow theorists would agree," said Julius. "I suspect they fancy that they are philosophers or mathematicians or something, and that because human thought is largely verbal they have plumbed its mysteries if they have invented what they imagine to be an ur-language. In fact if one opens their extremely dull books one finds that they usually cannot even write the natural language of their choice."

"No one denies that glossematics is in its infancy—"

" 'Glossematics'! Of course there has to be a pseudoscientific name. Phonetics I suppose is about something. Semantics is beginning to lose contact with reality. Glossematics is where we really take off! Oh, the bemused vanity of human beings! In all their tens of thousands of years of miserable toil the only genuine discovery they have made is mathematics, a discovery, incidentally, which will very soon finish them off altogether. And wherever they grub about they pretend if they possibly can to find mathematics at the bottom of the hole. The poor Greeks were typical. And you— really you make me laugh—with the intellectual equipment of a sixth form mistress or a literary critic, giving yourself airs because you imagine that you are manipulating an algebra of language!"

"At any rate, you must admit that comparative philology—"

"Now you're getting cross. Yes, yes, languages are useful. And I suppose genitives and subjunctives and such are even interesting to some people. The trouble with you, Morgan, is that you don't know who you are. The metaphysical search is always a sign of neurosis. Look at Rupert, for instance."

"Rupert—" Morgan's hand touched the paperweight and the surface of the envelope.

"At a superficial glance Rupert looks like a monument to patriotic toil and virtuous family life. But look closer and you will see a tormented man, a seeking man, a misfit. That book of his—well, you know I don't think highly of that enterprise—but its existence is a symptom of some deep grief, and that is what is really attractive about Rupert. If he were as comfortable and as satisfied as he sometimes seems he would be intolerable."

"You think he's—restless?" said Morgan. She was quiet and attentive now, studying Julius's vague beaming countenance. He was still sipping his whisky, as if licking it out of the glass with a delicate tongue, and glancing round the room as he talked with an air of enjoyment.

"He ought to have married an intellectual. That's part of the trouble. Not that he doesn't do his best. He's a loyal soul."

"I think Hilda and he are—very well suited," said Morgan.

"Phrases as conventional as that can hardly state facts! Oh, they both do their best. I was amused though that Rupert didn't think fit to tell Hilda that he'd lent you four hundred pounds. It shows he has his little prevarications."

"That's true," said Morgan. "And Hilda never told Rupert that she was subsidizing Peter."

"Well, these little weaknesses are endearing. But I feel a bit sorry for Rupert. There's a lost soul there crying for something stronger and more spiritual than dear old Hilda's solid common sense."

"A happy marriage is often based on somebody's common sense."

"Oh, yes. Arrangements like that can last forever, and it's probably just as well if they do. Good heavens, I'm not suggesting Rupert's marriage is rocky! It would have to be a strong inducement that would make *him* break out. No one will ever hear that wild sad voice with which he wails silently within." Julius got up and put his empty glass on the bookshelf, pushing the books back.

"Hilda is a marvellous wife," said Morgan. She felt a little confused and fuzzy. Words seemed to be meaning something different.

"Hilda is a darling and she's a very wifey wife. Cosiness is much. Perhaps cosiness is all. It's only outsiders like you and me who affect to despise it. And perhaps that's just because we can't have it."

"Outsiders, yes. I am an outsider," said Morgan.

"You're an unfettered nomad. Rupert admires you enormously, by the way. He was singing your praises the other night when I saw him at the club."

"Really?"

"He sees you as a sort of eagle. Or perhaps it was a hawk. Some sort of ornithological simile anyway. I couldn't entirely follow it, but it was certainly meant to be flattering."

"Did he say—"

"Dear me, look at the time, I must be going. I believe we're friends now, aren't we?"

"Yes, please!"

"I don't normally go in for friendships with women, but I dare say I can stretch a point. We must meet now and then and have a gossip. Do you think I'll get a taxi in the Fulham Road?"

"Yes, just start walking toward South Ken station."

"Well, that's all right. *Auf Wiedersehen.* And I hope that nice university job turns up."

After Julius had gone Morgan's fingers instinctively sought Rupert's letter. She began to pull it out from underneath the envelope. But she already knew its contents by heart. The incredible, the impossible had happened. "No one will ever hear that wild sad voice . . ." I have heard it, she thought. I have heard it and now nothing will ever be the same again.

🌩 | THREE

"Put the two chairs there," said Julius.

Simon moved the chairs.

"Now unlock the door."

"It isn't locked," said Simon.

"Good. Well, now we go inside."

"I don't understand!" said Simon miserably.

"Come, come. I promised you a puppet show. You will be immensely diverted. Inside, little one, I'll follow you. Then we shall sit upon the floor and talk. Quickly now, while no one is about."

Simon pushed the door. It was a big handsome door designed by Robert Adam soon after his return from Italy in 1785. It had once been in a baronet's mansion in Northamptonshire. It was now in Room 14 of the Prince Regent Museum.

The door was flanked by delicate scagliola pilasters, the panelling on either side of which was blood red, covered with elaborate symmetrical spidery patterns of shells and flowerets and creamy ovals containing dramas of nymphs and satyrs. A large medallion above the door showed Venus playfully depriving a chubby Cupid of his bow. This section of wall, with the door in the middle, was squared off with larger pilasters of a rich Pompeian green round the corners of which there were, on either side, two further painted panels portraying the revels of some disgustingly precocious baby fauns. The whole piece thus jutting out into the room, though sliced off and rather arbitrarily put together, provided a distinguished example of the neo-classical style. It also provided an excellent hiding-place.

Behind Robert Adam's door, between the panelling and the museum wall, there was a space of some four feet, open at the top and enclosed on the three other sides by the spoils of the baronet's house. Inside this box, once the door was closed, it was dusky but not dark because of the light coming in from above. Simon was completely mystified. He had done what Julius asked him to do because Julius had insisted. Julius's will had simply taken him captive.

"There's a packing case for us to sit on, what luck," said Julius in a low voice. "You sit at that end. I'll sit here and, yes, there's a splendid spy hole. I thought there might be. Now we won't have to rely just on our ears. I can see the door perfectly. I don't imagine many people come to study neo-classical interiors at ten-thirty in the morning, do they, Simon?"

"No," said Simon. He found himself whispering. Julius had drawn him down onto the packing case beside him. "But what on *earth*—?"

"The two chairs which you kindly rearranged are just a few feet away from us. They should prove irresistible, don't you think? Our puppets are sure to sit on them."

"Julius, I don't *understand*—" This is some sort of grotesque nightmare, thought Simon. It's something ridiculous and horrible. Here I am inside this false façade in a room in the museum sitting on a packing case beside Julius. I ought to say no to it all. But what *is* it all?

"You soon will, my pretty. Two people whom you know will very shortly appear upon our little stage. And you will witness a love scene which may surprise you."

"Julius, I don't want to, let me go—"

Julius's hand was round his shoulder, firmly pressing him down. "Sssh, you can't go now, it would spoil it, I won't let you. I am procuring you a rare amusement, sweet boy. You ought to be grateful."

"But what *is* it?"

"Just a midsummer enchantment. Be quiet now and wait. Quiet, quiet."

In the silence that followed Simon listened to his own quick breathing and to the deep drumming of his heart. He was closely pressed up against Julius in the half dark. He realized that Julius, one arm still weightily round his shoulder, had captured his hand and was now very lightly scratching the palm of it. Simon's head was swimming.

There was a sound outside. Someone had entered the room. There was a slight resonant sound of footsteps, the steps of a woman. Then a sigh. Simon twitched slightly, releasing his hand which Julius gently relinquished. After a short while there were more footsteps, heavier, a man this time. Someone spoke very close by. Simon gasped and clapped his hand over his mouth. It was Rupert's voice.

"Hello, my dear—"

A voice replied. "Oh—Rupert—"

The voice was Morgan's.

Simon pressed his hands against his mouth, against his eyes.

"Rupert, forgive me—I'm so moved—it's so awfully strange, seeing you again now—with everything different—"

"Don't worry, my child. There's nothing to worry about. Let's sit down on these two chairs, shall we? They don't appear to be exhibits."

"I can't help being—surprised— I never for a moment expected—"

"These things do take one by surprise, my dear."

"Everything seems changed."

"Change must be endured too. But we are still the same two people. And we have known each other a long time."

"Yes, that is so important, isn't it? I knew you'd be wise and sensible about it. You are so wise about everything."

"It's not easy to be wise in a situation like this."

"If any man could be it would be you."

"You see, my dear, I don't underestimate its gravity."

"Good heavens, neither do I! Oh Rupert, I'm so touched— you're so sweet to me—"

"How did you expect me to be? One mustn't get excited. One

mustn't run away either, must one? You agree about not running away?"

"Yes, I do. I've thought about it a lot. It would be such a *blank* thing to do. Rupert, you haven't told Hilda about this?"

"No. And I won't. It's better not."

"Yes. Better not. Though I feel— Oh Rupert, it will be *all right,* won't it? I don't want anyone to be hurt. You, Hilda—"

"I don't see why anyone should be hurt, my dear, if we just keep our heads. I suppose it's bound to be a bit painful—just now. But you see there can't be any drama, there simply can't be. We have always been fond of each other, Morgan, and we know each other well—"

"I hope we'll know each other better."

"So do I. As I see it, it's not a matter of going *round* love, it's a matter of going *through* love—through to a better love—much more sober, much more realistic. Nothing awful can happen."

"You don't see it as just a momentary thing, do you, Rupert? I feel—after seeing you in this new light—I couldn't bear to go back to how things were before—well, I *couldn't.*"

"I know. I couldn't either. And I'm sure it isn't momentary, Morgan. It's sincere and deep. Pay it that compliment."

"About going through, not round, yes, yes, how absolutely right you are. Thank heavens you're so calm about it, Rupert! I thought you would be when we actually met. Rupert, let's get out of here, out into the open air. I have a slightly eerie feeling in this room. Look, let's walk along to the park, shall we? You don't have to go back to the office?"

"Not yet. Yes, let's go to the park. There's plenty of time."

The chairs creaked and the footsteps receded. For some time Simon had felt Julius's shoulder shuddering. Now there was a low gurgling sound. Julius was laughing, his fingers stuffed into his mouth. He fell off the packing case onto the floor. "Oh, beautiful!"

"Sssh!"

"It's all right, Simon, they've gone. We can emerge."

Simon opened the Robert Adam door and they came out blinking into the bright light of Room 14. Julius sat down on one of the vacated chairs and continued to laugh quietly, moaning into his handkerchief. Simon secured the door again and dusted down his suit. He felt dizzy with emotion and a kind of nausea. He could hardly believe what he had heard. It had the quality of a bad dream, horribly immediate and clear and yet insane. Morgan and Rupert. There was something terrible here, dangerous, painful. Confusedly he recognized a feeling of jealousy. Rupert and *Morgan*. Morgan and *Rupert*. He sat down heavily on the other chair. "But Julius, however did you know——?"

"Let's go to your office," said Julius, calming himself at last. "Exquisite, oh, exquisite!"

In Simon's tiny office Julius occupied the only chair. Simon sat on the desk. "Julius, it was *awful* to listen to that conversation, *awful*. It was a *demon* thing to do. How did you know about Rupert and Morgan and that they'd be meeting there? And what was it all about? Are they really in love with each other?"

Julius looked at his watch. "Give them another half-hour!" He began to laugh again, taking off his glasses and wiping the tears from his eyes. "Didn't I promise you a capital puppet show? Aren't you pleased?"

"No," said Simon. "I'm not. I still don't understand. Will you please explain?"

"Tut tut, dear boy. No one will be hurt. As I told you, it's just a midsummer enchantment, with two asses!"

"But how did you know?"

"It was curiously convenient, wasn't it? I just couldn't resist hearing that conversation. Wasn't it *deliciously* high-minded?"

"But how did you——? Why did they——?"

"Never mind the details, my pet. Call it magic if you like."

"But you can't have *arranged* it."

"Oh, I have done very little. They will do the rest."

"But they—— I could see that they—but I couldn't really understand what they were talking about."

"I don't blame you! They didn't understand what they were talking about themselves!"

"What do you *mean*?"

"Sssh, keep your voice down, you are getting quite shrill. You see, each of them imagines that he has inspired a grand passion in the other. Each thinks the other is madly in love! Thus each will take the initiative instead of drawing back. Each will chivalrously imagine that he protects and elevates the other! Thus chivalry and vanity will lead them deeper in!"

"But why do they think that? How——?"

"Quiet, quiet, my child. Scarcely a device at all, chance could have done it. And by the time they discover, if they ever do, they will be completely involved with each other. They are ripe, oh, they are ripe!"

"Julius, you haven't explained. Just what——"

"Come, come. See how funny it is. There they were, pussyfooting round each other, full of tact and sympathy and consideration and unctuous nothings. 'You are so wise' and 'we must go through to a higher love' and so on! They will never talk straight to each other, they haven't that kind of honesty, and they are both such *gentlemen!* Oh, the refined and lofty muddle they will get themselves into!"

"But they love each other——"

"Can such beings love? Vanity not love conducts their feet. Each of them is thrilled and flattered at being an object of worship. That is all their love would probably amount to in any case."

"But this is *all wrong*," cried Simon. He held his head in his hands and shook it. "We mustn't let it happen. What about Hilda—what about——"

"Don't worry. I will undo the enchantment later. No one will be seriously hurt. Two very conceited persons will be sadder and wiser, that's all."

"It *can't* be right to deceive people like that. And how do you know——"

"But they deceive themselves! They are having an absolutely wonderful time at this very moment in the park!"

"Well, I won't stand for it," said Simon. He felt confused and wretched. If only he didn't feel *jealous* as well. The idea of Rupert and Morgan— But it was all too nightmarish and beastly. It must be made to go away.

"And what would you propose to do, my pet?"

"I don't know. Tell everybody—"

"Tell them what? No, no, it's already too late for telling, things have gone too far. And you're not going to tell Axel either. Axel would behave like a blunt instrument."

"Maybe we need a blunt instrument!"

"Now just think for a moment. How would those two feel if Axel came blundering round trying to sort them out? How would they feel if any outsider pushed his way into that deliciously delicate and private situation? Imagine the humiliation, the hurt vanity! Ouf!"

"But they'll be hurt anyway, you said yourself—"

"Not so much. They'll gain a little experience. It will all unravel quite painlessly, you'll see. Any revelations now would just be senseless and ugly. Let them have their little drama, their little dance together. Let them work the machine themselves. They'll feel the better for it afterward, even if they are a bit let down!"

"You can't play with people like that."

"Why shouldn't they be educated? They're keen enough on educating others, at least Rupert is."

"But that doesn't make it right to—"

"Enough, enough. Listen, Simon, did you tell Axel about what happened that day at my flat, when you were so delightfully deprived of your clothes?"

"No."

"Good boy, you're learning. And you won't tell Axel about this either."

"I will! I must tell Axel! I don't know what to do!"

"I'll tell you what to do. No, no, you'll keep quiet, Simon my boy. If you tell Axel—"

"Well, what?"

"I shall inform Axel that you have been making advances to me!"

"But I haven't!"

"Haven't you?"

Julius was smiling amiably, tilting his chair back, intent on cleaning his glasses with a blue silk handkerchief.

"Julius, you know perfectly well—"

"What do I know? Didn't you hold my hand just now when we were sitting in our little stage box?"

"You held mine!"

"What's the difference?"

Simon felt a flood of panic. He was blushing, breathless.

"You *couldn't* do that— Tell Axel—it would be—"

"Why of course I won't! And you'll keep quiet too, and not spoil things, won't you. If you reflect, you'll see it's far better. Make no mistake, dear Simon. If I chose to I could destroy your relationship with Axel very easily. No need even to tell falsehoods. A few jokes about your interest in me—for you *are* interested in me, Simon, and you can't deny it—would be quite enough. A few idle speculations, a few obscure references, nothing to be taken seriously of course. The poison would lodge and work. And the funny thing is that you would help! You would feel guilty and act guilty! Surely you realize how close Axel is to seeing you as a vulgar little flirt? And he's an extremely jealous man, as you know."

Simon was trembling. With an uncanny accuracy Julius had laid his finger upon the very quality of his secret fears. Axel might indeed see him, might see him at any moment, as a vulgar flirt. It was unjust, unjust, unjust. But how unutterably precarious his world was, how precious and how frail!

"You see, Simon, as in the case of the two enchanted donkeys whom we overheard just now, one has only to set the machinery going, and then it runs."

"All right," said Simon. "I won't tell Axel." He pressed his hands to his burning cheeks.

"You are wise, little one. Let me give you some advice, Simon, may I? I don't want to upset your little applecart, but it grieves me to see you so full of illusions. Human loves don't last, Simon, they are far too egoistic. You seem to imagine that your romance with Axel will last forever, yet just now you were prepared to believe that the tiniest strain would break it. Your fears are juster than your hopes, I am afraid. At present you think you are happy knuckling under to Axel and giving way to his moods and his ill-tempers. But human beings cannot live without power any more than they can live without water. Of course the weak can often rule the strong through nagging and sulking and spite. You choose at present to give in. But every time you give in you notice it. Later perhaps you will make Axel's life a misery. Then gradually the balance will tilt. You will get tired of being Axel's lap-dog. You are not at all monogamous really, my dear Simon. You miss your adventures, you know you do. And you will find out one day that you want to play Axel to some little Simon. The passage of time brings about these shifts automatically, especially in relationships of your sort. You are not at the beginning of a long marriage, my Simon, you are at the beginning of a series of love affairs of an entirely different kind. I don't say this to discourage you, but simply out of kindness so that you should not suffer too great a disappointment later on."

"Get out," said Simon.

"Axel will soon be putting on weight. Have you thought of that? Have you ever seen a picture of Axel's father? Axel will soon lose that lean ascetic look which you prize so much. Will you still care for Axel when he looks like an elderly teddy bear?"

"*Get out.*"

Julius got up, still smiling. "Come, don't be out of temper with me just because I have told you the truth. I like you, Simon. I liked you from the moment when you said that Tallis ought not to have taken my hand. Well, I will go, since I see you are upset. It would be nice to have you fetching and carrying. But perhaps things are better as they are. In a purely spiritual sense I am, like lucky Alphonse, always in the middle. Good-bye, dear boy, and remember to keep that pretty mouth shut, eh?"

Julius patted Simon's cheek. The door closed behind him.

Simon pulled himself off the desk. He sat in his chair and lifted the telephone. He held it in his hand for a while and then slowly laid it down again.

❦ | FOUR

Rupert and Morgan were sitting in the sun on the steps of the Albert Memorial. They had just walked from the Prince Regent Museum to the park.

Morgan had Rupert's letter in her pocket and she touched it from time to time with the tips of her fingers. She felt more at home with the letter now than she did with Rupert. She knew it better. In his presence she felt a paralysing mixture of exhilaration and embarrassment which made her both coy and effusive. She could not behave naturally and realized only now how thoroughly frightened she was of the situation. It was not a dull fright. She was frightened because so much was at stake, because it was all so exciting, because it was unprecedented and unique. She felt shy of this tall burly blond man whose nervous apologetic sympathetic smile was so new to her that at times she could scarcely recognize his face. It was like a momentous second encounter with someone whom she had met only once and who had suddenly and impetuously kissed her on parting.

Rupert plainly did not know how to behave either. He seemed at the moment more anxious to reassure her than to repeat any of the burning phrases of his letter. The anxious atmosphere of mutual consideration was not indeed conducive to any passionate confessions. But the amazing letter was there in her pocket. *The moment has come to tell you how much I love you . . . I cannot any longer now sustain the role of the detached and helpful friend . . . A long-felt need to come closer to you and know you better . . . I have so long admired you . . . Time will show us what to do* . . . And so on for pages of Rupert's tiny almost illegible script, with many erasures and the rendezvous mentioned in a scrawl at the end.

Morgan wondered if Rupert now regretted the letter. It was very possible from his embarrassed demeanour that he did. She knew that she could not possibly ask him. It was indeed an extraordinary letter for someone like Rupert to have written, impetuous, indiscreet, even inconsiderate. Yet Morgan was delighted, and had from the first moment been delighted, to receive this feckless homage from her sage and dignified brother-in-law. So there were surprises in the world. She recalled what Julius had said about Rupert's secret life, the lost soul, the private grief, the wild sad crying. Now she had seen these things, though perhaps only for a moment; and she wondered regretfully but bravely whether Rupert would not now simply require her assistance in resuming the mask. But of course the mask could never be entirely resumed. I have come closer to Rupert, she thought. Rupert needs me. We are involved with each other forever.

Rupert's letter had said nothing about Hilda except indirectly. *We both have our responsibilities.* And yes, there was Tallis too. How clear it had suddenly become to Morgan that she had somehow hoped that *Rupert* would clarify her feelings about Tallis! Only she had not expected quite this method of clarification. For what had become plain to her, as she brooded over Rupert's letter that morning before and after Julius's visit was that really she felt far more *at home* with Rupert than she did with either Julius or Tallis. Tallis was an eerie dream, Julius a beautiful but casual destructive force. Rupert was a man, an intellectual, a person rather like herself, a person who interested her profoundly and to whom she could *talk*. Rupert was someone who might have made her happy.

The unfulfilled conditional brought her uneasily back to reality. She was indeed excited but she was also afraid. It was inconceivable that she should meddle with Hilda's marriage. Yet here, full-fledged, was an extremely tricky situation and one which threatened her beloved sister. *Hilda must never know.* If there was pain she and Rupert must bear it. Almost with joy she felt herself able to take up that challenge. Hilda, who had shared all her troubles, must be forever spared this one. She would come close to Rupert, she would help him to bear his private grief, she would keep the secret of the wildness within, she would transform by patience the violence of his love. And if she was brave enough to undertake this dangerous, this heavy task, was it not because in the end she trusted in his wisdom and not in her own?

"I trust your wisdom," she said. "I trust it. I trust *you*."

"You have indeed shown your trust," he said. "I hope I shall be worthy of it."

"Hilda must not know."

Rupert was facing the sun, frowning. "One hates deception—"

"I know. But it's kinder. How could one tell her *that*?"

"I certainly think it must be our secret for the present," said Rupert, after a moment.

"Yes, yes." Morgan was finding the conversation difficult. She was fumbling carefully with words and phrases and she could see Rupert doing the same. With a certain painful joy she postponed the moment of taking hold of his hand.

"Rupert," said Morgan, "I think you said the essential things when you talked about going *through* and not running away. There has always been love between us, hasn't there?"

Rupert shaded his eyes. He looked uncertain, apprehensive. "Yes."

"What has happened isn't all that new and strange. Of course our relationship has altered, it must alter. Of course you must be feeling—well, anxious and upset. But once we're clear that we want to go on seeing each other, then should we not regard this new thing as a natural development of an old friendship? Would not that be the wisest way to look at it? And will not that development continue for us in a *good* way if we go on just keeping our gaze steadily and *seriously* fixed upon each other?"

"I admire your confidence, your sense—"

"You know, somehow I feel this had to happen, it was in the womb of time."

"I'm not sure that I feel quite that. Anyway, as I said, I take it as something deep and serious and not just a piece of momentary madness."

"Of course it's deep, Rupert. With *you* it couldn't be otherwise."

"Well, I suppose we must—ride out the storm."

"You sound so worired, Rupert, and so sad! Don't be, my dear. We'll meet regularly. We'll make each other's acquaintance quietly. We're both very rational, you know! Only you don't worry and I won't."

"I only hope it won't be all—too painful for you."

"How marvellously considerate you are, my dear. No. It'll be painful for *you*. But we must sustain the pain together."

"Not telling Hilda hurts me, but I see it's inevitable. Have you said anything to Tallis?"

"Good God no! It's no business of Tallis's."

"I should have said, my dear, that in a way it was—"

"I don't see that. Nothing's going to *happen*! And this is our private muddle, Rupert, yours and mine."

"I wonder if you feel—free of Tallis now—emotionally I mean."

How anxious he is, she thought. I must reassure him. "Yes, I think I do. There's still a lot of distress of course. But I'm out of that wood." Am I? she wondered. All that was perfectly clear at the moment was that her immediate task was one of absolute attention to Rupert.

"It's all very perplexing," said Rupert. "You are stronger than I am. Women so often are strong at these moments. You are so clear and so calm, now. But I can't help being worried on your behalf. I don't want as it were to lead you on into an even more painful situation. Imagine yourself in my position."

"But, my dear, I do! I can see it all, the puzzlement, the scruples, the pain. But once we've decided to ride out the storm as you put it we must simply trust each other and wait for time and affection to show us the form of a deeper and permanent relationship. Because that's what we both want, isn't it, Rupert?"

"Yes. I want it. Is it possible?"

"Your diffidence touches me so much! Do you really imagine that I'm going to rush off and abandon you? Of course it's possible!"

Rupert sat sideways, shading his eyes and regarding her. "I so much don't want you to be hurt. You don't think we're playing with fire?"

"Life is made of fire."

"Morgan, your courage is fantastic."

"So is yours, my dear."

"Look," said Rupert, "I must get back to the office. And I want to think all this over."

"You won't change your mind and say we should forget all about it and not see each other or something?"

"No. I won't."

"When shall we meet again? Soon?"

They began to walk down the steps in the direction of the High Street. "All the same," said Rupert, "I am worried. There's something—puzzling in it all. And I don't want to put an awful strain upon you."

"If you can bear the strain I should think I can! When? Let's have lunch tomorrow."

"I'm having lunch with Hilda tomorrow."

There was a silence. They reached the street and Rupert hailed a taxi. "Ring me up in the office," he said. "Not today."

"Tomorrow morning then."

"All right."

The taxi drew up.

"May I come with you in the taxi as far as Whitehall?" asked Morgan.

"No. Forgive me. Better not."

They stood in the sun beside the taxi, stiff, their hands hanging, multi-coloured shadows crowding past them. Morgan felt an almost intolerable physical tension. She wanted to climb into the taxi and seize Rupert in her arms and comfort him. He was looking at her with a frowning expression of pain. He turned to the taxi driver. "Whitehall, please."

"Oh Rupert—" She felt desolation, frenzy. She did not want to leave him like this, to be left like this. The separation was suddenly awful. She stood staring at him, her face ready for tears.

"Forgive me." Rupert got into the taxi and banged the door. The taxi sailed away.

What is happening to me? thought Morgan. She stood a while immobile on the edge of the kerb. Then following a sudden impulse she hailed another taxi and gave Tallis's address in Notting Hill.

🐚 | FIVE

"This matchbox is broken, look. It's quite squashed. You must have sat on it."

"I didn't sit on it."

"You must have done. It was all right yesterday."

"In a world reeling with sin and misery you prate about squashed matchboxes."

"I feel awful."

"So do I."

"I've got that bloody pain in my hip again."

"I thought you had it all the time."

"I do have it all the time! Only sometimes it's worse."

"I can't hear a word you're saying. I wish to God you'd get yourself some teeth."

"Well, why don't you treat yourself to a shave if it comes to that? You look like something growing on the side of a tree trunk."

"You could do with a shave yourself."

"The sort of thing you can't resist scraping off with your foot and then wish you hadn't."

"Either let your beard grow or don't let it grow."

"I'm an old piece of human wreckage, rejected long ago by society and shortly to be crushed by nature. I'd have one foot in the grave if I could still stand up. I don't have to worry about shaving. I don't consort with M.P.'s and that. Was that chap really an M.P. who came in yesterday?"

"About the housing committee? Yes."

"No wonder England's done for."

"I must go and write my lecture."

"Why don't you do something useful."

"Teaching people is useful."

"Adult education! All you do is sit middle-aged babies."

"We have jolly good discussions. Why don't you come along?"

"You'd be sick if I did! I'm going to be bed-ridden from now on. You'll be carrying bed-pans, my boy, not romancing about the Jarrow marchers and the General Strike."

"You do what the doctors tell you, Daddy, and you'll be perfectly all right. You see you didn't mind going to the hospital at all. The X-ray people were very nice to you."

"No they weren't. Yes I did. One of those pups in a white coat called me 'gaffer'!"

"He wanted to make you feel at home."

"I nearly dotted him one. 'Gaffer'! That's what the Health Service does for professional standards. When I was young doctors used to know their place."

"When you were young you couldn't afford a doctor."

"Don't start that. This world's a rotten oligarchy run by gangsters. Nothing in it ever gets better."

"Come, come, Daddy. You won't mind going in for the operation. That arthritis operation is quite simple now and it'll take the pain away."

"Who's talking about an operation? Perhaps I prefer to be in pain. It's my affair I should think!"

"All right then, only stop complaining!"

"Who's complaining? Yap yap yap yap. You never leave me in peace."

"Well, I'm going to leave you in peace now."

"You'll have to stop your gadding about when I'm lying here moribund."

"Oh, shut up, Daddy. Get up and shave and go and feed the birds, for God's sake."

"I don't want to feed the bloody birds. Anyway, the new doctor's coming. Little you care."

"Oh yes, I'd forgotten. What's he like?"

"A whelp."

"Do you want me to stay with you, Daddy, till the doctor comes?"

"I want you to bugger off."

Leonard was sitting up in bed, very bright-eyed, his toothless mouth sucking and chumbling as if he were trying to devour his gums. He was wearing an old shrunken blue shirt and an ancient shiny waistcoat with one button on it. The shirt was drawn in tightly at the neck by a safety pin over which the constrained flesh bulged out, pitted and cheesy. The tonsure of silver hair was *bouffant*, as if Leonard had been crowned by a small tire of foam rubber. Tallis went out and banged the door, opened the door, closed it again more quietly, and went off down the stairs. It was another hot day.

He had let the downstairs room where Morgan's things had been. The room now contained a divan bed with a genuine mattress, a chest of drawers, two upright chairs, and a useful hook for hanging things on. Tallis had promised the tenant a rug. The tenant was a Sikh who drove a London bus. The Sikh's turban occasioned recurrent tumults at a near-by bus station. The Sikh was dignified, silent, and obstinate, and so far the turban rode steadily onward. He was a lonely man whose only companion seemed to be his transistor set. Tallis felt he could not come between them. The Sikh's transistor set was now on, playing something rather old-fashioned which sounded like

> The sun has got his hat on,
> Hip hip hip hooray,
> The sun has got his hat on
> And he's coming out today!

The kitchen smelt of decaying matter. It was difficult to trace the source. I must get rid of all those milk bottles, thought Tallis. Some of them contained weird formations resembling human organs preserved in tubes. It was quite difficult to get these out of the bottles and the last time he tried to he stopped up the sink. He banged the kitchen door and a lot of things fell off the dresser. Some of them seemed at once to develop legs and scuttled about near his feet until he kicked them away. They squealed not with pain but with derision. The bitter smell mingled with the rest.

He did not feel strong enough to tackle the milk bottles so he sat down at the kitchen table where his books and notebooks were laid out on sheets of newspaper. He automatically laid his head down on the table and then lifted it again.

> The sun has got his hat on,
> Hip hip hip hooray . . .

Tallis had managed to find another evening class which paid five guineas a week, but it was out beyond Greenford and the return fare was nearly ten shillings. Also it was on the evening when the voluntary workers' subcommittee of the housing committee usually met, and he had so far not been able to shift either the one or the other. Also the class wanted the history of the European trade-union movement. Tallis's knowledge of this was rusty and sketchy in places and there were two silent sneering Central Europeans in the class who almost undoubtedly knew more than he did. He would just have to mug it up somehow.

How horribly all his work lacked dignity, he reflected. He never really *thought* about anything any more now. The stillness of thought was absent from his life. He was always scratching and patching, trying to fudge up some half-baked rigmarole which would get past without positive disgrace. He sighed and reached out for *Geschichte und Klassenbewustsein*. The traffic roared softly in his ears. The stifling stinking air of Notting Hill pressed down upon the top of the house, upon the top of his head. He imagined what it would be like to be in a *field*. He was in a field, full of tall fresh green grasses and little scrambling flowers and mossy earthy smells and moistness, lying down deep in the grass beside his sister.

"Tallis!"

Tallis woke up. Morgan was there.

Morgan was looking radiantly smart in a sky-blue linen suit and a white shirt. Her cheeks were flushed by the sun. She came in and closed the door. Tallis tried to rise and half fell off the chair, scattering books.

"You were taking a nap! I thought you were so busy!"

"I am busy," said Tallis. "Here, sit down."

"No thanks, not on that. This place smells."

"Must clean it," said Tallis.

"Can't you get a char?"

"No."

"You look a sight. Why don't you shave? It looks as if your beard is grey, but perhaps that's just dirt. And why are you wearing that piece of filthy white rag round your neck? You ought to wear a proper tie or else an open-necked shirt. And if you must roll up your sleeves roll them properly, not like an old rag bag."

"You look marvellous," said Tallis, "you look like flowers, fields, country things."

"You are poetical today."

Tallis felt an immediate thoughtless joy at her presence. He didn't feel sick this time. Just wildly joyful, like a dog. "Oh, God, I am glad to see you, Morgan. It's just *marvellous* to see you!"

"Well, don't take on so. Is Peter in?"

"No, he's gone to see Hilda."

"What's that ghastly row?"

"A Sikh playing a transistor."

"I've got a letter here for Peter. I wrote it in the taxi."

"Oh."

"Will you give it to him?"

"Yes."

"You seem put out."

"Didn't you come to see me?" said Tallis. Then he said imploringly, "*Please* sit down and don't look as if you were just going to go."

"Have you any clean newspaper in this dump?"

"Here's today's *Daily Worker.*"

Morgan put the newspaper carefully on the seat of the chair and sat down. Tallis hovered on the other side of the table staring at her.

"You won't forget to give Peter the letter?"

"No."

"All right, don't be cross. You aren't jealous, are you?"

"I told you not to mess around with Peter unless you meant to care for him properly."

"Well, who says I'm not caring for him properly?"

"You *can't*," said Tallis. "You haven't got the time. And you haven't got the *sense*."

"You are being censorious!"

"Peter's in love with you."

"You *are* jealous!"

"Well, all right, hang it, I am jealous!"

"You can't have it both ways, both lecture me and be jealous!"

"Why not? I'm quite clear-headed enough to see that you're being damned irresponsible. And now I suppose you're writing him love letters."

"If you could only hear your tone of voice!" said Morgan. "I'm *not* writing him love letters. You make me sick. Here, read the letter, I haven't sealed it!"

"I don't want to read the letter, it's none of my business."

"I'm glad you think so! Well, I'm going to read it to you."

Morgan pulled out the letter and read it aloud.

"Dearest Peter,

Just a little note to say that I shall be out of London for a while so don't try to get in touch. I have to go to Oxford and a whole list of other places about jobs. I'll let you know when I'm back. Be a good boy. Lots and lots of love to you, dear Peter.

Morgan

There, is that a love letter?"

"It's a lying letter," said Tallis.

"What do you mean?"

"It's untruthful."

"What makes you say that?" said Morgan, flushing.

"I can feel it. You aren't going to Oxford and a whole list of other places about jobs. Are you?

Morgan put the letter back into the envelope. Then with an exclamation of annoyance she tore it up into small pieces. She put the pieces on the table and glared at Tallis. "You are being very disagreeable."

"I love you," said Tallis.

"Oh, don't talk that weak-minded rubbish. I did come to see you, as it happens. Not just to deliver the letter to Peter."

"I'm so glad! Would you like some tea?"

"No. I've decided after all that I want a divorce, and I want it soon."

Tallis looked at her for a moment in silence. Then he turned away toward the gas stove.

"What are you doing, for heavens sake?" said Morgan.

"Putting on the kettle. I think we should have some tea."

Morgan lit a cigarette.

"What about all that stuff about being free and innocent and loving people?"

"Oh, I expect that will go on. But I suddenly feel capable of thinking and deciding. I feel lucid. Would you mind divorcing me for adultery?"

"Yes," said Tallis. He clawed the old tea leaves out of the pot.

"What do you mean, yes?"

"I don't want to divorce you. Anyway, Julius wouldn't play."

"What makes you think that? Yes, he would. Tallis, you're not going to be so inconceivably mean as not to divorce me?"

"Who've you met?" said Tallis. He held a tea-stained cup under the tap.

"I don't know what you're talking about."

"You want a free hand with someone else. That's the only motive which would make you lucid on that subject. Who is it?"

"Tallis, don't be an idiot. I've just been thinking. It's a pretty obvious conclusion, isn't it?"

"No. I've been thinking too. You're far too unstable to decide anything at present. Wait a year."

"A divorce takes time. I want us to start now."

"Wait a year."

"I haven't got a year! I want to get on with my life!"

Tallis dried the cup vigorously on a piece of newspaper. Some of the brown stain came off on the paper.

Morgan was quiet, regarding him and smoking. It was suffocatingly hot in the kitchen. She took off the blue linen jacket, rolled up her sleeves, and undid a button of her blouse. Tallis made the tea.

"Tallis, you are deceiving yourself."

"You are deceiving yourself. Oddly enough, you love me. You'll see this later."

"Stop dreaming."

"You are the dreamer. I took you on forever. That's what love is about. Forever."

"You're being solipsistic. I am an adventuress, Tallis. I doubt if I shall ever make any man happy. That's why—"

"You could make me happy. You need me. You will never be content frigging around with lovers. You'll only choose the wrong ones."

"That's the plea of a weak man. Stop, I've given up sugar."

"You have *forgotten* the quality of your happiness with me. We lived in an innocent world."

"That world has been smashed."

"No, it still exists only it is empty. You are my wife and you have not denied that you love me."

"Yes, but what's the use— Oh Tallis, you *mix* me so!" She took the tea cup. Tallis stood beside her. "It's no good, Tallis. You keep talking, but I can't hear you. I'm mechanical. I'm just a machine. I look like a human being but I'm really a robot."

"No. This is flesh and would bleed." He caressed her arm, and then moved away again.

"I wish you wouldn't *plead* with me, Tallis, though I know, what else can you do, and I ought to be grateful— Tallis, give me one good reason why I should come back to you."

"I'll give you two. I want a child."

"Really—"

"And you want a child."

"Oh—" The cup jarred abruptly onto the table.

"Of course," said Tallis, talking quickly, "that would bring us other troubles, children always do, and we'd be very short of money, and if you did decide to leave me later there'd be a problem about the child, or children they might be by then, and I know I'm not the only male in the world but I am convenient being your husband, although society is so terribly permissive these days of course, and you know you can trust me absolutely and who else can you really trust, at any rate it would take a long time for you to feel so right with somebody that you wanted him to be the father of your child, and after all you aren't all that young, you're over thirty, and it's time for this thing to happen to you if it's going to happen, isn't it?"

Morgan rose to her feet. She rolled down her sleeves and put on her jacket. "Tallis, I think you're *disgusting!*"

"I only said I was convenient," said Tallis.

"I'm going. I'll write to you about the divorce. Good-bye."

"Wait a minute." Tallis came round the table and stood in front of the door. "I've been bloody patient about this business of your clearing off and living with someone else for two years, and everyone nagging me to get tough with you, and now you

274 ☙ A FAIRLY HONOURABLE DEFEAT

come back and all you can do is talk a lot of slimy half-witted nonsense about your states of mind. Damn your states of mind. If you want me to co-operate with you either in continuing our marriage or in ending it you've got to talk to me properly. I'm fed up with your waltzing in and out with statements of policy and you feel this and you feel that. You can bloody well talk to me. You're my wife, and I want to know what you've been doing and what you're doing now. I want to know what *happened* in America, and if you now imagine you've fallen in love with someone else I want to know who it is."

"It's a bit late to start playing the jealous husband," said Morgan. "And you're not much good at acting anyhow."

"I'm not acting."

"Yes, you are. You put up with it all, didn't you?"

"I had to. I knew you'd come back."

"Don't, Tallis. When you pretend to be tough you're just pathetic and I can't bear it. Now get out of the way, please. Whatever's that you're wearing underneath your shirt? Good heavens, it's my amber necklace. I wondered where it was. You are sentimental, aren't you."

"You don't mean you forgot you put it round my neck?"

"Of course I forgot. And it's not the only male neck it's been round lately! I've got other things to think about besides you. As indeed you yourself were anxious to suggest!"

"So there *is* someone else!"

"No. Get out of my way."

"Who is it? *Who is it?*" Tallis took hold of the white blouse at the neck.

"Let go, you're tearing it. *Let go!* Or do you really want a fight?"

"I want you to stay here and talk to me properly."

"Well, just see if you can keep me here!"

Morgan crooked her left foot round the back of Tallis's ankle and pressed her right hand against his throat. They staggered together, knocking over a row of half-empty milk bottles. Tallis twisted the white nylon collar till it tore, and captured her hand, and began to bend it round behind her back. Morgan tried to bring her knee up but Tallis had drawn her too closely against him. Their faces touched, bone moving on bone. Morgan's free hand clawed the back of his shirt, her feet began to slip, and she came down heavily on the floor, pulling Tallis over on top of her. The string of the necklace broke and the amber beads pattered loudly to the ground all about them. Morgan twisted away from him and sprang to her feet. The kitchen door banged. The front door banged.

Tallis got up slowly. His neck was bruised, his knee was throbbing. The kitchen floor was covered with broken glass and stinking yellowish milky mess. He picked up a half of one of the bottles and threw it into the sink where it broke into further pieces. Bending down he began to pick up the amber beads here and there and stuff them into the pockets of his trousers.

"Oh, er, excuse me—" A round-faced young man with spectacles carrying a black bag and a nylon macintosh was standing in the doorway.

"What do *you* want?" said Tallis. He went on searching for the beads.

"I'm sorry—I thought I'd better wait until— I wanted to see you—"

"What about?" Tallis threw another piece of milk bottle into the sink.

"I'm the new doctor."

"Oh." Tallis straightened up. "Sorry. You've been with my father?"

"Yes."

"Sorry," said Tallis. "Won't you sit down? He's been rather in pain."

"We had a talk—"

"Can you operate for that sort of arthritis? We haven't heard anything since the X-rays."

The doctor, who had not sat down, closed the kitchen door. He drew his shoe along the linoleum in an attempt to scrape off the sour milk. He looked at Tallis with a rather odd expression on his face. "I'm afraid the news is not very good."

"You mean you can't operate?"

"I mean it's not arthritis. At least there is a mild arthritic condition. But—"

"It's cancer," said Tallis.

"Yes."

"I see," said Tallis. He picked up the two tea cups and put
them in the sink with the broken glass. "What's the outlook?"

"There's very little we can do, I'm afraid. Some deep ray treatment may ease the discomfort of course. But the condition being
already general—"

"What's the outlook?"

"Your father might live for a year."

"I see," said Tallis.

"Of course I haven't told him. He still thinks it's arthritis.
We naturally think it proper in such cases for the relatives to
decide—"

"Yes, yes. You'll let me know about the treatment. I don't
want—if it just prolongs life for a short while—if he's suffering
—but you said it might ease him—"

"It is thought to be advisable—"

"Could you go, please," said Tallis.

"If you'd like to see the specialist you'd be welcome at the
hospital, any time tomorrow morning, just telephone—"

"Yes, yes, I'll come. And now please go, forgive me. Thank
you."

The door closed.

The kitchen, where usually there were so many scratchings and
scufflings and patterings of claws, was completely silent. Even
the murmur of the traffic seemed to have been made still. Tallis
stared at jagged glass and crumpled newspaper and milk which
had already dried into thick yellowish pats and errant gleaming
globes of wine-dark Baltic amber. He stared down into a world
that had been utterly utterly changed.

᪈ | SIX

Hilda was cautiously stroking Peter's hair. Peter, politely affecting not to notice, had his noble far-away Napoleonic look on. They were in Hilda's boudoir, sitting side by side upon the small sofa.

"So I can tell your father that you'll definitely go back to college in October?"

"Yes. Haven't you told him already?"

"Well, sort of. But I wanted to be sure. I thought you might change your mind."

"I won't. I've given my word to Morgan."

Hilda sighed. She had perceived her son's love for her sister. She was not alarmed, but it made her feel sad somehow. It made her feel old.

"Your father will be so relieved."

"I don't care what *he* thinks!"

"Peter, do try to be a little more kind to him. You do hurt him so. He is your father."

"Precisely!"

Oh Peter, don't be so *boring!*"

"If only he'd just relax and stop *acting* father! It's like a rotten evening in the theatre."

"You might stop acting too!"

"All right, Mother, all right!"

Hilda thought, I must ask Morgan to tell Peter to be kind to Rupert. He'll attend to *her*. She sighed again. But that would have to wait, since Morgan had just rung up to cancel a luncheon date and announce her temporary departure from London.

"Morgan told me I ought to be nicer to him," said Peter, "so

I suppose I'll have to try!" He detached himself gently from the light pressure of his mother's arm and shifted a little way along the sofa.

"So she already— Will you come to that dinner party, Peter?"

"You mean to celebrate Pa's great book? I shouldn't think so. Is the ghastly masterpiece actually finished?"

"Yes."

"Is he going to read it aloud at the dinner?"

"Don't be silly!"

Rupert is sad that the book is finished, thought Hilda. He has travelled with it such a long way. And now that he's stopped working on it he probably feels all kinds of doubts and anxieties about its worth. Rupert had been in a strange mood just lately, nervy, preoccupied, worried.

"By the way, Peter, do you happen to know Morgan's address? She's away, isn't she?" Morgan had rung off so quickly, Hilda had not been able to ask for an address.

"She's visiting here and there and seeing somebody about a job, I think. She sent me a note, but no address. Look, I must go in a moment, Mother darling." He stood up beside her and put his hand lightly under her chin. Hilda captured the hand and quickly squeezed it and kissed his fingers, closing her eyes for a moment. Looking up at her tall son she felt an agony of anxious protective frustrated love. She yearned over his future, so full of terrible unknowns. She groaned with the weight of a love which she could scarcely begin to express. She had already released his hand.

"You are all right, aren't you, Peter?"

"Yes, Mother, I'm fine."

He looked well, calmer, plumper. That was Morgan's doing.

"Come again soon." She felt so sad at his going, sad at his inevitable separateness from her, sad that he had been so much taken over by Morgan, sad at her own inadequacy to the immense needs of his youth. "I do wish you'd come back and live here."

"I must have my own place. It's more than ever important."

"How's Tallis?"

"I think Tallis is going mad."

"You aren't serious?" said Hilda.

"No, I suppose not, but he's been very odd lately. Well, maybe no odder than usual. I must push along, Mama."

"You'll come again soon?"

"Yes, yes."

"When?"

"Oh, next week probably. I'll ring up. Cheerio and thanks for the mun!"

After Peter was gone Hilda uncurled herself from the sofa and patted the cushions back into shape. She teased out her hair which was still a little damp from a recent plunge in the pool. Then she went to her desk, where she had laid out all her arrears of correspondence. The Kensington and Chelsea Preservation Society. The West London Noise Abatement League. The Discharged Prisoners Help Society. Oxfam. Labour Party. Townswomen's Guild. The Bardwell Clinic for Unmarried Mothers. The Chelsea Pensioners' Christman Tobacco Fund. Friends of the Old Vic, the National Gallery, the Wigmore Hall, the Fulham and Putney Juvenile Delinquents. British Societies for Peace in various parts of the world.

Hilda found that she could not focus her eyes upon the letters. She felt vague and gloomy, she did not quite know why. She was a little worried about Rupert. Was it just his book or was he perhaps developing the flu? She had been very disappointed not to see Morgan and a little hurt at the brusque way in which Morgan had cancelled the appointment. The bond with her sister had never been more important. Hilda had expected much from Morgan's return, almost a renewal of life. She was well aware that she had felt gratified that the defeated Morgan should come back to her to be cared for, but she knew too that the gratification was an expression of love. There was some fruition of the past in this cherishing of her sister, some reassuring line of force from childhood which reached away onward into the future. Hilda needed to be leaned upon and confided in and Morgan could not have been more dependent and more frank. Thus far, in the chemistry of the world, all was well. Hilda had been sorry when her sister moved out of the house, but she had understood. Now she was troubled by this sudden breath of aloofness. Possibly Morgan regretted having talked so much.

She tried to be sensible about Morgan as she tried to be sensible about Peter, but it is not easy to cajole a naturally possessive temperament. Did Peter know what it was like for her when he walked out of the room vaguely saying he might turn up next week, vaguely saying he would telephone? Peter was uncaged and free, and although Hilda knew that her son loved her to an extent which was probably exceptional, and talked to her with an openness which was certainly unusual, she was after all only his mother. This meant that she was a unique and precious being to him, but it also meant that it was her special privilege to put up humbly and uncomplainingly with any degree of casualness and neglect. Peter knew that it was a metaphysical impossibility that her love for him should diminish by one iota whatever he might or might not do, and this precisely enabled him to dismiss her altogether from his mind.

Hilda brooded for a time upon these paradoxes, but she was not addicted to feeling sorry for herself and she soon began to try to concentrate upon the letters. She was just reaching for her pen when there was a sound upon the stairs. Hilda turned. It was much too early for Rupert. She thought it might be Morgan. Someone tapped softly upon the door.

"Come in," cried Hilda.

Someone opened the door rather deferentially and peered in. It was Julius King.

"Oh!" said Hilda. "Good heavens, you gave me a shock. Come in, Julius."

Hilda had seen Julius only twice since his return to England, on both occasions at Rupert's urging. Rupert was anxious that there should be no appearance of coldness on Hilda's part. She had joined Rupert and Julius for lunch once, and more recently Julius had come to Priory Grove for a drink, though he had only stayed for half an hour.

"Please forgive me for walking in. The door was open!"

"It usually is!" said Hilda. "I expect you want Rupert. I'm afraid he won't be in just yet."

"No, I didn't specially want Rupert. I was passing near by and I thought I might steal a brief refuge from the sun. You must forgive me for feeling so much at home here!"

"But I'm delighted!" said Hilda. "It is hot, isn't it. You wouldn't like a swim, would you? You could borrow Rupert's things."

"No, no, I'm nervous of water, even in swimming pools."

"Perhaps you wanted to see Simon? He's quite gone off his swimming lately, I'm sorry to say."

"No, indeed. But how modest you are! You imagine me to be anxious to see anyone rather than yourself."

Have I been rude? thought Hilda. She always felt a bit awkward with Julius. "No, indeed— But wouldn't you like some tea or a drink? I think it's not too early for a drink, don't you?"

"I'd adore some lemonade," said Julius, "or Coca-Cola if you had any in the fridge. I got so hot walking round the Boltons, and I must confess that the idea of a cold drink did figure in my plans for coming here!"

"Of course, of course, do come downstairs. I'm afraid we don't keep Coca-Cola but you could have some lemonade and plenty of ice."

Julius waited in the drawing-room while Hilda squeezed lemons and brought the lemonade and glasses from the kitchen. He had opened the french windows and a warm thick smell of garden came into the room.

"You wouldn't like some gin with it? No? Do sit down, it's a bit cooler in here. I expect you miss the air conditioning. But this is very un-English summer weather, you know, and I don't suppose it'll last much longer."

Julius merely smiled and sipped the lemonade. He was sitting in a small arm-chair half turned to the window. Hilda hovered about and then sat down near him. The room was shadowy and uncertain in the proximity of the bright sunlight. Hilda felt uneasy.

"I gather you may be our neighbour in the Boltons," she said. "You'll be very grand when you live there, we'll hardly dare to call on you!" I'm being idiotic, she thought. Why am I so inept?

"I hope *you'll* come," said Julius, politely. "Hilda, what perfectly delicious fresh lemonade. What are the more vaunted pleasures of the flesh compared with the wild joy of quenching one's thirst on a hot day?"

Julius was sipping his lemonade, smiling at her with an air almost of ecstasy, and his face looked like a mask. What pale hair and dark eyes he has, thought Hilda. He really is a very odd-looking man. His hair has a strange faded look, like old hair, yet his face is young. He's not exactly blond at all, and his eyes must be dark grey, or are they dark brown with a sort of tinge of blue? And how extremely long and curly his mouth is, like two mouths blurred into one.

She thought, I mustn't stare so. "It is a pleasant neighbourhood," said Hilda.

"I like that little backwater where Morgan lives too," said Julius. "It's quite near here, isn't it?"

"You've been to see Morgan—"

"Yes. Just as a friend, of course, the drama is over. I hope you didn't think too ill of me, Hilda?"

"I—no, I—how can I judge?"

"One does judge though. Morgan must have told you about it all?"

"She told me a little, yes, but—"

"But—?"

"But other people's lives are very mysterious," said Hilda. "One can hardly ever see what another person is like."

"You mean you can't see what I'm like?"

"No. I can hardly see what Morgan's like. Morgan talked about it but I couldn't really see—or presume to make any judgement."

"Thank you," said Julius, after a moment's silence.

He was rather solemn now. Hilda felt agitated by the conversation. Julius was studying her and she could not look at him. She looked at the sunlit garden and the sparkling water and the roses and her eyes dazzled. She shifted her chair and filled her sight with the soft blurred colours of the dim room, the figure of Julius vague and hazy in her attention. She felt nervous and yet at the same time almost sleepy.

"It may seem odd to you, Hilda, but I cared very much what you thought."

"What *I* thought?"

"Yes. Perhaps one instinctively selects one's judges. Perhaps there is deep significance in the selection. I always wondered: What will Hilda think?"

"But you scarcely know me, knew me."

"I am glad you altered the tense. Morgan talked a lot about you. And after all I have met you quite often, and you are not a person that one forgets. I dare say I have observed you much more closely than you have observed me."

"I can hardly believe you really worried about my opinion!" said Hilda. The idea rather pleased her, however.

"I did, I assure you! You are so much more grown-up than Morgan, so much more of a genuinely thinking being. When I tried to be objective I tried to see the thing through your eyes. Impossible of course, but I assure you it was a salutary exercise!"

Hilda was touched. It also occurred to her that she had not conceived of Julius as having scruples. She had been rather unjust to him. "I hope you were not too hurt by what you called the drama?"

"Thank you for asking, Hilda, thank you for *thinking!* I was hurt, I was after all very attached. But one recovers and the details don't matter. And I suppose my conscience ached a bit! A married woman and so on. I am old enough to be a very conventional person at heart. But one can deal with one's conscience. Morgan dealt with hers. And I can't pretend to be very saintly."

"I expect it was really a *muddle,*" said Hilda. "So many things in life are."

"So many things are. I'm afraid your sister has a compulsive genius for muddles."

"I think she gets entangled with people because she's so kind-hearted," said Hilda, "and then she finds she can't get out."

"Exactly. And it's very innocent really."

"You think Morgan has recovered?"

"From me? Well! Yes! Don't you?"

"Yes," said Hilda thoughtfully. "She is certainly quite absorbed in—being kind-hearted in another quarter!" She gave a little laugh. "And as you say, it's very innocent really."

"Good heavens," said Julius, "so you *know?*" He put his glass on the floor and stared at Hilda.

"Yes, of course," said Hilda. "But how did you know? Did Morgan tell you?"

"I—got to know."

"I hope it's not being talked about or made a thing of?"

"You're being very calm about it, Hilda."

"Why not?" said Hilda. "It's not in any way alarming, in fact it's been very valuable. After all, they're both fairly sensible people and the difference in their ages—"

"Hilda, you *amaze* me," said Julius. "I'll confess now that I've aways admired you. Now I reverence you."

"You're beginning to worry me, Julius!" said Hilda. "Have some more lemonade, no? Perhaps I ought to be more troubled. But I don't see that anyone is going to be hurt—"

Julius let out a long breath. "Hilda, you're marvellous. So genuinely unconventional! And you aren't just heroic, you're probably also wise. After all, as you say, two sensible people, these things blow over, if one has the sense just to wait and not to interfere, and of course it's probably just a sort of kind-heartedness on both sides—"

Hilda laughed. "I don't think it's kind-heartedness on Peter's side!" she said. "I think poor Peter has really fallen a bit in love with his Aunt Morgan. But it's just calf love and I know Morgan will deal with it sensibly."

There was a silence. The silence lasted oddly long. Hilda turned to look at Julius. He was looking at her with a strange horrified expression. "What is it, Julius?"

"*Peter*. I see. I'm sorry I—I thought we were talking of—something else— Oh dear—"

"What else could we be talking of?" said Hilda, surprised.

"Oh, yes, yes, what indeed. Yes, Peter, of course. Dear me, how late it is. Hilda, I really must go." Julius rose to his feet.

"But whatever did you think we were talking about?" said Hilda. She rose too.

"Oh, nothing. A complete misunderstanding. I mean, yes, of course I was talking about Peter. Morgan told me all about it. Excuse me, Hilda, I must go. I think I should call on Morgan since I'm so near. Thank you for the lemonade."

"Morgan's out of London," said Hilda. "She'll be away for a week or two."

"Well, well, she told you that, did she? I mean, oh, yes, I see, out of London! Yes, yes. Hilda, I must run."

They were at the front door.

"You've confused me, Julius," said Hilda. "What did you mean just now when you said—"

"Nothing, nothing. Just about Peter. Hilda, I— Forgive me, forgive me."

Julius kissed her hand. Then he departed rapidly with a wave and began to run away down the sunlit shadowed street.

Hilda held the hand which Julius had kissed in her other hand. She was not used to having her hand kissed. She returned slowly into the drawing-room. She felt completely puzzled. Then she began to feel frightened, as if her life was suddenly menaced.

🎎 | SEVEN

"I've put the irises in the white *art nouveau* jug," said Simon.
"I hope you approve."

"I defer to you in such matters, dear boy."

"But say you think they're nice."

"I think they're lovely."

It was Axel's birthday.

Simon had after all decided against the salmon trout. They
were to start with whitebait and retsina. After that a cassoulet
with rice and Nuits de Young. Then a lemon sorbet. Then a salad
of chicory and cos lettuce with a light dressing. Then white Stilton
cheese and special wholemeal biscuits from the shop in Baker
Street, with a very faintly sweetish hock.

It was of course rather hot weather for a cassoulet but Simon
especially enjoyed making this dish. Also it was an absorbing task
and just now he instinctively tried to find himself one absorbing
task after another. He had made a start on it yesterday evening,
cooking the beans with careful additions of onion, garlic, thyme,
parsley, basil, gammon, and pieces of sticky pork rind. That afternoon, which he had taken off from the museum, he had roasted
some mutton and half a duck while the beans were heating up
again to simmer quietly. After that the big brown earthenware pot
which they had bought in Besançon was packed with layers of
beans followed by layers of duck, mutton, and garlic sausage,
followed by more layers of beans, followed by more layers of duck,
mutton and garlic sausage, all the way up to the top. Then a slow
oven until the upper beans were crusty. Stir the crusty beans in

and let other beans get crusty. Stir these in. The climax had almost been reached.

"Doesn't the smell of this make you almost faint with joy?" said Simon to Axel. "I must say, I'm terribly hungry. We must be careful not to eat too much whitebait."

"I thought you never liked eating a fish if you could see its eyes. Perhaps whitebaits' eyes are too small to be accusing!"

"Axel, please, this is no moment for sentimentality! I hope you followed my instructions and had no lunch."

They were both in the kitchen holding glasses of sherry in their hands. Simon was wearing a very long plastic apron with pink and white daisies upon it.

"I thought it was rather quaint to be forbidden to have lunch on my birthday!"

"But in a cause like *this!*"

"I had a light lunch."

"You don't take food seriously!"

"Isn't cassoulet a bit rich for this weather?"

"It'll make you perspire and then you'll feel cooler."

"What a lot you've made. We'll be eating it for days."

"It's delicious cold."

"I'm afraid I don't take food seriously," said Axel. "I'm very puritan really."

"A fact which we've discussed in other contexts, darling!"

"Eating reveals the characteristic grossness of the human race and also the in-built failure of its satisfactions. We arrive eager, we stuff ourselves, and we go away depressed and disappointed and probably feeling a bit queasy into the bargain. It's an image of the *déçu* in human existence. A greedy start and a stupefied finish. Waiters, who are constantly observing this cycle, must be the most disillusioned of men."

"Really, Axel, in the presence of my cassoulet! I think it would be delicate to retire to the drawing-room."

They went up to the drawing-room. The picture of the *kouros*, briefly in eclipse, was back in its accustomed place. Simon began to rearrange the irises. They were tall bearded irises in a number of unusual colours, purples which were almost black, oranges which were almost brown, and extremely metallic luminous bright blues. They had cost Simon a large sum of money at Harrods.

"You do like your tie, don't you, Axel?"

"Yes, delightful."

Axel was wearing a rather dark and discreetly flowery tie which Simon had given him and which seemed rather like a piece of background from a pre-Raphaelite picture. The problem of Axel's taste in ties remained obscure. When Simon had first known him, Axel tended absently to wear the same tie every day, an extremely dreary darkish blue affair with white spots on it. Simon, in an effort to educate his friend, had at first made, as he now realized, the mistake of applying shock tactics. About ties Axel was impeccably polite and mysterious. He accepted with exclamations of pleasure the Matisse-like offerings with which Simon had hoped to enliven his sense of colour. However, Simon observed that these gifts were very rarely worn and that the white-spotted monstrosity tended, after a short interval, to reappear, until one day Simon quietly purloined it and dropped it into a waste basket outside Barons Court underground station. Later on, more tactful and with a deeper knowledge of his subject, Simon conceived a special style for Axel, something darkish yet rich in colour, intricate and yet not startling in design. Like someone studying an animal on a new diet, Simon watched Axel's tie behaviour. After a considerable repertoire had been built up Simon was even able to compile statistics and thus to discover the point at which his own taste and Axel's tended to converge. The birthday tie was, in Simon's opinion, bang on.

"And you like your shirts?"

"Yes, yes, just the right ones, thank you, my dear."

That was rather a dull present. Axel had insisted on instructing Simon exactly which shirts to buy him. This was, it is true, in the light of one or two rather expensive failures in the past. Axel was indeed not at all an easy man to give presents to. He tended to say, "But I've got one of those," when some carefully selected and

uniquely designed garment was presented to him. Simon mooted
the possibility that his friend was colour blind. Now I'm awfully
easy to give presents to, thought Simon. There are so many many
things that I like and want. He fondled the royal blue cravat with
emerald green acanthus leaves upon it which he was wearing
tucked into the neck of his palest of pale green shirts.

"You've got a new cravat, Simon. You are an extravagant boy."

"I'm always allowed to buy myself a present on your birthday.
It's a tradition. The house gets a present on your birthday too."

"Yes, yes, I've noticed. You've bought *another* piece of that expensive Irish cut glass. Do be more prudent, my dear creature,
we aren't made of money."

Simon loved that "we."

This was the sort of moment when he should have been feeling
very happy. And in a way he did feel happy. Since the incident
in the Chinese restaurant Axel had been entirely restored to good
temper. He was even exceptionally affectionate to Simon and
seemed to have completely forgotten his annoyance about Morgan.
What a proof of love this pardon was, thought Simon, and how
joyful it would have made him if only it were not for this compli-
cation about Julius. Simon found himself thinking obsessively
about Julius and about the curious situation in which Julius had
involved him, without at all succeeding in understanding what
that situation was. It was something bad and rather frightening
and it involved telling lies. It was also something somehow deeply
disgusting. Julius seemed to be trying to involve him in some
sort of conspiracy, but with what purpose? If only Simon had not
concealed from Axel that rather unpleasant scene at Julius's flat. If
only, for the sin went further back, he had not concealed from
Axel that Julius had asked him to go to his flat. If Simon had only
told the truth at the second stage, although he might have had a
rough time it would all have been over by now. Like a criminal
who asks for other misdemeanours to be taken into account,
Simon could by now have unloaded the whole thing and be able
with a clear and open heart to enjoy the latest proofs of Axel's

love. Was there not some moment when he could have told Axel everything? Should he not now perhaps tell him everything?

Simon was still in a condition of hurt shock about what he had been made by Julius to overhear at the museum. This particular secret was unutterably burdensome, and yet Simon felt forced to conclude that he must continue to carry it. The revelation would mean the telling of the whole story. And it was not just that he feared Julius's threats. He did fear them, deeply connected as they were with the permanent nightmares of his life. It was also that if he told Axel *this* it would be a betrayal involving other people. Would it be wise to tell Axel at this stage? Julius had pointed out the problem. What would Axel do? Would he keep quiet or would he rush round to Rupert or even to Hilda? Axel disliked Morgan. Would he not here blame her and wish to discredit her? And he hated concealments. There would be a terrible painful muddle, even perhaps a scandal. Simon was not helped to think clearly by his continued inability quite to believe that Julius was telling the truth. Had Julius really engineered it all, made Rupert and Morgan each believe that the other was in love? How on earth had he done it? And yet if he had not somehow arranged it how had he known where they would be meeting each other? Of course he might have intercepted a letter. This dreadful involvement of Rupert and Morgan might have happened quite independently of Julius, and Julius might have decided for obscure reasons of his own to mystify Simon about it. And if Julius really had started it could he also stop it, and stop it painlessly as he had boasted to Simon that he would? Could Julius at any point be trusted or believed? How could this tangle not have some agonizing denouement? If only it were not these particular two people! Simon felt an awful confused jealous pain about it on his own account. He hoped that it would all somehow end quietly, so quietly that later on it would seem never to have happened at all. It was partly this hope which persuaded him not to open his heart to Axel.

Simon was haunted. But human beings get used to leading

double lives. He avoided Seymour Walk and Priory Grove. And when he was with Axel these things faded, seemed not to matter too much, seemed quite likely to turn out all right after all. As Simon fussed about, rearranging the irises, patting the cushions, and pouring more very dry sherry into Axel's glass, he felt quite relaxed and cheerful.

"Oh, by the way," said Axel. "I forgot to tell you. Julius rang up and asked if he could come round tonight."

"Oh, *no!*" Simon put the bottle down on the table with a loud clack.

"I said that was O.K." said Axel. "I hope you don't mind. I thought it was rather brilliant of Julius to remember it was my birthday."

"Oh *God*," said Simon. He lifted the bottle and automatically wiped the wet ring off the table with his handkerchief.

"You don't mind, do you, Simon? What is it?"

"I thought it was going to be just you and me," said Simon. "I was so much looking forward to it."

"Don't be childish. After all we dine tête-à-tête a good many evenings in the year. Why worry so much about this one?"

"This one's special. Oh Axel, I do think you might have consulted me."

"Well, how could I, it would have seemed so rude. I had to say yes or no straightaway."

"You should have said no."

"Really, Simon! And suppose I rather like the idea of seeing Julius tonight?"

"Then why don't you go out and have dinner with him."

"Simon, stop it! You really must stop these irrational puerile bursts of jealousy, they spoil everything. Why don't you think a little before you speak? You're behaving like a child of three. Julius is an old friend, and I'm not going to give up my old friends just to humour your infantile possessiveness. I'm fed up with these sort of tantrums. You know perfectly well that I love you. I think you're being damned ungrateful."

"Oh, all right, all right, sorry. It isn't that anyway. I mean I'm not jealous. It's just— Sorry, Axel. But I did arrange everything so carefully, and now you suddenly spring this on me."

"Well, you can't claim there isn't enough to eat!"

"There won't be enough whitebait."

"You said yourself we shouldn't eat much whitebait. Come, Simon, it's my birthday, which you insist on celebrating. Don't be cross with me. Maybe I should have told you sooner, but I just forgot. So you see it can't have been all that important to me!"

"Yes, yes. Sorry, darling. When is Julius coming?"

"Now I come to think of it, he didn't say. He just asked if he could drop in."

"So I suppose we'll just have to wait for him indefinitely! The cassoulet will spoil."

Simon went down to the kitchen and stared at the big brown earthenware pot which they had bought in Besançon. Everything was suddenly blackened and deadened. Oh, if only he hadn't ever started telling lies to Axel.

"What ho, Axel."

"What *what*, Julius?"

"What ho. Isn't that what one says in England?"

"Not any more, I'm afraid. But never mind. What ho, Julius."

"Many happy returns."

"Thank you."

"Hello, Simon, you're looking very beautiful."

"Would you like a dry martini?"

"No, thank you. I find my touchy and fastidious inside has proved grateful for a moratorium on dry martinis since I came to England. And I think my migraine is better too. Just a little whisky, if you please. May I sit here?"

The cassoulet was overcooked. Simon had refused Axel's plea that as Julius was so late they should begin without him. He had insisted on waiting for Julius. It was now after nine o'clock.

Julius was looking rather immaculate and clerical in a black suit of very light material. He had brought in with him and placed without comment beside his chair an extremely large box wrapped up in brown paper. From the way he handled it the box appeared to be fairly light. Simon eyed it with uneasy curiosity. Whatever could it contain? It must be a present for Axel.

"What a very *English* interior this is," said Julius. He was sipping his drink and looking round the room with satisfaction.

"What's English about it?" said Simon. He was feeling nervy, irritated, and miserable. He had got into the mood when he wanted everything to be awkward, embarrassing, and awful.

"Oh, just that calm confident multi-coloured eclecticism! Americans are afraid of colours and afraid of muddling styles. The result is usually something dreadfully bare and ugly. One can't be *cosy* in America."

"You're looking very well, Julius," said Axel. "Life in England seems to be suiting you. I hear rumours of your settling down in London."

Axel and Julius were in the two larger arm-chairs on either side of the fire-place, their legs well stretched out. They looked maddeningly relaxed. The reproachful smell of the cassoulet crept about in the background. Simon was agonizingly hungry.

"Yes, I'm thinking of it. London is such a civilized city and so calming to the nerves. I don't think I *could* live in Paris now, could you?"

"No. I've never liked Paris much. I still imagine I could live in Rome, but it may be an illusion. I've always had a fantasy life in Rome."

"Have you really? Now isn't that odd, so have I. Though I've never actually been there for more than a few weeks at a time."

"Neither have I. But it does haunt one. That coagulated mass of history. The way the buildings jumble together. It's so gorgeously untidy, like London."

"Exactly. I love the village life of Rome."

"Those innumerable little squares."

"And the fountains."

"And the white statues among trees."

"And the ancient pillars built into Renaissance walls."

"And the neon lights at night on tawny-coloured houses."

"And the naked boys bathing in the Tiber."

"Ah, the naked boys bathing in the Tiber!"

This could go on forever, thought Simon. He was determined not to suggest dinner. Let the cassoulet burn.

"Of course the opera's not so good as Paris," said Julius.

"That's true. But one could always take a plane to Milan."

"I see they're doing Mozart at Sadlers Wells. Is that company any good this summer?"

"Not too bad. They did a very presentable *Così*. I forget what's on at the moment."

"*Die Entführung aus dem Serail*. Eh, Simon?"

"What?" said Simon. He had been standing morosely at the window, looking out.

"*Die Entführung aus dem Serail*."

"I can't stand Mozart," said Simon.

"Really, Axel, you mustn't let him say things like that. It makes me feel quite faint!"

"You enjoy some Mozart, Simon. You were humming *Voi che sapete* only yesterday."

"*Voi che sapete!*" cried Julius. "*Tiens!*"

"I only like what I can hum," said Simon.

"That's not a bad principle," said Julius. "At least it's an honest one. Humming is not to be despised. It is a starting point after all."

"I doubt if Simon will ever get beyond it, however," said Axel. "I've given up his musical education."

"What a pity. It seems so out of character for Simon not to like music."

"I agree with you."

"He's such a feminine person. All the little dainty touches in this room are obviously Simon's work. The cunning way those cushions are put, the graceful looping back of the curtains, the particular arrangement of the flowers, indeed the presence of the flowers. Am I not right? Simon provides the feminine touch. So he ought to like music. Most women are musical."

"Do you think so?" said Axel. "In my experience men are far more musical than women. In fact, I don't know any really musical women."

"You don't know any women," said Simon.

"One can't help feeling," Julius went on, "that it's awfully significant, who is musical and who isn't. Now Morgan, for instance, positively detests music . . ."

Simon looked surreptitiously at his watch. Ten minutes later they were discussing somebody or something called Dietrich Fischer-Dieskau. Simon went quietly downstairs.

He stood in the kitchen for a while drinking sherry. Let them talk. He hoped they'd go on for another hour. Only the smell from the brown earthenware pot was becoming almost unbearable. Simon savagely resisted the temptation to lift the lid and spoon out a few beans. He wanted to suffer. He could now hear from the drawing-room that Julius and Axel had got onto Wagner.

"Wagner was, of course, homosexual," Julius was saying as Simon glided back into the room. Simon refilled his own glass and sat down by the window. Even this information could not make him interested in Wagner. Now they were off again on the boring old *Ring*.

"But here I am prattling on," said Julius at last, "and I haven't given Axel his present. What am I thinking of!" He leaned over and began scrabbling with his fingers at the knot on the big brown paper package. "I never could undo knots!"

"How kind of you to bring me one!" said Axel. "Look, don't worry, I'll get some scissors." He got up and left the room.

"Simon," said Julius in a low voice. "Come here."

Simon automatically got up and approached him.

"Listen, Simon, *don't worry*. It will be all right. Do you understand?"

Simon looked down into Julius's eager smiling face. Then he shook his head and turned away. As he turned Julius reached up and pinched his bottom. Axel's foot was heard on the landing.

Simon stood looking out of the window, his face scarlet.

"Here's the scissors," said Axel behind him.

"I wonder if you can guess what it is?"

"I can't imagine."

"Simon, do come and look at Axel's present."

Simon turned round, trying to conceal his emotion. He felt shame and fury and a kind of horrid excitement.

Julius had the paper off and the box open. Something or other was concealed by tissue paper.

"You take it out, Axel."

Puzzled, Axel began pulling away the tissue paper. A pair of furry ears were revealed. A moment later Axel had lifted out an immense pink teddy bear.

"Isn't he lovely?" cried Julius. He smiled, giggled, laughed. Axel's face was certainly worth looking at.

"Good God!" said Simon.

"You must absolutely *love* him," said Julius, "both of you, or he'll be unhappy. I hope he won't end by making anybody jealous!" He nearly choked with laughter.

Axel was having difficulty in removing an expression of horror, disgust, and incredulity from his face. He achieved a blank frozen look. He put the teddy bear down on the floor. "Thank you, Julius. It was so clever of you to remember my birthday—" He leaned forward and began folding up the tissue paper. Over his stooped head Julius made a gleeful sign to Simon, putting his forefinger and thumb together.

"I think we should have dinner," said Simon desperately.

"*Dinner?*" cried Julius. "But I dined *hours* ago. I thought this was an after-dinner visit. Do you mean to say you two haven't eaten?"

"We were waiting for you," said Simon. "I understood from Axel that you'd invited yourself to dinner."

"No, no. I'm sure I said after dinner. I did think it a little odd when you offered me a martini, but I assumed it was just a tribute to what you took to be the barbarous habits of the U.S.A.!"

"Anyway, it was nice of you to come," said Axel. He was obviously still suffering from shock.

"You *do* like your present, don't you?"

"Certainly I do. Most original."

"I felt sure he'd be happy here. He hasn't told me his name but I'm sure he'll soon whisper it shyly to Axel. He has such a modest confiding expression, don't you think? Don't forget to give him lots of love. He's rather fat and lacking in confidence. 'A bear, however hard he tries, Grows tubby without exercise.' You see how well up I am in English literature. Dear me, look at the time, it's well after ten, I really must be going. I'm a fanatical early bedder. And you two poor dears must be starving. Good night, Axel. Good night, Simon love. I so *very* much enjoyed our last meeting. No, don't see me down the stairs, I can find my way. Good night, good night."

Julius departed and the front door closed. Simon, who had gone after him as far as the top of the stairs, returned to the drawing-room. Axel got up and kicked the teddy bear across the room.

"What's that about your last meeting?"

"He wasn't talking to me. He just meant both of us—"

"He didn't. He was talking to you. You didn't tell me you'd seen Julius. When did you see him?"

"Well, I didn't really see him— He rang up—"

"You did see him. When?"

"Well, only for a moment. He came into the office. It was only—"

"What did he want?"

"He wanted— He wanted to discuss what to give you for a birthday present."

"Birthday present? Do you mean to say you advised Julius to give me a large pink teddy bear?"

"No, no, of course not. That was Julius's idea. It was just a joke."

"I see, and you encouraged him. You had a good laugh together at my expense. Was that what he was signalling to you about?"

"He wasn't signalling to me."

"Stop telling lies. And you were whispering together when I was out of the room."

"Honestly, Axel—"

"And you were blushing furiously when I came back. Do you think I'm deaf and blind?"

"Truly, there was nothing—"

"Have you been to his flat?"

"No."

"Look at me. Have you ever been to Julius's flat?"

"No, no, never—"

"I can see you're lying."

"Axel, I swear—"

Axel turned and left the room. Simon ran after him into the bedroom. Axel was putting on his jacket.

"Please, Axel, *please*—"

"Get out of my way. I'm going out."

"But our dinner, the cassoulet—"

"Damn and blast the cassoulet."

"Axel, please don't go, I shall be wretched—"

"And you can get that blasted bear out of the house. I don't want to see it again."

"It wasn't my idea—"

"Don't touch me. And don't come near me later on tonight either. I don't want to see you or talk to you. You can sleep in the spare room from now on."

"*Axel!*"

Axel disappeared down the stairs and into the street. The front door slammed violently after him.

Simon went down slowly. He opened the door, then closed it again. He went into the kitchen. The cassoulet was burning. With tears streaming down his face he turned the oven off.

❀ | EIGHT

"I do wish you hadn't told them that," said Rupert.

"That I was leaving London?"

"Yes. It wasn't necessary. It's much better to stick to the truth as far as possible."

"I just had to, Rupert. I had to clear the decks. I don't want to *bother* with other people. And—with things as they are—I felt I simply couldn't face Peter. The poor boy can't help making demands. And I wanted, honestly, to give you all my attention, to be able to *think*. Was that wrong?"

"I'm very sorry we've had to mislead Hilda—"

"Well, we're already misleading Hilda, aren't we? And once I'd told Peter I was going away I had to tell Hilda the same story. Come, Rupert. You wouldn't like to feel *now*, would you, that Peter or Hilda was likely to come knocking on the door?"

"Suppose Hilda sees you somewhere?"

"She won't, Rupert. Don't *worry* so. Hilda never comes down the Fulham Road, except to come here. It's not her territory. You know she always goes by Earls Court."

"You'd better avoid the Earls Court Road."

"I will. The only nuisance is now I can't answer the telephone and it might be you."

"They won't telephone you."

"No, but someone might, and it could get round. I want to lie absolutely doggo for the present."

"Oh dear, it's all rather— You can always ring me at the office."

"I know, that's a blessing. You didn't mind my ringing today? I felt I just had to see you."

"Oh Morgan, Morgan. I wonder if we're being wise. It has upset me so much that you told that lie to Hilda."

"Rupert, you are being silly. We *can't* tell Hilda about the other thing, now can we? We've agreed to that. And this little falsehood is very unimportant."

"Have you told Tallis you'll be away?"

"Peter will have told him. There. Doesn't it make you feel more secure to know that we can be really private together?"

"It makes it all seem more clandestine."

"It is clandestine."

"And Julius?"

"I sent Julius a postcard. No one will call."

Rupert sat down on Morgan's sofa. He felt puzzled and troubled and anxious but also profoundly *interested*. He felt too an increasing tenderness and concern about Morgan. The girl seemed to be in a very strange frame of mind. In the last few days he had received at the office quite a stream of letters from her, all of which he read several times and meticulously destroyed. Some of the letters were reasonably calm, full of reassurances and worries about *his* feelings and *his* welfare. Others were the most frantic love letters he had ever received in his life. They upset and frightened Rupert considerably. Morgan seemed to be in a rather schizophrenic state about him. He was amazed too and indeed impressed by the firm way in which she insisted on seeing him. He thought that if he had been in her situation he would have *fled*. He felt, when she asked him to come, bound to come. A refusal might produce any degree of frenzy. And also he wanted to come.

"There's something very *odd* about all this," said Rupert. Morgan had taken a chair and pulled it up close to him. They regarded each other.

Morgan looked at him a moment in silence. Then she said, "You're behaving *beautifully*."

"I suspect I'm behaving rashly. I'm putting a burden on you which you probably shouldn't be expected to bear, even though you asked for it! There must be more pain than pleasure in seeing me like this."

"Don't worry about me. I can carry any burden. We must—come through to calmness—and we can only do it together. Don't be afraid."

"I'm not sure that there isn't some sort of contradiction in what we're trying to do. There's so much drama in these meetings, especially as they have to be secret."

"Of course at the moment it makes you feel more agitated. But if I were to go right away, wouldn't you, forgive me, feel frantic about it? *That* would be drama. We must try to do everything naturally. You must get used to me. Simply getting used to each other, to the feel of each other, will be half the battle. We've taken each other for granted for so long and only now do we realize that we are strangers. There is so much to learn. Rupert, we mustn't just give each other up because of what's happened. It's a challenge. It's something we've got to turn into a blessing, into something good. Isn't that so?"

"I suppose it is," said Rupert dubiously. "I certainly don't want to be just negative about it. That would be, I agree with you, a pity, a waste."

"A crime against life, Rupert."

"Mmm. Perhaps I don't think as highly of life as you do. It's very hard for me to be unemotional now, when I see you like this—"

"But why ever should you be unemotional? We've got to be realistic about the situation. We can't just ignore emotion! Here, take my hand." Morgan stretched out her hand toward him.

Rupert stared at her. Her face was hard, bronzed, stern. She looked like the totem of a bird. He took hold of her hand. The next moment he found that he had bowed his head and was pressing her palm to his forehead. He released her quickly.

"Oh Rupert, Rupert," said Morgan. "You remember that time in your room, just after I'd come back, the time when you were so kind to me, when you gave me the malachite paperweight? I was talking some rigmarole to you, and I said, I forget the exact words, something about 'One's lost inside one's psyche. There's nothing real. No hard parts, no centre. There's just immediate things, like—' And then I picked up the paperweight and said 'Like this,' and pressed it against my forehead. But what I meant, what I really wanted then, was to take hold of your hand instead and do just that with it, what you've just done with mine—dear Rupert—"

Rupert got up. He went and inspected the bookcase. "I think you'd better go on a world cruise."

"Oh, my dear, you're laughing at me, I'm so glad! If only we can both keep our sense of humour we're certain to be all right!"

"We need more than a sense of humour in this situation," said Rupert. "We need a damn clear sense of right and wrong, and I'm not sure that I can provide it."

During the last few days there had been fleeting, exciting, strange meetings with Rupert, tense lookings forward and end-lessly interesting reflections afterward about what had been said. Morgan felt extreme agitation but singularly little anxiety. It was a time of destiny, not a time of decision. Nothing terrible would happen. She and Rupert had simply to hold hands. The gods would do the rest.

About Rupert's own state of mind she had been at first a little puzzled. He had sent her several letters. Two of these were ex-tremely sober in tone, full of reluctances and doubts and tender concern that *she* should not suffer. The others seemed entirely mad, crazy violent letters, passionate declarations of love, pros-trations, beseechings, prayers. Rupert was certainly good at ex-pressing his love on paper, though when he saw her he was sadly tongue-tied. She destroyed all the letters, as he had instructed her to do, but she could not resist copying out some of the more eloquent passages into a notebook. Rupert was clearly struggling with himself—and equally clearly it was the wild impetuous Ru-pert, the deep hidden Rupert, that was winning. To have him thus at her feet was unutterably moving to her: she felt pity, compassion, delight. She felt, after a long time, a strange stirring of happiness.

Morgan had a capacity for dealing with one thing at a time, and not worrying about, almost not seeing, other features of the situation. Since she felt sure that she *ought* now to give Rupert her entire attention she found no difficulty in not reflecting too urgently about Hilda, about Peter, about Tallis. She was of course aware of these persons and even of their claims, but they seemed to inhabit some quite other time scheme. They were "pending": and Morgan did not feel, when she was with Rupert, that during *those* hours and minutes Hilda really existed somewhere else near by and might be wondering where her husband was. About Julius she thought in a different way. Julius remained large and omnipresent in her consciousness and somehow mysteriously involved in her new feelings. What is it? Morgan wondered. Is it that Julius set me free and *this* is the first manifestation of my freedom? Or is it that accepting Rupert's love is a kind of revenge? She would dearly have liked to discuss the whole matter with Julius. How *interested* he would be! She would like to have *boasted* to him of her conquest. Only of course that was unthinkable. It was certainly something big and something new: and to have, after Julius, something big and new and utterly unexpected in her life was an invigorating achievement. By it the old love was acted on and changed, and this, she felt, was good. Meanwhile her thoughts about Tallis, and she did think about Tallis, were vague, vague, vague. About Peter she scarcely thought at all.

It had also become even plainer to her, and she felt this as a sign of her own continued rationality, that as a companion and as a person Rupert suited and matched her more than any man she had ever met. The two other most important men in her life, Julius and Tallis, were, she now saw, simply not designed for her at all. Julius was far too erratic and domineering, and Tallis was too uncertain in his grip and too hopelessly eccentric. Tallis never really *held* me, she thought. Even a prostrate Rupert had over her a kind of authority to which her whole nature could calmly respond. It was, amidst all the hurly-burly of Rupert's passions and her own aroused feelings, the calmness and steadiness of this response which most of all made her feel confident of the rightness of her decision to go on seeing him. She knew that the situation was dangerous but could not feel it to be so. She had a deep trust in Rupert's sense and in his goodness. Perhaps indeed it was just from here that her warm sense of destiny arose. Rupert would help her to nurse Rupert through.

In her reflections on the matter Morgan was cheered by finding that there was really no conceivable alternative to the course which she was taking. She based this view, which she had worked out with some care, partly upon her knowledge of her own temperament, partly upon her hypotheses concerning Rupert, and partly upon the feeling that her conjunction with Rupert was the world's will. Morgan, smiling rather wryly at herself in the mirror, knew perfectly well that she was not capable of passing up this adventure. She had not invited Rupert's love. She had been astounded by it. But now that she had it she was certainly *not* going to go on a world cruise and trust to find a polite embarrassed cured Rupert waiting for her on her return. Whatever this thing was, she was determined to wade right through the middle of it. Rupert would be cured, of course, at least he would be, must be, somehow changed. And oh, in the change, she thought, let nothing be lost! Everything here was precious, precious. Rupert's own needs must dictate to her. Happily they dictated a similar policy. It would be unthinkable to abandon Rupert in this awful mess. It is rarely enough that two human beings really come within hailing distance of one another. It would be, at the very least, unfair to Rupert not to attempt to make this unexpected proximity into something psychologically and morally workable. We shall be very close friends, she thought, very very close, forever. No one will know. No one will be hurt. It can be done. And she felt that in this resolution life was on her side.

"The trouble is I'm getting so damnably attached to you," said Rupert.

"I adore your understatements! So indeed I gathered from your letters! I'm pretty attached to you if it comes to that."

"I enjoy seeing you so much," said Rupert. "Of course I always have done and this doesn't alter it—"

"I imagine not!"

"And you are able to be so wonderfully calm—"

"We have got to get used to each other again, in a new way, in a deeper better way. Rupert, it *is* all right, you know."

"When I hear you say this so quietly and firmly I want to believe you. But I somehow can't *see*, I can't *see*. In accepting that you love me—"

"And I do love you, Rupert, I do—"

"And in feeling—moved by you—myself—"

"There you go again! I can't help being glad that you're moved!"

"I, we, are creating a situation, a dramatic dynamic situation, which we may find we are unable to control."

"I think for the present we must simply surrender ourselves to it," she said.

"I'm not so sure," said Rupert. "There is however one fairly foolproof way of keeping the thing in order."

"What's that?"

"Tell Hilda about it."

Morgan was silent. She had been afraid that Rupert would suggest this. And the idea was intolerable. She could not bear Hilda to know. That would rob Rupert's love of half its sweetness. Her own quite special closeness to Hilda made this the one impossible revelation. Whatever this strange exciting new thing was in her life, Hilda's knowledge of it would kill it dead. How could she, without revealing all that she felt, dissuade him?

"It's just an idea, " said Rupert. "I don't know myself what exactly—"

"We *can't* hurt Hilda like that," said Morgan. Hilda's distress, Hilda's concern, Hilda's understanding? No.

"Hilda loves you. In a way, we're insulting her by assuming she couldn't bear to know how you feel—"

"How *I* feel? And what about how *you* feel! No, Rupert, this is the sort of thing people don't get over. It's so unpredictable. You might really damage your marriage—I mean more than it is already—I mean, after all, exactly this damage is what we're trying to avoid, isn't it?"

"I'm confused," said Rupert. "I wish I wasn't so uncertain about my own emotions. I wish I could be sure I—"

"Your last letter didn't sound as if you were uncertain about your own emotions!"

"My letters are calmer than my mind."

"Then your mind must be in trouble!"

"You are very perceptive, Morgan. My dear, I had better go. I'll think all these things over."

"You're always saying that! Rupert, you won't suddenly tell Hilda without warning me?"

"No, no. You may be right that it's better not to tell her, or not, anyway, until things have calmed down."

"I'm glad you agree. Oh Rupert, when you have that worried look you look so sweet! Like a dear puzzled animal!"

"I am a puzzled animal!"

"And your eyes are so very blue," she said. "I think the sun must be making your eyes bluer just as it makes your hair fairer."

Rupert smiled. He said, "God, I wish things were simpler. Good-bye, ring me."

They were standing close to each other beside the door.

Morgan said, "Rupert, I'm sorry and perhaps it isn't fair, but I've simply got to take you in my arms." She leaned up against him, passing her arms round his waist. Rupert closed his eyes and held her for a while in silence.

🐚 | NINE

"Where are you going?" said Hilda.

"To see Julius," said Rupert. "He asked me to drop over to-night. Or 'drop by' as he puts it. I said yes because I thought you'd be out too. Aren't you going to that committee meeting?"

"Yes, but it isn't till nine-thirty. I forgot to tell you Simon rang up."

"What did he want?"

"Nothing, just to say he couldn't come round about the bathroom after all. I'm afraid he's lost interest in our decoration problems."

"He seems to have lost interest in us. Better leave it then, it's all right as it is."

"Yes, leave it, I suppose. Are you feeling all right, Rupert? You hardly ate any supper."

"Yes, I feel fine."

"Don't be too late—"

Rupert turned to go. Then he came back and, very grave, kissed his wife. Then he went off again, leaving the door open. Cool evening air blew through the house.

Hilda went back into the drawing-room. She shivered and closed the french windows. Perhaps the weather was changing. She went into the kitchen and began putting the supper plates into the washing-up machine. She washed up the knives and forks. After a while she went restlessly back into the drawing-room. She lifted the telephone and dialled Morgan's number. There was no reply. She laid the telephone down on the table and let the number continue to ring. She had seen Morgan that morning in the Fulham Road.

Hilda still did not know what to make of the mystifying conversation she had had with Julius. The trouble was that she could not now properly *remember* the conversation. It was like a dream which the awakened mind feels and grasps at but cannot quite evoke. There had been a misunderstanding. But what did it mean, and what *exactly* had been said? Morgan was in love with somebody. Hilda was being heroic. Morgan had *said* she was going away. It was more sensible to wait. Some of the possibilities, as Hilda's frightened imagination with a mechanical speed deployed them, were so grotesque that she deliberately covered them with a haze. She knew that nothing really dreadful could happen to her. But Morgan had certainly behaved oddly. And had she really gone away or not?

Hilda telephoned Morgan's flat several times and got no reply. Then that morning she decided that she would go round and ring the bell. It seemed a rather pointless activity, but at least it was an activity. It was something she could do in connection with her restless worries. As she came out of Drayton Gardens into the Fulham Road she saw Morgan on the opposite pavement just going into a grocer's shop. Hilda for a moment felt almost faint. Then she turned quickly back and went home. She sat stiffly in the drawing-room for nearly an hour. Throughout the day, quietly, quietly, she brooded upon the mystery which had so suddenly and strangely arrived in the middle of her life.

The telephone was still ringing in Morgan's flat. Hilda had forgotten that she had laid the receiver down upon the table. She picked it up now, pressed down the receiver rest, and telephoned to the friend at whose house the committee was meeting to say that she was unable to come. She did not feel able to deal with those simple ordinary things any more. The world had changed.

Is it all a hallucination? Hilda wondered. Was Julius really talking about Peter, as he tried to say at the end that he had been? But no, he had clearly not been talking about Peter. And if he did not mean Peter, then— But this was all unthinkably absurd. She had indeed noticed that Rupert was behaving a little strangely even before that evening with Julius. She had noticed something to which, before that evening, she had not quite been able to put a name, something intensely distressing, which she now saw to be this. The deep rapport between herself and her husband was somehow broken. Hilda felt this as physical illness, as pain. In a happy marriage there is a continuous dense magnetic sense of communication. Hilda had enjoyed this with Rupert uninterruptedly for years. Even when Rupert was absent this magnetism filled the house, a web upon which Hilda's spirit rested, upon which it travelled. Looking, touching, the telepathy of speech, the telepathy of silence, the full mystery of trusting, married love, she had taken utterly for granted. Now she became aware that something had been altered. Rupert behaved very much, though not quite, as usual. He was nervy and abstracted and seemed to avoid her eye. The intonation of his voice seemed to be slightly different. There were a number of small things. The big thing was that her channels of communication with Rupert were indubitably blocked.

Hilda wondered if she should not say something to Rupert about it. She had not told him about Julius's visit. But supposing it was all a colossal mistake? At other times she wondered if she should not go and question Julius. Yet would that not be terribly indiscreet? On reflection it seemed absurd and everything that she feared so shadowy. She did not really think that Rupert and Morgan were involved with each other. Why, if either of them had seen *that* coming they would have run a mile. Besides, it was *impossible*. Perhaps Morgan was in some secret trouble and Rupert was helping her? Perhaps she was in some trouble which she would feel ashamed to confess to Hilda? This supposition had a ring of sense about it. Morgan had certainly lied about going away. If she had merely changed her mind she would certainly have told Hilda, whom she knew to be anxious to see her. Morgan was in trouble, Rupert was helping. Yet it was odd that they had told her nothing about it. And why had Julius spoken about Morgan being in love and called Hilda heroic? Surely he *had* said these things?

I must stop this, Hilda said to herself. There was panic in these thoughts. The lost contact with Rupert hurt and hurt. Even that exchange of words at the door just now had rung somehow false, as if for both of them there was a second meaning, something hidden. "Where are you going?" Surely even a few days ago she would not have said that? "Aren't you going to that committee meeting?" The tone was wrong. I must keep sane and calm, Hilda said to herself. Rupert loves me and nothing has changed, nothing can change. She gripped the side of her chair, feeling suddenly giddy. Supposing Rupert regretted having married her? She was not clever, she was not an intellectual. She had been a very dull wife for such a brilliant man. Why should he love me, after all? she thought. Perhaps there had been gradual slow regrets.

Hilda got up quickly. The room was twilit and seemed strange to her. Things could change, all things could change. She turned on one lamp in the corner and got out the decanter of whisky. She poured out a little whisky and sipped it. She felt an instant of false comfort. The whisky did not know of her troubles. She thought, Because Rupert was so much in love with me it all happened so quickly. We ought to have waited a little. But I was determined to keep him. Perhaps he ought to have married a quite different kind of person. Yet did these doubts make any sense after twenty years of quiet solid marriage?

"May I come in?"

Hilda jumped and set the glass down. Someone was standing in the half darkness near to the door. It was Julius.

"Oh *Julius*—" Hilda switched on another lamp and saw Julius, dressed in what looked like an evening cape, carrying a bunch of yellow roses.

"You look so— But what happened, did you miss Rupert, or what?"

"Rupert? Why, was Rupert looking for me?"

"He said he had an appointment with you. He left more than an hour ago."

"Appointment with me? No, he had no appointment." There was a moment's silence. Then Julius said, "Oh well, perhaps he did, I may be mistaken— Perhaps he said— I seem to remember something now—it must have slipped my mind—"

"All right, all right," said Hilda. "It does you credit." She switched on some more lights.

"I brought you these roses," said Julius. "I know it seems a bit idiotic, bringing you roses when your garden's full of them. But these are such a lovely yellow, and all the garden ones seem to be pink and white, so I thought at least they'd make a change."

Hilda took them. She felt ready to cry. "Thank you so much— I'll just put them in water." Out in the kitchen some tears did come, but she knocked them away, baring her teeth. She must keep her head now and get the truth out of Julius.

He was sitting down when she came back, rose, sat down again, and accepted whisky. He was in evening dress.

"Thank you for the roses."

"I just— I wasn't going to stay—in fact I'm on my way to a late evening party— I just felt I wanted to give you something."

"Julius," said Hilda, "what *is* going on?"

"Going on? I don't know what you mean."

"Yes, you do. Morgan said she was leaving London and she hasn't left. Rupert is being most secretive and peculiar. There's some drama going on. What is it?"

Julius was silent for a while, examined his fingers, examined his whisky, stared at the hazy dark blue screen of the uncurtained window, and cast a quick glance at Hilda. He said at last, "Well, I suppose you were bound to find out."

"Bound to find out *what?*"

"About Rupert and Morgan."

Hilda fought for control of her face and her voice. "You mean there's something going on between them?"

"No, no," said Julius, "that would be— I'm not quite sure what you mean—but one mustn't exaggerate—and with two such people—"

"But what *is* it?"

"Probably a nothing, Hilda," said Julius, giving her his full heavy stare. He seemed grave and upset. "Probably a shadow that will vanish away as if it had never been. A shadow which, believe me, it is very much wiser and *kinder* simply to ignore. I am afraid that our last conversation must have sounded to you rather portentous. And I would certainly not have expressed myself in that way if I had thought— You see, I imagined that they must both have told you everything—in fact, I took this as a proof that it was all really something quite unimportant. I must say, I was rather relieved."

"But they haven't told me everything," said Hilda. "They haven't told me anything." Her hand had begun to tremble. She put the glass down.

"Yes, yes, but I'm sure they will. Or no, it's much more likely that they won't. They'll feel it has all become exaggerated and if they tell you it will seem much larger than it really is. Honestly, Hilda, there's practically nothing to it. And after all, think who they are."

"But what is *it?*" said Hilda. "You keep speaking as if I knew. I know nothing."

"I've told you, it's nothing at all. Perhaps a little infatuation on one side, a little kindness on the other. Who knows how these things begin? Believe me, Hilda, just pay no attention. In a few months it will have passed away and you'll all have forgotten it."

"I couldn't—forget it—" said Hilda. "It changes—everything." She felt the tears again and pressed both her hands hard against her eyes.

"Hilda, Hilda, don't, you upset me terribly, I blame myself, I must have given you the wrong impression. There's no—there's no *love affair*, Hilda."

"No, but they're in love."

"Hardly that, a mere, shall we say, involvement. Oh dear, why ever did we start to talk about it. You've made me say all sorts of things I shouldn't have said. Dearest Hilda, you are so good. I can't bear that *you* should suffer."

"You've been very kind, Julius, and you mustn't blame yourself. I'm grateful to you. It's better to know."

"But truly, Hilda, there's nothing there, or practically nothing—a shadow, a fancy. Be generous. Don't speak of it to poor Rupert. Let those two deal with it themselves. Why, they may have done so already. In a long happy marriage there must be moments when one turns a blind eye. Be merciful to them and let it all be buried and forgotten. It's something very tiny and very momentary. And you know poor Morgan is in a thoroughly unstable condition."

"I must *think*," said Hilda. "I must *think*."

"I wish I could undo the effect of my words. There is really *nothing* between Morgan and Rupert. It would honestly be more true to say that than to say anything else at all."

"You are kind-hearted, Julius, and very loyal. You must go now, you must go on to your party. I don't want Rupert to come back and find us talking."

Julius rose. "May I come and see you again, Hilda? I don't mean to talk about *that*. That will soon be ancient history. It has sometimes distressed me to feel that you thought—less than well of me."

"I think very well of you, Julius." She got up and gave him her hand. He retained it, pressed it, began to lift it formally to his lips, turned it over, and let Hilda's fingers brush lightly along his cheek.

"I am glad, my dearest Hilda. You are a strong person and I admire you. More than that, more than that. I am a homeless man. I have no family and fewer friends than you could conceive of. A steady friendship with a steadfast woman— No dramas, no passions, no fear. Are such things possible? Who knows? I am tired of adventures, Hilda. But this is not the moment to tell you about myself. Perhaps another time. Good night, my dear."

A little later Rupert's step was heard below and he was switching on the lights in the hall. Hilda was standing near the top of the stairs. She had covered her face with cold cream to disguise the fact that she had been crying. She called down.

"Hello. Did you have a good evening with Julius?"

"Yes, fine. He sends you his greetings. How was your committee meeting?"

"Very amusing," said Hilda. She retired into the bedroom and switched off the light on her side of the bed.

🍀 | T E N

The pigeon was standing, almost invisible in the corner, behind a pile of wooden planks, just at the bottom of the first escalator on the Bakerloo side in Piccadilly Circus station. Morgan saw it with an immediate sick thrill of pain and fear.

She passed it by. She stopped and came back. She had just been paying an afternoon visit to the London Library and was intending to return to Fulham via South Kensington. She avoided Earls Court. She looked down at the pigeon. It stood there immobile, well back in the corner, its eye bright and inexpressive. Many people were passing by, most of them coming down the escalator. It was the beginning of the rush hour. No one paid any attention to Morgan or the pigeon.

Morgan stood there as motionless as the bird and her heart beat as hard. She had seen Rupert last night. It had been a terrible evening. As soon as he arrived the telephone had started ringing. She could not answer it. It had gone on and on ringing while she and Rupert sat eyeing each other, tried to talk, and then fell silent. It went on ringing for nearly twenty minutes. Then Rupert had broken down. She sat dry-eyed and stiff throughout his incoherent torrent of self-reproach. His letters were becoming more distraught than passionate and now he seemed to want to talk all the time about Hilda, about the terrible pain he felt at lying to her and the agony of having lost the daily contact of absolute trust and love. He besought Morgan to leave London.

Morgan said she would not, she could not, at least not yet. Where could she go where she would not be miserable? She turned away almost angrily from the distracted figure of Rupert, suddenly so undignified and pathetic. "Well, you started it!" No, *you* started it!" They almost quarrelled. Why do I have to suffer like this? thought Morgan. After so much misery and so many disappointments and so many people letting me down, I at last discover the one person who could really help me—and he has to go and make himself impossible. If only Rupert would *keep his head.* Everything could be perfectly all right. She tried to explain it to him.

"I love you, darling Rupert. And I trust your love for me. And you'll soon feel so much calmer when you get more used to seeing me. We're rational beings, we must construct a friendship here, we *can.* We mustn't just throw love away, it's rare enough in this beastly world. And real love is wise, you said so yourself. I need you, Rupert. No one will be hurt."

"I don't love you with a love that is wise," said Rupert. "It's all becoming a nightmare."

"You must try to. You must practise what you preach."

"I can't, I can't!"

Morgan moved nearer to the pigeon. It did not stir. It was a healthy-looking bird and seemed to be quite unhurt. Morgan laid her handbag down on top of the pile of wood. She edged round the wood and very cautiously began to bend down toward the bird, her hands spread out wide. Just as her fingers were almost touching the soft grey feathers the pigeon flew up into her face. It passed over her shoulder, glided over the heads of the hurrying people, and perched on top of a projecting poster facing the bottom of the escalator.

Morgan stood watching it for a moment. Then she edged her way through the criss-crossing crowd and approached the poster. She reckoned that she could just about reach the pigeon. If she could only get a firm grip on its legs. What would it do? Would it flutter wildly and be terrified, peck her perhaps? Birds sometimes died of terror if they were suddenly caught hold of. How would she capture and enclose those madly beating wings? Suppose a wing were broken? Morgan's hands sought her breast, her neck. Then she took several deep breaths and stood on her toes and began slowly to slide her hands up the face of the poster. With a quick clap of wings the pigeon took off again and flew this time half-way up the escalator. It perched on the sloping wooden surface between the up and the down escalators, quite near to the moving handrail on the up side. Morgan thought, Even if I can't catch it, if I could only drive it up into the upper part of the station, it might see the daylight through one of the exits and fly out. It would have more chance of survival there than if it stays down here. The idea of the bird trapped in that warm dusty electric-lighted underground place filled her heart with pity and horror.

Morgan got onto the upward-bound escalator, which was not too full at that time of day, and as she came near to the place where the bird was perched she stretched out her arm as far as she could to drive it on and upward. As the outstretched arm approached the pigeon flew up a few yards and perched again upon the wooden slope between the two escalators. As Morgan caught up with it again it flew a little farther on up toward the top. Then as her hand neared it for the third time, outstretched to drive it out into the space of the upper concourse, it rose with an agitated flutter of wings and flew all the way back down again to perch in its former place on top of the poster at the bottom of the escalator.

Morgan stepped off the escalator at the top. She could just see the pigeon, far below her now, perching upon the poster. She hurried across and pushed her way onto the descending escalator and tried to hurry down it. Tired thoughtless people were standing in her way. When at last she reached the bottom of the stair the pigeon was still sitting on top of the poster. Morgan stood below. Desperately and with more determination this time she reached up her hands. People hurried past her, shadows with anxious vague eyes. No one stopped, no one watched, no one paid the slightest attention to what she was doing. She touched the cool scaly feet and had them almost within her grip. But her fingers did not close in time. The pigeon took off again, flying sideways now, and disappeared through the archway which led to the second escalator descending to the Piccadilly Line. Morgan cried out in vexation and distress.

Pushing her way through the increasing crowd she entered the area at the top of the Piccadilly Line escalator. A great many hasty preoccupied human beings jostled her, passed her, and did not see her as she stared about wide-eyed and then began to search along the walls and into the corners for the poor pigeon. There was no sign of the creature. When she was satisfied it was not there she descended the next escalator as far as the level of the trains. She walked slowly along both platforms, looking with an agony of anxiety and hope into all little dusty corners, under seats, behind any object which could afford a refuge. She scanned the brightly lit curving roof. Two trains came and went. The platform emptied, filled, emptied again. At last she turned, still looking round about her, and went slowly back to the escalator. She felt dejection and confused defeated pain for her poor fugitive. Where could he be now? She set her feet upon the moving stair. Then she realized that she had not got her handbag.

Morgan flushed with shock. She recalled that she had left it on top of the pile of wood where she had first seen the pigeon. She began to run up. She reached the top and ran round through the archway to the place where the wood was stacked. There was no sign of her bag. Perhaps it had fallen down behind. She peered behind, she shifted the wood, she went on her knees. There was no doubt that the handbag was gone. Morgan stood and stared around at the people. Someone had picked it up, perhaps only a moment ago. Someone was carrying it, taking it away. She ran

a few steps. She must search, get help, tell somebody. Then she
stood still, her face burning with vexation and misery. How could
one expect to find a stolen handbag in Piccadilly Circus station
in the rush hour? She should never have put it down. She moved
back against the wall.

A woman who has just lost her handbag feels as if she has lost
a limb. Morgan felt maimed, naked. She told herself not to be a
fool. A lost handbag was not the world's end. Then it occurred
to her that her ticket was gone too and that she was inside the
Underground system with no ticket and no money. Tears began
to come into her eyes. She would have to go up and explain to the
ticket collector. Would he believe her, would he be unpleasant to
her? The idea of anyone being unpleasant to her brought on more
tears. She thought, I must get out of this ghastly underground
place as quickly as possible. I must get some money from somewhere. Perhaps she might meet someone she knew if she went
back to the London Library. Or perhaps she should take a taxi to
Priory Grove and—no, damn, she couldn't do that. Oh *hell*,
thought Morgan, all the rest and this as well! And, oh God, her bag
was full of credit cards, a banker's card, a full chequebook, a Post
Office savings book. An enterprising thief could rob her of all her
money in an hour and run up bills all over London in her name.
She dashed the tears from her eyes and got onto the escalator to
go up to the top again.

When she was half-way up the escalator she suddenly saw
Tallis. He was standing on the opposite escalator going down,
gliding slowly downward toward her, standing in the long line
of people on the right-hand side of the escalator. At first she was
not sure whether it really was Tallis or whether it was one of the
men whom she now noticed all the time who seemed momen-
tarily to resemble him. The scene shimmered and shook before
her eyes, the row of blurred faces moved onward with mesmeric
slowness. Morgan gripped the moving handrail, wanting to call out
to him, but her tongue was leaden and a sort of large bright humming electric silence all about her held her motionless and word-
less. Yes, it was really Tallis. Separated now from the hazy frieze

of other forms, she saw his face clearly: anxious, sad, and beauti-
ful-eyed. He was gazing far away and did not seem to see her.
Then he was gone, sinking downward past her, and a moment
later Morgan was stumbling off the escalator at the top.

She stood aside and let the people stream by. She felt shock,
fright, bottomless panic, a quick nausea in her throat. Lights flashed
in her eyes and there was a deep blackness near her into which
she might fall. She said to herself, I am going to faint. She put a
hand out to the wall and tried to breathe slowly and deeply. She
thrust her other hand deep into her pocket and touched a coin.
She drew out a half-crown. The flashing lights diminished. Morgan thought, I must follow Tallis. *I must see Tallis, I must see
him at once.* She pushed her way across to the descending escalator. The people ahead of her were moving very slowly. As she
pressed on down she was trying to think, Which way will he go?
How does one get to Notting Hill from Piccadilly? Her unprac-
tised mind tried to spread out the map of the London Underground system. She found she had forgotten it. Oh God, was Notting Hill Gate on the Bakerloo? But that wasn't Tallis's station
anyway. Tallis's station was Ladbroke Grove and whatever line
was that on? Some obscure line that went to Hammersmith.
Change at Paddington, change at Hammersmith, change at Char-
ing Cross? She stepped off at the bottom and stood in hesitation
beneath the poster where the poor lost pigeon had perched itself
such a very long time ago. Right or left? If only she could find a
map. The panic was still upon her and a terrible urgency racked
her bowels. She bit her fingers with incoherent doubt and fear.
Then she began to run along toward the Bakerloo line. Change
at Paddington. She ran down the next escalator and heard a train.
She saw it leaving as she reached the platform.

Morgan was shuddering and shivering so much that she had to
sit down. The platform filled up rapidly. Another train came. She
got herself onto it. It was very full and her arms were crushed to
her sides, her face close up against other faces. It was hot and there
was a smell of human sweat and the rubbery dark smell of the
Underground. Rupert is right, she thought. It is all becoming a

nightmare. The endless ringing telephone, the trapped pigeon, the lost handbag, the horror of the world. Then she thought, The line divides at Baker Street. Not all the trains go to Paddington. Am I in the right train? She had not looked at the indicator. She could not ask. Her tongue was stiffened and her eyes were hazy. Baker Street. Marylebone. Was that right? Edgeware Road. Paddington.

She pushed her way out of the train and raced up the escalator. She remembered now that to reach the Metropolitan line she would have to go the whole length of the Main Line station. She came out into the main station and began to run again. The station was very strange, it was dark, unless the darkness was only in her eyes. The huge cast-iron vaults were not glowing with light, they were obscure and yellow as if filled with steamy mist, and below them it was as dim and murky as a winter afternoon although the air was hot. Morgan ran past taxis which had turned on their headlamps, past stationary trains where people peered anxiously from lighted windows. She fled up a long flight of steps and down another and came out under the sky which was misty and sulphurous and overcast. As her train came in she heard a distant sound, and heard it again as she came out of Ladbroke Grove station, the sound of thunder coming from far away through still thick hot air. She stared about trying to recognize something, but everything looked unfamiliar. She had never come to Tallis's house this way before. She ran along one shabby street, paused, and then ran down another. She panted along between houses which were stripped and wrenched and torn, where people sat silently on doorsteps and waited. The horror, the horror of the world.

Tallis's house was before her and Tallis's door. The sky was darkening now as the deep yellow was slowly suffused with black. She was gasping for breath and tears like sharp points pricked her straining eyes. The door hung a little sideways, a little open. She pushed it and went into the darkness.

"Morgan!"

It was Peter.

Morgan pushed open the kitchen door and went in with Peter following. She sat down.

"Where's Tallis?"

"He's at his class at Greenford."

"I saw him half an hour ago at Piccadilly Circus."

"You can't have done. Greenford's the other way. He goes by bus. Morgan, how absolutely marvellous to see you! I thought you'd gone away."

"I went away. I'm going away—again."

"I'm so glad you've come. This light is so weird, isn't it. Like the end of the world. I was feeling quite odd. Why, you're out of breath and—what's the matter?"

"Nothing." There was a flicker of lightning, electrical and sharp, felt rather than seen. Then after a moment or two a long drum roll of distant thunder.

"Have you been running? You must rest a bit. I've got a hundred things to tell you! You will stay, won't you? We could go to the pub and have sandwiches, if you wouldn't mind paying."

"What time will Tallis be back?" said Morgan.

"He won't be back tonight. He's going on from the class to some place in Clapham where someone's ill and he's spending the night there. Oh Morgan, do let's go out and celebrate! Do you know I've actually been *working*, and—"

"It's so hot," said Morgan. The thunder came again like distant gunfire.

"Would you like something to drink here? Tallis has a few cans of beer. Morgan, you're looking so strange, what is it? Morgan, darling—"

"I've lost my handbag."

"Oh, I'm so sorry!" Peter had pulled another chair up beside her.

"And there was a pigeon—in Piccadilly Circus station—at the bottom of the escalator— I tried to catch it—"

The child, thought Morgan, the child might have existed. It would have been a few months old. It might have been the solution to everything. Why had she not understood what a terrible thing it was to deprive that child of life? She had killed it so casually and drunk half a bottle of bourbon afterward.

"The child—" The horror of the world.

"Morgan, are you feeling all right?"

The thunder was nearer, more explosive, cracking down upon London. A few huge drops of rain fell, hitting the houses, clattering like pebbles onto roofs and windows. A sudden coolness began to sway through the heavy yellow air.

It was dark in the kitchen. Peter pulled his chair closer still and began to try to take Morgan in his arms. She pushed him roughly away and rose to her feet.

"Don't touch me!"

"Don't look at me like that, Morgan."

"Leave me alone."

The rain was beginning to spill down like water from a tilted bucket. A huge flash lit up the kitchen for a moment with a cold pallid silvery light, showing Morgan's staring eyes and Peter's scared unhappy face. Then the rain itself darkened the scene, falling like a dense curtain of grey clangorous metal.

Morgan's figure merged into the darkness of the doorway and another flash of lightning showed the luminous lines of rain curtaining the street door. Then she was gone, running, fading, dissolving, instantly vanishing into the thick grey substance of the roaring downpour.

🐚 | ELEVEN

"Oh, it's you," said Tallis.

"Were you expecting me?" said Julius.

"I thought you'd turn up sometime. Come in."

Julius followed Tallis into the kitchen. There was a dull quiet mid-morning light.

The floor of the kitchen was extremely wet and sticky as if covered with black oil.

"I'm sorry," said Tallis. "We had a bit of a flood with that thunderstorm. I left the window open and the rain came in."

"Why is it so sticky?" said Julius.

"It's always sticky, I don't quite know why. The rain just seems to have amalgamated with all the other stuff. Stay where you are and I'll put some newspaper down."

Tallis laid sheets of newspaper on the floor and Julius stepped gingerly as far as the table and sat down.

"Shall I put the light on?" said Tallis.

Since the thunderstorm the weather had been cold and overcast and rainy, with a continuous slow bundling along of dumpy low-down grey clouds.

"As you like."

"Then I think I won't, if you don't mind. Electric light's always a bit depressing during the day."

"I entirely agree."

"I'm sorry it's so cold in here. The windows won't shut properly. I might light the gas stove." Tallis opened the oven door and put a match to the row of gas burners at the back. They lit up with a small explosion. He left the door of the oven open.

"Quite a change in the weather," said Julius.

"Yes, it's chilly, isn't it?"

"Such a damp cold. I'm not used to this degree of humidity combined with a low temperature."

"I suppose not."

"I hope I haven't interrupted you. Were you working?"

"No, no. I was just mending a string of beads." Tallis swept the dark brownish beads off the table top into the drawer. They pattered away. He closed the drawer and sat down opposite Julius.

"At any rate it hasn't rained this morning," said Julius. "Everything's quiet. It takes me so long to roll my umbrella to satisfy English standards, it seems a pity to undo the masterpiece directly." He leaned the slim rigorously rolled umbrella up against the table. Its black handle ended in a knob of ivory with a faint lotus design on it.

"You don't think my umbrella is too feminine, do you?"

"No, very elegant."

"One can get away with such things in London. In New York it would be quite impossible."

"I dare say."

Julius was neatly dressed in a rather old-fashioned way, with a dark suit, a white shirt, and a narrow tie with horizontal stripes. His colourless hair had recently been cut. He carried no hat.

"Are you working on a book?" Julius indicated the litter of papers, books, and periodicals at the other end of the table.

"No. Only lectures."

"I thought you were writing a book about Marx and de Tocqueville?"

"I gave it up."

"A pity. A most interesting subject."

There was a short silence during which Julius scrutinized the kitchen with a faint frown, noting the milk bottles, the dishes, the piles of newspaper, and the curious coagulated mess upon the dresser.

Tallis was looking at the window with big rather hazy eyes. He said, "My father is very ill."

"I'm extremely sorry to hear that."

"He's dying—of cancer."

"I am so sorry. Is he likely to live long?"

"Six months. A year."

"Perhaps that is just as well if the disease is incurable. I hope he is not in pain."

"Well, he is—in pain—" said Tallis. He was still looking at the window. "You see, we thought it was arthritis. He's had this pain in his hip for a long time and it's been getting worse lately. The doctor says some ray treatment may help, just ease the pain, that is, and some tablets, I forget what he said they were—"

"Does your father know that he has cancer?"

"No, he doesn't," said Tallis. "And I haven't told him. I've kept up the thing about the arthritis and how he may have to have an operation. It's something one can talk about and his thinking it's arthritis may somehow make the pain less dreadful; he's used to the pain, thinking of it in that kind of way. But it seems so terrible to lie to him and to go into all sorts of details about things which just aren't true."

"I can imagine how you feel," said Julius. It was beginning to rain a little. There was a murmur of wind, and rain swept in a long sigh across the window.

"It seems especially wrong to lie to someone who's dying. And yet this seems a silly abstract sort of an idea really. I've looked after him a long time now. I feel so hopelessly sort of protective. I want to spare him the misery and the fear."

"I quite understand."

"And in a way of course I'm protecting myself. It's much easier to live with him in the lie than to live with him in the truth."

"And because you are considering yourself you are more ready to doubt that you are right?"

"Yes."

"What kind of man is your father?" said Julius.

Tallis was silent for a moment. "It's hard to be objective about him. No one ever asked me to describe him before. He had no education. He was a porter in an *abattoir*. He used to carry the carcasses about. Somebody has to. Then he was unemployed for ages. Then he worked in a garage, only that was later. He came south from Derbyshire when we were kids. I had a twin sister only she died of polio. When we came to London my mother left us. She was posher, of course. Daddy fed us on bread and butter and stew. We were a hell of a burden to him. God, he's had a rotten life. We all have to go but I wish he hadn't had such a bloody rotten life."

"Are you on good terms with him?"

"Yes. We shout at each other."

"Perhaps the truth would embarrass you both. It might prove impossible to talk about."

"One couldn't talk about it anyway," said Tallis. "We can't talk about *that*. And when we think we do we don't."

"What's he like as a person, his character?"

"Disappointed. Bitter. Proud."

"His life belongs to him? Not all men own their lives."

"He owns his."

"Then you ought to tell him."

"Yes. Maybe. Would you like some beer?"

"No thanks. How's Peter?"

"Unhappy. He was happy, now he's unhappy. I don't know why. I ought to have found out. I haven't. Tell me something, by the way, you might know this."

"What?"

"Why is stealing wrong?"

"It's just a matter of definition," said Julius.

"How do you mean?"

"It's a tautology. 'Steal' is a concept with a built-in pejorative significance. So to say that stealing is wrong is simply to say that what is wrong is wrong. It isn't a meaningful statement. It's empty."

"Oh. But does that mean that stealing isn't wrong?"

"You haven't understood me," said Julius. "Remarks of that

sort aren't statements at all and can't be true or false. They are more like cries or pleading. You can say 'Please don't steal' if you want to, so long as you realize that there's nothing behind it. It's all just conventions and feelings."

"Oh. I see," said Tallis. There was a pause. "Do you mind if I have some beer? Would you like some coffee? No?"

He rummaged in the cupboard and produced a can of beer which he put on the table. Then he began to search the heaped-up mass of oddments on the dresser for an opener. Various things fell off. The oddments seemed to have become rather sticky too. There was no sign of the opener. Tallis began to bash the top of the beer can with a screwdriver. "Oh, *damn.*"

"You've cut yourself," said Julius, rising.

"It's nothing."

"Hold your hand under the tap."

Julius turned the tap on and Tallis washed off the blood which was flowing freely over his hand. When he took his wet hand away it reddened once more.

"Keep it there, you fool," said Julius. "You'll have to cover that. It seems quite a clean cut. I suppose you haven't any disinfectant? I thought not. No, *not* on that filthy towel. Is there nothing clean in this house? I'll dry it on looseleaf paper and tie it up in my handkerchief. You'd better get something at the chemist's."

Julius ripped several sheets of looseleaf paper from a pad upon the table and dried Tallis's hand. Then he took a clean white handkerchief from his pocket and tied up the cut, knotting the ends of the handkerchief round Tallis's wrist.

"You look quite shaken."

"Sorry," said Tallis. "I feel so rotten these days any damn thing makes me want to cry." He sat down.

"You'd better have some beer. I suppose there's nothing stronger in the house. You still haven't managed to open that tin. Why, here's the opener all the time." Julius poured out a glass of beer.

"Thanks."

Julius stood in front of him, looking down at him while he drank.

After a while he said, "I didn't quite take you in when I first saw you. However, I feel bound to say—you're a disappointment to me."

"I know," said Tallis, "I just can't— All I can think about at the moment is my father."

There was a minute's silence in the twilit kitchen. Tallis sipped the beer, gazing at the grey window down which the rain was noiselessly running.

"Has Morgan asked you for a divorce?" said Julius.

"Yes."

"You know why?"

"No. Well, why shouldn't she?"

"She's got herself involved with Rupert."

Tallis went on staring at the window. He said, "That simply cannot be true."

"Oh, well," said Julius, picking up his umbrella, "it's no good talking to you. I dare say it's all on the highest plane. I don't suppose she means to appropriate Rupert. He's just sorting her out. And tidying you away is the obvious first step."

"Oh, go to hell, will you," said Tallis. He reached out and poured himself some more beer.

"You need looking after," said Julius. "There's a most peculiar smell in here. The place must be crawling with germs. You ought to have it thoroughly cleaned up. Or better still, move somewhere else and start again. Look, I've got plenty of money. I never lend money on principle, it only causes trouble. Let me give you some."

"Don't be idiotic."

Julius sighed. "I won't say I'm misunderstood. I'm sure you understand me very well. But I am, as I say, disappointed, in more ways than one. Well, good-bye. It looks as if I am going to have to unroll my umbrella after all."

After Julius had gone Tallis sat for a long time watching the slow quick quick slow of the raindrops coming down the window pane. They glittered very faintly gold, like white sapphires.

The rain was noisier now, hissing, beating. The Sikh was out driving his bus and wearing his contentious turban. The Pakistanis upstairs had taken in a flood of new relations from Lahore, including several children. There was a faint continuous distant din. A policeman had called that morning and asked for someone with a name which sounded like one of the upstairs names. Tallis had said he knew nothing. Usually he helped the police. Sometimes suddenly on instinct he didn't.

He thought, Daddy must be still asleep or he'd be yelling his head off. Those new tranquillizer tablets must be very soporific. Tallis gave a long sigh. He finished the beer. Things which had scuttled away in terror on Julius's arrival had begun to come out from under the sink and the dresser. They watched him. He thought about Morgan and Rupert. Any serious involvement there was inconceivable. Hilda and Rupert were so married. And Rupert was an honest conscientious man. And Morgan loved her sister. That Rupert was trying to sort Morgan out, that he could believe, and also that Rupert might have advised her to get a divorce. Rupert was impatient with muddles.

I won't agree to a divorce, thought Tallis, I'll fight that. If there is no divorce she'll come back. Or am I just deceiving myself? I must do something, I must see her. But it's always such a rotten failure when I do. I'm so clumsy and stupid with her. I'll write to her today. Perhaps I should see Rupert too. If only I had some energy and could *think*. His heart lurched with the now familiar pain of remembering his father. Other thoughts came and went, they had to, but this deep thought hung like a leaden weight upon his heart, pulling his consciousness steadily back in the direction of pain. How soon would his father begin to suspect something? In these days he was accomplishing the tragic and final passage from being an ailing person to being a seriously ill person. Tallis had said, "You'll be up and about in a week or so." Had he been believed? He ought to tell his father. Julius was right. Leonard owned his life. He owned it down to its last miserable fragment. This terrible thing belonged to him too. And if he wanted to think his own final thoughts he should be allowed to think them. He should not be deceived. I ought to tell him, thought Tallis, yes, I ought to tell him. Only not today.

Every night now Tallis dreamed of his sister. Every night a lurid radiance hung like a canopy about his bed and a tall white-robed figure regarded him, formidably quietly, in silence. He could not see her eyes but he could feel their scrutiny, while he lay sweating with excitement and a sort of fear. The apparition never failed to amaze him. And he sometimes felt afterward that it wearied him. Something was spent. Had his nocturnal visitor changed in some way? Or was it that he had at last come to realize what had always been so? It was not a protective or a benign presence. It was not exactly hostile either, but ambiguous. Here something much greater and more august was watching him, but watching with a curiosity which was not totally unlike that of the creatures with claws and tails which had for so long inhabited the holes and corners of his world.

Tallis felt suddenly giddy. The giddiness came with a sense of large empty space, encircling him but not supporting him, as if he were spinning, spinning, spinning, but just about to tilt and fall. He held on tightly to the edge of the table, staring at his hand and at the bright red stain upon Julius's handkerchief. He could recognize but not understand these great moments of temptation. The formless light which he had once known had withdrawn from him, and he was now capable for the first time in his life of believing it to be illusory. Perhaps she was the queen of the other world after all and that glory had been just an empty reflection from the passing splendour of her robe?

🕸 | TWELVE

"So you don't feel that my visits are intrusive?" said Julius softly.

Hilda released his hand, which she had been holding. "No. You have been a tremendous comfort. I really don't know how I could have got through this time without someone to talk to. Without *you* to talk to. You are so wise."

"Not wise, alas, but your very devoted servant."

It had been raining, but now there was an obscure golden greenish light in the garden. It was afternoon. Hilda and Julius sat beside a tea table in the drawing-room. Tea had been drunk but no one had tried the walnut cake.

"I am sure you are right. You have convinced me," said Hilda, "that it is better just to wait and let *them* unravel it all." She stared out at the dripping roses.

"You see, they are so *proud*," said Julius. "Let us be tender to their pride."

"It goes against my instincts in a way—"

"I know. But remember, you are sacrificing yourself to them. You suffer. And you spare them suffering."

"You put it so clearly. Yes. I know Rupert *will* tell me about it. He will tell me, won't he?"

"Yes, of course. He may be in a tiny bit of a muddle at the moment. But it will all pass and he'll tell you. You must be patient, Hilda. After all, we don't suppose, do we, that anything much is actually happening?"

"Something is happening to me," said Hilda. "Something is—perhaps—irrevocably spoilt."

"I am glad that you say 'perhaps.' You simply must not give houseroom to that thought. It is your *duty*, Hilda, to keep unspoilt the thing of which you are the guardian."

"It isn't just Rupert, it's Morgan— Oh God— Sorry, Julius, we've been over and over this. You've been so kind, listening to all my obsessive worries—"

"I know, I know, my dear. You're hurt two ways. But one simply must not exaggerate. I blame myself in a way. We've so talked it over that it seems larger than it is. It isn't as if they were having a love affair or planning to run away or anything. It's just a momentary emotional patch in a brother-in-law sister-in-law relationship. This isn't at all unusual. Morgan needs help and Rupert can give it. It's as simple as that."

"You seemed to think more seriously of it when we had that first conversation."

"No, indeed, I never thought it serious. And you don't really either, do you, Hilda? Come now."

"I don't know," she said. "It's the deceptions— Sometimes it all becomes huge, like a nightmare, as if *they* were living in an epic world."

"Come, come. You must satisfy yourself. You must have been watching Rupert. You must see it's not all that important to him. What's a little prevarication about an evening's outing? I dare say it's happened before now! And I can just imagine him and Morgan sitting and discussing the economic situation or post-Christian ethics or something and forgetting to hold hands. They're such an intense pair."

"But then why— I can't get it into focus. I don't want to imagine anything. I'm sure Rupert's never deceived me before, even about the tiniest things."

"Your faith is touching, Hilda. Of course we know that Rupert is an exceptional person."

Hilda sat very still, looking out at the garden, where the light was growing pinker and the rose bushes were becoming plumper as the air became warm and the raindrops were drying upon their leaves. She sat carefully on her chair, very upright, her hands lightly resting on the arms, as if she had suddenly realized that she was made of very thin china. She had assumed that Rupert could not lie to her. Looked at from the outside it might seem a naïve assumption. But she was not on the outside. She had extra proofs, the proofs provided by a sense of connection, a loving communication which carried its own marks of truth. Just lately the communication had failed. But how well did she remember the past? Perhaps it had failed before? Had Rupert really been satisfied with his marriage? And would she, unless driven to it, ever have come to ask herself this question? Her own motives for self-deception were strong and for the first time visible to her.

"I've got to keep my head," said Hilda, thinking aloud.

"Don't *worry* so, Hilda." Julius was leaning forward intently across the tea table. His fingers touched the back of her tensed hand. His dark thickly lidded eyes gleamed at her, with reassuring humour, with pleading affection. His hair was a little shorter and more sleeked back, which made his face seem younger and more nakedly aquiline. His long curly mouth smiled, then drooped with sympathy. "My dear, relax. Remember that you are confronted with a number of little things, not with one big thing."

"A lot of little things make a big thing."

"No. Not in this region. Rupert's misdemeanours, if they are such, are quite scattered, probably quite momentary and random lapses. All right, suppose he did lie to you the other evening. Suppose he has given Morgan money. Suppose they have exchanged a letter or two, and been seen about together. These things should *not* be added up. It is far more just to see them as a series of impulses than as a deliberate policy."

"Given her *money?*" said Hilda. This was a new idea.

"Well, why not?" said Julius. "I confess this was just something which I assumed or guessed. Morgan seems to have got some money from somewhere lately. Consider all those rather expensive new clothes. And I certainly haven't given her anything."

Hilda blinked at the garden, which was damply sunny now, glittering here and there with sparks of light where some last drops of rain hung downward from the leaves. Well, why not? But the

idea of Rupert secretly giving Morgan money for clothes was somehow appalling. Perhaps he went with her to the shops— "No, no,"
said Hilda. "No, I doubt it—yet the clothes— I did wonder—"

"It's not a very grave matter, after all," said Julius. "Come.
Do you tell Rupert exactly how you spend your money? No little secrets?"

"No secrets at all." Well, almost none, thought Hilda. I never
told him I've been subsidizing Peter. But that's different. Different
yet still a falsehood, a rift in the structure.

"Well, I think these things are tiny," said Julius, "and you
ought to set your mind at rest. It's better to know than not to
know. I expect you've already had a quick look through Rupert's
desk."

"No, I haven't!" said Hilda. "I wouldn't dream of searching
Rupert's desk! Besides, he's such a careful man—" Where am I
going? she thought. I have leapt in a second from indignation at
the very idea to the thought that anyway it would be profitless.
How quickly can one lose one's faith and abandon one's standards.

"Hilda, Hilda, don't misunderstand me. I wasn't thinking of
a search for incriminating documents, for I'm sure there aren't
any. I merely thought that it might relieve your mind. I mean,
suppose you found some quite casual note from Morgan, affectionate, *ordinary*. That would give you an inside look at their relationship. And that is exactly what you need—to calm all those
ridiculous fears."

"Well, I'm certainly not going to search Rupert's desk!" said
Hilda.

"Quite right, my dear, if you feel like that. But do please believe
me that it's all just an unconnected pile of trivialities. No love
affair, no grand passion, nothing with consequences. You do really
believe this, don't you?"

"Yes," said Hilda. But the word felt dead in her mouth.

"Then relax a little. May I hold your hand again? I think physical contact is so important. Our foolish conventions are even now
too shy of it. Younger people know better. We beings are so

briefly in this vale of tears. We must neglect no method by which we can comfort and console each other."

"You are very kind, Julius," said Hilda, surrendering her hand. She returned the pressure of his and looked into the very dark brown almost black violet velvety eyes. The long mouth drooped and quivered.

"Dear Hilda, it is you who are kind to me. It is an act of kindness if someone lets you help them in however small a way. I am a lonely and deprived man, without family ties. I hope you will not mind my saying that you have given me a vision of friendship and affection."

"I am glad of that," said Hilda. "You must know now that you can always come to see me— Have you no living relations?"

"No, none. I have been what is called a successful man. I am well-known in my work. I have an independent income. I ought to have no worries. But it is hollow within, Hilda, hollow. One is so much alone."

"You've never seriously thought of getting married?"

"No. Forgive me, Hilda. Morgan is sweet, but she's—well, we both know her—she's unstable. And of course there have been others. I am no longer young. I don't want to sound sorry for myself. Women always leave me and then I feel relieved. I think probably marriage is not for me. I need the steady friendship of an older woman, married herself, someone wise and clever and warm-hearted. Someone like *this*." He pressed her hand. "You know that you are very much cleverer than your sister. There are many strange things I could talk to you about. One day I will tell you all about myself, if it wouldn't bore you and you would like to hear."

"Oh Julius, you know I'd love to hear, and you couldn't possibly bore me!"

"I am a homeless man—"

"Let this be your home. You know we would be so pleased—" Hilda stopped. That 'we' had been instinctive. But there was no 'we' any more. There was no home any more. Only a house where people watched each other. How mechanically she had reacted.

And how odd it was to be able at such a time to feel pleasure in the touch of Julius's hand, to feel deeply comforted by that warm strong grip and those velvet eyes, to feel flattered that Julius might tell her about himself so that she would know more about Julius than Rupert did. Rupert would be impressed. "Julius never reveals himself," he had said once. They would invite Julius. But there was the same mistake again, the same natural extension into a future which didn't exist any more. She must keep her head. There were only a lot of quite disconnected little things, quite unimportant, quite temporary. Nothing had happened, nothing had happened at all. Hilda burst into tears.

"My dearest—" Julius had come round the table and was kneeling beside her. "Now don't weep. The sight of tears upsets me so terribly. I shall start crying myself and then where shall we be!"

"Oh Julius, I know I'm being stupid, but I'm so *miserable*—" Hilda fumbled for her handkerchief and gave herself up to sobbing.

Julius patted her and rose.

"Mother!"

Peter had come into the drawing-room.

Hilda gave a little cry and buried her face in her very small wet handkerchief. Julius retired tactfully to the other side of the room. Peter threw himself onto the floor beside his mother.

"Mother darling, what is it, oh stop, stop please, *I can't bear it.*" He clutched her, one hand on her knee, one arm round her shoulder, pressing his face down into the crook of her arm.

Hilda tried to master the tears. "It's all right— It's nothing—"

"Something terrible's happened," said Peter. She could feel his lips moist on her dress. "There's been an accident—or you're ill—"

"No, no, no accident, no one's hurt. I'm not ill. I'm just being silly. Now, Peter, *please* don't panic, *help* me to be sensible by being sensible yourself. Nothing at all's the matter."

"Then why are you crying in this awful way? People don't cry like that for nothing."

"May I suggest some more tea?" said Julius. "Or possibly a drink?"

"Tea, yes, please, Julius, I'll—"

"No, no, I'll make it," said Julius. "You stay here and talk to Peter. I'll take the teapot into the kitchen and make us some more tea." He marched off, closing the door behind him.

"Mother, what *is* it? You've *terrified* me."

"Peter, it isn't *anything, truly*. I'm just overtired. These tears mean nothing. I cry very easily."

"That's not true. I've never seen you cry in my life before. Never ever in my life before."

"You must have done. Anyway it's all over now, see, no more tears. It was just a silly moment."

"You're ill, Mother. They've just told you. You've got cancer or something."

"No, I'm in perfect health. And so is your father. And everything is perfectly all right. I was just feeling tired and stupid, the way women do, and now it's over and you mustn't embarrass me by making such a fuss!"

"Do you *promise* that you haven't got some awful illness?"

"I promise. There. Now we're both quite sensible again, aren't we! How very very nice to see you, Peter. Have you been good and done some work like you said you would?"

Peter sat back on the carpet at her feet. His face was still creased up with pain and shock. "Mother, it was *awful* coming in and finding you like that. You've *frightened* me so."

"Stop it, dear. Now tell me about yourself."

"Oh, I'm all right. I've done some work. At least I read a book. I came really— I wondered if you knew when Morgan would be back. She said she was going away again, and I've telephoned a lot and she's not there."

"I'm afraid I don't know—when Morgan will be back."

"You haven't got her address?"

"No."

"Oh well, it doesn't matter. Is Father in the house, by the way?"

"No, he's working late at the office."

"I'm afraid I filled the electric kettle with *hot* water," said Julius, "so that it would boil quicker. I hope you have no superstitions about that? Some people think the tea doesn't taste right unless you boil the water from cold. Here, I've brought another cup for Peter. Delicious tea all round. And won't someone take pity on the walnut cake?"

"Bless you, Julius," said Hilda.

Julius began to pour out the tea.

"I won't have any, thanks," said Peter.

"Would he like a drink?"

"Would you like some sherry, darling? No? What about you, Julius. Something stronger than tea?"

"No, thank you. But let me get you some whisky, yes, I insist. I know where it lives."

Hilda sank back in her chair with a sigh, sipping tea and whisky. Peter was sitting on the floor in front of her, with his chin on his knees, regarding her under his flopping fair hair with anxiety and curiosity.

"There's something you haven't told me, Mother."

"No, nothing."

"Sorry, but I don't believe you."

"Oh Peter, stop it. I'm just terribly overtired and nervous—"

"Yes, if I may say so—" said Julius, "this isn't the moment—your mother is exhausted—all those committees—"

Peter bounded to his feet. "All right, I'll go!"

"Please, darling—"

"Don't fret, Mother. I'm not cross. I understand. You're tired. I'll come back tomorrow."

"Yes, yes, come back tomorrow, and we'll have a nice long talk. Tomorrow morning. You promise?"

"Yes, I promise. I'll ring up at nine and we'll fix things. I do promise."

As the door closed Hilda said, "How very unfortunate. He'll *worry* so. And he'll start wondering and—"

"What did you tell him?" said Julius.

"Well, nothing of course. I said nothing was wrong."

"Really, Hilda, you are hopeless. You should have thought of some plausible falsehood. Now of course he'll wonder and worry."

"I'm no good at plausible falsehoods," said Hilda.

"You should have said *something*. Would you like me to go after him and reassure him? I'll think of something quite harmless but definite. That will stop him from worrying. You don't want him to start *investigating*, do you?"

"No, no, that would be awful. Yes, do please go after him, Julius. You're so inventive and quick. Just say something to make him think it's all right."

Julius darted out of the room after Peter. Hilda poured a mixture of whisky and strong tea into the spare cup. She closed her swollen burning eyes. What a fuss about probably nothing. When Rupert came back she would look at him carefully and see how calm and ordinary he was after all, just as usual. Custom would console her, it would and it should. Unfortunately he was going to be working late at the office tonight. *Late at the office? Why?*

After a short while Julius returned. It was almost evening in the garden. The blackbird was singing.

"What did you say to him?"

"I told him you had just heard of the serious illness of your dearest friend at school, whom you hadn't seen for ages, and it brought back so many memories. I said you didn't want to tell him because you thought it would sound so absurd. I even told him her name and said he must have heard you talking about her."

"Julius! What is her name? I'd better know!"

"Antoinette Ruabon. She's French. Lives at Mont de Marsan. You always refer to her as Toni. You've been corresponding for years—"

"Julius, you really are—"

"You must learn to invent details if you want to lie well."

Hilda began to laugh helplessly. "Oh, you do do me good! I see I shall have to keep the Toni Ruabon myth going forever after!"

"Ruabon is her married name. Her maiden name was Mauriac. A remote cousin of the novelist. Her husband—"

"Oh, please stop, Julius. I can't bear it," said Hilda, putting her hand to her side. "When you make me laugh like that you make me feel suddenly as if I were happy and yet I'm miserable and it hurts! Did Peter believe you?"

"Absolutely! He even imagined he'd heard you speak of her! And I hope you don't mind, Hilda, I added a little passing reference to your age, the approach of the menopause, nervous symptoms in middle-aged women—"

"Well, that bit was perfectly true!"

"A good lie always has a spice of truth. Anyway, I think you'll have no more trouble on that front. And now, my dear Hilda, I fear I must go."

"Please don't go. I thought perhaps after Peter had gone you'd— But yes, of course you must go, I expect you're busy. Julius, I still can't make up my mind about that dinner."

"The celebration dinner for Rupert's book? But of course you must have it."

"But it's *tomorrow!*"

"Well, it would look very odd if you cancelled it now. You said you'd sent out the invitations? I've certainly had mine."

"I got as far as inviting the family," said Hilda. "Peter, Morgan, Simon, Axel of course with Simon. And you."

"I'm glad I count as family!"

"We were going to invite some of Rupert's office colleagues and their wives. And that philosopher with the funny name that he admires so. I was going to discuss the list with Rupert—but I put it off—and then I just didn't—and now—"

"Well, why not leave it at that, Hilda? That makes a nice little party."

"Oh *God!*"

"You can't cancel it, my dear, without letting them know that you know. You must go through with it. I'll support you."

"Julius, you're an angel. All right. Thank you immensely for your help and advice. I really don't know what I'd do without you. And please come again. Feel that you can always come. Another time we'll talk of you."

Julius's company had been a stimulus. Now that he was gone she felt utterly dejected and rather frightened. She took the tea things out into the kitchen. She realized that she felt very hungry, having had no lunch. She cut a piece of the walnut cake but found she could not eat it. She went upstairs to her boudoir, lifted the telephone, and dialled the Whitehall number. The telephonist at Rupert's office said there was no reply from his extension. That proved nothing. She went into the bedroom, bathed her face in cold water, and put on some more make-up. The garden was luminous with a heavy apricotish evening light, clear and faintly menacing. The house felt hollow and meaningless and sad, like an empty house. A homing aeroplane droned overhead. The sun and the evening time were desolate.

Hilda thought, I must do something to stop myself from getting panic-stricken. She went back to her boudoir and sat down at the desk and started fumbling with her papers. She could feel her eyes staring with fright. She thought, I must find something to hold onto, something to peg me down into the real world, something to make me believe in the reality of the past. Perhaps I might look at some of Rupert's old letters. A word from Rupert, even a years-old word, might ease this awful sick disconnected feeling. She had kept most of Rupert's letters dating from the earliest days of their courtship. There were few more recent ones since she and Rupert had always been together. The letters were in a secret compartment at the back of her desk. This consisted of a box tucked in behind the lowest drawer, which was correspondingly shortened. The lowest drawer was fixed so that it could not be pulled entirely out, and the box could only be reached by removing the drawer above and reaching in behind the drawer below. Hilda removed the upper drawer and her fingers scrabbled at the hidden box. Even before she was able to grip it and draw it out she realized that it was empty.

She sat still for a while with the empty box lying in front of

her on top of her papers. Then she began, slowly, she was breathless but deliberately slow, to examine the desk. She fingered about
above and below where the box had been, looking for cracks or
crannies. There were none. She opened the other drawers, though
she knew that this was futile. More frenziedly now she searched
the rest of the desk, she looked under it, she pulled it away from
the wall. Then she sat down in an arm-chair and thought.

The letters were gone. Only Rupert knew where she kept them.
Therefore Rupert must have taken them. Hilda sat stiffly in her
chair. What an absurd cruel strange *mad* thing to do, to take away
his old letters without telling her. The action made her with a
shudder intuit a whole dimension of otherness, Rupert's otherness. Rupert had all kinds of thoughts and needs and impulses
of which she knew nothing, of which she could not conceive. He
had wanted—what had he wanted? To meddle with the past?
To destroy the evidence? He had come into her room and with
some unimaginable expression on his face had furtively thrust
his hand in and drawn the letters out of the box. Had he assumed
that she would not notice their disappearance? It was indeed
nearly a year since she had looked at them. Was he testing her
perhaps? What was she to think?

Hilda found that she had risen. She went down the stairs and
out into the thickly darkly sunny garden. Long tongues of sunlight
crossed the pavement, casting camomile shadows, and the worn
surface of the old brick wall glowed patchily with golden browns
and rosy reds. Twilight was gathering in the shadowed places
where green things glowed with a momentary intensity of colour.
What does it *mean?* thought Hilda, and she clutched at her dress
with fright.

Then she saw, from the corner of her eye, that something
round and brown was floating on the surface of the pool. She
turned and looked quickly down. It was the hedgehog.

Hilda knelt and plunged her arms into the pool. The hedgehog
was floating half curled up, its brown prickly back uppermost.
She put her hands underneath it and felt the soft wet fur, the
little pendent feet. She lifted it out. It was quite dead. Hilda laid

the little light rounded body down upon the pavement where the water made a dark stain. The little black-tipped nose protruded toward her, the feet were limp and splayed, the eyes closed. Tears streamed down Hilda's face. She thought, I must tell Rupert and he will comfort me. She half rose, then sat back with a moan. She thought, I must bury the hedgehog; but the task was beyond her. She picked it up quickly and dropped it down behind some plants. Then she ran into the house and up the stairs, blinded with tears.

The letters, she thought, if only I could find the letters, where are they, are they safe somewhere near? He cannot have destroyed them? Is it possible that he wanted to see them somehow to comfort himself, to make him remember? She went into Rupert's study. In there his absence was terrible. She wanted to tell him about the hedgehog and to weep in his arms. She opened his desk and began helplessly to turn things over. Rupert did not keep his desk very tidy. There was a row of little compartments where he stowed receipted bills, insurance papers, stubs of old cheque books, old diaries, oddments of photographs, references, pamphlets. Hilda took a mass of tears from her eyes with the back of her hand and stared more intently at the desk. What Julius had said about relieving her mind, that was not absurd. Supposing she could find some communication from Morgan, something completely innocent and ordinary, something which would give her the *tone* of their relationship? It was that mystery most of all which troubled her. And it might prove to be a harmless one after all. Oh, how relieved she would feel! As for the letters Rupert might well have taken them just to look them over again. He would laugh at her terror.

Hilda began methodically to search the desk. She leafed through the photographs. They were all old ones of Peter and herself. There were a few letters, from an antique dealer about mending a bookcase, from a book-seller about completing a series of periodicals. Her fingers passed over the insurance papers and the old cheque books. Then she paused. Rupert threw his old cheque book stubs into the end compartment. After a year he destroyed

them. The latest one was always on the top. Hilda picked it up
and opened it. The last entry was a week ago. She began to run
through the entries. Here Rupert was meticulous. Bookshop,
drink shop, Harrods, New and Lingwood, Fortnum and Mason,
Commissioners of Inland Revenue, the Postmaster General,
the local builder. The next entry read simply "M. £400." Hilda
put the booklet back in its place. She sat down in Rupert's chair.

She began more hurriedly to search the rest of the desk. She
looked into all the drawers, pulling them right out and examining
their contents. There was nothing. The lowest drawer would
not pull fully out, it seemed to be jammed. Hilda tugged at it,
then thrust her fingers in and clawed its contents forward into
the light. Only a sale-room catalogue and some stamps. Then she
thought, The drawer is too short, there is a secret compartment
behind it, just as in my desk. The desks were of similar date and
style. Trembling now she pulled out the drawer above and felt
far in behind the lower drawer. Her fingers touched a piece of
folded paper. She drew out the secret box and lifted the paper
out of it. She saw at once that it was something in Morgan's
writing. It was a letter and it began as follows:

My angel, the ecstasy of your love makes me the happiest
person in the world. Was it strange that I cried yesterday when
I was in bed with you? I was crying with joy. Must we not soon,
somehow be properly together? . . .

Hilda read the letter through to the end. Then she folded it
and replaced it in the box and put the box back into its secret
place. She closed the drawers and arranged the contents of the
desk as they had been before and closed it up. She went slowly
downstairs to the drawing-room.

✿ | THIRTEEN

"I mustn't stay here any longer."

"But you told Hilda you'd be working late at the office. You don't have to go yet."

"You persuaded me to do that. I shouldn't have let you."

"You're such a coward, Rupert! She's not likely to go round to the office to look for you, is she! And even if she did you could invent some story. I think it's much more imprudent of you to have left your car outside the door."

"Yes, I know. I just drove it from Earls Court station, I didn't think—"

"Rupert, don't be so jittery! Just rest on *me*."

"I wish I could. I feel I just don't know what I'm doing at the moment. I hate telling lies to Hilda."

"Well, she doesn't always tell you the truth, you know."

"Yes she does!"

"For instance, she's never told you that she's been financing Peter lavishly ever since he chucked Cambridge. All the time you were making such a thing of making him live on two pounds a week or whatever it was!"

"Really? Is that true?"

"Do you doubt my word? Ask Hilda. I dare say there are other little things like that too. There are in any marriage. Why should yours be so special?"

"It was special," said Rupert. " 'Was.' Oh God."

"Well, don't whinge about it, for heaven's sake. You decided to break out. You didn't have to. Yet I suppose you obviously needed to. Men do after a while."

"I haven't 'broken out,'" said Rupert. "I'm married to *Hilda*. Have you forgotten?"

"I haven't forgotten. I thought you had."

"I think we're both behaving rottenly."

"Come, come, we're scarcely behaving at all! Anyway it was your idea."

"It wasn't my idea, it was your idea!"

"Well, never mind whose idea it was, we're both in it now and everything would be perfectly all right if only you wouldn't make so much fuss. You were the one who said we could sail through it all and build a marvellous relationship. I wouldn't have started anything if you hadn't been so confident and starry-eyed about it. You said you wouldn't let go. I thought you were damn brave. Now you're wrecking the whole thing because you haven't got a bit of sense and resolution. Decide what you want to do and do it, for God's sake. Or do you want me to go away or what?"

"I don't want you to go away," said Rupert miserably. "I couldn't just blankly send you off. I knew that from the start. But I can't carry on with this on a basis of deceiving Hilda. It's poisoning my life."

"If you tell Hilda, everything will be utterly different."

"Well, it'd better be!"

"All right then, tell Hilda!"

Morgan and Rupert were sitting opposite to each other on upright chairs in Morgan's sitting-room. They were huge-eyed and stiff, like a pair of Egyptian figures. They had both by now drunk a good deal of gin. The sun, sloping toward evening, was gilding a white wall across the street and the room was full of soft intense reflected light. The traffic was humming steadily in the Fulham Road.

"Oh Rupert, don't let's quarrel," said Morgan. "There must be some rational way of looking at this peculiar situation. I was so much wanting you to come this evening and now we're quarrelling."

"I was so much wanting to come too." He stretched out his hand and she gripped it hard. Then they resumed their stiff positions face to face.

"It's not that I'm against telling Hilda," said Morgan. "I just think there's no point in telling her *now*. This is the moment of maximum chaos. We wouldn't even know what to *say* to Hilda, and anything we said would be likely to mislead her and make her think there was more to the thing than there is. So in a way it's really more truthful not to tell her. I mean—"

"I'm afraid there is a great deal to the thing," said Rupert. "That's the trouble!" He got up and began to pace the room.

"Yes, I know," said Morgan. "I feel that too. Of course. But we *have* kept our heads. Quaint phrase!" She laughed and poured out more gin.

Rupert was thoroughly miserable. The loss of contact with Hilda made him feel reduced and mutilated. He hated telling Hilda lies and was in a state of abject fear in case his lies were discovered. At the same time, he craved for Morgan's company; even quarrelling with Morgan had become something necessary. They had endlessly discussed the situation and only succeeded in tangling it up to a mysterious degree. They had rationed their kisses. But he felt her passion and knew by now that she felt his.

At first it had seemed very clear to Rupert that he must *talk* to Morgan and not send her away, simply because the idea of sending her away in that peculiar state of wretchedness seemed so appalling. She had had a very unhappy time, she was seriously confused about her life, and she needed him. All this seemed to add up to some kind of duty. She had taken the responsibility of telling her love. He must take the responsibility of leading them both through to sanity.

Now it all seemed considerably less clear and somehow dreadful, yet he could not quite see what was the wrong step which he had taken. To deceive Hilda, temporarily of course, had seemed simply an essential part of doing his duty to Morgan. Of course he was well aware how fond he was of Morgan. Indeed it was on this fondness that he was prepared to build. Only love will do, thought Rupert, real love, real caring. He would not send Morgan away into bitterness and wretchedness. She needed love, as all human beings did. He would give her love, wise steady strong love, and this, he honestly believed, would set her free at last of the whole tangle, Tallis, Julius, himself. She would find then that she knew what to do about Tallis. She would become once more, or indeed perhaps for the first time, a whole person.

Rupert had been supported in this resolution by his deep age-old confidence in the power of goodness. Not that he located this goodness in himself. It was something very much exterior to him, but fairly near and very real. Rupert did not believe in God, in fact he even disapproved of belief in God, which he felt to be a weakener of the moral sinews. But in this he did believe, and under this star he would care for Morgan. He had loved people in this way before, though never anyone so close to him, and as far as he knew nothing but good had resulted. The top of the moral structure was no dream, and he had proved this by exercises in loving attention: loving people, loving art, loving work, loving paving stones and leaves on trees. This had been his happiness. This *freedom* had also been the keystone of his marriage. It was something, oddly, about which he had never talked to Hilda. He did not believe that she would understand. He had written about it, in a formal half-disguised way, as if it were a secret, in his philosophy book. When it was in typescript Hilda would read the book. And still she would not understand. And it would not matter. He loved his wife the more deeply because he felt he could love everything else in the world without depriving her at all. In fact this secret love enriched his marriage.

So it was that it had seemed to Rupert that it would be quite easy to control the situation with Morgan. Of course he would come to care for her more, but there would be no danger in that, only salvation. What was it that he had failed somehow to take into account? He had not realized how his life would be envenomed by the telling of one or two small necessary lies. He had not expected this curious breakdown of communications with Hilda. He had been quite prepared to be moved physically by

Morgan, to be moved by her more, and in a new way. All Rupert's affections had their physical side: and this was true also of his attachments to men, though he would never have confessed this to Axel. These were secret things over which he smiled. But he had not been prepared for the nervous craving for Morgan's company which was afflicting him now, nor for the precise temporally located urges to seize the girl in his arms. He had not foreseen the confusion, the arguments, the clouded sense of involvement and muddle. He had not foreseen that his own estimation of himself would seem suddenly in jeopardy.

"I think I've been a fool," said Rupert. "Maybe you'd better go away after all. I should have been tougher with you. Go away for six months. You know you can't lose me or my love. There's nothing to worry about. But I think we both need to calm down about this situation. While you're away I'll tell Hilda. I won't let it seem more important than it is."

"Where the hell am I to go for six months?"

"Anywhere. France, Italy. I'll pay for it. Let me do that anyway, now that we know each other better."

"Oh Rupert—your sweetness just cracks my heart. But my dear, I can't go away now. Even a week ago it would have been possible. Now it just isn't. I need to see you and talk to you. Seeing you is the only thing I've got to hold onto now. You took on this responsibility, Rupert, and you've got to see it through. If I went away I'd go mad with worry. You don't know what you're saying. Imagine me all alone in some ghastly hotel in Antibes! I'd go crazy. I've got to *talk* to somebody, that's the only cure, Rupert, talk, talk, talk, God, there are so many things bedeviling my mind, things I want to talk to you about, things I can *only* talk to you about."

"I'm sorry," said Rupert. He stopped in front of her and resumed his glass. "I'm being selfish and unimaginative. Yes, we must go on."

"I haven't told you about the child."

"The child?"

"I became pregnant by Julius."

"Oh Morgan—" Rupert sat down, pulling his chair closer, and took her hand. "Tell me, my dear."

"I had an abortion of course. I was by myself, I'd left Julius—or rather he'd somehow driven me out. I was all alone on the West Coast. It was a nightmare."

"Poor child— I am so sorry."

"I'll tell you all about it sometime—soon maybe. I need to tell somebody the details. I didn't know how to find a doctor. I went to one at random and he was just rude to me and charged a huge fee. Then I went to another and he was insinuating and beastly but said he'd do it and insisted on being paid beforehand and I thought he wouldn't do it and I was crying all the time and it was so utterly humiliating—"

"It's all over now, Morgan, don't cry now, my dear. Yes. I think you had better tell me the details."

"And it isn't only that, Rupert. I feel so guilty about it now, it haunts me, and I *regret* it so much. I want that child, I want *that* child—"

"Morgan, Morgan, don't upset yourself, here, have another drink. We will talk of all these things at great length, whenever you will. And of course you shan't go away. I'll manage, I'll *manage*."

"Thank you, my darling—"

Suddenly very close to them there was a sound so loud that they could not at first understand what it was. Rupert leapt to his feet. He looked round the room expecting to see that some large object had fallen heavily to the floor. Morgan was looking up at him with big startled eyes. The sound came again and Rupert realized that someone outside on the landing was hitting the door. It was not like knocking. It was more like an attempt to break in the door panels. Bang! Bang! Bang! Morgan rose and instinctively they both withdrew toward Morgan's bedroom, clutching at each other in panic.

"Who is it?" whispered Rupert.

"I don't know. It couldn't be Hilda. Sssh. Shall we just not answer it?"

They stood clasping hands, questioning each other's eyes. "It must be some mistake," whispered Morgan. "It can't be for me."

"Maybe you'd better answer it before the whole house comes to look."

The terrible banging sound had been resumed. Someone was thundering on the door panel with a closed fist.

"You go in here," breathed Morgan. "Keep quiet. I'll see who it is and send them away." She pushed Rupert into the bedroom and closed the door. Then she went to her front door and opened it.

Peter pushed past her into the sitting-room. He looked round and then immediately opened the door of the bedroom and looked in. Rupert emerged. He felt suddenly sick to fainting and sat down on a chair. Morgan closed the front door. They looked at each other.

"That's a very odd way to knock, Peter," said Morgan.

Peter seemed for the moment incapable of speech. Rupert knew that he could not utter any word himself. He gasped for breath and put his hand to his throat.

"Sit down," said Morgan. "Have a drink."

Peter said something. It sounded like "late at the office."

"What's that? Do sit down, Peter," said Morgan. "What is all this agitation?"

Peter continued to stand. He ignored his father. He said to Morgan, "So it *is* true."

"So what is true?" Morgan sat down and regarded him. She was blushing, but her expression was hard and calm.

"You are having a love affair with my father."

"I am not having a love affair with your father, you silly boy. Now calm down and—"

"Then why didn't you open the door at once?" said Peter. "And why were you in the bedroom and why is the bed all undone and why is he looking like that and—"

"Oh, stop it," said Morgan. "You'll make me angry. We were

just discussing something. And I never make my bed until the evening. And it was the way you knocked that made us hesitate to open the door."

"What were you discussing?"

"Something private."

"And why did he say he'd be late at the office when he was here?"

"He was going to be late at the office. Then I rang up and asked him to come round. And if you must know, we were discussing you. We were talking about your education."

"I am afraid," said Peter, "that I don't believe a word you say." He was pale and shuddering a little, his eyes fixed on Morgan.

"Look, Peter, I am *not* having a love affair with your father! The idea is completely unthinkable. Can't you see I'm speaking the truth? Come on, Rupert, or has the cat got your tongue?"

"It's true," said Rupert, "what she says." But he could scarcely raise his face and his voice sounded thick and jumbled. His mouth seemed to be filled with stones.

"What made you come round here and bang on the door in that horrible way?" said Morgan. "What put it into your head?"

"Someone told me—about you and my father."

"Someone *told* you? Who?"

"Never mind. I'm grateful. I just wanted to see with my own eyes. And I've seen. I could scarcely believe it. Then there was the car outside, and now that I've seen—both of you—I know— Don't worry. I'm going now. Then you can get on with it."

"Peter, this is a lot of nonsense," said Morgan, "and your father and I are very angry with you. Have you, or this other person, said anything about this fable to your mother?"

"No," said Peter. "She doesn't know. At least, she doesn't *know*. And I'm not going to tell her. You can keep your little secret. As long as you're enjoying yourselves."

"Peter, *really*. I'm very vexed with you—"

"You amused yourself with me," said Peter. "I should have seen the sort of person you were. You started it. Kissing me and rolling me in the grass in that railway cutting. You knew per-

fectly well you were making me fall in love with you. Then next
week you decide to drop me and take up with him. I expect it
will be someone else the week after."

"*Peter—*"

"All right, all right, I'm going." He turned toward the door and
then stopped. The piece of green malachite was lying on the
table in the little hall, weighing down a pile of letters. Peter turned
back to Morgan, who had risen. "I see he's given you *that*, that
bit of green stone. He gave it to me once, years and years ago
when I was a child. Then he forgot he'd given it to me and it
went back into his room He's simply forgotten about me, forgotten, forgotten. And what you said in the railway cutting just
isn't true, I know that now. *Full fathom five* proves nothing,
nothing at all. Except that everything's rich and strange all right,
rich and strange and foul. And the bells are ringing but they don't
sound pretty any more, not any more at all."

Peter's face had suddenly collapsed into tears. He covered it
with both hands, then turned and ran out of the door and out
of the flat. His running feet pounded down the stairs and the
front door banged.

"Oh dear," said Morgan. She closed the sitting-room door.
"Have another drink, Rupert. I think we need one."

"How can you be—so calm—" said Rupert. His tongue was
still impeded.

"I'm not calm, you perfect fool. I'm on the verge of hysterics.
But what good would it do us if I started screaming? I must say,
you were pretty helpful, weren't you, sitting there tongue-tied
and looking the absolute picture of guilt!"

"We are guilty."

"What do you say? Don't mumble so."

"We are guilty."

"Rupert, you make me sick. You entered this situation quite
deliberately, with your eyes open. Now when we get this awful
shock you just fold up. All right, go round and tell Hilda all about
it. And I'll go to Saint Tropez or Marrakesh or Timbuktu, and
not on your money!"

"Morgan, please don't shout at me. I'm very upset."

"I'm very upset too!"

"And we've got to *think*."

"You're right there. Please forgive me, Rupert. I'm very sorry. I'm just rather knocked out by that visitation."

"Who on earth could have told him?"

"Axel."

"*Axel?*"

"Yes. I've already worked that one out. I started doing my thinking at once."

"Why Axel?"

"He's the only person who detests me," said Morgan. "And he's about the only person who's likely to have found out. You must have left one of my letters lying about on your desk at the office. And I've been expressing myself rather warmly of late!"

"But I never left any letters lying about— I destroyed them all immediately—"

"All right, all right, I'm not blaming you, here, have a drink, for Christ's sake. I must say I hope Hilda *doesn't* know. And there's your ghastly celebration dinner tomorrow. What a moment for a family gathering! At any rate you won't have me there. I think I'll be genuinely out of town tomorrow."

"What was that about your rolling him in the grass in the railway cutting?"

"I kissed him on the way back from Cambridge. It was silly of me. It was a hot day."

"Did you let him make love to you?"

"No, of course not! Really, Rupert, are you going to start being jealous of Peter?"

"No," said Rupert. He got up heavily. "I'm much more troubled about Hilda—"

"Than you are about me? Thanks!"

"Oh Morgan, Morgan, my whole world is wrecked—"

"Yes, you are a *coward*," said Morgan. "I think it would have been better and more honest if we'd just gone to bed, we both want to. Instead of having this endless nerve-racking pulling sort of *discussion*."

"It's impossible."

"It isn't, but never mind. I'm not going to beg you for anything. I just ask you not to lose your nerve now and spill the whole thing to Hilda. I care about Hilda too, I care deeply, and I care about her opinion. I don't want her as a spectator of the jagged tangled snarled-up sort of muddle we seem to have got ourselves into at this particular moment. Just now we're both suffering from shock. And we can't really do anything but wait. Hold onto each other and wait. I do happen to love you, Rupert."

"Yes, yes. I love you too. Forgive me. I won't tell Hilda—yet."

"Come here, Rupert, let me put my arms round you. That's better."

"Suppose Axel tells Hilda?"

"There's nothing we can do about that. You'll soon know if he has."

"I must go home at once."

"Relax, relax. Come and lie down on my bed for a moment, I won't seduce you, I just want us to be quiet together for a time before you go."

She led him into the bedroom and they lay down in each other's arms upon Morgan's tousled bed. Rupert felt so sick and dazed with misery that he almost slept, and she had to rouse him at last when it was beginning to get dark. "I think you really must go now, my darling."

After Morgan had pushed Rupert out of the front door she saw that there was a letter for her lying upon the mat. It was from Tallis.

She climbed slowly and wearily back up the stairs. When she was alone in the sitting-room she stood there motionless for some time holding the letter and gazing at the white wall opposite, now illuminated by the light of the street lamp. She went to the window and pulled the curtains. She tore Tallis's envelope across and then across again. It was not easy to tear since the letter inside appeared to be a very long one. She dropped the pieces into the wastepaper basket. Then she went into her bedroom and, stuffing the sheet into her mouth, quietly had hysterics.

🦚 | FOURTEEN

"The weather seems to have quite recovered."

"I think it's not *quite* so hot, don't you?"

"What's the forecast?"

"Continuing warm. Won't you have a little more champagne, Julius?"

"Thank you, Hilda. Oh Axel, have I taken your seat?"

"No, no, don't stir. I am just going to inspect Hilda's roses."

"Bit battered, I'm afraid. Champagne, Rupert? Do you think it's iced enough?"

"Exactly right, I should say, my dear. Thank you, just a little."

"Is it cold in there, Simon?"

"No, the water's beautifully warm. Why don't the rest of you come in?"

"No, you're the water baby, ha ha."

"Have another black olive, Axel."

"What a pity Morgan couldn't be with us."

What a remarkable talent English people have for hiding their feelings, thought Simon, observing from water level the well-dressed convivial little gathering above him on the pavement. The men were in formal evening dress. Hilda was wearing an ankle-length shift of apple green silk with a slit at the side through which stockings of a slightly lighter green occasionally twinkled.

Corks popped, bottles tilted, glasses clinked, faces smiled, olives and savoury biscuits were enthusiastically selected. Simon had taken refuge in the pool.

The last few days had been a nightmare for Simon. A state of cold war existed between himself and Axel. Everything was difficult. Even getting rid of the teddy bear had been difficult. Never had a teddy bear seemed more like an albatross. Distractedly he had carried it down one street and along the next. "Disgusting!" said an old gentleman of military appearance as Simon passed him hugging his thankless burden. He had intended to leave it in the cemetery behind Barons Court tube station, but his arrival with a very large teddy bear and a very furtive manner had created so much interest that the gardener and several elderly ladies had actually followed him about all the time he was in there. After that he tried to leave it on an Upminster train, but had it helpfully thrown out after him with a cry of "Forgot your bear, sir!" just as the doors were closing. A Jamaican bus conductor prevented him from leaving it upon a bus, and when in desperation he tried to give it to a child in Kensington Gardens the child's mother almost called the police. Eventually he took a taxi to Great Ormond Street Children's Hospital and thrust it wordlessly into the arms of the receptionist.

Simon had made innumerable attempts to open negotiations with Axel, but it was simply impossible to get started. Axel was polite but distant and put on an air of boredom whenever Simon started to make a speech. Simon felt that if he could only gain the impetus which a genuine even acrimonious discussion would give him he would be enabled to confess. As it was he felt frozen and paralysed and also at first just sufficiently annoyed with his friend to be willing to let the situation continue and even deteriorate. He was getting into his old mood of "Let everything be awful": a kind of despair which he recognized, disapproved of, but seemed unable to check. Meanwhile he kept up an intermittent barrage, sometimes pleading, sometimes shouting. Axel replied with dreadful quietness. "Please don't be emotional." "Please don't shout." "This kind of talk is profitless." And "Please regard

yourself as entirely free." "I'm not free!" Simon screamed. "I
don't want to be free!" Axel coughed and looked at his watch.
Simon retired defeated to the spare room. Axel spent the evenings at the club, came in late, and locked his door.

At some point in every day Simon resolved to tell Axel everything. At some other later point he decided not to do so yet. He
began to feel with horror that if he did tell everything he would
be either not believed or not forgiven. The terrible terrible possibility lodged in him like an icy pellet that perhaps the days of
his liaison with Axel were numbered. It had all been an illusion
after all. Soon he would be a nomad again, looking back with
amazement upon his experiment in constancy. He could not face
or accept or even reflect upon this idea, but he knew that its
presence was poisonous to him and that to let it exist was to give
it power. He kept trying to impose some sort of pattern upon his
procrastination. If he could only find out more about Rupert and
Morgan. If he could only discover whether Julius had been speaking the truth. If he could only understand Julius's motives or if
only something *public* would happen. After that he might know
what to do next or at least be forced to do something. But Morgan
was out of London, Hilda told him. And he did not dare to seek
out Julius. Not that he feared that what Axel suspected might
become the truth. But Julius had this extraordinary power of
making him do things. And he did not want to add to the evidence
against himself.

It was a part of Axel's deadly policy that appearances should
be kept up. Of course they must both go to Rupert's celebration
dinner. The car was punctually at the door. On the way they had
a conversation which reduced Simon to a final frenzy of terror.

"Axel, please stop being so cold to me."

"Could you take your hand away, please?"

"I can't face this evening. I feel so bloody miserable."

"Your brother expects us. And I see no point in publishing the
breakdown of our little venture."

"But if only you'd *discuss* it—"

"There is nothing to discuss."

"You don't understand. There's nothing between me and Julius—"

"Please don't start that again."

"But, Axel, it's *true*— I haven't seen Julius since—"

"I don't want the details of your timetable. As far as I am concerned you are entirely free. Your private life is your affair from now on and mine is mine."

"I love you, Axel, we're bound together—"

"I have no taste for empty emotional badinage."

"You *must* talk to me properly."

"You can find someone else to talk to. I am sure you would have no difficulty in Piccadilly Circus station. Your old friends are doubtless still hanging round the public lavatory."

"No, no, no! Axel, I've been an awful fool—"

"On the contrary, the folly is entirely mine. I imagined you would be capable of changing your habits for my sake. It was a pathetic error and most unfair to you. I owe you an apology."

"But I *have* changed my habits! Oh Axel, you aren't really going to leave me, are you?"

"We happen at present to share a house."

"But you aren't making any other arrangements, are you? You said you didn't want Rupert to know—"

"One does not want day by day spectators of the breakdown of one's *ménage*."

"But you aren't going to go away, are you, Axel, please say you aren't, all this will pass, I swear it will. I love you and—"

"As I said, you are entirely free. And I regard myself as equally free, nor do I propose to consult you about what I do."

"Axel, how can you be so cruel! I can't exist without you—"

"I detest these profitless scenes. Here we are at Rupert's. Try to behave naturally, will you."

Simon got into the pool so that his face should be wet anyway.

"Dinner! *Messieurs sont servis!*" came Hilda's voice from the house, a little shrill. "Togs on quick, Simon dear!"

Axel and Rupert, who were discussing tax relief as an incentive for lower income groups, began to move off toward the french windows. Julius lingered beside the pool. He was wearing a midnight blue velvet evening jacket which made his pallid hair look blond and brought out the violet light in his dark eyes. He gazed down, smiling at Simon.

Conscious suddenly of his thinness, Simon swam to the shallower end to get out, and Julius walked round to meet him, placing his back to the house. Rupert's pool, minute and designed for swimmers, sloped sharply to a depth of six feet, and there was very little standing space where it was shallow enough to stand. Simon's feet touched the slippery bottom and he reached for the aluminum ladder. Then as he put one cringing foot onto the lowest step of the ladder and started to pull himself up, he felt a light tap on his chest. He lost his balance and fell backward with a splash, swallowing a large mouthful of water. Julius had touched him with his foot.

Simon spluttered.

Julius laughed. Then he went down on one knee on the pavement, leaning toward Simon. "Have you been a good boy, Simon?"

"Damn you," said Simon.

"Don't worry, they've all gone into the house. They've gone through into the dining-room. We can have a little private talk."

"I don't want to talk to you."

"Naughty temper. You haven't discussed any of our little secrets with Axel, have you?"

"No, but I'm going to!" Simon began to climb the ladder again.

"I should advise you not to," said Julius. "Wait, I want a word with you." He thrust his knuckles into Simon's shoulder and Simon flopped back again into the pool.

Simon could not now touch the bottom. He trod water and glared at Julius. "Let me out! I must get dressed for dinner."

"No, not yet. I want to relieve your anxiety."

"You're driving me mad! What's happened to Rupert and Morgan?"

"I wondered when you were going to ask me that."

"Well, what *has* happened?"

"Oh, a lot of things. But you can't expect me to tell you now,

with Rupert and Hilda twenty yards away. You must come round
to my flat. I've been expecting you, you know."

"I won't come! I don't want to have anything more to do with
you!"

"You want to know about Morgan, don't you? Didn't I tell
you I'd unravel it all quite painlessly? I may even need your assistance."

"I won't help you. You've done me enough damage already.
Now let me out."

Simon swam forward, gripped the steps, and started to mount.
Julius, laughing, lifted his hand again. Before Julius could push
him, Simon fell back, swam as fast as he could to the other end
of the pool, and began to pull himself out. There was no ladder
here and the smoothly rounded edge of the pool was slippery.
Julius strolled round, waited until Simon had got one knee upon
the edge, and then tipped him back in again with a touch of his
patent-leather shoe. "You are my prisoner, little one."

Simon, spitting water and panting, stared furiously up at his
tormentor. "Stop doing that. I'm getting cold. And I'm not a
strong swimmer."

"In the soup. That is an English expression, isn't it? You have
to swim when you are in the soup."

"I'm going to tell Axel everything," said Simon.

"No, you aren't, little one. If you do I shall give Axel a circumstantial account of how you and I had our little romance."

"But we haven't had any little romance!"

"Come, come, have you forgotten our intimate luncheons at
my flat at Brook Street and the long afternoon you took off from
the museum?"

"He wouldn't believe you. Anyway, everything's so terrible
now—"

"Do not imagine that it could not be worse. That would be a
great mistake. Axel is deeply attached to you. Your little tiff will
probably pass. Nothing irrevocable has happened—yet. If you
are good I may even help you to regain Axel's confidence. If you
are not good—"

Simon made a dart for the other side and had one leg stretched sideways on the pavement before Julius's foot hooked him gently in the stomach. He rolled back into the pool with a loud splash and the foaming water closed over his head. He rose gasping.

"You'll drown me. Let me out."

"Don't be silly. I just want your assurance that you will be discreet."

"I'm cold and exhausted. Let me get out. I shall get cramp."

"No. I am going to step on your fingers. Look out."

Simon withdrew to the middle of the pool. He was beginning to feel very cold and very tired.

"Please, Julius."

"That's better. I will let you out if you will say after me—"

"Oh, *damn* you!"

"If you will say after me, 'I will not tell Axel.' "

"What's the use of my—"

"Say it. Fingers! Say it."

"I will not tell Axel."

"All right. Now you may get out."

Simon held onto the edge of the pool and struggled to pull himself up. He felt limp with exhaustion and sick from swallowing water. He fell back, hauled himself up again with weak trembling arms, and got one leg out onto the slippery edge. Julius, who was watching and laughing, did not assist him. Simon got onto his knees on the pavement and slowly rose to his feet. He was shivering with cold. Then he turned and with a quick rush, hands outstretched, he pushed Julius into the deep end of the pool.

At that moment Axel and Rupert and Hilda emerged from the drawing-room. Hilda screamed.

The pool surged and boiled, suddenly filled by an immense bulk of struggling blackness. The water tilted and leapt up. Julius's limbs were everywhere. A dark-sleeved arm lifted and clawed the air. Julius's head seemed to have vanished. It emerged for a brief moment, red-faced, gulping, gasping, the mouth round and open. Julius's tongue showed red, his eyes were visible suddenly like wild sea-eyes in a contorted creature, his arms whirled aimlessly, and his head sank like a great stone. The frenzied water rushed back and closed again above the bulky twisting helpless mass.

"Simon, you crazy fool, he can't swim!"

Simon threw himself onto the ground and stretched out his hands. The others were rushing forward. He felt his wrist gripped and jerked. The next moment he had been dragged head first back into the pool and something was clasping him about the neck. His body was liggoted, weighted, sinking. He choked and fought desperately with knees and arms to free himself. Green water was arching over his head, a green glassy dome was above him, an iron bar was pressing on his throat. My next breath, he thought, my next breath, my next breath. There was agony in his mouth and lungs.

Then his head was in light and air and he was gasping and spitting. His breath came in with a moan, with a screech. He saw, very clearly and brightly coloured, the sunny garden above him, the roses, frightened faces, blue sky. Something broad and dark in front of him was Julius's back. Julius had been drawn up against the edge, with Rupert and Axel supporting his arms.

"Hang on, Julius, you're all right, we've got you, just breathe quietly, we'll pull you along to the steps, you'll be able to stand in a minute."

No one paid any attention to Simon. He tried to put his hands onto Julius's waist from behind and help him along, but there was no strength left in him and he found that he was clinging weakly to the soaking velvet of Julius's jacket. He let go. Julius was being towed toward the steps. He was being steadily hauled out. Simon followed.

Julius lay immense and limp upon the stones, water pouring off him. Hilda, her green dress darkened and stained, was kneeling beside him. Axel and Rupert, their sleeves soaking, were jostling each other, both talking at once.

"Turn him over."

"No, not like that."

"Artificial respiration."

"Water in his lungs."

"He's lost consciousness."

"No, he hasn't," said Julius. "I am perfectly all right. I am breathing normally. Just let me be for a minute, *let me be.*" He lay with his eyes closed, breathing deeply. Then he turned slowly on his side and began to sit up. He pulled at the neck of his shirt. Rupert began to unbutton it.

"Have you become dangerously insane or what?" said Axel savagely to Simon in a low voice. Simon was shivering, hopping from one foot to another.

"Bring that towel, would you," said Rupert. Simon's towel was brought. Julius began to mop his face and push back his hair, darkened by the water, which had been plastered to his cheeks and brow.

"I think I'm going to faint," said Hilda. She sat down in one of the chairs and drooped her head between her knees. Rupert ran to her. Julius began to get up.

"I'm terribly sorry," said Julius, "to have occasioned all this fuss."

"You didn't occasion it," said Axel.

"I'm all right, I'm all right, leave me alone!" said Hilda. She began to cry.

"Are you really recovered, Julius?" said Axel.

"Yes, I'm fine. A change of clothes, if Rupert doesn't mind. Hilda, my dear—"

Hilda ran into the house. A low weird wail echoed in the drawing-room.

Rupert hesitated, turned to Julius. "Yes, yes, come inside— I'll give you some clothes—"

"I think we'd better go," said Axel. "It's scarcely the evening for a dinner party."

"If you don't mind—" said Rupert. He half ran toward the drawing-room, then came back again. Julius was standing, rubbing his face and neck with the towel.

"*Get dressed,*" Axel said to Simon.

They began to move toward the house.

"One moment," said Julius. He beckoned to Simon.

Julius's back was toward the others. Simon stepped toward him. Then he thought, He is going to hit me. He began to raise a hand to protect himself. Then he saw Julius's eyes glowing at him. His hand was seized, lifted, and he felt the warmth of Julius's lips upon his cold fingers. Julius murmured something. It sounded like "Well done!"

❧ | FIFTEEN

"Hilda! Hilda! Open the door!"

Julius was changing his clothes. Simon and Axel had gone.

The lock turned in the bedroom door and Rupert went in. Hilda had gone back and was sitting on the bed. She had taken off the green silk dress, which lay damp and twisted across the back of a chair. She was wearing a white lacy petticoat, sitting hunched and shuddering, staring away into the corner of the room.

"Hilda, what is it? What's the matter?"

"You know what's the matter," she said in a dull heavy voice, still staring and frowning a little as if she were trying to discern something in the corner.

Rupert felt terror. He moved closer, made as if to kneel but did not, touched her light green stockinged knees with a finger. She flinched away, not looking at him.

"Hilda—I beg you—whatever—"

"Oh, *don't*," she said. "Don't pretend. It makes it worse. It makes me sick. And don't come too close to me, please."

"Hilda, I don't know what you think, but—"

"Don't lie any more, please. Oh Rupert, if it had been anybody but Morgan. I wouldn't be silly and conventional about a— At least I'd try— But *this*— You don't know what you've done to me between you, you've simply killed me."

"Hilda, there's nothing between me and Morgan, it's just—"

"I know everything. So don't talk. I won't stand in your way."

"Hilda, listen," said Rupert. "There has been a misunderstanding, which I will explain. Meanwhile, just keep sane, will you, and help me to keep sane. We must hold up the world and not let it collapse on top of us. I love you and you are my wife. I will tell you the whole truth, as I ought to have done at the start. I blame myself terribly—"

"Don't you see it's no good? There is nothing you can say. The facts say it all. You can't *explain* something like this. You have this pathetic belief in words. But words can't console me or make whole again what you've irrevocably spoilt and broken."

"But nothing is spoilt, Hilda, nothing is broken! I'm not having a love affair, I swear to you—"

"I am afraid that I know otherwise. And I hate to see you lying so shabbily and so *stupidly*. Can't you see the extent of what you've done?"

"You can't know what isn't the case."

"You shouldn't leave ecstatic letters lying around."

"I haven't left anything lying around, I destroyed—"

"All right, there were ecstatic letters, only you destroyed them. You can't even lie efficiently. Oh Rupert, I loved you so completely, I revered you, I admired you, I trusted you—"

"Hilda, *listen*." He sat down on the bed. "I have deceived you a little and I have acted wrongly, but it's not what you think. You see, Morgan fell very much in love with me—"

"I don't want to hear the details," said Hilda. "These anecdotes about who first caught whose eye are for you and Morgan to entertain yourselves with. I don't want to hear." She got up and went to sit before the dressing table. She began with slow weary movements to smooth some lotion into her face.

"Will you *listen*. She fell in love with me. I couldn't ask her to go away. I was trying to talk her out of it—"

"Of course. Such fascinating talk. And then you talked yourselves into bed. You're not denying that you're in love with her."

"I care for her," said Rupert. "I love her. But—"

"Oh well, what does it matter," said Hilda. "Men of your age often fall in love with younger women and have love affairs with them. I should be thankful it hasn't happened before. Well, perhaps it has happened before, for all I know. On all those evenings when you said you had to stay on at the office and I felt so sorry for you when you came home tired! It's just that here you've chosen the one person whom I can't and won't tolerate in this role. Because I love her as well as I love you. I don't mean that I'm going to insist that you part. It wouldn't make any difference to me anyhow; if you and Morgan never met or communicated from this day forth, it wouldn't be any good. Something like this is eternal, it lives inside one forever, and what you have broken you have broken forever and there is nothing that either of us can do to re-establish our marriage as it once was."

"But, Hilda, *nothing's* happened— I feel I've already exaggerated it— Morgan was emotional and upset— I just talked kindly to her—we were both very worried about you—"

"How extremely kind of you to be worried about me. I'm sure you were both very concerned about poor old Hilda. I find your solicitude *vile*. As vile as your treachery." She turned to him for a moment, her face glowing and shining with the lotion, her mouth and eyes wrinkled up. Then she gave a sob and turned back to the mirror.

Rupert stood in the middle of the room gasping for breath. He could not believe that something so unspeakably dreadful was happening to *him*. There must be some way to halt the destruction, to switch off the machine.

"Hilda, I will not let you destroy our marriage."

"I am not destroying it. Rupert, don't you see that these things are completely automatic? My will can do nothing here. I can't undo this change any more than I can make the sun turn back. You and Morgan have simply altered the world."

"But nothing is altered, Hilda, nothing! There must be a mistake somewhere, you've made a mistake. I am *not* in love with Morgan, I am *not* having a love affair with Morgan—"

"Oh, do stop, Rupert. I don't want to discuss it all. Maybe you shouldn't have ever married me. You and Morgan are obviously ideally suited to each other. In a way I'm sorry for you, having to step over me. I won't roll about and scream, I assure you. In fact I'll do whatever you want, except that I think I must just go away for a little while to rest and be by myself. I suppose I shall have to learn to be in myself alone. Later on if you want me to stay in this house and keep things going I'll do that. Only I don't want to see Morgan any more. You must see her somewhere else and not talk to me about it. I dare say it could all settle down into some sort of— Except that, oh Rupert—how could I bear it—when we've been so happy—" She began to sob, working her hands into her eyes.

"Hilda, Hilda, my darling!" He knelt beside her now and smelt the soft familiar cosmetic smell of her body and saw the white satiny shoulder straps pressing into the plump flesh of the shoulder. The humble friendly familiarity of these things came to him with a sense of terrible doom. "Hilda, we will be happy again, we will— You'll understand how it was— I'll explain—"

"Please go away, Rupert. I'm suffering from shock. I don't see how I'm going to be able to live with myself any more. My whole being is connected with you, we've grown together. But now I see you so differently. I don't know whether I could stay with you in a sort of pretence. And anyway Julius seems to think that everybody knows—"

"*Julius?* Does he know?"

"Yes. He's been wonderfully wise and sympathetic. Oh Rupert, that everyone should see you in that horrible light—you, whom they all admired so and looked up to—and they'll be so pleased to find out—that you're just like they are after all—"

Rupert clutched his head in his hands. "Julius? How on earth could Julius have known?"

"Oh, apparently everyone does."

"But it's *impossible*. Besides—"

"Oh, I'm sure you and Morgan were very careful and discreet," said Hilda, "but people are so curious and it's not easy to conceal these things. I seem to have been the last one to find out." She began to brush her hair.

"But this is just a nightmare," said Rupert. "I don't understand. Morgan and I—it was just beginning—we only met a few times—it's only a short while—no one could have known—"

"A lot can happen in a short while," said Hilda, "and there can be a lot of talk. If it was, as you say, 'just beginning,' you certainly got off to a flying start. Could you leave me now, please, Rupert. I'm weary weary weary of the whole thing. I think I'll probably go away somewhere tomorrow."

"But you must *believe* me!" cried Rupert. "It's all become exaggerated and twisted somehow. Morgan will tell you how it was. Morgan will be horrified when she hears—"

"She's already heard," said Hilda. "I wrote her a long letter this afternoon and delivered it by hand. I've asked her not to communicate with me any more. Now go away, will you, please, Rupert, *go away*, and don't come in here tonight. You can spend the night wherever you like. And don't worry about me. I'm not going to commit suicide or anything. I just want to be by myself. You'd better go and look after Julius. I suppose he's still in the house."

A door banged loudly downstairs.

"Nothing's—hurt really—" said Rupert. He could hardly speak now for the utter heaviness of his whole being. "Nothing's hurt, Hilda—you'll understand—and we'll be together always—"

"Go away, please."

Rupert went out of the door. He heard it being locked behind him. He went down the stairs and into the drawing-room.

Julius rose politely. He was wearing Rupert's dark blue silk dressing gown and holding a glass of whisky.

"I hope you will forgive me for having helped myself to a drink, Rupert."

"Why are you—still here—" said Rupert. The sun had stopped shining and the garden was darkening, full of dark brown sombre light. A small wind touched the roses. Julius had turned on a lamp but the room was dim.

Julius was standing, leaning forward a little, his face blurred, large and pale, smiling, his hair dry and fluffy after its immersion. "I quite appreciate, it's not a very good evening. But I could hardly go away in your dressing gown, and I hesitated to choose one of your suits without consulting you. I'm afraid my own clothes are still rather damp."

"Did you tell Hilda I was having a love affair with Morgan?" said Rupert.

"No," said Julius. "I know there's a rumour to this effect. I told Hilda not to pay too much attention to it."

Rupert stared at Julius's blurred face and at his big shadow on the wall. He said, "Something insane has happened."

"I know how you feel," said Julius. "Here, let me give you some whisky. Did you meet Peter, by the way?"

"No. Was he here?" Rupert automatically accepted the glass of whisky.

"Yes, he was here. He left a few minutes ago. That was him banging the door."

"What do you mean, you know how I feel?" said Rupert. "The rumour is entirely false."

"Yes, of course," said Julius.

"Then what on earth are you talking about, and why have you been discussing the whole thing with Hilda?"

"My dear Rupert, Hilda was anxious to discuss it with me. I did my best to reassure her. I told her that these things soon blow over and it's better to pretend not to notice—"

"You've been encouraging her to think things about me—"

"Now don't be ridiculous, Rupert. And please don't get so hot under the collar. Your wife needed comfort, even perhaps advice.

I told her, and I do in fact believe, that very little has happened and there is no grave cause for alarm."

"But *nothing* has happened."

"Of course, Rupert, if you say so."

"Don't you believe me?"

"Of course."

"It's just a muddle, a nightmarish muddle, and I simply can't think how this rumour—"

"Well, you know how malicious and sharp-eyed people are. And how they love to discover faults in those they envy and admire."

"But I am to blame," said Rupert. "Something has happened. Of course the rumour isn't based on nothing. I am terribly to blame." He sat down.

"It's probably wiser to admit that to yourself," said Julius. "Why should you not be a little to blame, after all? You are upset because your image of yourself is shaken and because Hilda's image of you is shaken. A trifle chipped or cracked perhaps. You have expected too much of yourself, Rupert. No marriage is as perfect as you have imagined yours to be and no man as upright as you have posed to yourself as being. It was perhaps a pity that you chose your sister-in-law to go to bed with—"

"But I *didn't*—"

"Well, never mind the details, Rupert. You have just admitted that something happened. From Hilda's point of view the details don't even matter all that much. She sees you utterly involved with Morgan and an idol falls to the ground. So much perhaps the better. Doubtless things can never be quite as before, but your marriage can continue and be no worse than the next man's. A little realism, a touch of shall we call it ironical pessimism, will oil the wheels. Human life is a jumbled ramshackle business at best and you really must stop aspiring to be perfect, Rupert, especially after this latest piece of evidence! As for Morgan, the poor girl is a natural man-chaser and a hopeless muddler and self-deceiver. She sees herself as a sort of intellectual eagle, whereas she is blind with sentiment and feeble with self-indulgence. But she's a very sweet person all the same and of course you were right to be kind to her. She's very attractive and she needs you. In the circumstances a love affair was practically inevitable and you mustn't blame yourself too much—"

"But there wasn't a— You're deliberately confusing things— I couldn't live like that. I couldn't *live* like that."

"Like what? Without a false picture of yourself?"

"No. In cynicism."

"Why use that nasty word? Let us say a sensible acceptance of the second-rate."

"I won't accept the second-rate."

"If you stay in the same house as yourself you may have to. Come, there will be a few smiles at your expense, but why worry? The smilers merely demonstrate their own tawdriness. But human life *is* tawdry, my dear Rupert. There are no perfect marriages. There is no glittering summit. All right, Hilda will stop admiring you. But when have you really merited her admiration? Haven't you deceived yourself, just as Morgan has deceived herself? All right, Hilda won't love you quite as she did before. She may feel sorry for you, she may even despise you a little. And you won't forget what you've learnt either, how to pretend, how to lead a double life. It's natural to you, Rupert, you all do it. There will be those late nights at the office, and Hilda will sort of know and sort of not know, and it won't matter anything like as much as it seems to do at the moment."

"Stop," said Rupert. "There's something I can't live without—"

"A mirage, my dear fellow. Better the real world, however shabby, than that condition of high-minded illusion. By the way, have you been into your study in the last half-hour?"

"No."

"Well, I think you had better come up and see."

"See what?"

"I will come with you. Come."

Julius left the drawing-room and led the way up the twilit

stairs. At the door of Rupert's study he said, "Prepare yourself for a shock." He opened the door and switched the light on.

Rupert followed him in, blinking. The room seemed to be paler, different. He stared about.

It seemed to have been snowing in the room. The floor, the chairs, the desk were covered in drifts of white. Rupert looked more closely. It was torn paper. Paper torn up into very small pieces. He picked up one of the pieces. He saw his own writing upon it.

"Yes," said Julius, "I'm afraid it's your book."

Rupert picked up a few more pieces. He let them fall. He looked at the table where the stack of yellow notebooks had been.

"I'm afraid it's all gone," said Julius. "It was Peter. I came upstairs wondering if you'd stopped talking to Hilda and I heard this curious tearing noise in your study. He'd done about half of it when I came in."

"You didn't—stop him—"

"How could I? I could hardly use force. I reasoned with him a little. Then in the end I helped him."

"*Helped* him—to destroy my book?"

"Yes. Perhaps it was silly of me. But I could see that he was determined to finish the job, so I thought I might as well tear up one or two notebooks too. Besides, to be perfectly frank, Rupert, I don't think it was a very good book. I don't just mean it wasn't true, it wasn't even particularly clever, at least not anything like clever enough for its pretentions. You haven't got that kind of mind. It wouldn't have done your reputation any good."

Rupert turned back toward the door, leaned against the doorway, switched the light out. "Could you go now."

"Not in your dressing gown, please, my dear Rupert."

"Take any suit—there in my dressing-room—and then go. I don't want to talk to you again tonight."

Rupert went down the stairs. A few minutes later he heard the front door shut quietly. He turned the lamp off and stood in the dark drawing-room. His body ached with misery and with tormented love for his wife. Tomorrow he would talk to Hilda. He would persuade her not to go away. But of something, he knew that he would never persuade her and never persuade himself ever again. There was something which had vanished away out of the world forever.

✿ | SIXTEEN

Morgan laid down Hilda's long letter. She had read it through carefully once. Then she tore it into small pieces.

What a long distance lies between an act and its consequences. How *could* her dreamy converse with Rupert have occasioned, have *caused*, this terrible violence? It was like the humming of a song causing an aeroplane crash. Had she deserved this awful rejoinder from Hilda and the horror of seeing Hilda's pain? It's all a mistake, she thought, I'll have to explain. But now that this had happened *could* it be explained? Rupert's love was a fact and her acceptance of it a fact. She had even started to imagine that she was in love with Rupert. And now it had all been made to look so dreadful.

How did it happen? she wondered. Hilda did not say how she knew. Axel must have told her. Morgan imagined it all. Axel's hints, Hilda's quick suspicion, her certainty, her taxing of Rupert, Rupert's breakdown. That was pitiful to imagine. Rupert was, after all, so weak. How had she ever imagined him as a hero? Rupert would break down, would confess everything, would tell Hilda all the details of his love for Morgan, swear to get over it, weep probably, promise never to see Morgan again. No wonder Hilda thought it had all been so terribly serious. And this has happened because I was kind to him, she thought. It was his idea that we should meet and talk, his confidence that made it all seem permissible. And now Hilda writes to me as if I were trying to steal her husband from her.

Morgan sat down. She was dry-eyed. Anger, contempt, remorse kept her rigid. They shall not overcome me, she thought. I will not be an object of disapproval and ultimately of pity to the married pair. How idiotic of her to have encouraged Rupert so. Of course she was fond of Rupert and of course it had been *interesting* and she had spent enough years admiring the huge seamless edifice of her sister's marriage. But she should have seen from the start that Rupert was a muddler. He must have left letters lying about in the office. How else could Axel have known? Rupert's soft, she thought. Someone tougher and braver would not have let me be hurt like this. Rupert will be on his knees to Hilda at the first word of reproach. He will scarcely have confessed his love before he will start denying it. He will drop me. He will abandon me absolutely in his heart.

How was I so taken in? she wondered. What was it in Rupert that seemed so remarkable? Was it just his horribly perfect marriage? Some moral glory had seemed to shine round about him. I believe I was simply impressed by his own self-satisfaction, she thought. Some people are like that. They are so profoundly pleased with themselves that they mesmerize others into admiring them. Perhaps in Rupert's case it had something to do with his particular sort of theories. Of course she hadn't read any of Rupert's stuff, but it did somehow come out in his conversation, even in his manner. Rupert imagined that he knew all about goodness. He imagined that it was permitted to him to love and do as he liked. But what was he in reality? A hedonistic civil servant, an easygoing member of the establishment, with a marvellous wife and a lucky disposition. Well, his luck had abandoned him this time.

How little he deserves Hilda, she thought. How often he had seemed to be, about his wife, the least little bit patronizing: Hilda was not an intellectual but of course she was a wonderful woman. Couldn't he see that Hilda was a much cleverer and better person than he was? Hilda was no muddler. Being the sweetest person in the world did not prevent *her* from being steely truthful and clear in the head. *She* needed no steamy visions of moral altitude to make her and keep her a decent human being. Who was always talking about helping people? Rupert. Who was always really helping people? Hilda. Only one failed to notice Hilda's virtue because she was unaware of it herself. And she treated her good works as jokes.

Morgan sat there stiff, with her eyes half closed, leaning forward, and her face became hard and strange to her like a mask and she felt the deep obscure bases of her life shuddering and stirring. I have not known who I am, she thought. But I will know. I will. She sat thus quietly for a long time. She wished that she had not torn up Hilda's letter for she was collected enough now to meditate upon it. It had caused such shock and such pain that her instinct had been to destroy what had hurt her so. She could not conceive of reading it a second time. Yet already that was possible. She reached for the wastepaper basket and began to pick out the pieces of the letter.

She found she had something in her hand in Tallis's writing and she dropped it quickly. It was part of the letter which she had torn up unread. Tallis's letter and Hilda's letter now seemed inextricably jumbled up together in the basket. She began to pick up pieces and look at them and let them flutter down again: *really remember our life together?* was Tallis, *even our innocent childhood* was Hilda, *and by a family bond I mean* was Tallis, *warned by your casual treatment of* was Hilda, *to buy you an engagement ring* was Tallis, *Rupert misled you? Our happiness* was Hilda, *lot of tommyrot, my darling* was Tallis, *only this particular treachery* was Hilda, *position to command not beg* was Tallis, *vulgar deceptions and lies* was Hilda, *unharmed and bright* was Tallis, *blackened and destroyed* was Hilda, *always always* was Tallis, *never never* was Hilda.

Men, thought Morgan, all the trouble in my life has come from men. The only time I was ever really happy was when Hilda and I were together, long ago when we were young. And not just long ago, but ever since in a way Hilda has been the guardian of my happiness. I never came to claim it, but I knew it was there, and that was my only deep and enduring comfort. All through that awful time in America I rested upon the thought of Hilda, and when I came back it was to Hilda that I came home. How childish of me to have tried to deceive her. As if it could even have been *possible*. The flirtation with Rupert was a piece of idle folly. But the deception of her sister was a crime for which she deserved to suffer, to suffer with meaningful and purging pain, with Hilda as judge and executioner and healer.

As Morgan surveyed her life and the deep interlocking of her past and her present she felt in all her being which still ached from the shock of Hilda's letter a kind of bitter confidence and a sense of being at last in the truth. Compared with her bond with Hilda, these matters of men, of lovers and husbands, seemed utterly flimsy. And, it came to her, compared with Hilda's bond with her, even Hilda's marriage could be seen as an interlude. Something might be blackened and destroyed, but it was not the tie that united Hilda and Morgan. That tie could not ever be broken. Of course she had acted wrongly. But it was to Hilda that she would come for judgement.

Morgan lifted her head and a ray from the far past, from the dark forgotten beginnings of her existence, shone through her eyes and made them glow like amber. Hilda must know of this, Hilda must know that there was no horror, no shock, and no crime which could in any way undo that ultimate belongingness.

The sun had ceased to shine and the room had become dusky and brown. Morgan rose and turned on a lamp. She went to her writing table.

To Rupert she wrote at considerable length. Her letter began thus.

My dear Rupert,

I have received an emotional letter from Hilda which leads me to assume that you have by now told her everything about your initiative with me. As I can scarcely believe that your feelings can sustain the shock of Hilda's discovery of them, I am also assuming that our curious interlude is now over. I cannot help feeling slightly resentful that you should have so signally mismanaged the drama which you yourself occasioned and that you should have exposed me to Hilda's anger. You were, I am afraid, over-confident. Your choice of method might have suited the saint which I fear you are not. For ordinary mortals, more conventional reactions are doubtless safer. I am of course to blame for having followed your "high style" rather than my own more mundane instincts. These things, your tactics and my ill-considered response, are regrettable but possibly not very important. Remorse and hurt pride are stings which are cured by time. And it seems to me now that your emotions were stormy but not profound. What is important to *me*, and for this I find it harder to forgive either you or myself, is the damage done to my relationship to Hilda: a relationship older and, I venture to say deeper, than the relation of either of us to you. What you may decide now to think or do about your marriage is of course your affair. But I would like to say this. I will not be a sacrifice to the restoration and celebration of your married bliss. In brief, you shall not separate me from Hilda. I do not propose to save you from embarrassment by shunning the house, though I may henceforth shun you. And the explanation of our little drama which really matters is the explanation which Hilda will receive from *me* . . .

To Hilda, Morgan wrote only:

Darling, hang on. *We will not be divided.* M.

✥ | SEVENTEEN

"Axel, stop the car will you, anywhere."

Axel did not reply, but he turned the car down a side street and stopped it and switched off the engine. Then he took out a cigarette, lit it, and sat looking straight ahead of him. They had just left Priory Grove after the immersion of Julius in the swimming pool.

"There's something I want to tell you," said Simon.

Axel said nothing.

"A lot of things have happened which you don't know of—" Simon found it hard to talk. His throat was still hurting. He was blushing with emotion and something like a sob impeded his tongue.

Axel still said nothing, looking away down the road and smoking his cigarette.

"Listen," said Simon. "I must tell you everything. I should have from the start. But I was afraid to, afraid of you, afraid you'd be angry or not understand or something or that you wouldn't believe me or that you'd suddenly see me in some ghastly new way. But now it's getting so awful and Julius—I feel he's taking me over—I mean just sort of controlling me—and what you said on the way to Rupert's was so terrible. I almost feel I've nothing to lose any more. I mean, you couldn't think worse of me. And I'm sure you suspect all sorts of things which aren't true. And if I tell you the whole truth perhaps you'll see that it's the whole truth and believe me."

He paused. Axel still sat motionless, one hand on the steering wheel, the other holding his cigarette, staring ahead.

"It all started," said Simon, "on the day when Julius first came to dinner. Just as he was going he whispered to me that I should come round to see him on the following Friday evening. That was the evening when you were going to *Fidelio*. He said, come round, but don't tell Axel. I thought this was pretty odd but I imagined Julius wanted me to help him about giving you a present or something on your birthday, so I went round—I'm sorry, all this is going to sound pretty mad but every word of it's true— I went round and Julius wasn't there but Morgan was there with no clothes on."

"With no clothes on?" said Axel. He threw the cigarette away. He was still expressionless.

"Yes. Something had happened between her and Julius, I don't know what, and he had destroyed all her clothes—all right I know it sounds mad—and then locked her out of the bedroom and gone off, and there she was by herself with no clothes on when I arrived. Then Morgan persuaded me to give her my clothes so that she could go and fetch some of her own from Priory Grove, so I gave her my clothes and I was there with no clothes on when Julius came back."

Simon paused. Axel said nothing.

"Julius just laughed at me. He said he'd forgotten he asked me to come and he'd just asked me for the hell of it to see if I would come. Then Morgan came back and gave me my clothes again and they persuaded me not to tell you anything about it. They both thought it rather funny. Then about—"

"Wait a minute," said Axel. "One or two questions. Why did they want you not to tell me and why did you agree?"

"Morgan didn't want it known that she'd been with Julius and that this peculiar thing had happened. And they said that you would find it all very absurd and think that I'd been ridiculous and undignified and that you'd hate me being involved with them in something like that. And I thought they were right. Well, then—"

"Wait. Is that the whole of the story so far?"

"Yes."

"You didn't have any sort of love passage with either Morgan or Julius?"

Axel had turned now in the seat to face Simon. Simon looked back at him. "No."

"Go on."

"Do you believe me, Axel?"

"Go on."

"Then the next thing was that Julius appeared one morning at the museum. He said he wanted me to come and watch something, he called it a puppet show. You remember, well perhaps you don't, there's a false façade in Room 14 with an Adam doorway and a piece of wall and there's a space behind it where some-one could hide. I'm sorry this all sounds crazy, but this was exactly what happened. Julius made me go in behind the façade with him and we sat there and he seemed to know exactly what was going to happen and a few minutes later Rupert and Morgan arrived in the room at some sort of love rendezvous."

"Rupert and Morgan?"

"Yes. I was stunned. I've no idea how Julius knew they'd be there, but they had a few minutes' rather intense conversation and then they went away and Julius and I went back to the office and—"

"You say a love rendezvous. What was going on exactly?"

"I don't know. I was pretty upset and confused. It sounded as if they'd been making declarations of love to each other. They were both rather agitated too."

"So it wasn't something which had been going on for a long time?"

"No. In fact Julius then explained, only I couldn't really quite believe him, he went off into some rigmarole about how he'd fixed up the whole thing himself and somehow made Morgan think that Rupert was in love with her and made Rupert think that Morgan was in love with him. And he seemed to imagine that this would make them really fall in love with each other."

"Did he say why he was playing this trick on them?"

"Something about punishing them for their vanity."

"I see. Go on."

"He said it was a sort of midsummer enchantment and that he would unravel it all later on quite painlessly and no one would be really hurt."

"What were your reactions to all this?"

"I was horrified," said Simon. "I said I'd tell you, I'd tell everyone."

"And why didn't you?"

"Because Julius said that if I did he'd make you believe that I'd been making advances to him."

"And had you been making advances to him?"

"No!"

Axel was silent for a moment. Then he started the car. He said, "I think I'll drive us home. Just go on talking."

"I now think I was mad," said Simon, "but at the time I didn't feel I had any alternative. I was so damn frightened of Julius. He threatened to break up things between you and me. And I somehow felt that he could. Not that he could do anything to my faith in you. But he could do things to your faith in me, he could make you see me as—something worthless—a sort of slut—or so I felt."

Axel said nothing.

"Well, that's the main part of the story, the rest is just consequences. On your birthday—I had nothing to do with that ghastly bear, by the way, that was entirely Julius's idea—on your birthday he would stare and whisper and he touched me when you were out of the room and then he dropped that hint at the end about my having been to see him. I think he did it on purpose to make you imagine there was something going on."

"And was there something going on?"

"No, no, no! I'm telling you the whole story, the *whole* story! Then I didn't see him again after that until this evening when he talked to me in the swimming pool after you'd all gone in. He kept pushing me back into the water when I tried to get out. He asked me if I'd said anything to you and I said I hadn't and he said that's just as well and if I did he would give you a circumstantial account of how he and I had had what he called a romance!"

"And after that you pushed him into the pool?"

"Yes."

"One thing. What was the date when Julius came to the museum, when he made you spy on Rupert and Morgan?"

Simon reflected. "I think it was a Tuesday. Yes, three weeks ago next Tuesday."

The car stopped outside the door of their house and Axel got out. Simon followed him as he fumbled with the front door key, went in, and went on upstairs to the drawing-room. Simon came on into the drawing-room and shut the door. Then suddenly he felt weak at the knees. In the car, the narrative itself had carried him, the deep surrendering sense of telling the truth at last. Now standing in the enclosed darkening room he felt very much afraid.

"And what about Rupert and Morgan?"

"What about—oh, I don't know," said Simon. "I've no idea what's happened to them."

"You mean you didn't bother to think or to try to find out from Julius?"

"No. Maybe I should have done. I was worried about them. But I was in no position to find out things from Julius. I wanted to avoid Julius. And just lately I've been very much more worried about you."

"Haven't you been seeing Morgan?"

"No. I haven't seen Morgan since that day when she was here and you came home and—found us—that day."

There was silence. Axel was looking out of the window. Simon could not see his face. After a little while Axel moved to switch on a lamp. He began to draw the curtains.

"Axel, you do believe me, don't you? You do believe all this? I know I've been very stupid. But there isn't anything else, there isn't anything else at all."

Silence.

"Axel—"

"Come over here a moment."

Simon came and faced him.

"Yes, I believe you."

"Oh God—" said Simon.

"No demonstrations please, dear boy. Sit down. Let's have some gin, we need it. Here."

"Do you blame me terribly?" said Simon. He was feeling limp with joy. He tried to control his face and his voice. He would be quiet, dignified, sober, all that Axel would wish him to be. But whatever came next, he was home and safe.

"Of course I blame you. That you might be thoroughly confused by Julius or even frightened of him I can understand. But I can't see how you could have gone on lying and mystifying me when you saw how bloody miserable it was making me."

"Miserable—" said Simon. They were sitting close to each other now drinking gin. He had been miserable. Axel had been fierce, dangerous, terrible.

"I think I got into such a state of guilty terror worrying about myself, I just didn't see what was happening to you. I thought how angry you would be with me. I thought how Julius might make you see me differently. I didn't think you were miserable."

"Then you were damn stupid."

"Yes. I was. I see it now."

"As for seeing you differently, it isn't as if you had a halo to lose. I've known the worst for years, you little fool. And can you really have imagined that Julius could make me believe something entirely untrue about you? Think, Simon! I believe you now because you're telling the truth and this is completely and absolutely evident—just as it was evident before that you were lying. Julius couldn't have duped me and I doubt if he ever even intended to try."

"No, I suppose not. The trouble was that as soon as I started lying I felt so guilty that I imagined Julius could hang anything round my neck."

"Precisely. Julius is very clever. You did all the work of deception! I thought I'd lost you."

"Axel, you can't have done—"

"I was stupid too. And I blame myself. You oughtn't to have been so afraid of me."

"I always have been and I thought it didn't matter, it was just a sort of thrill. But when it got mixed up with deceiving you it was nightmarish. Then everything mounted up and mounted up and it got harder and harder to tell the truth. It was only—what you said in the car really, when we were going to Rupert's— and then somehow Julius not letting me get out of the pool— it suddenly made me feel that anything was better than going on in that sort of hell."

"A pity you didn't come to that conclusion a bit earlier!"

"Axel, you weren't really going to leave me!"

After a moment Axel said, "I don't know. I did absolutely believe that you were having some sort of love affair with Julius. I'd imagined it all into existence with all the details and everything seemed to fit. Have you ever noticed that Julius wears a particular sort of rather expensive American after-shave lotion?"

"No, not specially."

"Well, once you came home absolutely reeking of it, and then when I asked about your day at the museum you were rather evasive. I didn't draw any conclusions at the time, but later it seemed pretty damning evidence."

"Good God, that must have been—"

"Yes, that was the day when you and Julius were sitting together behind the arras!"

"He sat very close to me. He even took my hand. Oh Axel—"

"It's all right, I don't mind Julius having taken your hand. Now. Actually it's all rather in character. I knew Julius do something like this once before, mystify people and make them act parts. Never mind."

"I knew you suspected something. But if you really thought I was carrying on with Julius I'm surprised you didn't—"

"And you didn't think I was suffering! I was nerving myself to throw you out! It just turned out to be very very very difficult."

Simon took this in. He looked up at the ceiling. "More gin, Axel?"

"Thanks. I wonder about Rupert and Morgan and whether there's anything we ought to do."

Simon considered this for the first time. "It's a bit difficult without knowing whether anything's happened. Honestly, I don't even know whether Julius was speaking the truth. I heard them talking to each other of course— Do you think we ought to see Julius and make him explain it all?"

Axel was thoughtful. "I can't help wondering how he did it. If he did it. But I don't think I very much want to see Julius just at the moment."

"Me neither!"

"You haven't any further evidence at all?"

"No, none. Had you noticed anything unusual?"

"No, nothing. Well, Rupert was a bit nervy. I had my own troubles."

"Hilda was rather on edge tonight."

"I think we'd better let that one drift," said Axel. "If there's any obvious drama we might consider dropping a word to somebody, but even then it's rather tricky. One doesn't want to be indiscreet and raise a false alarm. If there's no muddle then all's well. It there is a muddle we aren't likely to be able to understand it anyway and our helpful revelations might just make things worse. It's probably better to let them sort it out for themselves."

"I entirely agree!" cried Simon. "Let it drift. It isn't any thing to do with us really, is it? Oh Axel, my darling! Axel, Axel, Axel—"

"All right, dear boy. All right, all right, all right!"

🔅 | EIGHTEEN

"Oh, hello."

"Am I disturbing you?" said Julius.

"No," said Tallis. "Come in."

Julius walked after him into the kitchen, stepping cautiously. The newspaper which Tallis had laid down on the floor was still there, now entirely black and slightly rubbery in texture. Tallis took some dirty plates off the chairs and put them under the sink.

"What are you doing?" said Julius, looking at the table.

"Addressing envelopes."

"Isn't that a waste of your intellectual powers?"

"Someone's got to do it. Anyway, I haven't got any intellectual powers. Sit down."

"Thank you."

One end of the table was covered with a disorderly heap of brown envelopes, some of them plain, some of them addressed in Tallis's large hand. The other end of the table was piled with books and notebooks, on top of which lay a screwed-up copy of the *Statesman* in which some bony remnants of kippers had been rather unsuccessfully wrapped. Tallis removed the kippers and put them on the floor.

"Have some tea?"

"No, thank you."

"Beer?"

"No, thank you. How is your hand, by the way?"

"Hand?"

"You remember you cut your hand last time I was here."

"Oh, yes. I put some sticking plaster on it. I'd forgotten all about it. It's still on. Must be O.K."

"Hadn't you better take the sticking plaster off," said Julius, "and see what's going on underneath it? Come here. Let me look. I'm going to pull it off. May hurt."

Julius ripped off the plaster.

"Ouch!"

Tallis stood patiently and looked vaguely out of the window while Julius examined his hand. The cut had almost healed. The skin about it was pocked and puckered and slightly paler than its surroundings.

"Better leave it uncovered now," said Julius. "Let the air get at it. You might try washing your hands occasionally. An old-fashioned device, but quite effective."

"Sorry."

"Not a criticism. I am thinking of your welfare."

Tallis went and sat at the other end of the table among the envelopes. He put his head down on the table and then raised it again. He saw Julius through a haze of tiredness and gloom. Julius was wearing a navy blue polo-necked sweater and a jacket of soft grey tweed. He looked relaxed and youthful. The kitchen was rather cold, lit by weak reflected late evening sunlight. A watery ray had even managed to find its way between two walls to cast a triangle of clarity upon the wooden draining board, showing the ragged rotting wood at the end and the green filaments of the mould which had covered the contents of a white porcelain bowl. Things which had been jerking about on the dresser became still. Tallis began to rub his eyes and then to poke his fingers into his ears. His eyes itched. His ears itched deep into their cavities and on down into the throat. The roof of his mouth itched and there was a small inflammation on his tongue.

"What?"

"I said you ought to clean this place up. It can't be good for your health."

"Haven't time," said Tallis.

"Then you must make time. All this ridiculous activity isn't necessary. You just do all these things to stop yourself from thinking."

"Maybe."

"You ought to get some sensible person to help you clear up all this mess. Why don't you get in touch with the local Samaritans?"

"I am the local Samaritans."

"Oh. How's your father?"

"All right. I mean much the same."

"Have you told him?"

"No," said Tallis. He stopped poking into his ears. He gave a long sigh. "I think you were quite right to say I ought to. The truth belongs to him. He is a person who could even *do* something with it. But it's so damned hard. There doesn't seem to be any moment which is better than any other moment to tell him. It seems so arbitrary, at any particular instant of time, to change the world to that degree. And he's a bit better just now. The pain's less and he's quite optimistic. He's got out of bed. In fact he's out at this moment feeding the pigeons."

"Has he had any deep ray treatment yet?"

"No. I was afraid he'd guess when that started. But they're going to tell him it's heat treatment for the arthritis. He's always reviling the doctors, but he believes everything they say all the same."

"I sympathize with you," said Julius, "about there never being the right moment to tell him. I'm sorry."

They were silent for a while. Tallis found half a packet of peppermints underneath the letters.

"Have a peppermint?"

"No, thank you."

Tallis started to eat one.

"Have you seen Morgan lately?" said Julius.

Tallis swallowed the peppermint. "No. I've written to her. Had no answer."

"What's the good of writing, you fool?" said Julius. "You must go round and see her."

"I know," said Tallis. "I will. I just feel so bloody tired and discouraged at the moment. I know I'll bungle everything if I go and see her. There's a sort of pattern to it. She's got a picture of what she wants me to be and I'm just not it and it simply exasperates her. I can't bear that exasperation. I'm bloody miserable enough at the moment without a ghastly interview with Morgan to look back on. I suppose it's cowardly to write letters. But if one writes letters one can go on hoping."

"Your particular kind of tenacity amazes me," said Julius. "I could understand your going round and making a scene and I could understand your switching off altogether and looking for someone else. This dull holding on and hoping I find incomprehensible."

"It's a form of cowardice."

"I don't know. Perhaps it's a virtue. I suppose there are such things. You know the latest round at Priory Grove?"

"No."

"Simon pushed me into the swimming pool."

"Did he?" said Tallis. "Why?"

"Well, it's a long story. Have you got a bit of time? Perhaps I can help you with the envelopes?"

"No, I can manage."

"I was in evening dress. Everything was ruined, of course."

"I haven't seen Simon for ages. Is he all right?"

"He's fine. Others not so fine, I'm afraid."

"Why did he push you in?"

"Oh, I was tormenting him. I was very impressed by his spirit, I must say. I didn't expect it. However, he isn't important really. Shall I tell you all about it?"

"Yes, if you want to."

"You know that Hilda's left Rupert?"

"No!" said Tallis. He jerked up, scattering envelopes. "Why ever—?"

"Well, that's the story. It's not without interest. Hilda has fled from Priory Grove and gone to the cottage in Pembrokeshire. Only she hasn't told Rupert that. She's told him that she's gone to Paris. She doesn't want him to follow her, you see."

"Surely she hasn't really left him, she can't have—"

"Time will show. Meanwhile—"

"But *why?*"

"Because Hilda thinks that Rupert is having a love affair with Morgan."

Tallis stared at Julius's bland judicious face. Julius had the air of one explaining something to a pupil. "You said something about Morgan and Rupert when you were here last—only I didn't believe you. I thought—naturally Rupert would want to help Morgan—it could be nothing important— I thought—"

"And in a way you thought right," said Julius.

"It's impossible that they should be having a love affair."

"Here you are doubtless quite right. They are not having a love affair, I imagine."

"Then why—"

"However, they are certainly rather involved with each other, and from Hilda's point of view—"

"But what has happened? And why should Hilda—"

"Wait, wait, one thing at a time. I must admit it is rather complicated. Your picture of Rupert and Morgan is entirely just. And if they had been left to themselves there would have been no involvement, beyond the little bit of sentimentality which you so properly conjectured. Only they were not left to themselves. Someone intervened."

"Who?"

"Me."

"Why?" said Tallis.

"You are jumping ahead. Don't you want to know exactly what happened? Anyway, you know why. As I say, it is rather complicated and it's not easy to know exactly where to start."

"Go on, go on."

"You see, it all hinges upon letters."

"Letters?"

"Yes. Human beings should be awfully careful about letters. They are such powerful tools. Yet people will write them, in moments of emotion too, and other people will fail to destroy them."

"What letters? Whose letters?"

"Don't hurry me. It all started—well, I don't know when it *started*—in a sense I suppose in South Carolina—but then where does anything start? It started in a more immediate sense when I was prowling round one evening by myself at Priory Grove. You know how they always leave the door open. Well, no one seemed to be in so I started exploring. I'm afraid I rather enjoy poking round people's houses. You'd be surprised what one can find. Considering how nasty the human race is, it's amazing how carelessly trusting it can be too. Anyway, I went into Hilda's study, what she calls her boudoir. There were a few letters lying about and I read them. I always read any letters I find. Nothing of interest, all about her various charities and so on. I was rather idly wondering whether Hilda had any secret life. Most people have, after all. And I began to search the desk. That sort of eighteenth-century desk has always got a secret drawer, only it isn't secret because they all have them and it's usually not too difficult to find. I fiddled round and found the secret drawer in Hilda's desk and sure enough it was full of love letters. Only they were from Rupert. Hilda's secret life was her husband. Do you mind if I drink some water? No, don't get up, I'll just wash this cup under the tap."

Julius resumed. "I put the letters back and smiled over Hilda's virtue and then I strolled downstairs and there was Rupert, who had in fact been out in the garden, and we had a drink and started to talk about his book. And that I must confess rather annoyed me. I don't suppose Rupert's ever bored you with his ideas; I think he would probably feel that theorizing was quite out of place with you. But he always makes a dead set at me. Anyway, the book was mentioned and then Rupert started to hold forth about goodness, and this sort of talk sickens me, as I expect it does you. And I couldn't help wondering how old Rupert would stand up to a real test and what all this high-minded muck could really amount to in practice. You see what I mean?"

"Yes," said Tallis. He was leaning tensely forward, the table pressing into his chest. The room was getting darker.

"About the same time, or a little later, I began to get really bored with Morgan. Well, bored is the wrong word perhaps. I began to feel a sort of disgust. I imagined she'd have the sense to leave me alone, but of course she hadn't. I kept stepping on her everywhere I went. Morgan has a remarkable capacity for making false images of people and then persecuting the people with the images. Well, you know that. Anyway, she'd cast me in some sort of role as a liberating force and then she started talking some nauseating drivel about freedom. I expect she talked it to you too."

"Yes," said Tallis.

"About freedom and love and about loving without bonds or conventions like a noble savage; I forget how it ran. In a way it was a broken-down version of Rupert's stuff. And she seemed to want my imprimatur on this tosh, or rather she seemed to assume that she'd got it. Then I'm afraid I did rather lead her on."

"How, lead her on?"

"I just wanted to make her make nonsense of her ideas, at least that was all I wanted at first. I wanted to see how far she'd go, without even noticing it, into frivolity and cynicism. I was amazed to see how readily she responded. I was talking about the frailty of human attachments and she was pretending to disagree and egging me on at the same time and I said that anyone's faith in anyone could be broken in no time by the simplest of devices. She said No! all big eyes and lip-licking sophisticated superiority, and bet me it couldn't be done. So then we selected a victim."

"A victim? Who?"

"Simon."

"Simon?"

"Axel and Simon, that is. Morgan bet me ten guineas that I couldn't detach Simon from Axel in three weeks."

"My God," said Tallis.

"Yes. I was pretty disgusted. On reflection, very disgusted. And then one day when I was thinking about Morgan, and then thinking about Rupert, and how in a way they were quite a pair, I suddenly decided that I might as well set them at each other."

"I see," said Tallis. "Go on."

"Morgan wanted a demonstration of the frailty of human attachments. I decided that she should provide the demonstration. I also wanted to get her off my back and it was a way of doing it. You understand?"

"Yes."

"As for the method, as I said, it all depended on letters, and when it came to it it was surprisingly easy, as almost all attempts to beguile human beings turn out to be easy. There's hardly any deception, if you choose it carefully enough, with which people will not co-operate. Egoism moves them, fear moves them, and off they go. Now, I had kept all the love letters which Morgan wrote to me in South Carolina, when our thing was just getting going—"

"You'd kept them?"

"Yes. You mightn't expect it, but I am rather sentimental. Anyway, I had those letters with me. And there in Hilda's desk was an excellent set of Rupert's love letters to her. I went in quietly one afternoon and purloined them. I now had a splendid pack of cards and had only to play them with care. I went through the letters and crossed out any local references. Almost all the letters began "Darling" or "Angel" or something equally ambiguous. In fact the style of love letters in a certain class of society is remarkably similar. This is particularly true of women's letters, even of intellectual women's letters. I've had hundreds of them. That sort of ecstatic self-indulgent running on has an almost impersonal quality. And of course vanity blinds the reader. So it was not likely that the recipients would realize that the letters were not really intended for them at all. I set the whole machine going by sending off simultaneously a carefully selected love letter of Rupert's to Morgan and a love letter of Morgan's to Rupert. In each letter I appointed a meeting place. It was quite easy to produce a scrawl, like a hastily written postscript, which looked sufficiently like the writing up above it. People don't examine writing carefully, especially if they know the writer and are reading something which titillates their vanity and their curiosity. They both came, of course, to the rendezvous. I had arranged to be a witness of this, and I took little Simon Foster with me. I won't bother you with the details of my eavesdropping, which were ingenious. As for Simon, as I said, he's not important. I did torment him a little, I confess, but he was a side-dish. I didn't ever really intend to take him away from Axel. Well, Rupert and Morgan arrived, both bursting with curiosity and interest and excitment at having so unexpectedly inspired passionate love in the other one, and both resolved to carry the whole thing through with discretion, compassion, wisdom, the lot, this to be compatible of course with extracting the utmost fun from a fascinating situation. You follow me?"

"Yes," said Tallis.

"Of course," said Julius, "the plan might have fallen to bits at the start if those two had been a little more down to earth, but it was of the essence of the business that they were away up in the air. No one said anything as crude as 'Look here, I didn't quite understand this letter of yours,' or 'I am very dismayed to learn that you are in love with me.' They set off straightaway with delicate references to the situation and considering each other's feelings and how each should be most chivalrous to the other and so forth and so on. I was sorry that I couldn't overhear more than the beginning of the conversation, but it was obvious that they were well away. And one could be quite sure that a few days of this sentimental pussyfooting around would produce such a web of emotional confusion that they would soon no longer be in a position to verify anything. In the days that followed I sent off some more of the letters, choosing ones that looked as if they'd be suitable. It was really rather fun choosing the letters. Then after a while I stopped because I judged that by now they would both be quite capable of writing their own love letters. You see, since each thought that the other was bound, while they themselves were free, they could become thoroughly absorbed in the drama while feeling superior and even innocent. Mix up pity and vanity and novelty in an emotional person and you at once produce something very much like being in love."

"What about Hilda?" said Tallis.

"I'm coming to Hilda. I did not neglect Hilda. I know it sounds heartless, but my curiosity was aroused and I wanted to see how far everyone would go. You know, any woman can be flattered into doing anything. You just can't lay it on too thick. Just flatter them outrageously, it simply doesn't matter how outrageously, and they will lose their minds, like some birds and animals when they're tickled in a certain kind of way. However, I was, I confess, a trifle disappointed in Hilda. I don't always care for easy successes and I expected Hilda's case to present interesting difficulties. But a few hints soon made her suspicious. And by this time there really was something to be suspicious about. I brought the thing to a climax by a real master stroke. I had already discovered earlier on, during one of my little prowls, that Rupert's desk contained a secret drawer, rather like Hilda's. Rupert's secret drawer was empty, rather dusty, and obviously not in use. Hiding things in secret drawers is a female occupation. I took one of Morgan's ecstatic missives, one written soon after she and I had first been to bed and full of more than suggestive references, and tucked it into the secret drawer in Rupert's desk. Then I half suggested to Hilda that she might relieve her mind by searching her husband's desk. Of course she indignantly denied that she would do any such thing, and of course she went straightaway and did it. And found Morgan's letter."

"How do you know?" said Tallis.

"Hilda told me. She has been a very willing informant throughout. I must say, I do respect Hilda and I don't blame her too much for getting lost. She is a very good-natured and kindly person who doesn't think too much about herself. She's not *interested* in herself, the way the others are. This is what makes her so restful to be with. She used to be a bit hostile to me, you know, but I'm glad to say she's entirely got over it. I so much enjoyed talking to her and being with her. She's entirely truthful and genuine, unlike her sister. In fact in other circumstances Hilda— There is something so relaxing— Well, I suppose I always did rather want a mother figure— However, I didn't come here to talk about myself."

"What's happened now to Rupert and Morgan?"

"I don't know the *very* latest, but Hilda told me all she knew before she took off for Wales. Rupert is so tied up with guilt and damaged vanity and loss of face he can't say or do anything straight. Morgan, with her eternal determination to have everything all ways and eat all cakes and have them too, has been appealing to her sister to go on loving her in the sacred name of childhood days. I must say, they have behaved predictably to an extent which is quite staggering. Indeed, if any of them had been less than predictable the whole enterprise would have collapsed at an early stage. They really are puppets, *puppets*."

"You haven't talked to Rupert or Morgan about it?"

"I've kept clear of Morgan. I find her company very lowering; even the pleasures of curiosity have palled. I had a few words with Rupert. He was mainly concerned with the destruction of the big spotless Rupert-image which he's been living by, and which he mistakes for some sort of vision of goodness. He was also rather down in the mouth because Peter had destroyed his book."

"Peter destroyed Rupert's book?"

"Yes. Tore it up into small pieces. And unfortunately it's the only copy. Still, I don't think the world has lost a masterpiece."

"But why did Peter—"

"Well, poor Peter's always been in love with Mama and lately he's been in love with Aunty too, and when he found out that Papa was betraying Mama with Aunty it was a bit too much for the poor lad."

"How did he find out?"

"I told him. He came round once when I was with Hilda and Hilda was in tears. I told her I'd see him off the premises and tell him some reassuring story. I told him in fact, in a curtailed version, the truth, and his imagination did the rest. He then set off to make a scene and doubtless caused much dismay. Maybe I shouldn't have told Peter, it was just my instinct as an artist, it was entirely impromptu. And I suppose he would have found out anyway."

"When did Hilda go to Wales?" said Tallis.

"The day before yesterday. I would have come to see you yesterday, only I had the most terrible migraine. Indeed, I might have told you all about it last time I came, I half intended to, only you started telling me about your father and then it seemed out of place to start on this rather peculiar story."

"Why are you telling me now?"

"Oh, you know why. And I didn't really intend things to proceed quite so far. It all got rather out of hand. I expect you have this sort of experience too. And honestly, I'm getting a bit tired of it and I don't know what to do next."

Tallis sat for a moment reflecting. Then he jumped up. "We must telephone to Hilda."

"You mean tell her all this?"

"Yes. They must all be told. At once. Not the house phone, everyone hears every word. There's a phone box down the street. Come on."

"Are you going to talk to Hilda?"

"No. You're going to talk to Hilda."

✿ | NINETEEN

It was raining. The wind rattled the windows and bore down over the wet grass, flattening it, shaking it. Twilight was coming over the treeless land with a chilly brownish greenish autumnal glow, bright in the light rain.

Hilda had imagined that the solitude of the cottage would be a refuge, that it would provide a kind of freedom. She had imagined herself sitting there and steadily thinking things out. She had been careful to deceive Rupert into believing that she was going abroad. After two days, however, the loneliness and all sorts of physical fears which invaded her weakened organism had reduced her to such a state of panicky misery that she was quite incapable of thinking at all. She had never been alone at the cottage before. There had always been Rupert's strong, full, reassuring presence, a completely effective bulwark against anxiety of any kind. The cottage made her miss him dreadfully in an instinctive way, and she wept. Day-time and night-time became equally terrible. Strange distant figures appeared on the horizon during the day, seeming to watch. Things disappeared from the outhouses. Windows opened and banged horribly. At night there were noises to which Hilda sat breathlessly listening. Bodies seemed to brush against the walls of the house. Latches were quietly lifted and bolted doors quietly pressed upon. There were sudden near sounds, rustlings and little murmurs, and mysterious distant incomprehensible booms. Hilda imagined ferocious animals, gipsies, murderers, and beings from beyond the bounds of the human world whose presence she even more indubitably felt as they detached themselves quietly from the heather and crept slowly toward the cottage. At night she sat by candlelight and the light of the fire. There were oil lamps but she did not know how to light them. Rupert had always lit the lamps.

After the first night Hilda told herself that she must get out or lose her reason. But the weakness which attracted the terrors made her also unable to decide or move. This had seemed to be a safe place, at least it was familiar, it made some kind of sense to be here. Where else could she go, to whom could she go? Could she live in a hotel, sit in a bleak bedroom, take her meals alone in the dining-room? If she went to stay with somebody she would be incapable of pretending, and there was no friend to whom she wanted to talk about the carnage which had taken place in her life. The only person she felt in any way inclined to see was Julius; him she even at moments craved to see, but it was an odd craving, as if for something unreal. A very few days of not seeing Julius had made him seem once more unapproachable and remote, and she had not had the spirit to telephone him, though she had written him a long letter just before she left London.

There had been no grand explanation with Rupert. In fact Hilda had avoided one. On the first evening Rupert had seemed quite dazed. Hilda had locked the bedroom door. Rupert had tapped on it late at night. From his voice it had sounded as if he were rather drunk. Next morning it appeared that he had drunk almost a whole bottle of whisky and had gone to sleep fully clothed in his dressing room. Hilda had left the house before he woke up and installed herself in a near-by hotel. For the moment she could not bear the sight of Rupert. Once the first shock was over jealousy inhabited her like a fever, making her shake and sweat. She had to get away from the house, where all the ordinary things did not yet know of Rupert's faithlessness and where sweeping brushes and tea cups and cigarette boxes and little innocent unconscious knick-knacks told her at every moment the extent of her loss. Something very like embarrassment, only embarrassment potentiated into agony, made her anxious to shun her husband. She did not want to look into his guilty eyes and to see the man whom she had worshipped shorn, defeated, utterly at a loss.

It was also very necessary to avoid Morgan. About Morgan, Hilda felt a sickness too deep to be identified as misery or anger. That particular betrayal had injected its venomous power into the whole of her past, changing all that was good into rotten specious appearance. Everything was different now right back to the start. To cherish her sister had been the chief business of her life, a constant unfailing source of warmth and sense. She had received a note from Morgan saying *we will not be divided* and she had thought how ridiculously characteristic it was before she had realized with a jerk that such a thought could now no longer be a vehicle of affection.

Hilda came back and fetched her clothes. She saw neither Rupert nor Morgan. Letters from both of them were lying on the hall table at Priory Grove and she read them later in her room at the hotel. Rupert's letter was hopelessly confused, full of self-accusation and pleading, and at the same time denials that anything worth mentioning had really happened at all. She tore it to pieces with misery and disgust. Morgan's letter made a good deal more sense. Morgan explained how Rupert had suddenly fallen desperately in love with her, how they had decided not to tell Hilda, how they had hoped that the situation could be contained. Hilda set this letter aside more thoughtfully. On the spur of the moment she wrote a very bitter letter to Rupert. She ended by telling him that she was going to Paris to stay with her old friend Antoinette Ruabon. She conveyed the same information more curtly to Morgan on a postcard. Then she hired a car and drove to Wales.

The cottage, which was six miles from the main road and farther than that from the nearest village, was approached by a rough track which ran between mossy brambly mounds which had once been stone walls. The only habitation near it was a farm-house now empty and for sale. The sea was two miles away. Hilda had imagined herself staring at the sea and receiving from its indifferent immensity some old grey weary sort of wisdom. In fact she had not been to the sea. She set out toward it on the first morning, tore her leg on some barbed wire, and returned to the cottage in tears.

She decided, I must go back to London tomorrow. Oh God, I wish I hadn't written that awful letter to Rupert. There'll have to be *talk* and it's unkind as well as cowardly to run away like this. They must both be in torment. I see now that I ran away in order to punish them. Then she began to wonder: What are they doing at this moment? Then she thought, Holding each other's hands and taking counsel about what to do. Comforting each other. Discussing me. And she cried out with pain, alone there in the dusky comfortless room. She thought, I am the one that is destroyed, by that particular alliance, by that special and absolute cruelty. They have futures, I have none. Can Rupert and I, in the end, attempt to go on as before? Things can never be as before, and whatever they do, what has happened has happened forever. She remembered Morgan's letter, and thought, I cannot exist without Morgan and yet now it is utterly impossible to exist with her. I cannot accept her back into my life. Oh, what will become of me now?

Hilda rose and bolted the doors. It was dark outside, windy rainy rumorous darkness coming from far away across the empty coast and the sea. She lit three candles and put dry wood onto the fire and carefully pulled the curtains, thinking how solitary and strange that square of lighted window must look, glowing and flickering in the middle of nowhere. She hoped that no being was watching it now. She sat by the fire and began to cry quietly. She had been happy and protected for so long. She was too old to find her way in this wilderness of unpredictable violence and naked personal will.

A sudden loud shrill noise filled the room. Hilda sprang up with a little shriek of fear before she realized that it was the telephone. Her instant thought was: Rupert. She ran to the instrument and lifted it with clumsy frightened fingers.

The remote unmoved voice of an operator said, "Professor

King is calling you from a London call box. Will you pay for the call?"

"Professor—? Oh, yes, yes, please, yes—"

"Hello, Hilda," said Julius's voice.

"Oh *Julius*, thank God, I've been just going mad down here, I shouldn't have come, I can't think and it's all turning into nightmare; how I wish I'd seen you before I left London, but I wanted to rush away and I see now it was crazy, I'm simply going to pieces here, oh Julius, I'm so grateful to you for ringing, it's such a blessed relief to hear your voice, can we talk for a bit—"

"Hilda, *listen* please—"

"Have you seen Rupert or Morgan?" How terribly real and present Julius's voice made London seem.

"No, I haven't. Hilda, I want to tell you something important and I want you to listen carefully."

"Something about—them?"

"Yes. You have—"

"Julius, I've been so wretched, I know I shouldn't have left London—"

"Hilda, please just *listen*. Can you hear me all right? You have been the victim of a trick."

"A trick—"

"Yes. Rupert and Morgan did not fall in love with each other and they have not been having a love affair. What you have seen is simply a façade of falsehoods. You have all three of you simply been duped."

"I don't understand," said Hilda. "What on earth are you talking about?"

"A trick has been played upon them and by extension upon you. Each of them was falsely convinced that the other was in love. Their kind scrupulous natures produced the rest of the confusion. There has been nothing else, no love affair and indeed no love."

"But—a trick—who could have—"

"I was the magician, Hilda. It started as a sort of practical joke but it got rather out of hand, I fear. But never mind about me.

You must attend carefully while I tell you exactly what happened so that you can understand that they are entirely blameless."

"*You*, Julius—but—"

"I stole your letters, the ones that Rupert wrote you, from the secret drawer in your desk, and I sent them to Morgan as if they came directly from Rupert. And I sent Rupert letters which Morgan once wrote to me. Never mind the details. They were each persuaded of the other's love. They met a few times to discuss the situation. Nothing else has happened at all, there is nothing else to it, and when they find out, apart from being naturally a trifle annoyed with me—"

"I can't believe you, Julius," said Hilda. "Please don't jest with me, this is making the nightmare worse, you are just trying to help us by inventing this, I *know* about this thing, I've got proof, I've seen—"

"What have you seen, my dear Hilda? You found a letter from Morgan in Rupert's desk. That letter was written to me, and I planted it there for you to find. They've both behaved like people with a guilty secret, but their secret was simply the mutual delusion of each other's love. There is *nothing there*—it is all a magical emanation which the utterance of the truth will blow quite away. You have all three been deceived by mere appearances and apparitions."

"Julius—this can't be— Rupert behaved so strangely and—"

"Rupert is always irrationally anxious to blame himself, and he thought that he was protecting Morgan."

"But how could they both be *mistaken*—"

"Quite easily. People are never too unwilling to believe themselves valued. Ordinary natural vanity led them into this maze. I will tell you the details later. The important thing now is that you should *believe me*. I invented it all, Hilda, I invented it and made it happen."

"Julius, I can't accept this, it's too fantastic, why should you do something so extraordinary, and anyway, it's utterly impossible that—"

"She won't believe me. Would you like to have a word with Tallis? He's here beside me. Wait a moment."

Hilda heard Tallis's voice saying, "It's true, Hilda. Julius has deceived all three of you, and Rupert and Morgan are quite innocent, they're simply victims like you. Julius really did send the letters as he said and made both Rupert and Morgan imagine that the other had fallen in love. There is honestly nothing more to it than that. It was a sort of joke, that's all. And no one else knows anything about it, there haven't been any rumours or any talk. So you see, nothing's changed really—"

"But I— Have you told them, Rupert and Morgan?"

"Not yet. What do you want us to do? You do believe this, don't you?"

"Yes—if you say it—but it's so weird—"

"Yes, it is. But Julius will explain later. Listen, Hilda, shall I telephone Rupert?"

"Yes. No, I'll telephone him. I'll tell them both. Don't you do anything more. Please leave it to me now. Thank you for— Tallis, did Julius *really* do that?"

"Yes, he did. You will ring Rupert at once, won't you?"

"Yes, at once, at once. Thank you, Tallis. Good-bye."

Hilda began to put the telephone back onto its rest. Her hand was shaking and she pushed the instrument a little toward the edge of the table. The next moment it had tilted and crashed to the floor. The receiver clattered away under the table. Hilda knelt awkwardly in the obscurity, pulling at the tangled wire. She lifted the telephone up, replaced the receiver, and began to dial for the exchange.

But something seemed to have gone wrong. The telephone was an old-fashioned one with a projecting dial. As Hilda put her finger into the hole to spin the dial she realized that something or other must be broken. The outer part of the dial moved easily, too easily and unresistingly, while the inner part with the circle of numbers appeared to be shifting too. In the receiver the dialling tone continued unchecked. The dial was no longer properly attached to the interior of the instrument. Hilda stared at it. It was projecting too much and tilting slightly sideways. She tried to push it back into place, to screw it in, but could get no purchase, and there seemed to be some sort of resistance behind it. She tried again to turn the dial and again it spun idly and the numbered circle lurched round together with the outer casing. She looked at the machine and tried to think. In a second the telephone had been transformed from a natural means of communication, an extension of herself, into a grotesque senseless object, useless and even sinister. Hilda shook it desperately and put it down.

She lit two more candles and ran to the kitchen and found a screwdriver. She turned the instrument over and began to unscrew the bottom of it. A mass of little worm-like wires of different colours were swarming about inside the dark box. What *happened* inside a telephone when one dialled? It wasn't magic. There must be some way of doing what the dial did. Something had broken. Could she not see what it was and mend it? If only she could get through to the exchange. She put the telephone down on the table and it fell apart, disgorging entrails of pink wire.

This is no good, thought Hilda, I must put it together again. But now there was too much wire, fat coils and bundles of it, hanging down and refusing to go back inside. The dial was hanging off the instrument like a dislodged eye. She began to pull on the wires from within, hoping to pull the dial back into place. It seemed to be coming back into position. Only now the moving section of the dial had shifted round so that only half the holes were opposite the numbers and the other holes were blank. Moaning with exasperation Hilda seized the outer casing and tried to twist it back. Something cracked and the metal disk came away loosely in her hand. She threw it on the floor and tears streamed down her face. She must talk to Rupert, she must talk to him *at once*, she must tell him that all was well, that all was unchanged, she must ask him to forgive her. Why had she in an instant judged Rupert? Why had she had so little faith in her husband and her sister? All those years of love and trust should have made her at least wait, at least keep quiet. Hilda pulled on her macintosh. She would have to drive to the village, to the telephone box there.

The rain was sizzling down, thickening the air, as Hilda splashed her way toward the car. She tumbled into the driver's seat and switched on the headlights, which revealed lines of rain, tumbled yellow stones, nettles. The ignition key was still in the dashboard. She turned it. There was a brief fruitless mutter from the starter motor. She turned off the headlights and pulled out the choke and tried again. The same dry empty whirring sound. Again. Again. Again. Oh, *no*, thought Hilda, and the tears were leaping out of her eyes. She sat still for a minute, then tried once more to start the car. The starter motor whirred idly. The engine would not turn over. "Rupert!" cried Hilda aloud, "*Rupert!*" She jumped out of the car and found a torch and opened the bonnet with the intention of drying the distributor head. Perhaps rain had got in. But so much more rain immediately rushed past her in the light of the torch, blown by the wind in great watery gusts, that she began hastily to close it up again. In any case the engine looked incomprehensible and lumpish and she could not remember what it was that she was supposed to do.

Hilda turned and began to run, stumbling along the muddy stony track, lamenting as she went. Her torch jerked and flickered over glittering boulders and black pools and brambles and heather and watercress and swathes of old wire. Calling out to Rupert she plunged ahead into darkness and the square dim-lit window of the cottage grew smaller and smaller behind her.

✿ | TWENTY

Morgan rang the bell at Priory Grove. It was ten-thirty in the morning. Rupert would be at the office. There was no reply. She tried the door. Locked.

When Morgan had written her *we shall not be divided* to Hilda she felt cold and hard. Her love had been resolute and purposive. She would not be destroyed, she would survive this mess, she would regain her sister. It could all be explained, after all, and Hilda would see that it was certainly not Morgan's fault. As she wrote her second explanatory letter she felt, as she covered the pages, that the nightmare thing was really being unravelled. Telling Hilda the truth calmed her heart and made her feel confident that all would be well. She delivered the letter by hand late at night.

The next day she felt a little less certain. She telephoned Priory Grove several times but got no answer. She went round, risking Rupert, and knocked on the door. No one there. Then came Hilda's curt card to say that she was going to Paris. This frightened Morgan. She ran to the public library and asked for the Paris telephone directory. There were several Ruabons. She telephoned them all but none of them was Hilda's friend. Hilda had said Paris, but of course she might have meant somewhere, anywhere near Paris. Morgan then cautiously telephoned one or two of Hilda's charitable acquaintances, but none of them could help her. Morgan's need to see her sister was by now becoming extreme. It seemed idiotic to cross to France and search, but she felt almost ready to do so out of the sheer need to do something. She told herself that of course Hilda would very soon come back. It was not in Hilda's nature to leave everything in confusion and run away. She might return at any moment. Indecision and the sheer multiplication of possibilities racked Morgan. She lay aching and sleepless till the early hours of the morning and then dozed wretchedly to see in dreams Hilda's dear face, that orb of kindliness which had always shone forth in her life with more than a mother's love. She awoke again to tormented puzzlement. If only she could see Hilda, hold her quietly by the hand and *explain*.

Morgan could not bring herself to ask Rupert for Hilda's address. Rupert might not know. In any case communication with Rupert had now become unimaginable. Morgan now saw Rupert as a blind instrument of destruction. In tampering with his marriage he had damaged more than he knew. Rupert's grand passion had been essentially something frivolous, or so it now seemed in the outcome. And Morgan blamed herself for not having rejected this dangerous frivolity at the very beginning. She ought to have *laughed* at Rupert's love. She could not even quite remember what she had felt about Rupert at the start. She had been touched, tender, sentimental, and she supposed somehow rather thrilled. She groaned with remorse. The sight of Rupert now would make her sick with shame and about the future of her relations with him she forbore to think. She reproached herself constantly with Hilda's voice, falling down in abject and passionate supplication before that accusing shade.

Everything that I have done lately has been a disaster, thought Morgan, and yet each thing when it came along seemed absolutely *natural*. It was natural to fall in love with Julius, it was natural to feel sentimental pity for Rupert. How can one live properly when the beginnings of one's actions seem so inevitable and justified, while the ends are so completely unpredictable and unexpected? The only thing I ever did in my life, she reflected, which was unnatural was to marry Tallis. And that turned out to be a disaster too. That had seemed inevitable and unnatural. Whatever had she hoped for? She had certainly hoped for something. Had she simply *forgotten* that hope? The idea came to her sometimes that she should go to Tallis and tell him all about Rupert and Hilda, tell him everything, everything, everything. If only Tallis had that much more authority, that much more dignity and stature, she could have put her head on his knees. As it was he could not compel her at a distance. And it seemed to her that to confide in Tallis would be disloyal to Hilda.

Morgan began to walk down the side of the house, through the wooden gate into the garden. She had decided that she must get into the house somehow and find out from Hilda's address book the whereabouts and telephone number of this Ruabon.

A little rain was falling and the wind was beating the roses against the trellis. Wet rose petals adhered to the pavement in a design of heart-shaped pink and white blobs. The rain pitted the surface of the swimming pool, making it look like a grey metal grill. Morgan tried the kitchen door, but it was locked. With less hope she tried the french windows and found that they were open. She stepped in on tiptoe, closed the doors carefully behind her, and stood quiet and suddenly breathless in the drawing-room. A clock was ticking. The house felt inward, mysterious, full of thoughts. It brought to Morgan quite automatically a breath of peace, though she told herself at the next moment: All is changed. Only the house does not know it yet. The house still keeps for me a smiling Hilda. Then she told herself, Perhaps the change is not too terrible after all. Hilda will forgive Rupert. But she will ever after be closer to me.

Morgan opened the cupboard where the drink was kept. There was no whisky, but she found the remains of a bottle of gin and poured some into a glass. She had drunk a good deal in the last two days. Then holding her glass and instinctively treading quietly she went on up the stairs. She went into Hilda's boudoir. The room was tidy, full of stretched velvets and fragrant chintzes. There were some dead roses in a silver cup. Morgan dropped them into the wastepaper basket. Then she began to search Hilda's desk. Piles of impersonal letters, bills, pamphlets, circulars. She soon had her hand on the address book and with triumphant anticipation turned to the letter R. No Ruabon was listed. Morgan put the book down in puzzlement. Hilda was usually so methodical about these things. Then it occurred to her that of course if this Ruabon was married and was an old friend Hilda might have listed her under her maiden name. Morgan sat down and began to go through the whole book. There were no Antoinettes and no addresses in France. Hilda's note had just said "old friend." Had they been at school together? Would it be any use asking the school? Owing to the difference in their ages Morgan had not known many of Hilda's school friends. She could not recall Hilda mentioning this Antoinette. Or had there been some talk about a French girl, a long time ago? She dimly remembered something of the sort. It came to Morgan that of course the reason for the absence of the address was that Hilda knew it so well that it was unnecessary to record it. Morgan began to think seriously about this Antoinette Ruabon.

After all, she really knew very little about Hilda's personal life. She had, she now realized, rather taken it for granted that Hilda *had* no personal life. Happily married people don't. Hilda was Rupert's wife and Morgan's sister and Peter's mother, and, so Morgan had assumed, into these eminently satisfying relationships the whole of that generous being was without residue absorbed. Of course Hilda had lots of friends of a luncheon-party, bridge-playing, sherry-morning-for-the-local-charity kind. But no close friends. Could it be that this picture was all wrong? Why after all had Rupert so suddenly fallen in love with Morgan? Was it conceivable that he was being neglected? Could this flight to Paris be something really significant? Morgan thought, I talked so much about myself when I came back. I did not ask Hilda one single searching question. Oh God. Morgan suddenly began to feel jealous and frightened in an entirely new way.

She decided, just to occupy herself, to search the rest of the house, just in case papers of Hilda's elsewhere might reveal the coveted address. She looked into the bedroom. The bed was unmade, the drawers open, underclothes of Hilda's strewn here and there, a bottle of brown cosmetic lotion broken upon the carpet. Morgan examined the dressing table and the cupboard. There were no papers. She looked into Rupert's dressing room, where the divan bed was also unmade, and into Rupert's study. Rupert's study was full of little piles of torn paper, like autumn leaves, and something about it made Morgan shudder. On the table by the wall some of the scraps of paper had been laid out, as if in an attempt to reconstitute the torn pages. Morgan closed the door quickly. There would be nothing of Hilda's there. She went downstairs and began to search the drawing-room and the kitchen. There was nothing to be found. She poured the rest of the bottle of gin into her glass and wondered what to do next. She was curiously reluctant to leave the house. Getting into it had seemed to be an important action. Then she thought, Letters. Might there not be letters from this Antoinette? When she had been looking for the address book she had only glanced cursorily at Hilda's letters. She ran upstairs again and started once more to forage in Hilda's desk. The letters there yielded nothing. Morgan drank the rest of the gin and went over gloomily to the window. It had stopped raining.

Morgan looked down on the familiar garden. The sun was just beginning to come out and a faint steam was rising from the wet pavement. The swimming pool looked somehow odd. Morgan gripped the window ledge. Something weird and awful was in the pool, seeming to occupy nearly all of it. Something dark, like a huge dangling spider. A great bundle, some immense animal or— Morgan's glass fell to the ground. She ran to the door and fled moaning down the stairs. The french windows of the drawing-room had swung open. Morgan reached the edge of the pool. Her legs gave way and she sat down with a whimper. A fully clothed human body was floating in the pool below the surface, arms and legs outspread and dangling. It was a man. It was Rupert.

Morgan could not see the face, but she knew the clothes, she knew the form. She tried to scream but her throat was so constricted that she could scarcely breathe. She sat there gasping, raucously drawing her breath. Then she reached out and tried to catch hold of some part of the terrible dangling object. Her hand brushed a sleeve but she could not get a grip on it. She got to her knees and staggered up. She began to climb down the steps into the pool but the water was so intensely cold that she instinctively drew back and climbed up again, her soaking skirt clinging to her knees. One shoe came off and the rungs of the aluminum ladder cut into her foot. She lost her balance and plumped back into the shallow water with a splash. Water filled her eyes and her mouth, and her feet slithered on the slippery sloping floor of the pool. Then she was able to cry out. She gave a choking sobbing wail and stretched her hands out blindly. She touched something, gripped it, pulled, and felt another human hand in hers. She let go, tried to scream. Then she was holding onto material, clothing, pulling again. Something huge and dark moved slowly up against her in the water.

Rupert was floating face downward, his head drooping down toward the bottom of the pool, his arms and legs spread out and more buoyant. Morgan, her mouth wide open and frothing with terror, tried to pull his shoulders upward. She found herself gripping his hair. The sodden waterlogged thing was heavy, heavy. The back of the head slowly broke the surface and Morgan had a terrible glimpse of a darkened swollen nearly unrecognizable face. Then the weight of the body broke from her again and the head sagged.

Morgan began to climb out of the pool. She felt that in another moment she would faint. She could hardly pull herself out. She crawled onto the pavement and began to struggle to her feet. Get help, she thought, get help. She was not able to utter a sound. Her soaking wet clothes constrained her, she shuddered with cold, she could hardly walk. She got into the drawing-room. The telephone rang.

The familiar sound of the telephone bell sounded like a signal from another universe. But Morgan automatically picked up the receiver.

Hilda's voice said, "Rupert."

Morgan sat down in an arm-chair holding the receiver against her breast. Then she lifted it again.

"Rupert, darling. It's Hilda."

Morgan swallowed something in her throat. She said in something like her own voice, "Hilda, it's Morgan."

There was a moment's silence. Then Hilda said, "Is Rupert there?"

"No, he isn't."

"Well, look, never mind. Give him a message, will you? I'm at Newport changing trains, I can't talk more than a second. I'm on my way home. Please tell Rupert that everything is absolutely all right. And you too, darling—it's all right. There's been an extraordinary mistake. No one's to blame. I shouldn't have gone away. I'll tell you both when I see you. Just give Rupert my love, my very special love, and tell him not to worry. And don't you worry either. Nothing terrible has happened after all."

Morgan put the telephone down. The clock ticked. Then she lifted the receiver again and dialled for the police. In a sense there was no hurry now. Rupert was indeed not there.

⚕ | TWENTY-ONE

"It does me no credit," said Julius. "I just have a passion for cleanliness and order."

With neatly rolled sleeves he was washing the dishes, while Tallis sat at the kitchen table and watched him. The table had been scrubbed and Tallis's books and notebooks put into orderly piles. The newspaper and other debris had been removed from the floor and the floor had been swept and the bins emptied. Julius lowered another collection of plates into the steaming water.

"What did you do with all those milk bottles?" said Tallis.

"I washed a few and put them outside and I put the rest in the rubbish tip across the road. It's just as well I thought to bring you some new drying-up cloths. I've soaked several already."

"There were one or two somewhere here—"

"I've thrown them out. They would not have made self-respecting dusters. I also brought you this thing for cleaning the pots and this thing for mopping the sink. I hope you didn't mind my starting before you arrived?"

"No, not at all. It's very kind of you."

"You were expecting me?"

"Some time."

"I cannot make any great claims for the floor," said Julius. "A rather superficial job, I'm afraid. It needs to be scraped all over with a knife and then thoroughly washed."

"It looks fine to me," said Tallis.

"And I hesitated to deal with the stuff on the dresser. I suspect a good deal of it ought to be thrown away. But you'd have to sort it out yourself."

"Yes, yes, I will."

"How's your father?"

"In bed."

"Have you told him?"

"No."

"Has he had any treatment?"

"Yes. But I'm pretty sure he thinks it's for arthritis."

"Are you going to tell him?"

"Yes." Tallis began automatically to spread out his books and notebooks in front of him.

"You ought to stop this lecturing nonsense, it wears you out and it's completely unconstructive. Can't you find some easier way of earning money? You should be doing proper research in a university. Surely you know somebody who knows somebody?"

"No."

"Don't be so down in the mouth. It wasn't your fault about Rupert."

"Possibly."

"How were you to know that Hilda would break her telephone?"

"True."

"Or that she would get lost on the moors and wander around all night?"

"Yes."

"In any case, it seems that Rupert may have been already in the water when we telephoned Hilda."

"Maybe."

"And of course you don't imagine it was suicide?"

"No."

Rupert had died of drowning, but with a large dose of sleeping pills and alcohol in his body. It was presumed that he had fallen into the pool accidentally. The verdict at the inquest was death by misadventure.

"But really, how terribly stupidly they all behaved. Don't you agree?"

"Mmm."

"Human beings set each other off so. Put three emotional fairly clever people in a fix and instead of trying quietly to communicate with each other they'll dream up some piece of communal violence."

"Yes."

"It's all egoism of course. They will do the most dreadful things to each other rather than seem to be made a fool of or seem not to be in control of the situation."

"Indeed."

"And sex— They get so agitated, they crave and muddle so. I must say, it's always seemed to me a very overrated phenomenon. Where do these plates go?"

"In there."

"God, what a mess. I think this stuff, whatever it is, can be thrown away, can't it?"

"Yes."

"Hilda, for instance, of whom one might have hoped better

things. Why did she have to run off like that? They all do of course. She should have stayed and talked and listened. But the hurt pride of the outraged wife had to be satisfied by some sort of violent gesture. She wanted to make the other two feel wretched and then, if they consoled each other, even more guilty. And why when we telephoned was she so keen to tell the other two herself? *She* had to be the good fairy, the one with the knowledge and the power."

"Maybe."

"And Rupert and Morgan. Of course they were flattered into a state of stupefaction at the start by finding themselves adored. Then they each thought they were so wise and good they could manage the whole situation and change passion into spotless love without in any way endangering their loyalty to Hilda. Then suddenly being found out is ugly, nothing lofty and dignified there. Morgan turns nasty and blames Rupert. Rupert just folds up. He cannot endure the destruction of his self-respect. Rupert didn't really love goodness. He loved a big imposing good-Rupert image. Rupert didn't die of drowning. He died of vanity."

Tallis was silent.

"You're looking very tired. Are you all right?"

"Didn't sleep much last night," said Tallis.

"Why not? Do you suffer from insomnia?"

"No. The police were here."

"What for?"

"They were arresting somebody upstairs."

"What had he done?"

"Something to do with motor-cars."

"How's Peter, by the way?"

"I don't know. He's disappeared. Hilda doesn't know where he is either."

"Where is Hilda?"

"At Lyme Regis."

"Lyme Regis. How splendid. Alone?"

"No, with Morgan."

"I believe the house at Priory Grove is for sale?"

"Yes."

"You don't happen to know what she's asking for it? I'm looking for a house in that area."

"I don't know."

"I'd prefer the Boltons, but there's nothing available there at the moment. Where did you get these rather pretty cups and saucers? I believe they're real Worcester."

"They're old family things," said Tallis. "We've always had them. I think they belonged to my mother's family."

"I'll stick them up on this shelf on the dresser. The cups can hang and the saucers can sit upright. Better clean it first though. There, they look charming. I've got an awful lot of nice stuff in store in New York which I haven't seen for years. I really must get a house to deploy it in. My parents had excellent taste as well as a very good eye for an investment."

"Are they still alive?" said Tallis.

"No. I lost touch with them ages ago in fact. We were scarcely on speaking terms."

"Why was that?"

"Because they changed our name to King. And because they were converted to Christianity."

"What was your name before?"

"Kahn."

"Why didn't you change yours back?"

"I don't know. A sense of history perhaps. I have a strong sense of history. What has happened is justified somehow. At least it's one up on what hasn't happened."

"You are an only child?"

"Yes. And you had a sister. Only she died of polio."

"She didn't actually," said Tallis. "She was murdered. She was raped and killed by a sex maniac. She was fourteen."

"Ah— I'm sorry—"

"I don't tell people," said Tallis. "Because it remains—too dreadful."

"I understand. Where do the knives go?"

"In the drawer of the table. Here." Tallis shifted his chair back a little and opened the drawer.

"Any special order?"

"Any old how."

Julius leaned forward and began to stow the knives into the drawer. He closed the drawer.

"Wait a moment," said Tallis.

Julius shirt sleeves were rolled up to the elbow. Just above the elbow something was visible upon his arm. Tallis took hold of Julius's wrist with one hand and with the other rolled the sleeve back a little further. There was a blue tattoo mark, a number inscribed in a circle. Tallis released him.

"So you were in a concentration camp?"

"Yes," said Julius. He added apologetically, "I spent the war in Belsen."

"Morgan must have noticed that mark," said Tallis.

"Oddly enough she didn't. Perhaps it is only visible in certain lights. You need a little line here to hang your drying cloths on. They're all quite wet now. There. I think that's all I can do at the moment."

"Thank you," said Tallis.

Julius rolled down his sleeves and began to pull on his jacket.

"The sun's coming out. That's nice. Well, I suppose I'd better be getting along."

Tallis rose and Julius fingered the door. They looked at each other and then looked away.

"I'm sorry," said Tallis. "But there it is."

"I quite understand. Well, what am I to do?"

"What do you mean?"

"You know what I mean."

"Oh, just go away," said Tallis. "I don't think you should live in the Boltons or Priory Grove. Go right away."

"Yes, yes, of course. I didn't really intend to settle here. I was only playing with the idea. I'll go abroad. I may take on another big assignment quite soon. This was just an interim."

"Naturally."

"Do try to get yourself a decent job. As things are, what does your life amount to? I suppose it's always like that, but it does pain me. After all, I am an artist. This is just a mess."

"Yes, I know," said Tallis.

"Let me lend you some money," said Julius. "Or rather, let me give you some. As I explained, I never lend."

"No, thanks."

"Why not? I know you refused before, but we do know each other better now. Think again. I have money, you need it. Morgan owes you money. Let me pay her debt. She owed you four hundred pounds and paid you a hundred. Let me give you the remaining three hundred. Come, be generous."

Tallis reflected. "All right. It would certainly come in handy. Thank you."

Julius wrote out the cheque.

"Yes, well, I must be going," said Julius. "Good-bye. I suppose in the nature of things we shall meet again." He still lingered. "You concede that I am an instrument of justice?"

Tallis smiled.

The door closed behind Julius and immediately the house was full of noises. Squealing in the kitchen, jazz music in the room opposite, altercation in Urdu upon the stairs, and Leonard calling out loudly for his son.

"Coming, Daddy, coming, coming."

🦋 | TWENTY-TWO

The pale blue Hillman Minx was heading south. The sun-striped poplar-shaded road ran straight on ahead, on and on and on. Simon's arm was stretched along the back of the seat.

"We thought of ourselves."

"We were so damn relieved."

"If only we'd thought a little more carefully about *them*."

"Yet at the time it did seem rational to keep quiet."

"But, oh God, if only we hadn't."

"Don't keep on about it, Simon."

"We were so relieved," said Simon. "We'd found each other again. Being back home inside our own love was so wonderful. I was nearly faint with joy that evening. I just felt I was right out of the tangle. The rest of it was so messy and obscure. I didn't want to think about it any more. I felt all my own guilt had been left behind *there*, and I had no responsibility any more outside my love for you."

"We have lived too much inside our love for each other."

"Axel, you don't mean—"

"No, no, stop being so frightened. I just mean I think we should see more people and live more in the world. We've been so shut in with each other."

"Yes. You know, I think if we saw more people and went about more together it would sort of give me confidence."

"It's probably to do with being homosexual. We're all a bit afraid of society. There's a tendency to hide. It's bad."

"You don't want to send that letter to *The Times* or tell all Whitehall?"

"No. It's not their business. But we shouldn't hide so. I think if we'd been living more in the open we mightn't have been involved in this terrible muddle."

"Oh God," said Simon, "I know. It was all my fault, all my doing—"

They had been through it all over and over and over again. With a melancholy patience Axel had led Simon round the circle of accusation, explanation, exculpation, accusation. Each time Axel said a little more, was a little more definite, a little more pressing, attempting to clarify both charge and excuse, trying to help Simon to accept and understand the full awful detail of what had happened.

"No," said Axel. "If you think of the terribly tangled network of causes which led to Rupert's death and how very little any of us actually knew at any given moment about the whole situation and about the consequences of our actions—"

"But I acted wrongly, knowing it was wrong," said Simon. "Everyone else was just in a muddle. If only I hadn't started telling lies to you, if only I'd told you everything right from the start—"

"If you had, Julius probably wouldn't have told you about his little plan at all."

"But if I'd told you *then*, after Julius came to the museum—"

"We might still have decided to keep quiet—in fact we almost certainly would. The only person about the place with really sound instincts is Tallis. He led Julius straight to the telephone."

"Yes, Tallis was right. He saw how awfully perilous it was."

"And we didn't because we were so damn self-absorbed. We thought the others would manage."

"All the same, Axel, I can't help feeling I'm more to blame than anyone. I simply let Julius enslave me."

"Dear boy, I am to blame too. I just didn't take Julius seriously enough as a possible mischief-maker. Yet I've seen him do something like this before. And I did nothing about it then simply because I was flattered at being Julius's friend, at seeing how dangerous he was to other people and yet not to me. Similarly now, I let myself be flattered by Julius, and when I did begin to be suspicious all I could see was his connection with you. That day when we left Rupert's, after you'd pushed Julius into the pool, when you said, 'Stop the car,' I thought you were going to announce that you were going off with Julius!"

"Oh Axel, Axel—"

"It seems mad enough now, thank God. As for your telling me lies, why did you do so? Because you were afraid of me. That fear ought not to have existed. It's not just that I've always bullied you. A little bullying between lovers needn't matter. But I've always withheld a bit of myself. And you have felt this and it has made you frightened."

"Yes, I have felt it," said Simon, "but again I blame myself. Why should *you* be interested in *me* at all? I'm so flimsy compared with you. And I know you've always hated *that* world, and I did so absolutely belong to it. It was very easy for Julius to make me think that for two pins you'd throw me over."

"Well, you should have had a bit more guts at that point. Hope and faith are courage too. But if you've had these doubts I've really prompted them by holding back from you, by keeping in reserve some corner of my personality, something which you never saw at all and which might be taken away intact to some other place. This was partly failure of nerve, partly pride. I wanted to feel that if all this came to grief there was a part of me which had never engaged in it and which was not discredited or even disappointed. It was a failure of love. You held nothing back, but I played for safety. I haven't deserved your full and absolute faith."

"Axel, you aren't going to go away to some other place, are you?"

"Don't keep asking that ridiculous question. You know we are much closer to each other now than we have ever been before."

"So you won't leave me?"

"No, you fool. You won't leave me?"

"Axel, what can I swear by—?"

"All right, all right."

"You'll *never* leave me?"

"How do I know? I don't intend to leave you, that's all. I love you, that's all."

"You won't flay me in the end?"

"How do I know, child?"

"You're right that I should have had more guts with Julius."

"You should have been brave, like you were that night in the restaurant."

"Will we be all right, Axel?"

"We've got a reasonable chance. Mutual love is something in this vale of tears and it's rare enough. But this sort of thing can be precarious, as you know."

"Will you, after this, open up that reserve, not shut me out?"

"I'll try. I've never done so with anyone else. But love is awfully difficult, Simon. One learns this as one grows older."

"It seems easy to me. Nothing in the world is easier for me than loving you."

"My dear."

"I say, I can't help being rather glad Hilda didn't come with us! I hope we pressed her enough?"

"I think so. It may be better for Hilda not to see us at present. We're all of us still a bit shell-shocked."

"I wonder if it's good for her to be so much with Morgan?"

"We can't know what passes between those two."

"It's almost as if Morgan's—taken her over."

"Hilda must be suffering terribly. And there are very few people in the world whom one can really talk to. Think how much more dreadful it would all have been for us if we hadn't been able to talk endlessly to each other."

"You don't think we've somehow—cheated—Axel? I mean, that we've too much taken refuge in our love and not really faced what happened, suffered it properly?"

"Of course our love is selfish. Almost all human love is bloody selfish. If one has anything to hang onto at all one clings to it relentlessly. We've tried to face it and to suffer it. To take refuge in love is an instinct and not a disreputable one."

"I feel so damned responsible and so guilty. If I could only *see* it all clearly—"

"You may never be able to do that."

"If only I'd told everybody—"

"Don't begin again, darling. Not today. Now perhaps if you'd just look at the map—"

"Oh Axel, if only—"

"Stop it, Simon. You said there was a village with a Romanesque church."

"Yes, we must be almost there. Shall we stop and look?"

"There's your village, I think. We may as well stay the night there, if there's a decent little hotel. We needn't rush. We can cross the Alps the day after tomorrow."

"That's right, we needn't rush, need we. What a marvellous strange light. The sun's shining but I can just see a star. Look."

" 'The evening star is the morning star.' Frege."

"Come, Axel, that's poetry, not logic."

The solid grey forms of the village rose from behind a meadowy hill-side where the strange light had turned the grass into furry green velvet. The light blue Hillman Minx took the hill at a rush and glided into the grey square where the declining sun was making shadows between the cobblestones. A little *mairie* with a glittering high-pitched roof of bluish slate faced the façade of the church. The church tower reached upward in crazed irregular lines of arcades and archlets to a slender spire of matching blue slate whose weathercock had become a blurred spear of gold. In the tympanum above the doorway a very battered Christ wearily opened long arms and huge hands, receiving, judging.

"Let's go in at once!" said Simon.

"No. It's already too dark inside. We'll see it tomorrow."

Simon did not argue. He felt that he would never argue with Axel again.

"There's our hotel," said Axel.

The modest-looking Hotel Restaurant du Commerce occupied the corner of the square. The Hillman Minx stopped outside it.

Simon followed his friend in, and stood aside while Axel asked the *patron* for a room. Simon could read French but could scarcely speak it. He liked Axel to be the one who knew such things.

The little hallway of the hotel was dark and smelt of something very good to eat. Simon looked through and saw that there was a garden beyond where the sun was shining onto a clipped lawn and onto a vine which had trailed over a trellis to make a little arbour where there was a table and two chairs.

Simon went on through the hallway and out into the garden. The sun was still warm and bright, though the evening star had strengthened. The vine was hung with glassy green translucent grapes and the leaves and tendrils glowed with a pale green radiance, outspread and welcoming and still in the quiet sunlight. Simon moved toward the vine, bowed his head under its shadowy arch, and touched the warm pendent beads of the grape bunches.

Axel came out, removing his jacket and rolling up his white shirt sleeves. The sun made gold in his dark hair. "I've asked the *patron* to bring us a carafe of wine out here straightaway. I'm just going up to look at the room. You stay here."

Simon sat down at the table. The *patron* bustled over, wearing purple braces, with a carafe and two glasses. "*Merci.*" Simon poured out some wine and tasted it. It was excellent. The serrated green leaves extended above him, before him, their motionless pattern of angelic hands. The air quivered with warmth and a diffusion of light.

Simon thought, It is an instinct, and not a disreputable one, to be consoled by love. Warily he probed the grief which had travelled with him so far, and felt it as a little vaguer, a little less dense. His thoughts of Rupert now reached back further into the past, to good times which had their own untouchable reality. He drank some more wine and raised his face to the dazzle of sun among the leaves and felt his youth lift him and make him buoyant. He was young and healthy and he loved and was loved. It was impossible for him, as he sat there in the green southern light and waited for Axel, not to feel in his veins the warm anticipation of a new happiness.

🌀 | TWENTY-THREE

"Even matchboxes aren't what they used to be. When I was young a matchbox looked like something, it had personality. Now they're just insipid trash or else garish catchpennies for tourists."

"I've brought you a cup of tea, Daddy."

"The world is poisoned and starving and on the brink of nuclear war and all you can do is bring a cup of tea. *And* you've slopped it in the saucer."

"Sorry."

"I've got the most frightful pain in my hip, little you care."

"Have you taken your tablets?"

"Yes. They're no good. Just placebos. Probably made of sugar. There's the Health Service for you, *and* you have to pay a shilling."

"Let me do your pillows, Daddy, they're all over the place."

"I can do my own pillows. You might bloody well spend some of your valuable time cleaning this room out. It's a wonder I'm alive at all with all the germs there must be crawling about here. That piece of toast I threw at you last week is still there going mouldy underneath the dressing table."

"I'll take it away."

"No, no, leave it, I'm getting quite fond of it. It's nice to see a familiar face. Since you never seem to bother to come and see me."

"I'm sorry, Daddy, I have to go to my classes and—"

"The idea of you teaching anybody anything is a laugh all right. I don't know what I did to deserve such a stupid son. I

suppose you are mine. Other men of your age manage to live all
right. They have proper jobs and decent houses and wives that
don't run off with Jews."

"Drink your tea, Daddy, you'll feel better. Would you like
some cake?"

"No, I wouldn't. And I feel perfectly all right except for this
ghastly pain. I'm not going to go to any more of those heat treat-
ments. They aren't doing any good. I feel worse than I did when
they started."

"It's the damp weather. You'll feel better soon."

"And those whelps at the hospital talk about me as if I were
some sort of animal or moron. 'Shove him along, Joe,' one of
them said last week. 'Shove him along,' I ask you! I wonder they
didn't say 'it'! And they chatter to each other all the time and
giggle and ignore the patients. I bet they're all pansies."

"If you hate it," said Tallis, "you shan't go any more."

"Well, and why shouldn't I go! It's a chance to get out of this
shit house. Makes a change from these four bloody walls and you
and your cups of tea. And the blasted Welfare State may as
well do something for me, even if it's completely futile, since
I've been paying through the nose all these years. And to think
people are dim-witted enough to be grateful, after the state's
stolen nearly everything they earn and given them some rotten
slapdash medical attention at the end when they've got one and
a half feet in the grave and they don't realize they've already paid
for it fifty times over! People as blockheaded as that deserve a
government like this one. They deserve to be treated as they are
treated, like sheep."

"People are a lot better off now—"

"Now that they have television sets to make all the horrors of
the world into an evening's entertainment. It all went wrong from
the start. It's no better now and no worse, only stupider and
more vulgar. The sooner it's all bombed into oblivion the better."

"Daddy, I must go and write my lecture—"

"I wish I had half a crown for every time you've uttered that
inane formula so as to get away from me."

"It's true—"

"You and your lectures. You're like an old maid with her crochet work. Except that crochet amounts to something."

"Can I do anything for you?"

"No, just clear off. Yes, you can take some of the newspapers off the floor. Not those ones. Those ones. They've been here for weeks. Be careful, there's some muck inside one of them; God knows what it is, you'd think half the dogs of Notting Hill had been shitting in here."

"You haven't drunk your tea."

"Your stench spoils the taste of it. And it's cold. No, I don't want any more. And you can tell that bloody nig nog to turn off his blasted transistor."

"I'll ask him to turn it down."

" 'I'll ask him to turn it down.' You talk like a blinking constipated deb. I sometimes think you're just a girl in disguise. You're afraid of those nigs, afraid you might say something nasty and hurt their precious feelings. They're all a bunch of crooks anyway."

"All right, Daddy, I'll—"

"Filthy habit wearing a turban all the time. I wouldn't be surprised if he wears it in bed. Don't suppose he's washed his hair in years. We'll have lice in the house at this rate. Don't suppose you've washed your hair in years if it comes to that. All right, go away, go away."

Tallis retreated. Through the closing bedroom door he saw his father sitting bolt upright in bed dressed in an old tweed jacket and dirty crumpled blue shirt. Leonard's eyes were brilliant with aggrieved vitality. His face was losing the podgy wrinkled look and was gaunter, paler, transparent, the skin pulled and smoothed and yellow, the nose sharper. The tonsured bush of silver hair was flatter, thinner.

Tallis went down the stairs and knocked. The Sikh, asked to turn down his transistor, turned it off altogether. He inquired kindly about Leonard. Tallis inquired about the dispute at the bus depot about the turban. It appeared to be over. The men had got used to their outlandish fellow worker. The Sikh was now happily united with his fellow males in an attempt to sabotage a campaign for women bus-drivers. Tallis was offered tea but refused. He looked with gratitude into the gentle dark sympathetic eyes of the man from so far away. He had heard the story of the Sikh's life. It was not a happy one.

Tallis went into the kitchen and closed the door. There was a dead sallow light of late afternoon and it was just beginning to rain. He threw the old newspaper down underneath the sink, where a row of half-choked milk bottles had congregated once again. He closed the window. A lot of dead leaves seemed to have got inside and were blowing about in the draught. He thought for a moment of the Sikh and of the Pakistanis upstairs, who had come, no doubt with hopes, for who can prevent the human heart from hoping, from their own troubled lands into this alien milieu of poverty and racial tension and petty crime.

The remains of Tallis's lunch-time baked beans were still upon the table. He scraped the bean juice into a screw of newspaper and put the plate into a basin on the draining board. The sink had been blocked for several days and was full of dark brown greasy water. Perhaps the dead leaves had clogged it, or perhaps some hot fat which he had poured down the other day. Now he washed up occasionally in the basin and threw the water down the drain outside the window.

He had still not managed to tell his father. Did Leonard already know, had he guessed and was a comedy being played out between them, a comedy which would continue to the end? "You'll feel better soon, Daddy dear." "You'll get better when the warm days come." Tallis could not believe that his father had understood. And he still knew that he ought to tell him, that the freedom of this last thing ought not to be denied him. But when and how to tell him? Should he go up to him *now*, mount the stairs, open the door, interrupt Leonard's sarcastic welcome? "There's something I must tell you. You are iller than you know." What tone, of all the possible tones of their converse, could suit itself to this theme? The usualness of Leonard, his special predictable liveliness, gave comfort. Perhaps it made unreal what was to come, extending a veil over it from the past. Human beings cannot live without custom. Leonard had always been so. How could he cease to be so, how could that fearfully *characteristic* vitality ever come to an end?

I ought to tell him, thought Tallis. I'll tell him tomorrow. He sat down at the table and made the accustomed gesture of spreading out his books. The class at Greenford were hostile. They seemed to enjoy catching him out. But perhaps it was all imagination. He gazed ahead of him. On the dresser were the pretty cups and saucers which Julius had arranged there, the cups hanging from hooks, the saucers upright upon the shelf. Seeing them there so neat and clean reminded him of old quiet things almost beyond the reach of memory, his earliest childhood, an orderly world, his mother. Near to the cups upon another hook hung the amber necklace which Tallis had mended again. He had still not had time to sort out the coagulated junk on the lower part of the dresser. It spilled over to the floor during the regular search for the tin opener. Would it not be possible to assign some special place to the tin opener? Why did his nervous fuzzy mind just refuse to think about these simple matters?

The air was dense with subdued noise. Tallis was used to it. The endless din of motor-cars made the room vibrate, made the pretty cups and saucers tinkle. There was a faint squeaking and shrieking, metallic sounds of grinding and jarring, sounds that set the teeth on edge, the minor pandemonium with which he had lived intermittently for so long. Once he had feared that this would get steadily worse until it overwhelmed him with horror. Now he treated it merely as a nuisance, as a mechanical accompaniment of his consciousness. And even when he saw with clarity some weird crawling thing he felt pity rather than disgust. Other things he feared. The ambiguous presence of his sister. Her visitations disturbed him with the sense of an alien and somehow dangerous reality which increasingly jostled him close. Here perhaps one day some thin partition could break down. He had come into his bedroom and thought that he saw his sister lying on his bed. Only that must have been a dream.

For the rest, he seemed to have nothing left. No experiences, no certainty. Had there ever been certainty? There had been experiences. He remembered something, like a kind of light, nothing with form. Perhaps that had been a dream too. He never knelt down now; that act of homage to elsewhere had become impossible, would have seemed obscene. Perhaps it had always been just a mucky sexual ritual after all. Any kind of prayer would be superstition now. But sometimes he caught hold of things, edges of tables, sides of doors, books, the bakelite handles of knives. Caught hold of them and held them tight, not so as to perform any act himself, but so as to immobilize himself for a moment to be, if that were possible, perhaps acted upon, perhaps touched.

Meanwhile Tallis's days went on much as usual. Classes, preparation for classes, committees, aftermaths of committees, writing manifestoes, fetching them from the printer, putting them in envelopes, seeing clergymen, seeing probation officers, seeing police officers, seeing people in tears. He thought a good deal about Rupert. The image of Rupert spreadeagled in the pool often came to him involuntarily, with the clarity of a memory, and regularly appeared in his dreams. He did not believe that Rupert had taken his life. But this was little consolation. The accident was deeply the product of its circumstances. Tallis did not try to unravel these nor did he speculate about the guilt of any person, not even about his own. He grieved blankly over something which seemed, in its disastrous compound of human failure, muddle, and sheer chance, so like what it was all like. It went wrong from the start, he said to himself. But these were not his words and this was not his thought, and he put it away from him as a temptation. Then he tried just to remember Rupert and keep the memory clear and feel the pain of it mindlessly.

An air letter from Hilda which had arrived by the morning's post was lying on the table. Hilda and Morgan were in America. Morgan had taken a university job on the West Coast. They had bought a pretty modern house with eucalyptus trees and a view of what Hilda called the ocean. Hilda wrote regularly. She sent news of Peter. Peter had eventually been caught on a massive shop-lifting spree. He was put on probation and was to have psychological treatment. Then Hilda took him away with her, and he was now undergoing prolonged psychoanalysis in California. A good start had been made. He was living with his analyst. Later, Hilda sent colour photographs of the house. Of the view from the picture window. Of the patio with the Spanish tiles. Of the Chevrolet in the carport. Her letters were chatty, mentioning Morgan in a casual way, as if this were a dear friend with whom she had always lived and whom she took entirely for granted. Morgan never wrote. And Tallis in his chatty replies never mentioned her. He told Hilda anecdotes of his classes, little dramas of the house and the street, political chit chat. He did not fail to describe the weather. Why Hilda wrote him in this way he did not know. Probably out of pity.

He thought about Morgan, but rather vaguely, with disconnected images of the past. He often saw her eyes, glaring at him with affectionate exasperation, through those steel-rimmed spectacles. He remembered the house where they had lived in Putney and he even visited it one evening when he had business in that part of London. It seemed to be full of Chinese. He recalled how awfully untidy that house had been, but with a cosy organic sort of untidiness, quite unlike his present jumble and clutter. He recalled a small tabby cat which had adopted them for a short while. Morgan had called it Mackintosh after one of her early swains. They never discovered its sex. The nervous anxious tenderness which had pervaded his marriage came back in clear moment-visions and cloudy swirls of atmosphere. He remembered Morgan's jokey self-consciousness about her wedding ring and the peculiar shy ache of his pleasure when she displayed it. He never bought her an engagement ring. In fact they were never really engaged. They just suddenly found that they were married. Hilda was annoyed that the engagement had never been properly announced. He remembered the dreadful anxiety of going to bed, Morgan's extraordinary sweetness, the things she said, always the same things like a liturgy, to comfort him, the strangeness of it all. They had never got used to each other. He thought of these things now vaguely and without urgency. He did not even wonder if he would see her again. He simply let her continue to occupy his heart.

Yes, thought Tallis, tomorrow I will tell him. Tomorrow, oh God, tomorrow, not today. It was cold in the kitchen. He lit the gas oven and opened the oven door. He found his pen and turned the pages of his notebook. If Leonard stopped the treatment would there be more pain? The doctors were so evasive. Perhaps they were just experimenting. What was the pain like, would it become terrible, unbearable, before the end? I must tell him tomorrow, thought Tallis. He must know what is happening to him. I must explain it all and I must look into his face while I do it. God, he's had such a bloody rotten life, he thought, and now it's nearly over. And he thought, How can I endure my dear father's death, how can I live through his dying? Tears welled from his eyes and soaked into the stubble on his cheeks. Blinking, he leaned forward and began to write. *It was not until 1860 that the Coal Mines Regulation Act enjoined that children under twelve years of age should not be employed in the mines. Previous to that date . . .*

❦ | T W E N T Y - F O U R

The rich autumn sun flattered Paris. The Seine was enamelled with blue and silver under a lapis lazuli sky, and green chestnut leaves with golden rims lay about motionless like bright discarded fans upon the warm stony paths of the Tuileries gardens.

Julius was crossing the iron footbridge. He paused awhile to look down toward Notre-Dame and to feel the obscure pleasure of many overlaid and inexplicit memeories of previous visits to Paris, all happy ones. The memories were cloudy, sugary, making the quiet brilliant outward scene into an inner one of even greater vividness.

He had spent the earlier part of the morning at the Louvre. Painting may not be the greatest of the arts, he reflected, but perhaps it gives the purest and most intense pleasure. At least it does to me. I love music, but my pleasure in music remains always a little muddied by emotion. My pleasure in painting is, as pleasure should be, absolutely cold. After leaving the Louvre he had procured a ticket for the opera, L'Incoronazione di Poppea, a work to which he was devoted but which he had seen performed only once. He greatly looked forward to a second experience. The cast was said to be very good, with a Canadian soprano to whom he was particularly partial. After that he had walked along the Rue de Rivoli and impulsively purchased some mauve shirts. Julius was usually rather sober in his dress, almost clerical. Was the spirit of the times taking hold of him after all? He adjusted his collar and tie. He was wearing a dark grey suit of fine worsted with an almost invisible stripe, a white shirt, and a black tie with scarlet rosettes upon it. He was carrying a thin black silver-topped cane which, although he thought it a trifle ostentatious, he always took with him when he felt especially at leisure.

He was staying at the Crillon, but of course one didn't eat there. He felt in a mood for exploring little restaurants, tiny bars, places where the petty bourgeoisie consumed in silence the best food in the world. He walked on across the bridge, breathing in the warm fresh watery smells, and felt his step so light that he almost floated in the air. He was so much better now that he was not closely involved with human beings. Involvement was always bad for his nerves. He had friends in the biology department of the Sorbonne, but he felt no inclination to telephone them. He was happy, for the present, to be by himself in Paris, an outsider, even a tourist. He paused at the quai, waiting to cross, watching the cars speeding by. The traffic was certainly much worse. Yet perhaps he had been wrong to say he could not live in Paris. He might even look at a few apartments while he was here. It would pass the time.

He walked under the Institut archway and up the Rue Mazarine. He was beginning to feel that a quiet apéritif and then one of those really serious meals would be just what was required to complete a very satisfactory morning. He found that his digestion always improved when he was completely on his own. He turned to the right, through streets that he remembered well, and found himself at the corner of the Rue Jacob. Somebody had mentioned a restaurant here. Oh, yes, it was Rupert. What was it called? A la Ville de Tours. Julius walked along a little and saw the sign. It looked a promising place. Dark inside, red-and-white-check tablecloths covered with sheets of white paper, flaking brown paint, a fat cat, and an aspidistra. The food would probably be excellent. He would book a table and then return to the Place Saint Germain for a leisurely apéritif. He began to examine the menu. The sun was warm upon his back. Life was good.